RECONNECT

OTHER BOOKS AND AUDIOBOOKS BY TRACI HUNTER ABRAMSON

UNDERCURRENTS SERIES

Undercurrents

Ripple Effect

The Deep End

SAINT SQUAD SERIES

Freefall

Lockdown

Crossfire

Backlash

Smoke Screen

Code Word

Lock and Key

Drop Zone

Spotlight

Tripwire

Redemption

Covert Ops

Disconnect

Reconnect

LUKE STEELE SERIES

Hometown Vendetta

ROYAL SERIES

Royal Target

Royal Secrets

Royal Brides

Royal Heir

Royal Duty

GUARDIAN SERIES

Failsafe

Safe House

Sanctuary

On the Run

In Harm's Way

Not Dead Yet

Unseen

DREAM'S EDGE SERIES

*Dancing to Freedom**

An Unlikely Pair

*Broken Dreams**

Dreams of Gold

*The Best Mistake**

Worlds Collide

FALCON POINT SERIES

Heirs of Falcon Point

The Danger with Diamonds

From an Unknown Sender

When Fashion Turns Deadly

PEN AND DAGGER SERIES

Novel Threat (April 2025)

STAND-ALONES

Obsession

Proximity

*Twisted Fate**

*Entangled**

*Sinister Secrets**

Deep Cover

Mistaken Reality

Kept Secrets

Chances Are

Chance for Home

A Change of Fortune

The Fiction Kitchen Trio Cookbook

Jim and Katherine

* Novella

RECONNECT

THE FINAL SAINT SQUAD NOVEL

TRACI HUNTER ABRAMSON

COVENANT

Cover image: *Military Soldiers* by Fukume, AI generated © stock.adobe.com, *Red Map Pin* by Atchariya63 AI generated © stock.adobe.com, *Abstract Brown Dust Explosion* by Faiza © stock.adobe.com, *Military Soldiers Running to Helicopter* by Meysam Azarneshin© stock.adobe.com

Cover design by Kevin Jorgensen

Published by Covenant Communications, Inc.
American Fork, Utah

Library of Congress Cataloging-in-Publication Data

Name: Traci Hunter Abramson
Title: Reconnect / Traci Hunter Abramson
Description: American Fork, UT : Covenant Communications, Inc. [2025]
Identifiers: Library of Congress Control Number 2024939251 | 978-1-52442-790-0
LC record available at https://lccn.loc.gov/2024939251
Printed in the United States of America
First Printing: March 2025

31 30 29 28 27 26 25   10 9 8 7 6 5 4 3 2 1

for all of the readers who have supported both me and the Saint Squad through all our ups and downs

ACKNOWLEDGMENTS

As this series comes to an official close, I want to thank everyone who has encouraged me to keep going and to tell stories I didn't even know needed to be written. Thank you so much to my amazing editor, Samantha Millburn. You have helped me so much in my growth as a writer, and you truly are the secret to my success.

Thank you as well to Mandy Biesinger and Lara Abramson for your help during the early editing process and to my fabulous critique partners, who are always pushing me to improve: Ashley Gebert, Daniel Quilter, Eliza Emma Jackson, Connor Olsen, Eliza Sanders, Jack Stewart, Steve Stratton, Millie Hast, Ann Feinstein, Brian Godden, Dave Elliott, Ellie Whitney, Paige Edwards, Kyla Beecroft, and Kori Pratt.

Thanks to Amy Parker and Lauryn Blume for pushing me to try something new and to Sam Millburn for making sure it worked.

As always, thank you to all those at Covenant who help me in so many aspects of launching my books into the world, especially Shara Meredith, Ashlyn LaOrange, Brookelyn Jones, and Tracy Bentley.

I'd also like to express my continued appreciation to the CIA's Publication Classification Review Board for your continued support.

Most of all, I want to thank my family for sharing me with my fictional worlds and the readers who have made them come to life. The Saint Squad series might be over, but the characters still have many more stories to live. I hope you all will come along on their continued journeys.

SAINT SQUAD CAST OF CHARACTERS

SEAL TEAM 8

COMMANDING OFFICER

KEL BENNETT

& Marilyn
Backlash

SAINT SQUAD COMMANDING OFFICER

BRENT MILLER

& Amy Whitmore
Freefall
Disconnect
Reconnect

TRISTAN CROWTHER

& Riley Palmetta
Lockdown
Redemption

SETH JOHNSON

& Vanessa Lauton
Crossfire

QUINN LAMBERT

& Taylor Palmetta
Smoke Screen

JAY WELLMAN

& Carina Channing
Code Word
Lock and Key

DAMIAN SCHMITT

& Paige Vickers
Drop Zone

CRAIG SIMMONS

& Sienna Blake
Spotlight
Tripwire

1

COUNTRY, FAMILY, TEAM, HONOR. BRENT fought for all four as gunshots fired across the expansive lawn that separated two naval helicopters from the fortress, the ten-story building filled with Morenta's men.

Or it would be filled with his men had they not all come outside to shoot at Brent and the other thirty navy SEALs now scrambling for cover.

Brent tapped on the comm unit in his ear, but nothing happened. Yet another equipment failure in this nightmare operation on the edge of the Nicaraguan jungle.

Gunfire punctuated the air in Morse code: *Retreat*.

The other SEALs loaded into the two waiting choppers, but Brent remained where he was. If he retreated, no one would be left to face the imminent threat: the man in front of him holding a rocket launcher. He had to stay so his teammates and the valuable asset they had liberated could leave.

And they were running out of time. Something was zapping battery power from everything nearby, and it was only a matter of minutes before their transportation would fall victim to the same fate. This wasn't a matter of *if* but *when*. Brent's squad had already experienced the equipment failure on a previous mission, and it was clear that the blocker was active now.

Someone shot at him, bits of bark flying into the air above his head. Brent ducked and quickly changed out the magazine on his assault rifle, but before he could take aim, the man with the rocket launcher disappeared behind the jeep.

His options limited, Brent rushed out of the jungle and circled behind the vehicle to where the man was, then took aim and squeezed the trigger. His weapon jammed. A sense of urgency swept through him. He was out of time.

The man disappeared around the other side of the jeep. Brent dropped his jammed rifle and, careful to stay clear of the back-blast area, sprinted around to the man again and dove at him just as he fired the missile.

The projectile shot through the air, whipping between the helicopter still on the ground and the one that had just taken off. It missed both targets, and relief flooded through Brent. His teammates were on one of those choppers. His brothers-in-arms.

The shooter threw an elbow into Brent's ribs, but Brent ignored the pain. He grappled with the man—another elbow, a fist to Brent's jaw. Brent countered with a few blows of his own, but the man broke free and quickly reloaded. He lifted the launcher again. Brent grabbed him from the side as the weapon jerked from the force of the missile shooting out of it. The projectile whizzed between the two helicopters once again, and the recoil of the weapon knocked Brent backward, but his grip remained firm on the gunman.

Both thudded to the hard-packed earth, and again the two men wrestled. The man broke free and grabbed for a second loaded launcher. Brent fought for control of the weapon. This time he managed to yank it free of the other man's grasp, and the weapon fell to the ground.

His opponent lunged for it, and Brent kicked it under the jeep, then scrambled to his feet, his enemy doing the same. Brent reached for the backup weapon holstered at his back, and the other man's hand went to the holster at his waist. Brent lifted his gun at the same moment the other man raised his pistol, but Brent fired first.

The man crumpled to the ground, and Brent rushed to where the launcher had landed.

Shouts rang out, and gunfire punctuated the air as the two helicopters lifted off.

His teammates were leaving him. They didn't have a choice.

Through the fog, they wouldn't be able to see that he had the rocket launcher. Even if they could come back for him amid the dozen guards shooting at them, they couldn't be sure how long their aircraft would continue to function.

The helicopters backed out of range of the automatic rifles firing at them. His friends were safe. So was the man who could help the United States defend against the new electromagnetic weapon they had discovered.

The flood of guards turned their guns from the choppers and headed toward Brent. He ducked as more bullets whizzed in his direction and sparked off the jeep.

Staying low to use the jeep for cover, Brent rushed to the nearby trees. He made it only halfway there before his toe caught on something on the ground.

Brent stumbled and fell. His heartbeat quickened as he rolled over and shouldered the rocket launcher.

The guards raced toward the jeep, their rifles nearly clear of the one obstacle between them. Outnumbered, Brent aimed the rocket launcher, and despite his dangerous proximity to the vehicle, he squeezed the trigger.

* * *

On the screen in the Situation Room, a ring of fire engulfed the area where Amy had last spotted her husband. Her breath caught. Her heart stopped.

She dropped into the nearest chair as flames illuminated the fog on-screen. Amy had worked as the intel officer for the Saint Squad for years, always hoping and praying this moment would never come. But it had. Her husband, the man who was her everything, was gone.

She fought that thought away. He couldn't be dead. Brent was invincible. He always came home.

Her hand went to her stomach, where a new life grew within her, a life Brent didn't yet know about.

"Amy, I'm so sorry."

The whispered words jumbled in her mind, but she didn't have to look to know the attempted comfort came from her father, the same man who, only a minute earlier, gave the order to leave her husband behind. The pain of that moment crashed over her, and she fought against it.

Brent had chosen to stay. Deep down, Amy knew it. He had stayed to make sure the other SEALs made it out safely.

A reverent hush came over the White House Situation Room. On the screen, the video feed from the naval helicopters continued to play. The fortress disappeared into the mist, the glow of red and orange fading in the distance. Then the image distorted, and the screen went black.

The comm officer in the corner of the room broke the silence. "We've lost all communication."

Seth Johnson, a former member of the Saint Squad, stepped in front of Amy. He lowered his six-foot-seven frame until he was on his knees so he could see her clearly. His dark skin glistened as though he had been out on the mission with his former teammates rather than watching with her. "I'll go after him. I'll bring him home."

The secretary of the navy spoke before Amy could. "Commander, don't make promises you can't keep. We can't send anyone in there until we can do so safely."

The safety of the Saint Squad and two dozen other SEALs had been the reason Brent had remained behind. Amy had worked with the SEALs long enough to understand their methods, and she knew her husband. He had sacrificed himself for his men, just as he had sacrificed himself for her the first time they'd met. They had come home from that mission. She had to believe he would come home from this one.

Conversation hummed around her. Talk of the devastating power outage in Kansas City. The potential terrorist attack in Las Vegas. The professor who was being transported to the United States to help counteract the attempt to plunge the entire country into darkness.

Amy processed only bits and pieces of the words as the image of the explosion played over and over in her mind.

From where he still knelt in front of her, Seth had listened quietly, but now he focused on her again. "Don't give up hope, Amy. If we don't have proof, we have to believe he's still alive."

"But you saw—" Secretary of the Navy Hartley began.

"I saw an explosion," Seth interrupted. "That's all."

"Seth is right," Amy's father said, his voice thick with emotion. He put his hand on her shoulder and swallowed hard before speaking again. "When it's safe, we'll send someone in."

"Sir, I advise against a rescue mission," Secretary Hartley said.

Amy's father faced Hartley. "Work with Commander Johnson to formulate a plan. Until we have proof to the contrary, we assume Commander Miller is alive."

The secretary of the navy nodded. "Yes, Mr. President."

"In the meantime, we have a lot of people at risk from the power outages. We need solutions," Amy's father said.

From his seat across the room, Doug Valdez, the new director of Homeland Security, spoke. "We're working on it."

Her father nodded. "Keep me apprised of your efforts."

"Yes, sir."

* * *

Tristan Crowther didn't want to believe Brent had been caught in the blast. He prayed his former commanding officer had survived, that somehow a miracle had kept him alive. He remained in the helicopter doorway until Quinn and Craig pulled him inside. Had they seen where Brent was when the explosion had occurred?

The Saint Squad had experienced one miracle after another over the years, and not once had they suffered a casualty. Of all the statistics the navy tracked, that remained the only one his squad cared about. They were brothers.

Tristan scrambled into a seat and gripped the edge as the helicopter jerked to the left. His two squad members who had yet to buckle in lost their footing and skidded across the floor.

"Hang on!" Tristan grabbed Quinn by the arm to prevent him from sliding toward the open hatch. In the same instant, Quinn caught hold of Craig's ankle.

Tristan's muscles flexed as he fought against gravity and the sudden movements of the aircraft. Beside him, Damian reached over and gripped Quinn. Like a human chain, they pulled Quinn and Craig to the empty seats on the other side of Tristan.

"Strap in." Tristan shouted the words over the rumble of the engines.

Another missile ripped past them.

"That was close," Craig said, his voice barely audible.

"We have to go back for Brent," Quinn shouted.

Webb, the commander of the Gamma squad, shook his head. "We have our orders. If we stay, we lose power, and we all go down."

Webb was right, but logic paled to the urgency rushing through Tristan. His gaze swept over the other ten men in the helicopter, one of whom was currently bleeding from a bullet wound in his leg. Damian sat beside the civilian they'd rescued from the hideout behind the fortress. The professor had been kidnapped nearly a year ago, and from the sound of it, his knowledge had been used to create an electromagnetic pulse weapon unlike anything they had ever seen before.

Tristan turned to the men beside him. Damian was still beside the professor, but the other three squad members stared at him. The unspoken question shone in each of their eyes. "We'll go back for him," Tristan said, praying that he could follow through and that Brent would still be breathing when they returned to Nicaragua. "It won't be tonight, but we'll go back."

Quinn blew out a frustrated breath, then finished strapping himself into his harness. The last buckle clicked into place as another shout carried over the engines.

"Incoming!"

2

Evidence to the contrary. Those words repeated in Jim Whitmore's mind. As much as he wanted to believe Brent had survived tonight's military action, he couldn't imagine how it was possible.

Jim should go to his room and wake up Katherine to let her know what had happened, but she'd been sleeping so peacefully when he'd poked his head in earlier that he hadn't had the heart to disturb her. There would be plenty of sleepless nights in their future.

Jim paced the main hall of the White House residence, guilt eating at him. He'd given the order for the navy SEALs to leave Brent Miller behind. Three men injured, one missing. And that was assuming the two helicopters made it out of Nicaragua safely. Then there were the hundreds of thousands of people without power in Kansas City, Missouri, as a result of what had likely been a terrorist attack.

When Jim had stepped into the role of president, he'd known he would face challenges as well as casualties during his term. He hadn't expected a major attack to occur only three weeks into his presidency, and he certainly hadn't anticipated the first death to be his own son-in-law. His stopped and stared at his daughter's door as that almost-certain fact replayed in his mind.

The Secret Service agent down the hall glanced in his direction as Jim paced in front of Amy's room for the sixth time in as many minutes. He supposed it had been overkill to have one of the White House physicians called to his daughter's room, but Amy's lack of color and the shock of what she'd witnessed had left Jim erring on the side of caution. He couldn't bear it if she lost both her husband and her unborn child.

Maybe Seth was right. Maybe Brent had survived, but even if he had managed to escape the explosion, Jim couldn't fathom how he could have escaped Morenta's men.

The knot in Jim's stomach tightened. How could Amy ever forgive him? How would he ever be able to forgive himself? And how would tonight have played out if his opponent had won and different choices been made?

The possibility that another president's decisions could have created different outcomes, some different decision that could have spared his son-in-law's life, rocked Jim to the core.

Hushed voices carried to him from the stairwell. Jim turned as Seth passed the Secret Service agent and approached.

Jim met him halfway. "Any updates?"

"Comm is still out, but the USS *Harry S. Truman* has two aircraft approaching on radar," Seth said, the cadence of the South hanging in his voice, a stoic expression on his face. "It looks like they made it out."

"Thank goodness." The relief offered from the news did little to ease the ache that had penetrated Jim's entire body. "How long until they land on the carrier?"

"Ten to fifteen minutes," Seth said. "Once we have the intel from Yago Paquito on how to neutralize whatever is zapping our power, we'll finalize the rescue plan."

Jim swallowed hard. He glanced at Amy's door before returning his gaze to Seth. "I'm surprised you're up here. I thought you would still be in the Sit Room."

"I would be if Secretary Hartley hadn't ordered me to get some sleep," Seth admitted. "We won't be able to go in until we know more about the weapon that's draining our equipment's batteries."

"You're welcome to stay in the guest room upstairs."

"I was hoping you'd say that. I'll text Vanessa to let her know I'm staying over." Seth put his hand on Jim's shoulder. "Tonight wasn't your fault."

"I gave the order."

"Brent chose to stay behind," Seth corrected. "And you saved more than thirty men by giving that order, including men who were injured. Don't second-guess yourself."

"It's hard not to when we could be planning Brent's funeral in a matter of days."

"Unless we have proof, he isn't dead." Seth gave Jim's shoulder a squeeze. "Don't forget that."

Jim swallowed hard and nodded.

Seth's hand dropped, and he took a step back. "Good night, Mr. President."

"Good night, Seth."

Seth disappeared into the stairwell leading to the third floor. He was barely out of sight when the Secret Service agent down the hall spoke into his comm unit.

The agent stepped forward. "Mr. President, Secretary Valdez has asked to see you."

"Where is he?"

"In the Sit Room."

"Tell him I'll meet him in the Oval Office." Jim moved toward the staircase. "And make sure I'm notified as soon as the doctor is finished examining my daughter."

"I'll see to it, sir."

"Thank you." Jim started down the stairs, his heart heavy and his silent communication with the Lord constant. Under his breath, his utmost prayer escaped. "Please let Brent be alive."

* * *

Tristan kneaded the back of his neck to alleviate the tension that had settled there after the helicopter had jerked hard to the right to avoid the missile that had narrowly missed them. They were lucky to be alive. He prayed that luck extended to Brent.

Though he couldn't see outside, Tristan sensed their change in altitude. They were almost to safety. The helicopter touched down, and Tristan immediately unclipped his harness and pushed his way to the door. He didn't know whether Brent had survived the explosion, or whether it was even possible for him to have escaped capture, but Tristan wasn't going to rest until he had answers.

The rest of his squad fell in behind him. Knowing what it was like to lose a teammate, Commander Webb and the other SEALs aboard waited respectfully for the Saint Squad to exit before following.

Damian escorted Yago Paquito off with them. Brent had sacrificed himself to liberate the professor and ensure his knowledge made it out of Nicaragua. Now it was their duty to make sure this man helped them counteract the weapon that had caused widespread equipment failure during their mission.

A master-at-arms crossed the *Truman*'s flight deck and approached them.

"Damian, go with him to help translate," Tristan said. "I want to know everything he tells you as soon as they finish debriefing him."

Damian nodded before he issued instructions in Spanish to Paquito.

Tristan pulled the sling of his rifle over his head and handed his weapon to Quinn. "Take this for me. I'll meet you in our ready room in a few minutes."

"Where are you going?"

"To see the XO," Tristan said. "We need a plan for going back in to get Brent."

"I'm coming with you." Quinn unslung his weapon and handed both his and Tristan's to Craig. "Take care of our weapons, and talk to N4 about getting new comm gear and night-vision goggles."

"I'll try, but I doubt they'll issue new equipment until we have orders."

"We'll get the orders sorted out," Tristan said, determined.

Craig nodded. "Good luck."

Tristan and Quinn crossed to the catwalk at the edge of the flight deck and made their way inside. They descended one level and went only a few steps before the executive officer approached, but the XO's focus was on the men filing in behind them. Tristan moved into his path. "Commander Chang, we have a man missing. We need to get back out there."

"Sorry, Petty Officer," he said, sympathy in his voice, "but we're in a holding pattern until the White House clears us for further operations in Nicaragua."

"Does the White House know who was left behind?" Quinn asked.

"They're aware."

Tristan's eyebrows lifted. If Jim Whitmore knew Brent was their missing man, surely he would authorize them to go back in to get him.

"Sounds like we need to make a call," Quinn said.

"We're River City," the XO said, referring to a ship-wide communications blackout. "Official communication only until further notice."

"The call we need to make falls under the 'official' umbrella," Tristan said, urgency rising within him. "We need to talk to the White House."

Commander Chang gave a skeptical look. "Sorry, men, but that's not going to happen. We can't let everyone who loses a man in combat demand an audience with the president."

The muscle in Tristan's jaw jumped. "He'll want to talk to us."

"Not going to happen."

Tristan's hand fisted. Quinn gripped his arm. "Come on, Tristan. Jim knows how to find us."

Commander Chang moved forward. "You men need to get some sleep."

"Come on," Quinn repeated.

Tristan forced himself to fall into step with Quinn.

As soon as they were out of earshot, Quinn said, "You weren't seriously going to punch an officer, were you?"

"I thought about it." Tristan drew a deep breath and let it out in a huff. "You saw the look on his face when we asked to call the White House."

"I hate to break it to you, but calling the president isn't a normal request."

Tristan stopped walking and studied his teammate. Quinn, a voice of reason? Miracles really did happen. "How are you so calm?"

"I'm not calm. I'm hungry." Quinn grabbed his sleeve and tugged. "I say we find some food. Then we plan our attack."

"You heard the XO. He said they're not letting us go back to Nicaragua."

"I wasn't talking about our attack on the fortress," Quinn said. "I'm talking about taking over the bridge."

Tristan couldn't help but laugh. Though he suspected Quinn was exaggerating his intention, they were unified in purpose. One way or another, they were going to get off this ship and bring Brent home.

* * *

Amy was living her worst nightmare. She vaguely remembered the doctor escorting her upstairs to the bedroom reserved for her in the White House residence.

An ultrasound had confirmed that the life growing inside her was still safe, the rapid heartbeat visible on the screen. She'd been briefed with the rest of her family on the medical resources available at the White House, but she hadn't expected to use them, especially not so soon after her father had taken office.

Commander Landero asked questions. Amy was pretty sure she answered them.

She sat up higher and leaned against the headboard, then reached out a hand and ran it over the thick comforter on the empty side of the bed. A new wave of despair clogged her throat. He should be here.

"I'm going to give you something to help you sleep," Commander Landero said.

Amy stared blindly at her for a moment before shaking her head. "No. I don't want to risk the baby."

"We have several options that are perfectly safe." She opened a medical bag and searched through it, finally coming up with some Benadryl. "Here. A little of this will help you relax and get some sleep tonight."

Amy's eyes watered. "I don't think anything can do that."

Sympathy shone in the doctor's eyes. "You and your baby both need rest." Commander Landero measured out a dose of medication and set it on the bedside table. "I'll leave this for you in case you change your mind."

"Thank you."

The doctor nodded, then pushed the portable ultrasound machine toward the door and made her way into the hall.

The door had barely closed behind her before a knock sounded. Amy straightened. Maybe it was someone with news about Brent. "Come in."

The door swung open, and her mother walked in.

The mere presence of her mom brought tears to Amy's eyes. Her parents had enjoyed nearly forty years of marriage. She and Brent had barely made it six before . . . She couldn't finish the thought. The first tears spilled over and ran down her cheeks.

Her mom rushed to where Amy still lay on the bed. "I heard the doctor was with you. Are you okay? Did something happen with the baby?"

Amy blinked back tears and shook her head. She had no idea what her mom was doing awake in the middle of the night, but her presence couldn't have been timed better. "The doctor said the baby's fine."

"That's a relief."

Amy swallowed hard. "The baby's fine," she repeated. "But Brent's missing."

"Oh no." Her mom pulled her close.

A sob broke from her, and Amy leaned into her mother's embrace.

"Oh, honey." Her mom rubbed her back in a soothing rhythm. "What happened?"

Amy swiped at the tears on her cheeks, and she forced her gaze to meet her mother's. "There was an explosion." She gulped in air. "Brent was right there when it happened."

Her mom's eyes widened. "Are you saying . . ."

"Everyone thinks Brent's dead." Amy drew a shuddering breath, daggers of truth unraveling every aspect of her world. "And it's Dad's fault he didn't come home."

3

Jim had never prayed so hard for a miracle, but thus far, every tidbit of information gave him little beyond the current party line: they didn't know anything. He paced to the fireplace at the far end of the Oval Office before circling to the windows, the light from the West Colonnade spilling onto the dormant rose garden and the lawn beyond.

He lowered into his chair and ran his hand over the glossy wooden surface of the Resolute desk. Did all presidents experience moments like this, moments of helplessness and reflection? Moments when they could do little but beg the Lord for help and guidance?

Jim's most recent meeting with Doug had confirmed that the emergency responders in Kansas City had calculated the range of the pulse weapon that had taken out the city's power system. The governor of Missouri had called up the National Guard, which was en route to provide support, both to the motorists still stranded along the roads leading out of the city as well as to protect against potential looting or any other problems that a widespread power outage could create.

The locals had been creative in their efforts to help those whose cars had lost power. Bonfires along the side of the road. School buses from some of the suburbs transporting people to emergency shelters.

Despite the ongoing efforts, Jim feared how many lives might be lost to the below-freezing temperatures.

The phone on his desk rang. Jim plucked it up. "Yes?"

One of Jim's secretaries spoke. "Mr. President, I have Secretary Hartley on the line."

"Put him through."

After a cursory greeting, Hartley said, "We heard from the *Truman*. Both helicopters arrived safely back on board."

"Thank heavens," Jim said. "Do any of the men have additional insight on Commander Miller or updates on the wounded?"

"The three wounded are being evaluated right now on board the *Truman.* We don't have anything yet on the commander."

"I want to talk to one of the men who was there," Jim insisted. "How do I make that happen?"

"I can arrange it," Secretary Hartley said. "I'll contact the carrier and have them put the call through as soon as they have the commander from SEAL Team Six on the line."

"I don't want to talk to the commander of SEAL Team Six. I want to talk to someone on the Saint Squad."

"I'll take care of it," Hartley said.

* * *

Tristan's patience had run out. Surely Jim Whitmore would want to talk to him or someone else on the squad about Brent. And if Jim wasn't calling them, why wasn't Amy? Surely her status as First Daughter should count for something.

"I've had it." Quinn pushed his plate back on the table. "I say we go to the bridge and talk to the captain."

Tristan cast him a sidelong glance. "You aren't really planning to take over the bridge, are you?"

"I haven't decided yet." Quinn stood. "Come on."

A dozen reasons for why this wasn't a good idea flew through his mind. Tristan ignored all of them. He pushed out of his seat and followed Quinn out of the enlisted mess and down the corridor. "The XO isn't going to be thrilled to see us."

"Commander Chang is an idiot."

The Saint Squad's past dealings with the *Truman*'s executive officer had rarely resulted in problems. Then again, Brent and Amy usually dealt with him. And when it wasn't one of them, Brent sent Seth. Maybe the man didn't respond well to demands from enlisted men. Tristan briefly questioned whether he should have become an officer, but he quickly discarded the thought. He didn't want to be an officer. He wanted to do his job, not play politics.

They approached the bridge.

A seaman a short distance in front of them opened the hatch, and the captain's voice carried to them at full volume. "Where are they now?"

"I'm not sure, sir," the XO responded, his voice much more subdued.

"Find them," the captain roared. "The last thing I need is to get dressed down by some White House bureaucrat because of your assumptions."

"Sorry, sir. I'll find them right away." The XO appeared in the doorway, and his eyes widened when he practically ran into Tristan. "You two. The captain wants to see you."

"Yes, sir." Quinn snapped a salute, but sarcasm dripped from the two simple words.

Tristan entered the bridge and introduced himself.

The captain merely nodded and turned to his communication watch officer. "Get the White House on the line."

"Yes, sir."

A moment later, Tristan took the phone the comm officer handed him, and the president's tense greeting came over the line.

"I didn't think they were ever going to let me talk to you," Tristan said.

"What do you know about Brent?" Jim asked, jumping straight to the heart of the matter. "Is it possible he's still alive?"

"I didn't see him go down." Tristan replayed those few seconds in his mind, his doubts competing with his hopes. "Last sighting was a few yards from where the explosion originated, but that was at least twenty seconds before it happened."

"Twenty seconds?"

"Brent can cross a good distance in that amount of time."

"Assuming he had the opportunity," Jim said. He paused for a moment before he asked, "What are the chances he survived?"

"Either he did, or he didn't," Tristan said bluntly. "My question is, When are you going to let us go back in to get him?"

"As soon as we find a way to get an aircraft or boat in there without risking your safety."

Quinn stepped in front of Tristan, his hands spread out to demonstrate his impatience. Tristan ignored him. "It's Brent's safety I'm worried about right now."

"I know. I'm worried too," Jim said. "We have people working on how to counteract whatever is causing your equipment failures."

"We successfully inserted by inflatable before. We can do it again."

"That's a possibility," Jim said. "We have a satellite tasked to pick up images in a few hours. Seth will work on a plan and have something for you by morning."

"They have the ship under a communications blackout, I assume to protect the intel that Brent is missing." Tristan glared at the XO before adding, "We won't be able to call you."

"Get some sleep," Jim said. "Seth or I will have an update for you in the morning."

"I hate that we have to wait," Tristan said.

"I know. So do I."

* * *

Jim ended the call and blew out an unsteady breath, his emotions in turmoil.

With nothing more that he could do for Brent at the moment, Jim made his way upstairs. He probably wouldn't sleep, but he had to try. Tomorrow would be a challenge even if he could get a full night's sleep. But since there were only a few hours until daybreak, he had little chance of getting even half of his recommended eight hours.

He reached his bedroom, surprised to find the light on and his wife absent. His eyebrows furrowed. Katherine had been asleep when he had come upstairs a short while ago.

He headed back into the hall and made it as far as the main hall before Katherine emerged from Amy's room.

Jim crossed to her. "What are you doing up?"

Katherine didn't speak until she passed the Secret Service agent and reached him. "I woke up and went to get a glass of water. That's when Gray told me the doctor was in with Amy."

A new avalanche of guilt crashed over him. "How is she?"

"What in the world happened?"

Jim put his hand on her back and nodded toward their bedroom. He led her inside and closed the door behind him. "What did she tell you?"

"She said Brent's missing." Katherine turned to face him. "And that it's your fault."

The arrow of truth speared through the center of his heart. Jim's hope for a miracle deflated, and he forced himself to accept the likely outcome from tonight's events. Amy's child, his grandchild, would grow up without a father.

Katherine's voice wavered when she said, "Please tell me Brent's still alive."

"We don't have confirmation, but it doesn't look good." Jim collapsed onto the sofa in the seating area and lowered his head into his hands. "I can't believe this happened."

"What did happen?" Katherine sat beside him and put her hand on his knee.

Jim let out a shaky breath. "Brent couldn't make it to the helicopter. It looked like he was trying to protect his men."

"That's not surprising." Katherine turned so she was facing him more fully. "What else can you tell me?"

"The helicopters were pulling back when an explosion happened right where we last saw Brent." Jim pressed his lips into a hard line. "The fire must have gone out a good twenty yards in every direction."

Katherine's hand found his. "And you saw Brent by this explosion?"

"We couldn't see him by then. The fog was too thick."

"So you can't be sure if he's alive or not."

"That's what Seth said. So did Tristan." Jim ran a hand over his face. "I want to believe he's alive." He broke off and tried to swallow the lump forming in his throat. He drew a deep breath. "But we have to face the facts." Moisture sprang to his eyes, and he blinked it back. He swallowed again. "It's highly likely Amy is a widow, and she'll have to raise her child on her own."

"Why do we have to face those facts?" Katherine shook her head. "If Seth and Tristan think there's even the smallest chance Brent is still alive, then we need to cling to that possibility. Our daughter deserves nothing less."

Katherine was right, but would pretending Brent was alive help or hurt when the confirmation came that Jim's orders had resulted in his death?

"Amy must hate me." He leaned back and gazed upward. "This is all my fault."

"Don't do this to yourself." Katherine put her hand on his cheek and turned his head so he didn't have a choice but to look at her. "Brent chose to be a navy SEAL long before he met you. The risk has always been there. Amy knew that when she married him."

"But when she married him, she didn't know I would someday be the president who would send him into harm's way."

"Why did you order the helicopters to leave Brent behind?"

He hadn't had a choice. Even as that thought formed, he second-guessed himself all over again. "There was a possibility of mechanical failure. If they had waited for Brent, it's very possible they all would have died."

"If Brent were in a situation where he had the choice to sacrifice his life to save the lives of his squad, would he do it?"

Yes. What he had seen on the screen tonight was proof of that. The truth didn't take away Jim's role in the disaster. "I'm still the one who gave the order."

"An order Brent not only would have agreed with but one he also would have given had he been granted the authority to do so."

"Katherine, don't you understand?" He stared down at her, not bothering to fight the tears that spilled over. "He could be dead because of me."

"I understand that you're taking blame that isn't yours." Katherine's brown eyes darkened. "What did you do that any other president wouldn't have done?"

Her question jumped to the heart of the issue, and he faced it again. Would his predecessor have acted differently in a similar threat? What would his opponent have done had she won the presidency? The answer to those questions circled, and this time, Jim found answers. "I don't know what I could have done differently."

"You feel guilty, and Amy may be casting blame your way, but both of you have to step outside of your feelings long enough to face the facts. You made the best decision you could with the information you had at the time. Any other president would have done the same. And no matter what orders you tried to give Brent, you know he would have protected his men no matter what." Katherine paused, and her eyes misted. "Whether Brent survived or not, this is all in the Lord's hands. Trust Him to guide you through this."

"I don't know if I can."

"You can," Katherine insisted. "And if you stumble, I'll be right here to help you back up."

* * *

Tristan jerked awake when the hatch opened. Though he had ordered Craig and Quinn to get some sleep, he had opted to wait in his squad's boardroom for Damian to give him an update. A power nap in an office chair wasn't as restful as six hours straight in his bunk, but only sheer willpower had allowed him to turn his brain off long enough to sleep at all.

Damian entered and closed the hatch behind him.

Tristan checked the time on the wall: 4:15 a.m. "Took you long enough."

Damian stifled a yawn and sat beside him. "It took a while to get the professor to calm down enough to talk."

"What's the latest?"

"I learned a lot about how the weapon works, but how to stop it may be more complicated than we expected."

"How so?"

"The electromagnetic pulse weapons are relatively small and portable, but the core of how it works is through the electronic virus that disables battery power for anything that gets infected."

"Are you saying our comm units and our night-vision goggles were infected by computer viruses?"

"I'm not sure. The professor suspects Morenta had a pulse weapon operating in the woods somewhere near the hideout to neutralize enemy forces," Damian said. "The range would wipe out the battery power for everything within a five-mile radius."

"I don't get why our comm and goggles failed, but the listening devices we planted last week were still operating when we went in." Tristan contemplated the challenges of living in an area where battery power couldn't be used. "And how are the people at the fortress functioning? Their jeep worked fine."

"Yago said something about how copper shielding could be used to protect batteries. That makes sense since all the computer equipment at the hideout was encased in copper."

"The listening devices have technology to keep them from being detected," Tristan said. "That must have included a copper coating of some sort."

"That's my guess."

Tristan swiveled toward the computer behind him. "Has a message already gone out to the White House?"

"*Sí.*" Damian yawned. "A yeoman took the professor to guest quarters to get some sleep."

"I guess we should get some too. The sooner the higher-ups consider us operation ready, the sooner they'll let us go back in after Brent."

The weariness on Damian's face faded, replaced by concern. "I don't even want to think about where he is right now."

Death, torture, injury. Tristan clenched his hands. He couldn't think about any of those. Positive thinking. Brent was okay as long as they didn't have proof that he wasn't. They'd been through this before, and he'd come out alive. They would bring him home again.

"Get some sleep," Tristan said. "Tomorrow, we start planning our rescue mission."

"It already is tomorrow." Damian stood and took a step toward the door. "Aren't you coming?"

"I'll be there in a minute. I need to do one thing first."

Damian nodded and disappeared out the hatch. As soon as it closed behind him, Tristan rested his elbows on his knees, clasped his hands, and bowed his head. In a matter of hours, they would plan the rescue mission, but it never hurt to ask for some divine guidance along the way.

4

Vanessa Johnson paced along the front window of the enormous great room. Her hand gripped her cell phone while her eyes followed one light after another that lined the currently empty driveway leading to the beautiful mansion where she now resided.

When she and Seth had moved into the Whitmore family home, it had felt like a dream. An immense house to raise their daughter in as they worked in DC, horses in the pasture up the hill, a reasonable commute to the White House. After receiving Seth's text early this morning, though, she was now bracing for a nightmare.

Staying at Jim's. Say extra prayers.

The meaning between the words had been simple enough to decipher. Her husband had spent the night at the White House, and his squad was in trouble.

Seth had only transferred from the Saint Squad last week. He would never forgive himself if someone were injured in the field when he might have been able to protect them had he and Vanessa not opted to take advantage of new opportunities here in the DC area.

The progression of her career from deep undercover work for the CIA to teaching at the farm to now acting as liaison between the guardians and the president of the United States still continued to amaze her. In truth, her relationship with Seth had prompted all her career changes: first, her change to teaching at the farm when she and Seth had married, and now her new position working in DC while her husband served as one of the president's military aides.

Her phone rang, the letter *K* illuminating her screen. Kade. The guardian she worked with most frequently.

She hit the Talk button. "Any word on the Saint Squad?"

"They're back on the carrier, but they're a man short." Kade's frustration carried over the line along with his typical impatience.

Technically, they had gone in two men short—Seth, who had just transferred from the squad, and Jay, who was out on paternity leave after the birth of his first child. "Who are you talking about?" Vanessa asked.

"Brent Miller. He didn't make it out."

Vanessa's breath caught, and she gripped the back of the nearest chair. She gathered her courage. "Define 'didn't make it out.'"

"Officially, he's listed as MIA, but the reports don't look good." Kade detailed the after-action report as well as the video feed from the helicopter when the explosion had erupted where Brent had last been seen.

Vanessa lowered her head and muttered a silent prayer for Brent and Amy. "What do we know from the guardian in Central America? He must have some idea of what really happened."

"We haven't had any contact from him since his update that he was going to the fortress to provide support."

"Not even on the guardian message board?" Vanessa asked. The guardians not only supported intel and military personnel in locations where the government couldn't operate openly, but they also had access to a highly effective communication system.

"Nothing. He's gone dark, even from us."

Vanessa's grip tightened on her phone. "You don't think Morenta has him, do you?"

"No. The SEALs extracted Morenta last night. He's currently in custody aboard the *Truman*."

"Then, why wouldn't the guardian down there check in? What's his name anyway?"

"Manuel," Kade said. "And if the equipment failures the SEALs suffered during their op last night are any indication, the lack of communication isn't intentional."

* * *

The chill of the early morning air nipped at Jim's exposed skin when he stepped outside onto the West Colonnade. He tucked his hands into his pockets and quickened his pace as he traversed the lighted space between the exterior wall and the columns that ran the length of the walkway.

More than twenty of his predecessors had made this same journey on what was often referred to as the shortest commute in DC. Thank goodness he didn't have to drive to the office. He already didn't know how he would manage to concentrate today without that added stressor.

He entered the Oval Office as the clock across the room chimed the half hour. Five thirty in the morning. Another half hour until the daily brief would arrive.

Jim glanced across the room at the door leading to his private study. His desk behind that closed door was stacked high with work, but he didn't have the emotional strength to face so many tedious tasks right now. Instead, he took his spot behind the desk in the Oval Office and opened his secure laptop.

As suspected, the presidential daily brief had not yet arrived, but a report from Homeland Security topped his unread messages.

Doug must have gotten less sleep than Jim had. The bad news came first. Three dead in Kansas City, all of whom had been on life support in local hospitals that had lost both their primary and generator power.

What he read next sparked a new light of hope. Local farmers had worked through the night using horses to transport stranded motorists outside the affected area to where buses and tractor trailers shuttled them to churches and schools that had been set up as shelters in outlying areas. Cell phones were being collected before transport to ensure the computer viruses infecting them wouldn't potentially spread the power outages. Other local volunteers were knocking on doors to inform residents without heat where emergency shelters with kerosene heaters were located.

Transporting critical-care patients from the Missouri side of Kansas City to the Kansas side still proved to be problematic, but copper-shielded batteries had been delivered to two of the main medical centers so their generators would function again.

A knock sounded on the door before it opened. Sawyer Gaines, Jim's chief of staff, walked in wearing the same suit from yesterday. "I had a feeling you'd already be in here."

"Have you been here all night?" Jim asked.

"I wanted to stay on top of the intel reports coming in." One shoulder jerked up, and he sat in the chair beside Jim's desk. "Our search team in Vegas finally found the pulse weapon."

"Thank goodness."

"I'm afraid it's not all good news. The weapon had already activated, and it took out the power in North Las Vegas."

"Can't they deactivate it?" Jim asked.

"I'm afraid it's not that simple. The ripple effect of the embedded software virus is already complicating the battery drainage issues."

"How widespread is the outage?"

"Just like in Kansas City, it's limited to one area. Las Vegas proper is still operating normally."

"I would think they would have gone after Las Vegas itself. That would be more impactful."

"The Strip going dark would have made a bigger headline," Sawyer said. "I can only think that the cascade effect of a nationwide power outage would have been greater through North Las Vegas."

"Maybe, but I'd like the data on that to be sure."

"I'll take care of it."

"Put in the request, and then go get some sleep."

"I already took a nap on the couch in my office." Sawyer motioned to Jim's laptop. "Any update on Brent?"

Jim swallowed the emotions that the simple question stirred inside him. "Nothing yet."

"I hate to bring this up, but we need to write a press release. If the wounded SEALs haven't already been transferred stateside for care, they will be soon. It's only a matter of time before the information leaks about the mission."

"The SEALs know how to keep a secret."

"Mostly, yes, but I'd still prefer to control the narrative," Sawyer said. "We don't want some well-meaning information specialist with the navy leaking something prematurely without understanding the full ramifications of what happened last night."

"What do you recommend?"

"We have Morenta in custody. We lead with that and the recovery of the SEALs."

"What about the power outages?"

"That's trickier because we don't want to talk terrorist attack and potentially create a panic. For now, I say we focus on the rescue-and-recovery efforts. We get the Red Cross to set up a relief fund. People like to help when they can."

"I'll leave the details to you and Eva," Jim said, referring to his press secretary. "Make sure she knows that nothing goes out about Brent or that we have a SEAL missing."

Sawyer stood. "Yes, sir."

5

Tristan approached the enlisted mess. The scent of burned toast and fried mush did little to stir his appetite. The instinct to have one of the officers in his squad bring him food from the officers' mess surfaced only to be immediately discounted. His squad didn't have any officers at the moment.

Tristan paused by the mess entrance, debating whether he should go inside or not. Maybe they would have a muffin or something he could take with him.

Commander Webb approached. "What's the latest on your missing man?"

"No news yet," Tristan said. "We're supposed to have satellite photos sometime this morning."

Webb's jaw clenched briefly. "This is when we need our own intel officer on board."

"Yes, sir." Tristan's gut twisted uncomfortably. If Amy were here right now, would she help or hinder their efforts? He couldn't imagine what she must be going through. Stateside or aboard ship, she no doubt was well-informed of their mission status.

"Let me know what I can do to help your squad."

"Thank you, sir." Tristan took one step toward the mess but reconsidered. Instead, he bypassed the entrance and started toward his squad's boardroom.

"Not interested in what they're serving this morning?" Commander Webb asked.

Tristan turned. "Have you ever eaten in the enlisted mess?"

"Can't say that I have."

"Good decision."

Webb's lips quirked up. "Can't be worse than the ration bars my men will be living off of by this time tomorrow."

Hope stirred. "Where are you going?"

"Morenta's place in Colombia," Webb said.

"Why?"

"That's where Morenta's Z-10 was last spotted."

The attack helicopter was supposed to have been at the fortress when they'd inserted two days ago in Nicaragua. "They think Morenta might have been developing weapons there too?"

"No one knows, but so far, Morenta isn't talking. The higher-ups don't want to get blindsided again if they can help it."

"Does my squad have orders too?"

"Last I heard, you're on standby to go back in to get Commander Miller." Webb shook his head. "Personally, I'd prefer that that mission take priority."

Tristan didn't disagree, but even though the extra support could work to their advantage, the Saint Squad worked best when they were on their own. Or they did when they had access to the information that flowed through their intel officer and their chain of command. "Any chance you can get our squad looped in for the intel reports on Commander Miller? I doubt the XO is going to send them our way since Amy and our officers aren't on board."

Webb jutted his chin in the direction of the Saint Squad's boardroom. "I'll take care of it."

"Thanks." Tristan worked his way through the maze of corridors until he reached his intended destination. The moment he opened the hatch, voices carried to him.

"What about the duty officer from last night?" Craig asked.

"I think we'd have better luck with the communication watch officer from the bridge," Quinn said. "He was there when Tristan talked to Jim."

"Craig, don't you have any more autographed pictures of your wife?" Damian asked from where he sat by one of the computer terminals.

Craig swiveled in the chair beside Damian. "I only have a couple left, and I promised those to the NR who promised to get us our new equipment."

Tristan closed the hatch behind him. "It's pretty bad that one of us had to marry a movie star to get what we need."

Craig offered a halfhearted grin. "She's a television star now."

"Whatever." Tristan turned his attention to Quinn, who was pacing the narrow space by their worktable. The fatigue on his face was visible, no doubt caused by the worry they all shared about Brent. "What are you negotiating for anyway?"

"Expedited intel reports." Quinn gestured toward the hatch. "Without an officer, we're having trouble getting everything we need."

"Webb's taking care of that for us." Tristan motioned to Damian's computer screen. "What's the latest?"

Quinn tapped a finger on the papers spread out on the worktable. "We've been going over the latest satellite images, but this one is from before we went in. The fog last night made it impossible to see anything."

"What about the video feed from the helicopter cameras?" Tristan asked. "Do we have access yet?"

"I asked," Damian said. "They didn't answer."

Tristan glanced at Craig. "We may need one of your wife's photos to get that first. It may be faster than waiting for Webb."

"What about the equipment you wanted?"

"Quinn can go have a nice chat with the XO about what we need to increase our operational readiness."

"Me?" Quinn's dark eyes narrowed. "Why me?"

"Because he'll remember you from last night. After getting dressed down by the captain, I suspect he'll be eager to help us."

"You were there last night too. Why can't you do it?"

"Because you're less likely to punch the guy." Tristan folded his arms across his chest. "Besides, I outrank you."

Quinn bristled. "What? Because your name is before mine in the alphabet?"

"By my calculations, I figure I've got at least six, maybe seven minutes' seniority on you."

Quinn shook his head. "You're delusional."

"Yet another reason you should deal with the XO."

"What are you going to do?" Craig asked.

"I'm going to start on our mission plan." Tristan moved to the worktable. "And, Quinn? While you're at it, see if the XO can shake loose the latest sat images."

"And the helicopter video feed," Craig added.

"What? I have to do all the work?"

"Fine." Craig stood. "I'll come with you, but I'm saving Sienna's photos until we absolutely have to use them."

"Do you know something we don't know?" Tristan asked.

"They're making chocolate éclairs for dinner tonight in the officer's mess."

Tristan barely suppressed the smile trying to form. "Get the equipment and intel we need. We'll worry about dessert later."

Craig let out a sigh. "I really miss Amy. She always got us our intel *and* dessert."

"We all miss her *and* Brent," Tristan said. "And we're not going to waste time getting the two back together again." He prayed that reunion wouldn't include the need for a casket.

* * *

Adrenaline rushed through Vanessa along with a sense of helplessness that she couldn't leave yet for the White House. She hated not knowing what was going on.

From her spot in the center of the living room carpet, one-year-old Talia babbled as she stacked blocks three high only to knock them back down again. Her giggle cut through Vanessa's worry for a brief moment.

Eager for a distraction, Vanessa sat beside Talia. "Hey, little one. Want to build a tower?" Vanessa stacked several blocks. Talia promptly waved her chubby little hand and sent them tumbling back down. Another giggle.

Vanessa gathered her daughter close and kissed her cheek. "I'm going to miss you today."

Talia snuggled closer for a moment before squirming so she could reach the blocks once more.

Vanessa released her and stood to look out the window again. She checked the time on her cell phone. No word yet from Seth this morning. Nothing new from any of the guardians either.

Not willing to wait any longer for word, she called Kade.

"Hey, I was just about to call you," Kade said in a greeting far more cordial than his usual "What do you want?"

"Is a rescue operation for Brent underway yet?" Vanessa asked.

"The navy won't send anyone in until they can protect against the equipment failures, especially after the helicopters barely made it back to the ship."

She paced the room again. "What are you talking about?"

"The battery power on both helicopters was in the danger zone. If they'd been in the air another ten minutes, they would have gone down."

Vanessa's insides churned, both at the thought that so many men could have been lost and at the knowledge that Brent's fate remained unknown. The deep-seated relief that Seth wasn't in danger flowed through her and left her with a seed of guilt. Her husband was safe, but Amy must be going through pure torture.

"As soon as my babysitter gets here, I'm heading to the White House."

"Word is that the man who helped develop this weapon is also on board the *Truman*. Something has to come out soon."

"I'm praying for that." A car pulled into the driveway. "Call me as soon as you hear anything new."

"I will, but I expect the same from you."

"You can count on it." Vanessa hung up the phone and moved to the door. She pulled it open as her mother rushed up the front steps, pulling a suitcase behind her. "Thanks for coming," Vanessa said.

Her mother enfolded her in a hug. "I'm afraid to ask what happened that you needed me to drive down from Pennsylvania at this hour of the morning."

"I can't tell you much, but I have friends who need me." Vanessa glanced at Talia, and a rush of regret overwhelmed her.

"I'll take care of Talia. You do whatever you have to. We'll be fine."

Vanessa gave her mother another hug. "Thanks, Mom."

6

Jim's chief of staff had barely left his office when Seth appeared in the open doorway.

"Sir, have we heard anything new from the *Truman*?" Seth asked.

"Not yet." Jim picked up the phone. He was too tired to identify the voice of the secretary who came on the line, but as soon as she greeted him, Jim said, "I need to speak with the captain of the *Truman*."

Seth continued into the room and closed the door behind him. He held up a manila envelope. "We have the first satellite photos of the fortress since Morenta's extraction."

Jim straightened. "Any sign of Brent?"

"No." Seth pulled the photos from the envelope and slid one onto Jim's desk. "This is the best shot of the area where we saw him last."

Jim cringed when he lowered his gaze to the charred ground and the bodies still visible near a mangled mass of metal. Jim was still trying to process the contents of the photo when Seth pointed at a scorched tree.

"Look here. I don't see any bodies."

"I'm not following."

"Brent was on this side of the jeep." Seth tapped the downed tree. "There's a chance he was under that tree or could have been thrown into the trees."

Hope lit within him. "And you think he could have survived?"

"I want the chance to find out." Seth set another photo in front of Jim. "This is the latest image of Morenta's villa in Cali. The reports show the Z-10 helicopter is there, but it looks like it's getting ready to move."

"I'm sure this is all leading up to something."

"It is." Seth straightened to his full height of enormous. "If Brent is still at the fortress, especially if he's wounded, he won't be able to stay hidden for long if the Z-10 starts scanning for heat signatures."

"What do you propose?"

"Let the Saint Squad go in there. Now. Before Morenta's men have time to recover from last night's conflict."

"Now?" Jim glanced at the light breaking over the horizon. "In daylight?"

"They aren't far off the coast," Seth said. "If you give the order, they can slip in and do a quick search-and-rescue during the morning hours. Then they can rendezvous tonight."

"And if Brent is wounded?"

"They'll adapt."

Jim wavered. He wanted to give the order, but what if more of the Saint Squad went in and didn't come home?

Seth lowered into the chair beside Jim's desk. Determination and compassion filled his eyes. "You can't afford to wait on this. Son-in-law or not, we need to give him the benefit of the doubt."

"I agree, but what about the risk to the rest of your squad?"

"They know the area, and they know how to stay invisible."

"And the communication problems?" Jim asked.

"They'll plan for it." Seth motioned to the phone. "I guarantee my men already have a plan. Before they go in, I'll walk them through the new intel we've gathered over the past few hours."

Jim replayed Seth's last comment. They were Seth's men now. Even though Seth had transferred from the unit, they were his friends, his brothers-in-arms.

The phone on Jim's desk rang. He picked up the receiver.

"The Situation Room has the captain of the *Truman* on the line."

"Thank you." Jim hung up the phone and stood. "Let's go talk to the captain." He skirted around the edge of his desk. "And you can brief your men."

"Thank you, sir."

* * *

Tears gave way to sheer exhaustion in the early morning hours, and Amy was finally able to fall asleep, though only about as well as a rabbit in its burrow with a fox waiting outside. Her uneasy stomach pushed her out of her deep sleep, but she curled up on her side, determined to ignore it. Minutes ticked by, the discomfort growing.

Even as she slowly came awake, she fought to stay in that semiconscious state, where she could alter her reality. Her hand went to her stomach. At least part of her reality.

A baby.

The image of creating a nursery in her home in Virginia Beach, Brent painting the walls while she put together the crib, filled her mind. He never was good about taking the time to read the assembly instructions. They would finally have a reason to shop for baby clothes and car seats and strollers. She would have to decide whether she wanted to keep working after the baby was born. Could she be content being a full-time mom? Would it drive her crazy not knowing where the Saint Squad was and whether they were okay?

Amy's eyes opened, and her breath caught. Brent wasn't okay. Being in the inner circle of intelligence didn't take away the questions. It only brought the hard truth forward that her husband was missing in action.

Fresh tears flooded her eyes. Had any new information been uncovered about her husband? Had he miraculously survived the explosion and been able to call to let someone know he was alive? As much as she prayed that was the case, she had no doubt such news would have warranted her parents waking her up to give her the update. No, if she hadn't heard anything, only two possibilities existed: either no one had any new information, or her husband's death had been confirmed.

Amy curled her body tighter. If her only two choices were the unknown or the unthinkable, she didn't want to start this day. Maybe she could hide in sleep for a few more hours.

Her stomach roiled. Acid rose in her throat.

The discomfort stole Amy's first choice from her, and she sat up. That was a little better.

Drawing slow, steady breaths, she swiped at her damp cheeks. Whether she was ready for this day or not, apparently her unborn child wasn't going to let her wallow much longer.

She made her way into the bathroom, deliberately avoiding her reflection in the mirror. She didn't need to see her face to know her eyes were swollen and her cheeks tear-stained.

A shower, a couple of cold compresses, and some concealer to hide the dark shadows under her eyes were enough to make her look almost normal. Now, if she could get her stomach to settle, maybe she could find the courage to face what the day had in store for her. After she dressed, she moved to her bedroom door.

The aroma of bread baking scented the air. Amy's appetite stirred.

She walked out the door and started down the wide hall. When she got closer, the Secret Service agent outside the kitchen turned his head long enough to acknowledge her but then averted his eyes.

Amy forced her shoulders back and lifted her chin. She would make it through the day.

With sustenance being the only item on her current to-do list, she passed the agent and entered the kitchen.

Inside, her mother sat at the square table that abutted the island in the center of the room. Several cloth-covered pans lined the counter beside the oven, and a scatter of papers lay on the table.

Her mom looked up. "Honey, how are you feeling this morning?"

Amy dragged a hand through her hair. "I don't even know how to answer that question."

Her mom rose and gathered her close. "Everything is going to be all right. I know it."

Logically, Amy knew the words were meant to soothe, but she couldn't stop the anger from rising within her. She pulled back. "You can't know that, Mom. No one can."

"Have a little faith, Amy." Her mom grasped both of Amy's arms. "Hope for the best. If the worst does happen, we'll all be here for you. And know the Lord will carry you through your trials, no matter what."

"It's a nice sentiment, but I'm not feeling very uplifted at the moment."

"You'll feel better after you've eaten." Her mom motioned toward the table. "Have a seat. I'll fix you something."

Amy doubted food would help, but she sat anyway.

The timer buzzed, and her mom grabbed an oven mitt before pulling open the oven. She slid out a tray of rolls before uncovering another one and sliding it onto the rack.

"Why are you making rolls at"—Amy glanced at the clock on the wall—"eight o'clock in the morning?"

"This was one of the few things I could eat when I had morning sickness." She retrieved a cooling rack from a lower cabinet and set it on the counter. "Dry toast gets pretty old after a while."

Amy's gaze swept over the counters again. "Don't you think five dozen rolls is overkill?"

"We can share, and they freeze well." She transferred the rolls onto the rack. "You can take a couple dozen home with you after Brent gets back."

"If Brent gets back." Amy clenched her teeth.

"Don't do that to yourself." Her mom set the spatula aside and turned to face her. "Isn't it better to believe he's okay, to keep your hope alive?"

"What if he's not?" Despair clogged her throat. She swallowed hard. "What if he doesn't come home this time?"

"You're borrowing trouble, Amy." Her mom set a roll in front of her and put her hand on her arm, squeezing gently. "You can't hurt any more than you do now. Give yourself the gift of hope and faith. Let yourself believe in the future you always wanted."

The future she always wanted: Brent, children, a life with purpose. She needed that purpose now. She swallowed hard. "No guarantees, but I'll try."

"Good. Now, eat your breakfast. You need to keep your strength up, for both you and your baby." Her mom moved back to the counter and set the empty cookie sheet in the sink.

Amy took a bite, the taste of home giving her both strength and comfort. "Your rolls really are the best."

"Glad you think so because if I'm going to send half of these rolls home with you, it's only fair that you help with the dishes."

Amy's lips twitched into a half-smile. Leave it to her mom to use cooking and chores to make things better. Amy ate slowly as her thoughts churned. She tried to grasp the gift of home and faith her mother offered, but she doubted anything would give her the comfort she needed. But as much as she feared what she might find when the next intel reports came in, she couldn't stand by and hide forever.

She stood and moved to the counter to get another roll. "I'm going to head downstairs. I need to check the new intel reports."

Her mom's eyebrows lifted. "You're trying to get out of doing dishes again, aren't you?"

"Maybe." Amy's heart lifted ever so slightly. "Thanks, Mom."

"You're welcome. Let me know when you hear anything."

Amy pressed her lips together as she fought against another rush of fear. "I will."

7

Tristan was in command. That thought alone terrified him as their inflatable boat cut across the waves, the spray of water misting over the four SEALs and the boat operator at the helm. But the unorthodox decision to send the four enlisted Saint Squad members into Nicaragua without an officer in charge had come straight from the top. The very top.

President Whitmore had been right there on the screen when Seth had briefed him and the rest of the squad members on their mission. The captain and XO had little choice but to follow the president's directive. Now here they were, once again inserting into enemy territory in a country that was considered an ally.

Their objective: find Brent and bring him home. Tristan prayed they would find their commanding officer both alive and mobile.

The landing zone they'd used for their alternate exit point if they couldn't reach the helos in their last mission came into sight. The first part of today's mission would be to remove the tree that blocked their primary entry point, which was significantly closer to the area where they'd last seen Brent.

The early morning sunlight glistened on the whitecaps as they approached shore.

Tristan lifted his binoculars and scanned the cove and the trees encircling it. A doe feeding in the clearing beside the water lifted her head. A bird took flight.

"Anything?" Craig asked.

"No," Tristan said, then added, "We go in and clear the area. If we don't see any sign of him, we regroup at the boat."

"Got it." Damian unslung his rifle so it was at the ready.

"We'd better find him quick," Quinn said. "We don't want Tristan to get used to being in charge."

The simple comment broke through the tension.

"Ignore him," Tristan said. "He's just jealous."

"Of you?" Quinn lifted his rifle and peered through the scope. "Not a chance."

They drew closer to shore, and the chatter ceased. As soon as they reached the beach, Tristan signaled for his teammates to proceed.

The four men spread out, fanning through the nearby trees. Whatever footprints his squad had made when they'd inserted last night had been washed away by the tide. The few footprints that remained farther inland were pointing toward the fortress, not away. Nothing in his path appeared to be recent beyond a few deer tracks.

Tristan doubled back to the boat. Quinn, Damian, and Craig joined him.

"I don't see any fresh tracks," Craig said.

"Me neither," Quinn said.

"Craig and Damian, work your way down the beach to the other cove. Clear that tree out of the way," Tristan said. "Quinn and I will meet you there with fresh comm sets."

"Got it."

Tristan and Quinn returned to the boat. If today's experience was anything like the last several times they'd inserted here, staying clear of the magnetic pulse weapon would extend the battery life on their equipment.

Quinn climbed in and took his seat. "I'm surprised you didn't send me down the coast."

"I thought about it, but you probably would have told me no."

"Yeah." Quinn sighed. "I was kind of looking forward to it."

"Once we find Brent, I'll tell you to do something so you can ignore me."

"That'll work." Quinn sat down and laid his weapon across his lap. "Especially if you tell me not to borrow your last pair of clean socks."

Tristan glared. "You didn't."

"I can neither confirm nor deny."

Tristan took his seat. "It's official. We have to find Brent. He may be the only person who can save you when we get back to the ship."

Tristan gave the order to the boat pilot, and they pulled away from shore. They navigated back out to sea before approaching the next landing area with a tree that had fallen into the water and impeded their path.

"Craig, Damian, what's your ETA?" Tristan asked over his comm set.

"Almost there," Craig said.

"Do you want me to approach?" the boat pilot asked.

"Not yet." Tristan shook his head. "We want to stay as far away from whatever is killing batteries as we can."

"Roger."

Tristan opened a plastic case and fished out a new battery for his comm set. He switched it out with the old in case the first one had been drained during their few minutes ashore earlier. He handed a second battery to Quinn before he lifted his binoculars again. Two minutes passed before Craig and Damian dragged the tree onto land just enough to let their boat pass.

"Let's go." Tristan grabbed two extra batteries. As soon as the boat reached land, Damian and Craig came into view and grabbed the front of the boat to steady it.

Tristan and Quinn stepped ashore, and Tristan handed each of them fresh batteries. As soon as everyone put the new ones in, they did a quick comm check.

"*Está bien*," Damian said.

Tristan looked behind him briefly before he remembered. None of the officers was here. He was in charge. A weight of responsibility pressed in on him, but he drew a quick breath and gave the order. "Move out."

* * *

Amy walked along the colonnade, the frigid air a reminder that the sun hadn't been up long enough to bring the temperature above freezing. She stuffed her hands into her coat pockets, a Secret Service agent trailing behind her.

The rolls she'd eaten for breakfast had conquered the worst of her nausea, but the fatigue from lack of sleep slowed her steps. The tightness at the corners of her eyes and puffiness beneath them would be yet another reminder of her lack of sleep and the worry that caused it.

Hope and faith—Amy tried to muster both.

One of the Secret Service agents opened the door leading into the West Wing. Amy passed through and mumbled her thanks.

She drew a deep breath and struggled against the mopiness that pressed down on her no matter how much she tried to find a glimmer of positivity.

Oval Office or Situation Room? The thought of facing her father right now made the decision for her.

Her limbs heavy, she turned toward the stairs. She was nearly to the Situation Room when someone called her name.

Vanessa hurried toward her. Amy didn't even have a chance to utter a greeting before the shorter woman wrapped her arms around her in a hug.

The unconditional love flowing off her friend brought fresh tears to the surface. Amy fought against them and tightened her hold on Vanessa.

Vanessa held her for a long minute before she finally stepped back and studied her. "Tell me what you know."

Amy glanced around the hallway. A Secret Service agent stood behind her. A navy steward was positioned beside the Navy Mess. Amy took a step away from the mess doorway so they could speak without being overheard.

She swallowed hard and struggled to choke out the words. "Brent didn't make it out." She drew a breath. "There was an explosion."

"What did you see?"

"I couldn't see anything through the fog when the fire burst into the air, but it was right where Brent was."

"Any updates today?" Vanessa asked.

"I'm gathering my courage to find out."

Vanessa put her hand on Amy's arm. "Come on. We'll find out together."

The two approached the Situation Room. As soon as the agent at the door verified their identities, he opened the door and let them pass.

They entered the main briefing room, which, despite the early hour, was nearly full.

Her father sat at the head of the table, looking every bit as presidential as he had before Brent had disappeared beneath the fog and flames. Resentment bubbled inside her. In her head, she knew her father had done what needed to be done when he'd ordered those helicopters to retreat to safety, but the veracity of the situation didn't translate to the heart.

From his seat beside her father, Seth stood. "Amy, sit here."

Amy shook her head and motioned for him to reclaim his chair. She should have known he wouldn't comply. The man had Southern gentleman too deeply ingrained in him to let her stand while he was sitting.

Even though she would have preferred to keep some distance between herself and her dad, she took the offered seat. Her weary muscles sighed in relief, but when she looked up, she immediately tensed. An image of dense woods blurred as the camera holder moved stealthily forward. The angle of the lens and the deliberate movements of the person it was attached to screamed special forces.

Light filtered through the blurred leaves. An op in daylight? Had her father's concern for Brent impacted his judgment already?

Amy turned to Seth. "Who is it?"

"Tristan. He's on point."

On screen, Tristan slowed, and the barrel of his rifle lifted into view.

"They're at the fortress?" Amy asked incredulously. Despite her prayers that her husband was still alive, she had expected the soonest anyone would go in looking for him would be tonight. Was her father really risking the rest of the Saint Squad to find him? Even as that thought flitted through her mind, she knew the answer. Brent's men would move heaven and earth to bring him back home. Her father didn't have to order them back into that enemy camp. They volunteered.

Seth's presence beside her brought up a different question. "Who's in command?"

"Tristan," Seth said.

Vanessa shook her head. "Heaven help us."

Amy let out an unsteady breath. "I'm praying heaven will help all of us."

8

Tristan sidestepped a motion detector and moved through the dense woods. Quinn followed several yards behind him with Damian and Craig taking a parallel path.

Tristan couldn't remember the last time they'd inserted during daylight, and he wasn't about to be the person to demonstrate why the SEALs preferred to operate at night. Despite the sunlight already streaming through the trees, they had to stay invisible both while they searched for Brent and when they left this compound that had become his squad's Achilles' heel.

Tristan reached the edge of the grassy area by the fortress. He signaled Quinn to clear the wooded area to his right. Damian and Craig fell in behind him, keeping deep enough in the shadows to avoid being seen. They needn't have bothered. Only a single guard was visible, and he was over three hundred yards away by the front gate.

Tristan didn't blame the guards for steering clear of this side of the fortress. The gruesome sight of the burned-out jeep was bad enough, but the carnage from the blast remained.

Tristan drew a deep breath and slowly let it out. He wasn't here today to identify Morenta's men who had died. He was here to prove Brent had lived.

The charred ground between the woods and the jeep was completely barren, except for the remnants of a tire that had landed a short distance away. Tristan moved forward a few steps to get a better view of the area beyond the jeep. Though several victims of the blast were visible, none was where Tristan would have expected Brent to be had he been too close.

He motioned to Craig and spoke quietly into his communication headset. "Go up that tree. See if you can spot any sign of Brent or where he could have gone."

"I really miss Jay," Craig muttered.

Tristan couldn't help the beginnings of a smile. Even though Jay was an officer, he often ended up taking lookout duty. While he was on paternity leave, the job had fallen to Quinn last night and Craig today.

Craig moved to the base of a nearby oak and silently started his climb. He was almost to the top when Quinn's voice came over Tristan's headset.

"I found something," Quinn said. "Tracks."

His gaze still on the guard, Tristan asked, "What kind of tracks?"

"Footprints. Looks like someone was dragged out of here." Quinn described his location.

Tristan sidestepped another motion sensor and made his way to Quinn's side. He slowed when he caught sight of the disruption on the forest floor, two parallel lines that made faint indentations in the dirt and underbrush. Tristan tracked the impressions back to the yard and judged their position, comparing them to where he had last seen Brent. Had Brent been captured? And if so, where was he being held?

The very thought of him being held prisoner curled Tristan's stomach. Tristan stepped behind a tree, keeping himself hidden from the guard who still occupied the space by the front gate.

The niggling question of why the guard had positioned himself there instead of by the woods or the beach surfaced, but Tristan focused again on the tracks that stopped short of the charred grass.

He knelt and took a closer look at where the tracks stopped. Or rather, where they started. Whoever was being dragged through the woods wasn't being taken to the fortress but away from it.

"Craig, check my position. Could Brent have landed here during the blast?"

"I think so."

Tristan followed the tracks back to Quinn. "It looks like someone was pulled to safety."

"If it was Brent, he's still alive. At least, he was when someone hauled him out of here." Quinn leaned down and pointed at a leaf that had some dried blood on it. "He left a trail."

"Follow it."

"I already did. The trail ends after another twenty yards."

"And what do you mean 'the trail ends'?"

"It just ends. Vanishes."

"We didn't have any other SEALs left behind," Damian said from where he stood a few yards away.

"If Morenta's men captured him, they would have taken him to the fortress."

"So, who did take him out of here?" Tristan asked. "And don't tell me he vanished. I don't believe in ghosts."

The moment the words left Tristan's mouth, a new thought formed. He looked at Quinn, and awareness lit his expression.

"A ghost," Quinn and Tristan said in unison.

"You think there was a ghost down here?" Damian asked.

"It's possible."

The thrum of a helicopter in the distance cut over the sound of the nearby surf.

"I hate to be the bearer of bad news, but I found the Z-10," Craig said. "And it's headed our way."

* * *

The rumble of a helicopter sounded in the distance, and air stirred in time with the thrumming in Brent's head. Where was he? He reached out an arm. Where was Amy?

He cracked his eyes open, the bamboo blades of a ceiling fan overhead providing a subtle breeze in the already cool room. Not the room he shared with his wife at home. A room he had never been in before.

A door opened, and a male voice broke into his thoughts. "About time you woke up."

Brent pushed up on his elbow and winced. The pounding in his head increased, each heartbeat sending a new series of aches and pains through his entire body.

"Take it easy. You didn't do yourself any favors last night when you shot off that rocket."

The rocket launcher. The jeep. The guards. His men. "Did my men make it out?"

"As far as I can tell. Comm is still down."

Brent gingerly sat up and took in the simple bedroom with the tile floor and bars on the single window. "Where am I?"

"We're in a safe house a couple miles from the fortress," he said.

Brent pushed himself higher on the bed, a sharp pain ricocheting through his leg when he bent his knee. He sucked in a breath and fought for calm before he asked his next question. "How did I get here?"

"I brought you here."

Brent's eyes narrowed. "Who are you?"

"You can call me Ghost."

Ghost? Another one? He wasn't the ghost Brent normally dealt with, nor was he the one who had worked with him in Europe a couple of years ago. Though he had dealt with guardians in the past, Brent had no idea how he had come into the care of one in the middle of a military operation.

Brent studied the dark-haired man before him who could easily pass for a local. "Exactly how many ghosts are there?"

"Sorry. That's need-to-know."

"Can you tell me what you were doing at the fortress?"

"I was feeding intel to the powers that be in Washington until my phone died." Ghost motioned to the rickety wicker table beside the bed, where a water bottle sat beside a protein bar. "You should eat something."

Brent lifted his hand to his throbbing head. "How long was I out?"

"About ten hours," Ghost said. "Of course, most of that was because I sedated you."

"Why would you do that?"

"So I could get you out of Morenta's fortress without being heard." Ghost waved at Brent's leg. "It also made it easier to patch you up. You took some shrapnel in your leg."

"Are you a doctor?"

"No, but I've had advanced medical training, just like you. The wound was deep enough that you needed a few stitches and some antibiotics, but I doubt it'll keep you down for long."

Brent looked at where his pant leg had been cut away, a clean white bandage encircling his thigh. "Thanks."

"No big deal." Ghost shrugged. "I was just glad I was able to pull you out of there before the next set of guards reached the burned-out jeep. I couldn't very well have the president's son-in-law dying on my watch."

Brent's eyes widened. He and his wife had gone to great efforts to hide his association with Amy's family so Brent could continue his work as a SEAL even after Jim had been elected president. "How did you know . . . ?"

"I'm a guardian." He cocked an eyebrow. "I know everything."

"Then, what's the deal with this new weapon Morenta developed?"

"I know *almost* everything." Ghost lowered himself into a chair in the corner of the room. "We've been tracking activity in Morenta's compound, but I hadn't ever experienced a communication failure until tonight."

"The same isn't true for my squad. We lost comm on this mission and on our sneak-and-peek at the fortress a couple weeks ago."

"I read about the first one, but we thought it was a bad batch of batteries."

"So did we." Brent grabbed the water bottle by the bed and unscrewed the cap.

"How long did it take for your comm to go down the first time?"

"I don't know." Brent took a drink. "Maybe twenty minutes."

"And this time?"

"A bit less than that."

"Did you insert at the same place?" Ghost asked.

"No. We had to divert to a secondary landing spot."

"Could be the source of the problem was closer to your second insertion point than your first." Ghost stood. "I'll be right back." He disappeared from the room and returned a moment later with a folded map in his hands. He spread it out on Brent's bed.

The map revealed the entire grounds of the fortress as well as the surrounding area. The front gate, the beach, the ten-story building beside a helicopter landing zone. Woods surrounded the side and back of the structure and extended several miles to where the beach gave way to rocks and then a narrower strip of sand beyond.

"When I did my surveillance, the only spot I could get a clear view from was right here." Ghost tapped the map a short distance from the front gate. "Where did you come in?"

Brent identified the cove where his seven-man squad had landed, nearly a mile from the main beach by the fortress. "Right there the first time." He tapped the map and pointed to his secondary landing spot. "This was where we came in yesterday."

"And the hideout?" Ghost asked.

"You know about that?"

"I know everything." Ghost's eyebrows lifted. "Remember?"

"Right." Brent studied the topography, identifying various obstacles and landmarks he and his squad had encountered in their path. "It was somewhere in this area."

"I came in through the woods tonight too," Ghost said. "Whatever is causing these power failures has to be back here somewhere."

"According to the civilian we liberated yesterday, we know what's causing the power failures," Brent said. "It's an electromagnetic weapon that has been paired with a computer virus. Combined, the two can wipe out the power of an entire city." Brent took another sip.

"They already have."

Brent lowered his water bottle. "What?"

"Right before I inserted into Morenta's compound, I saw a message that Kansas City, Missouri, had a citywide power outage. They were having issues with car batteries dying too."

"This is a nightmare."

"It's not going to get any better until we neutralize Morenta's organization."

"My men grabbed Morenta last night," Brent said. "That should cripple them for a while."

"Don't count on it." Ghost shook his head. "Morenta is far too paranoid to leave anything to chance. I guarantee he already has his successor chosen."

"Any idea who that is?"

"It's either Osman Robleto or Elena Laceres," Ghost said. "I'm praying it's Laceres, because if Robleto is the one who takes over, he's going to make Morenta look like a minor pest compared to what he has planned."

"What does Robleto have planned?"

"A complete destruction of the American way of life."

"That's what Morenta was attempting."

"If his track record is anything to go by, Osman Robleto doesn't just want to see Americans suffer. He's interested in how high he can make the body count."

9

THE ATTACK HELICOPTER LOWERED TO the landing pad between the ten-story building of the fortress and the front gate. Tristan took a step back to ensure he wasn't visible to the new arrivals.

"We've got movement," Craig said, his voice flowing through the comm headset that was thankfully still working.

Damian ducked behind a tree.

Quinn lowered himself to the ground and used a fallen log as cover, his rifle barrel peeking over the top as he aimed in the direction of the helicopter.

"Six men approaching from the fortress," Craig continued. "Make that . . ."

Static filled the line momentarily before Craig's words cut off.

Tristan tapped his ear. "Craig, do you copy?"

No response.

"Damian, can you hear me through comm?"

Damian shook his head.

"What did Craig say?" Tristan asked Damian, his voice low.

"We've got six men heading for the helicopter. Seven more moving into the woods by our exit point, and two more toward the beach."

Four men emerged from the helicopter, but the pilot remained. The engines shut off as a truck approached, a fuel tank visible in the back. The driver parked beside the helicopter and went about refueling the aircraft while more than a half dozen men searched the beach and the nearby trees, their guns at the ready.

Damian said something in Spanish to Craig. Then he pressed a hand to his ear. "Craig? *¿Escuchame?*" He shook his head. "My comm is out."

"Mine too," Quinn said.

"Great," Tristan muttered. He looked up at where Craig was still perched in the tree above where Damian had taken cover. Using hand signals, Craig communicated the same information Damian had just relayed.

The men who had approached the helicopter joined the four who had gotten out of it at the side door and unloaded several crates.

Tristan lifted his binoculars for a better look. The first crate was unmarked, as was the second. The men set them on the concrete helicopter pad. Two more crates followed. When all four were in place, one of the men signaled to the others. Tristan shifted his gaze to the person who appeared to have taken command of the situation.

The man motioned to the crates before he turned and scanned the area. When he turned toward Tristan, recognition dawned. Osman Robleto. One of Morenta's top advisers. Was he taking over Morenta's self-made empire? And if so, was he following through with Morenta's plans, or did he have his own agenda he planned to follow?

Craig quietly made his way down the tree and to Tristan's side. "I don't know what they're up to, but it looked like they're doing a full-on search of the woods."

"The pilot stayed with the helo," Tristan said. "They may be sending him back up to do a search."

"That's not good," Craig said. "It's one thing to pretend we're wildlife when it's dark. I'm not a fan of trying to be invisible in broad daylight."

"Think we can get back to our extraction point?" Damian asked Craig.

"It's risky," Craig said. "The men heading into the woods looked like they were going hunting. We might make it. Not sure we can make it unseen and uninjured."

Tristan looked down at the tracks on the ground from where someone had been dragged out of here. Whether Brent was the one being dragged or doing the dragging didn't matter at the moment. They couldn't rescue their commanding officer if he wasn't here.

With a change of focus, he said, "Craig, Damian, see if you can get close enough to hear what they're saying. I'd like to know what's in those crates. We'll stay out of sight until tonight and try for the secondary extraction point."

"That's risky," Craig said. "Especially if the helicopter goes up for a search."

"He's right. We hijacked a plane to get back for Craig's wedding." Quinn jutted his chin in the direction of the Z-10. "I say we hijack a helicopter to get out of here."

Even though Quinn hadn't technically hijacked a plane, his idea had merit. The Z-10 wasn't that different from the Apache helicopters Tristan had trained on, and the risk of discovery was far lower if they had to go only as far as the helipad instead of fighting their way through the woods, especially without their comm operational.

Tristan motioned to Damian and Craig again. "Go see what you can pick up from their conversation."

The two men nodded and silently made their way deeper into the woods so they could approach without being heard.

As soon as they were out of earshot, Tristan repositioned himself beside where Quinn lay, his rifle pointed at the men who were now loading the crates into the back of the jeep.

"What do you think? Weapons?"

"Yeah, but who knows what kind."

Over the next fifteen minutes, the men finished their various tasks. The loaded jeep pulled away, and the refueling truck followed. Osman spoke with the half dozen men and two women who remained behind before one moved to the main gate and another headed for the beach. The remaining men headed toward the fortress. They were nearly to the entrance before everyone except Osman and one other man broke off toward the woods.

The pilot stepped out of the helicopter and began what appeared to be a preflight check.

Craig and Damian approached.

"Anything?"

"We didn't find out what's in the crates, but Osman seemed very concerned about finding someone."

"Who?"

"I don't know, but they're searching the woods, looking for tracks. The helicopter is going up again any minute."

"It's only a matter of time before these guys search over here."

"Like I said, time to hijack a helicopter."

"I can't believe I'm saying this, but Quinn's right," Craig said.

"Okay, but if we do this, let's do it right." Tristan jutted his chin toward the pilot. "Damian, you take out the pilot. Craig, you take the guard by the gate. Sedate them if you can. We want to stay silent."

"And I'll hijack a helicopter," Quinn said.

"I'll hijack a helicopter," Tristan corrected. "You can cover me."

"But—"

"You're qualified on fixed wing, not helicopters."

"I can fly a helo," Quinn insisted.

"Sure, in an emergency." Tristan held up a finger. "We want it to look like their pilot is the one flying."

"Fine." Quinn gripped his rifle. "Can we go now?"

"Yeah. We can go."

* * *

Amy clasped her hands together in her lap, fear and hope twining through her. She clung to the hope even as she analyzed the obstacles in front of the Saint Squad. She should be waiting for mission updates on board the *Truman*, but the Situation Room wasn't a bad second choice. At least here she was sure to get news as soon as it was available. Unfortunately, at the moment she had nothing but a blank screen in front of her and static coming over the speaker.

From where Vanessa stood behind her, she put her hand on Amy's shoulder in a gesture of comfort. Seth had taken position on the opposite side of the room beside the communications officer.

"Whatever killed the batteries on our last two missions is still operational," Seth said.

"I agree, sir," the communications officer said. "The comm issues are originating from their end."

Her dad looked at the clock on the wall. "How long until they're supposed to get picked up?"

"Two minutes."

"Bring up the video from the boat operator," Admiral Moss said.

"Yes, sir." The comm officer clicked on his keyboard, and the video of the shoreline came into view.

Someone stepped onto the narrow beach of the cove, an automatic rifle in hand.

"Is that—" Jim started.

"Call him off." Seth pointed at the screen. "He's not one of ours."

Admiral Moss nodded. "Do it."

The comm officer relayed the command. The boat operator changed direction an instant before gunfire sparked in the air.

The hum of the single engine increased in volume.

"Status?" the comm officer asked.

"Taking fire." The clipped voice fell silent, the video demonstrating the change of direction as the boat cut through a wave and sped up even more.

"What are our options?" her dad asked.

"Send the boat to our secondary extraction point," Admiral Moss said.

The command was given, and the boat operator altered course.

Tension hung in the room for the next several minutes while the boat moved into position.

"Sir, I have activity on the beach," the boat operator said. "Looks like they have patrols all along the coast."

"Send him back to the ship," Seth said, his voice eerily calm. "If hostiles are all over there, the Saint Squad is somewhere else."

"Agreed," Admiral Moss said.

"Then, what do we do?" her dad asked. "We can't leave those men stranded."

Like Brent. The now-familiar dread that Brent might not come back flooded through Amy. If they didn't find a solution for the Saint Squad now, four of her friends would be experiencing these emotions all too soon.

Silence filled the room for a moment, and Amy surprised herself when she spoke. "We should wait until the squad tells us what to do."

"Their comm is out," her dad reminded her.

"Yes, but they're resourceful. If there's a way out, they'll find it."

"She's right," Seth agreed. "If we don't hear from them in the next forty-eight hours, I'll fly down and find them."

"Sorry, Seth, but we can't keep sending people in only to lose contact," her dad said.

"They'll make contact." Amy lifted her gaze to meet Seth's. "One way or another, they'll find a way."

10

Tristan timed the steps of the guard on the beach that stretched out on the far side of the wide yard between the helicopter and the sand. As soon as he disappeared from view, Tristan lifted his hand and signaled his men.

Moving as one, Damian and Craig darted out of the trees, syringes at the ready. Craig reached the guard first, covering his mouth and injecting the fast-acting sedative into the man's thigh. Damian was only a second behind in neutralizing the pilot.

Damian and Craig dragged the now-unconscious men into the woods. Tristan checked the other guard's position and rushed to the helicopter. He did his own quick check of the aircraft, keeping to the side of the helo, where he would remain out of sight. Once he was satisfied that everything was in order, he climbed into the pilot's seat and pulled on the helmet that the pilot had left behind.

He started a mental countdown in his head. Only an estimated six minutes until the guard would return to the fortress side of the beach, six minutes until he would be in position to see that the gate guard was missing.

Hijacking a helo. Really. Quinn was turning into quite the bad influence. Then again, if this would get them safely out of Nicaragua, who was he to question his brother-in-law's judgment? He doubted the whole thou-shalt-not-steal commandment applied right now. After all, they would happily give the helicopter back if the current owners wouldn't try to kill them.

Five minutes. Four. Three. Tristan started the engines, the rotors slowly coming to life. Then he switched frequencies to make sure no one at the fortress could monitor their communications.

Quinn emerged from the woods, his rifle raised and aimed toward the beach. Damian and Craig rushed to the helo and climbed in. A moment later, Quinn followed.

"Let's get out of here," Quinn shouted over the engines. He grabbed the spare helmet on the copilot's seat and put it on. Juggling his rifle in one hand, he took his spot beside Tristan.

The guard on the beach strode into view.

"Duck!" Tristan reached out and pushed Quinn's head down. The front of Quinn's helmet knocked against the control panel.

"Hey!"

"They only had one pilot," Tristan said through the communication headset built into the helmet. "If the guard sees two, they'll know something's up. We don't need to see if they still have antiaircraft guns lying around somewhere." And they needed to buy time for the engines to warm up and reach full capacity.

"Get us out of here, and it won't matter," Quinn grumbled.

"Another minute." He hoped. Tristan checked the instrument panel. Seconds ticked by.

"The guard knows something's up," Craig said, his voice also coming through his helmet. "He's heading our way."

"We're out of time."

"The engines aren't ready to take off yet," Tristan said. "I need another forty or fifty seconds."

"Craig and Damian, buy us some time," Quinn ordered.

"Wait as long as you can before you let him see you," Tristan added. "The longer we can go without gunfire, the better."

"Yeah." Craig climbed out of his seat and moved to the side door. "We don't want a repeat of last night."

"Isn't that the truth," Quinn muttered. He lifted his head enough to peer out the windshield.

Tristan stared at the instrument panel, willing the engines to come to life faster. "Come on."

The guard continued closer.

He was a hundred yards away when Quinn said, "Now."

Tristan wasn't sure who pulled open the door and who shot at the hard-packed dirt in front of the guard, but Craig and Damian achieved their objective. Out of the corner of his eye, Tristan saw the guard dive for the ground.

"We woke up the lion's den." Craig scrambled to close the door again. "We've got a flood of guards heading our way."

"How many more guards can they have here?" Tristan asked. "There are at least a dozen in the woods."

"I don't know, but can we please get out of here?" Craig asked.

Tristan stared at the readiness indicator. Four seconds later, it finally turned green. Immediately, he lifted off. Gunfire sounded. Bullets sparked off the front.

Tristan focused on the controls and continued higher until he could clear the trees. More bullets sprayed in their direction as he turned the helo toward the water.

"We've got a launcher down there," Quinn said. "Ten o'clock."

Fight or flee. Or both.

"Man the guns," Tristan told Quinn. He turned the helo back toward the threat. As soon as the gunman came into view, Quinn fired, the bullets from the guns strafing through the yard and toward the guard with the rocket launcher on his shoulder.

A projectile flashed into the air.

The proximity alarm rang.

Tristan banked hard right.

The whole helicopter vibrated as the missile whizzed by them.

Quinn's hand relaxed, the position of the helicopter now making it impossible for him to shoot with any accuracy. "I'm tired of getting shot at."

"Me too." Tristan accelerated, but this time, instead of trying to move farther out to sea, he headed for the nearby trees. To protect them from becoming an easy target, he lowered his altitude so that the helicopter was below the tree line but still over the ocean.

The proximity alarm sounded again, warning about another incoming missile. This time, the projectile impacted a tree and exploded.

Tristan kept going.

"We need to get out of Nicaraguan territory," Craig said. "This daytime stuff makes me nervous."

"Me too." Tristan followed the shoreline for two miles before he once again turned toward the ocean. Once they cleared Nicaragua's territorial waters, he let out a sigh. "We're clear."

"Finally." Quinn fiddled with the radio controls. "Let's hope we can raise the *Truman* before one of our own decides to shoot us down."

"That would be bad," Damian said.

Tristan let out a chuckle. "Yeah, it really would."

* * *

Jim resisted the urge to lay a comforting hand on his daughter's arm. Even though Amy had finally broken the silence between them, the tension in her posture communicated that she wouldn't grant forgiveness anytime soon.

Amy's certainty that the Saint Squad would find a way out of Nicaragua sparked hope that she also believed Brent could return home too. If Brent had survived the explosion, it would be nothing short of a miracle, but Jim still believed in miracles. Didn't he?

He shook the doubts from his head. "I want recommendations on how to proceed, both on extracting the Saint Squad and how to locate Commander Miller."

"At this point, sir, I believe the best option is to wait," Admiral Moss said. "Give the Saint Squad time to find a way out."

"And Commander Miller?"

"We need more intel. The Saint Squad knows more about the situation than we do," Admiral Moss said. "Until we know what they found, we can't do anything for the commander."

Jim hated the helplessness that came from the waiting option, but his impatience wasn't a good enough reason to override common sense.

"Mr. President, you have a briefing in ten minutes," Sawyer said.

Even though Jim would have preferred to stay in the Situation Room until word came in about the Saint Squad, he had no idea how long that would take.

He stood, and despite the high-ranking officials present, Jim focused on Seth. "Keep me informed. I want to know as soon as they make contact."

"Yes, sir."

Jim's gaze lowered to Amy. She blinked hard against what appeared to be more tears threatening. He put his hand on her shoulder now and squeezed. "I'll be in my office if you need me."

Amy swallowed hard and nodded.

Jim and Sawyer left the room.

"How are you holding up?" Sawyer asked.

What could he say? He wasn't sure he could describe the gnawing sensation in his gut or the ache in his chest that kept shooting into the rest of his body until paralysis threatened to take over his very being. Despite the friendship he shared with his chief of staff, he didn't attempt to put those feelings into words. "I'll be better when we have answers."

They entered the Oval Office, and everyone stood.

"Please, everyone, have a seat." Jim pulled a chair from the side of his desk and turned it to face the seating area in the center of the room. After he sat, he focused on Doug. "What's the latest in Kansas City and Las Vegas?"

"The *Truman* has been relaying information from Yago Paquito, the professor who was kidnapped by Morenta and who helped develop the weapon,"

Doug said. "We have a company in Pennsylvania and another in California retrofitting generators, car batteries, and other emergency devices with copper shielding. We'll have the first shipments to Kansas City and North Las Vegas by tonight."

"What about restoring the actual power grid?" Jim asked.

"We have technicians working on it, but until they can find a way to counteract the virus affecting the equipment, there's not much they can do," Doug said. "Our priority right now is getting people into shelters that have gas heat and establishing emergency power at the hospitals."

Jim nodded and turned his attention to his director of Central Intelligence. "Director Gibson, any luck with Morenta?"

"Nothing. He hasn't said a word since he was brought into custody." The director continued with the basic update of other happenings around the world: a report of fifty Afghani soldiers crossing into Uzbekistan, a dozen Turkish citizens arrested for speaking out against their president, a possible uprising in Abolstan.

The secretary of state was giving the latest update on some recent tension between North and South Korea when a knock interrupted.

The door opened, and Seth peeked his head inside. "Sir, I'm sorry to interrupt, but we have a Z-10 helicopter on approach to the *Truman*. It's the Saint Squad."

"They stole a helicopter?"

"It appears so," Seth said. "After identifying themselves, they went to radio silence. That's protocol when operating an enemy aircraft. They should be aboard the *Truman* in approximately ten minutes."

"I'll be in the Situation Room shortly."

"Yes, sir." Seth left the room and closed the door behind him.

"Is there anything else that needs our immediately attention?" Jim asked.

Sawyer shook his head. "I'll reschedule your meeting with the economic advisory committee for after lunch."

"Thank you." Jim stood. "And thank you, everyone. Doug, keep me apprised on the power situation."

"Yes, Mr. President."

Everyone stood and filed out of the room, leaving only Jim and his chief of staff.

"We need to prioritize who to drop from your schedule today," Sawyer said.

"I want to meet with the economic advisory committee, but you take the congressional leadership meetings."

"How much do you want me to tell them?" Sawyer asked.

"Stick with the facts about the power-grid problems and that we captured Morenta."

"Nothing about the Saint Squad?"

"No. I don't want to risk someone putting the pieces together that my son-in-law is part of that squad," Jim said. "If Brent is alive, we need his identity to remain classified."

Sawyer pressed his lips together before he nodded. "I'll take care of it."

11

Brent sat at the rickety kitchen table across from Ghost, a detailed map of the area spread between them. His leg throbbed with each heartbeat. He ignored the pain and focused on their objective. "My men and I did a thorough search of the hideout. If there was a pulse weapon generating from there, we would have found it."

"You inserted here and here." Ghost pointed at the two coves the Saint Squad had used for their landing spots. "That means you never would have passed through any of this area." He pointed to the farthest corner inland of the fortress property.

"No, we didn't." Brent tapped on the spot where the hideout was located. "We wouldn't have even found the building here had Seth and I not needed to divert to the secondary extraction zone during our first mission."

"And you said you lost battery power faster on your comm when you came in over here."

"Which is closer to that dead area we haven't explored." Brent nodded. "You're right. It makes the most sense that the source of the problem is over there."

"As soon as I get you on a plane to DC, I'll come back and check it out."

"Or we can go in together and check it out."

Ghost motioned to Brent's leg. "No offense, but you're not in top shape at the moment. Besides, I don't want our president sending people in looking for you. We need to get word out that you're alive."

The events of last night replayed through Brent's mind, only this time from his squad's point of view. Would they think he had died when he'd fired the rocket launcher? "You really think they'll believe I'm dead?"

"You would be had that tree not been between you and the jeep when you fired," Ghost said. "That shrapnel in your leg went straight through the tree to get to you."

"Thank goodness my wife wasn't aboard the *Truman*."

"Your wife is the daughter of the president. Will he tell her you're missing?"

"I don't know, but she has access to the reports." That thought pushed Brent to stand despite the pain in his leg. "You're right. We need to get word out. I don't want my men risking themselves to come back in after me."

"I have a car outside." Ghost folded the map and pulled his keys from his pocket. He checked out the window before he pulled open the door and used a key to unlock the storm door beyond it.

"This way." Ghost motioned to a detached garage, which he unlocked when they reached it. He opened the main door to reveal a small hatchback. Not exactly Brent's idea of a getaway car, but here in Nicaragua, it would blend in well enough.

Brent climbed into the passenger seat as Ghost slid behind the wheel and put the key in the ignition to turn it on. And nothing. He tried again with the same result.

"How far away are we from where you think the source of the battery drain is?" Brent asked.

"As a crow flies, we're about two miles from the back corner of the fortress wall." Ghost pulled the key back out of the ignition. "Looks like we're within its range."

Brent climbed back out of the car and looked up at the sun's position. "We have about nine hours of daylight left. Time to plan how we're getting into the fortress tonight."

"You want to go back into the fortress?" Ghost's eyebrows lifted. "Are you crazy? You're injured, and we don't have transportation."

"But there's transportation at the fortress and means of communication." And Brent probably was crazy. "It's possible that if we can locate and neutralize whatever is draining battery power, my squad will be able to come in safely."

"Safely? Going into the fortress is never safe."

Brent had learned that the hard way. Twice. "Like you said, as a crow flies, we're only two miles away." Brent ignored the twinge of pain in his leg and tried not to limp as he walked back into the house. As soon as Ghost locked the door behind them, Brent continued. "We can head out at dusk. That way, we'll have enough light to find our way, but it'll be dark enough by the time we get there that we won't be seen."

"You really want to risk going in there again?" Ghost slipped his keys back into his pocket. "You barely made it out alive last night."

"I want to get home. Neutralizing the problem is the fastest way to my intended destination."

"Fair enough." Ghost spread out the map on the table again. "Any thoughts on how to get over that wall?"

Brent sat at the table and studied the map again. Determined, he nodded. "I have a few."

* * *

Vanessa sat at the conference table between Seth and Amy. The senior officers who had been present during this morning's operations had left to go about their duties. Only Admiral Moss remained.

The communications officer in the corner had also changed over. She looked up from her station and addressed the group. "I have the captain of the *Truman* on the line."

"Put him through," Admiral Moss said.

The captain came on the screen. "We have the Saint Squad onboard, along with the Z-10 they liberated from the fortress."

"Liberated," Vanessa whispered under her breath. "That's a nice way of saying *stole*."

The captain motioned to someone off screen. "Chief."

A moment later, Tristan stepped into view beside the captain.

Seth stood up. "Any sign of Brent?"

"We found tracks of someone being dragged away from the fortress, but they only went about twenty yards. It was like they vanished." Tristan focused on Vanessa. "Any chance one of your friends might have been nearby?"

Vanessa nodded once, but her words contradicted the movement. "As far as I know, we don't have any CIA operatives in the area."

"Got it," Tristan said. "Let us know if you get any updates on that."

"I will."

"What else did you find?" Seth asked.

"The Z-10 was back. We had to use it for our ride out of there."

The captain tilted his head to his left. "Some technicians are going over the aircraft now to see what alterations were made to it to protect the battery and electrical systems."

"I want that information as soon as it becomes available," Admiral Moss said. "We may be able to protect our aircraft in the same way."

"My thoughts exactly," the captain said.

"What about Commander Miller?" Amy asked, breaking her silence for the first time since the call came through. "Did you find any indication of whether he survived the blast?"

"The scene of the explosion was pretty gruesome, but it looked like all the casualties were Morenta's men," Tristan said. Determination shone in his eyes.

"What's the activity level of the fortress now?" Seth asked.

"They either got reinforcements, or Morenta had more men there than we realized," Tristan said. "According to Craig and Damian, they're looking for someone."

"Any idea who?" Admiral Moss asked.

"No, sir, but they had dozens of people scouring the woods."

The conversation shifted again to the technical aspects of the Z-10.

"I have a few things I need to take care of." Vanessa stood. "Let me know what I miss."

"You know I will," Seth said.

Vanessa left the Situation Room and made her way to the currently unoccupied Roosevelt Room. She pulled out her guardian cell phone and dialed Kade.

"What's the inside scoop?" Kade asked in lieu of a greeting. "I don't have anything yet on Brent."

"Someone was dragged away from where the explosion occurred," Vanessa said, her voice low. "Any word from our friend down there?"

"No. Still complete silence," Kade said. "We did come across several reports of people who have had car problems near the fortress. Looks like the battery problems are more widespread than we realized."

"Are these new, or have they been going on a while and no one noticed?"

"Still trying to piece that together. I've only seen the three from this morning: a produce truck that broke down at the market, a man trying to take his laboring wife to the hospital, and a police car that tried to respond to the pregnant woman's call for help."

"See if you can find anything that dates back to before last night."

"Renee and I are already on it," Kade said, referring to his wife, who also served as an intel officer for the guardians. "Who knows, maybe the explosion last night caused some of Morenta's safeguards to crash."

"I'm on my way to brief the president. Call if you find anything."

"Will do."

Vanessa crossed to the Oval Office, choosing to approach through the secretaries' office. She stopped at Sarah's desk.

"Who's in with the president?" Vanessa asked.

"Doug Valdez."

"Do you think you can squeeze me in before the president's next appointment?"

Sarah nodded. "I already cleared most of his appointments today. The CIA director also asked to speak with him."

"I only need a minute."

"I'll see what I can do."

The door opened, and Doug walked out, Jim standing right behind him.

"We're off to a good start, but make sure you check in with Admiral Moss. You need that information about battery protection as much as the navy does."

"Yes, sir." Doug nodded a greeting to Vanessa before continuing through the secretaries' office and into the main hall.

"Sarah, have we heard anything from President Aviles yet?"

"No, sir."

"Interrupt me if he calls," Jim said.

"Of course." Sarah motioned to Vanessa. "Director Gibson requested a meeting, and Mrs. Johnson asked for a minute."

"Let me know when Director Gibson is available." Jim waved Vanessa inside. "Come on in."

Vanessa passed through the door into the Oval Office. She waited until Jim closed the door before she asked, "You called the president of Nicaragua?"

"Yes." Jim waited for her to sit before he did the same on the couch across from her. He glanced at the glass door leading outside, where a Secret Service agent stood watch, before focusing on her again. "We received a report about unexplained battery problems in Playa Azul."

"The village beside the fortress." Vanessa's muscles tensed at the thought of that small area of the world where she had nearly lost her life. "I just received the report on that."

"I'm hoping President Aviles can shed some light on how widespread the problem is and when it started." Jim clasped his hands together and leaned forward. "How's Amy doing?"

"It's hard to say, but I think getting the report from the Saint Squad helped," Vanessa said. "They didn't find evidence of Brent's body, but someone was dragged through the woods. Putting the pieces together, I'd say it was Brent and Ghost pulled him out of there."

"But we have no idea if Brent is still alive?"

Vanessa's shoulders stiffened. "No, sir. Protocol would be to pull both our wounded and our casualties out of enemy territory."

"This not-knowing has got to be killing Amy."

"It's not the best for your mental health either."

The phone on Jim's desk rang, and he rose to answer it. "Yes, send him in."

Jim returned to his seat as the door opened and the director of the CIA entered. "Come join us. You know Vanessa Johnson, don't you?"

"I've seen her in a few meetings." Director Gibson looked from Vanessa to Jim. "Sir, I'm sorry, but this is highly confidential information. Perhaps we should speak privately."

"Vanessa is fully read in on all current intelligence operations."

The director hesitated briefly before he sat beside Jim. "We have a breakdown of the hierarchy in Morenta's organization. Fort Huachuca intercepted a transmission last night from Morenta's villa in Cali. Voice identification software indicates the caller was Osman Robleto."

Vanessa stiffened. Osman Robleto, one of the men who had been dominating the weapons trade in Central and South America for more than a decade. The one time Vanessa had met him in person, she'd been wearing the alias of Lina Ramir, but she remembered his arrogance and his security precautions well.

"What do we know about him?" Jim asked.

"He's a small-time arms dealer, operates out of the Caribbean most of the time," Director Gibson said.

"Small-time?" Vanessa repeated the unexpected phrase. "Since when?"

"You have a different opinion?" Jim asked.

"I do. Osman is the gateway for arms deals in this part of the world. I wouldn't categorize him as small time," Vanessa said. "And his hatred of the United States is well-known."

Director Gibson cocked a brow. "The intel I have on him doesn't show any strong allegiances one way or another. And from what my analysts have gathered, he's only been involved in a handful of deals over the past few years."

"Just because he stayed under the radar doesn't mean he wasn't involved," Vanessa said. "You must have had some turnover in your Central American division if your analysts didn't have that intel."

"That may be, but it doesn't discount the validity of this information."

"I'm sorry, but they clearly didn't go back to the intel reports from five years ago. Those would have detailed his involvement with Akil Ramir before Ramir was arrested."

"How do you know about these reports? Are you intelligence?"

"I am, and I'm the one who wrote those reports."

"Wait." Director Gibson's eyes widened. "You're *that* Vanessa?"

Vanessa fought against her surprise that the director would know her name.

When Vanessa didn't respond, Director Gibson pointed a finger in a circle to encompass himself and the president. "We're all in the need-to-know circle here," Director Gibson said. "You're Vanessa Lauton, the agent who infiltrated Akil Ramir's family."

"That was a long time ago."

"But it was you."

"Yes, sir."

"Vanessa, tell us what you know," Jim cut into the conversation.

Vanessa gathered her energy to pull out the memories of her years working undercover. "This could take a while."

"That's okay. Getting an accurate picture of who we're dealing with is worth the effort," Jim said.

Director Gibson nodded. "I agree."

12

Jim digested the information Vanessa had laid out. Not only did she have knowledge of Osman Robleto's past arms deals, but she was also well-versed in his personal vendetta against the United States. The details of how Osman's sister had been killed while attending college in California were vague, but the incident appeared to have been a turning point for Osman. According to the rumors Vanessa had heard, he had transitioned from an electrical engineer to an arms dealer almost overnight.

"You said Osman travels with at least four guards?" Director Gibson asked. "That's a lot but not enough to necessarily stand out, especially in that part of the world."

"I suspect it's probably more." Vanessa's eyes lit up. "Osman is good at staying below the radar, but maybe we can track his guards. It's possible some of them are the same as when I saw him last."

"You know their names?"

"I'll have to access my notes, but I can get them."

"Is that something you can have someone else do for you?" Jim asked.

"Maybe." Vanessa pulled her cell phone from her pocket and typed in a text message, probably to either Kade or Paige, Vanessa's former assistant. As soon as she finished, she said, "We should also look at passport records for people who could be traveling with him."

"That's a needle in a haystack," Director Gibson said.

"Why would it matter?" Jim asked. "If Osman is at the fortress, his guards are likely there too."

"Possibly, but they could also be among the people trying to deploy these electromagnetic pulse weapons," Vanessa said.

Awareness dawned for Jim. "If we can identify them and determine if they're in the US, we may be able to stop them."

"Yes, sir."

"It's worth a try." Director Gibson nodded.

Vanessa's cell phone buzzed. Her lips curved slightly. "I've got the names of the four guards who checked in with Osman when he stayed at Akil Ramir's resort in Punta Cana."

"That's a start." Director Gibson fell silent for a moment. "But maybe we have another way to gather intel."

"What did you have in mind?" Jim asked.

Director Gibson motioned toward Vanessa. "If Vanessa goes to the fortress as Lina Ramir, she could find out firsthand what's going on."

Jim's gaze darted to Vanessa. Her face paled. His long friendship with her and Seth along with his former position on the Senate Intelligence Committee had given him knowledge of Vanessa's undercover work. He also knew how dangerous that work had been. "That sounds extremely risky to me," Jim said.

"The fortress still belongs to Akil Ramir." Director Gibson waved a hand toward Vanessa. "Her uncle."

"My *supposed* uncle," Vanessa corrected. "I haven't worked undercover for some time."

"But your cover is still intact."

Vanessa drew a deep breath and lifted her chin. "Theoretically, yes."

Apparently satisfied with her answer, the director turned his attention to Jim. "Mr. President, we need to explore every option to ascertain what Morenta's men are doing. If Osman already knows Vanessa as Lina Ramir, she could gain us valuable intel."

"Assuming she would even be able to pass it along to us." Not to mention she had a one-year-old at home. At his home. Jim shook his head. "Even if she manages to get inside with a communication device, there's no guarantee it would work long enough for her to transmit any information to us."

"We're working on ways to counteract the problem."

"I want other options," Jim said. "Let's start by tracking Osman's guards. For now, sending Vanessa to the fortress is a last resort."

"Yes, sir."

Jim stood, signaling the end of the meeting. "Keep me apprised of your progress."

"Yes, sir." Director Gibson led the way toward the door and opened it for Vanessa.

They had barely left the room when Jim's phone rang. He moved to his desk and answered it.

"I have President Aviles on the line," Sarah said.

"Thank you, Sarah. Put him through." Jim settled into his chair.

"*Señor presidente*," Jim said, setting the tone that he was willing to have the conversation in Spanish.

"*Habla español*?" President Aviles asked.

"*Sí*." Thanks to his two years living in Ecuador during his early adult years. He continued in Spanish. "What do you know about the battery problems in Playa Azul?"

"It's a mystery."

"Did this happen before last night?" Jim asked.

"Not that I know of." The president discussed the efforts his local police were making to identify the source of the problem.

When he finished, Jim asked, "What do you know about Osman Robleto?"

"He has been challenging my authority since the civil unrest started a few years ago. Why do you ask about him?"

Jim debated how much information to share. "We believe he could be involved in these battery problems as well as the power outages we have experienced in two of our cities."

"He does know about power systems," President Aviles said. "He worked for our power company in Managua before he started his own business."

The fact that President Aviles was aware of Osman's background proved the arms dealer was enough of a problem to keep him on the Nicaraguan government's radar. "What can you tell me about his business?"

"Officially, he's in the furniture business."

"But you don't believe that?"

"No. Smuggling is more like it. What and how much continues to be a mystery," President Aviles said. "I suspect he has someone feeding him information out of our police and border patrol departments, because every time we conduct a search, they don't find anything."

"What makes you so sure he's doing something illegal?"

"I have my reasons."

Recognizing that the topic was closed, Jim said, "Please let me know if you learn anything more about your problems in Playa Azul."

"And you will share what you learn about your power outages?"

Since intelligence would not approve of such an agreement, Jim chose his words carefully. "If we find anything that will help your people, we'll be certain to share."

Jim ended the call and leaned back in his chair. Brent was still missing, Morenta wasn't talking, and they had a potential new enemy to face. And at the center of it all was the knowledge that the fastest way to a solution could be sending Vanessa into harm's way. Why had he thought running for president was a good idea?

13

AMY JOTTED DOWN POSSIBLE SOURCES of intelligence based on the information Tristan had shared. The navy had taken the lead on analyzing protective measures for electronics, Homeland Security was working with Professor Paquito, the CIA now had custody of Morenta to ascertain whether more attacks were imminent, and she suspected Vanessa was in contact with the guardians to make sure nothing fell through the cracks in interagency communications. All these people were working toward protecting their country, but all she could think about was where her husband was now and what else they could do to find him.

Seth sat beside her at the conference table in the Situation Room, where she had set up with a secure laptop.

Amy glanced over. "Anything new?"

"I've been studying the area around the fortress. With what Tristan said, it sounds like we had two people: Brent and someone else. Whoever pulled our injured person out of there went back to cover up their tracks."

"Why only cover up part of their tracks?" Amy asked.

"Probably so we would know what happened." Seth shrugged his wide shoulders. "That's what I would do. I'd cover the tracks enough to make sure I wasn't followed, but I'd also know that my squad or someone would likely come back looking for me."

New hope bloomed. "You think Brent was the person who was okay?"

"I think Brent was alive if someone took the trouble to stop and cover their tracks," Seth said. "And whoever it was, it was someone with training."

Seth's words made sense. Brent was the only American left behind. No one else had been near him when he had last been spotted on the helicopter's video feed.

"It must have been a guardian or an intel operative there to support the mission," Seth said.

"I think so too." Amy drew a deep breath and let it out slowly. Uninjured was her first choice for her husband, but she'd take injured over dead. She rested her left hand on her stomach. A protectiveness swept over her, as did a sense of determination. She needed her husband back, and her child needed his or her father. "I can't stand sitting around here waiting. I need to get on board the *Truman*."

"You and me both. Look at this." Seth set an iPad on the table in front of her. "The reports of car batteries dying came from this area right here."

"The village beside the fortress. Yes, I know."

"If cars can't get out of there, Brent has to be close by."

Amy's heart lifted. "The village can't have more than a few hundred people in it. If the Saint Squad goes in, you might be able to find him."

Seth nodded. "I've narrowed down the areas where I think he could be hiding."

"How did you narrow it down?"

"If Ghost is there, he must have some kind of a safe house," Seth said. "Only eight houses in the village are close enough to the fortress for someone to carry a wounded man out of there without being seen and are also built well enough to be used by a government operative."

"Brent is missing, you've been reassigned, and Jay is on paternity leave." Amy pondered how to move past their typical procedures. "Who do you suggest we approach to get orders?"

"Since I'm not technically part of the Saint Squad any more, I say we go straight to the top."

"To my father?" Amy's eyebrows lifted.

"Okay, a couple steps below the top." Seth motioned to the videoconferencing room they had been in a short time ago. "I was thinking of Admiral Moss."

"He may be easier to get a yes out of anyway," Amy said. "I'm sure my father would prefer to keep me home." A little flicker of doubt surfaced. Maybe she should stay home to protect the life growing inside her.

"We need you on that ship as much as the Saint Squad needs a commanding officer to fill in until Brent gets back," Seth said. "Letting them go in on recon without an officer was a stretch. There's no way the navy will approve them running an op in the village without me or Jay there, and we need an intel officer on board to watch our backs."

Seth's words swayed her. She wouldn't be the one on the front lines. Surely, she could handle this one trip. "Does Jay even know Brent is missing?"

"No. I didn't want to risk someone intercepting my call, and there's nothing Jay can do besides worry anyway." Seth picked up the iPad and stood. "I'll get our orders sorted out. You'd better pack."

"My go-bag is in my closet upstairs." Amy swiveled in her seat. "I'll check with the CIA to see if they can help me pull some new intel. I want to have every possible detail on that village before you go in to bring him home."

"Better call now," Seth said. "If I have my way, we'll be out of here as soon as they can get us a ride."

Amy pulled out her phone. "I'll be ready."

* * *

Brent needed a visual before he could formulate an effective action plan. He took a sip of his bottled water and tapped a finger on the map. "I hate to wait, but I think we need to do some surveillance tonight."

"I already have my notes for the guard rotations and when people have been coming and going into the fortress for the past few weeks."

"I'm sure those have all changed," Brent said. "They took on some pretty heavy casualties, and we have no idea if they had any reinforcements show up. Plus, I heard a helicopter earlier. If it's back, who knows what other defenses they may have set up that weren't there before we inserted."

"You're right, but maybe you should leave the surveillance to me." Ghost motioned to Brent's leg. "Making that walk two nights in a row isn't going to help you heal."

The need to be on the front line, to make sure they had all the information necessary for success coursed through him, but Brent couldn't deny that Ghost's proposal made sense.

"I don't suppose you have any comm or surveillance gear that still works, do you?"

"We can check, but I doubt it." Ghost crossed to a cabinet in the corner of the living room and unlocked it.

Brent shifted his position so he could see inside when Ghost opened it. His eyes widened. Shelves lined with laptops, surveillance equipment, and an assortment of other electronic gadgets. A stack of what appeared to be passports and boxes of new cell phones occupied the top shelf. On the next shelf down, larger sheets of something he couldn't identify were stacked vertically beside the surveillance gear.

"What's that on the top?" Brent asked.

"I keep a few blank passports for when I need to help someone leave the country," Ghost said. "We should print out a photo of you while we still have electricity."

"I was talking about that stuff on the next shelf down."

"Some leftover EMF shielding."

An electromagnetic field. They were safe from being overheard or having their electronic signals picked up, but they didn't have a way to generate signals.

Ghost retrieved a communication earpiece like the ones the Secret Service used. "This one is still working."

Brent's spirits lifted. "What else in there is still operational?"

"I already checked all the cell phones and laptops while you were sleeping. They're all dead." Ghost checked another earpiece and returned it to the shelf and retrieved another one. "This one's dead too."

"Hand me the stack. I'll check them." Brent motioned to the other equipment inside. "We should check the laptops and phones again, just to be sure."

Ghost handed him some more comm gear and returned to the cabinet, this time pulling out four laptops that were stacked on top of each other. He carried them to the table. Then he handed Brent a stack of cell phones.

One by one, Brent checked the cell phones, and Ghost checked the laptops.

"You're right." Brent blew out a frustrated breath. "These are all dead."

"The laptops too." His brow furrowed. "Why wouldn't the batteries in the earpiece be affected like all of these?"

"Do the other ones work?" Brent asked.

Ghost carried the laptops back to the cabinet, placed them back inside, and inspected the equipment beside the earpiece. "Almost all of these are still operational."

"Why would everything else in that cabinet not work except for the stuff on that shelf?" Brent stood and limped across the room. A few spare batteries, headsets, a surveillance camera, two listening devices, some odd-looking cell phone contraption attached to a hotel key card.

Ghost picked up the gadget. "This is the only thing that doesn't have a working battery."

"What is it?"

"Sorry. That's need-to-know." Ghost moved it to the top shelf.

Brent picked up one of the comm earpieces and checked the power for himself. Sure enough, it turned on. His gaze landed on the EMS shielding that was the same copper color as the computers they had discovered in the hideaway behind the fortress.

"That shielding is made of copper." Brent reached out and retrieved a piece. "That must have given everything on this shelf extra protection against the electromagnetic field."

"That makes sense, but unfortunately that also means that as soon as we pull this stuff out of here, it's only a matter of time before the batteries die. Unless . . ."

"Unless we use the shielding to protect the batteries," Brent finished for him. "Any chance you have a blowtorch?"

"Yeah. I've had to cut through metal more times than I care to admit," Ghost said. "I'll get the torch; you check the kitchen for something we can use to collect the copper when we melt it down."

Brent glanced at the handful of batteries on the shelf. "We don't have a lot of room for error with this."

"Then, we'd better take the time to get it right," Ghost said.

14

TRISTAN WALKED INTO THE SQUAD'S boardroom, not surprised to find Quinn, Damian, and Craig waiting for him.

Quinn looked up from the worktable where they all sat. "We got the latest satellite images from the fortress."

"How did you get them so quickly?" Tristan focused on Craig. "I thought you used the last autographed pictures of your wife to get those éclairs from the officers' mess."

"I did."

Humor hummed through Quinn's voice. "The intel officer was very cooperative when he found out our commanding officer wasn't available to come down himself because he was talking to the president."

Damian motioned to the screen of the laptop in front of him and said something in Spanish.

"I don't speak Spanish, remember?" Tristan asked.

"I didn't either until I started hanging out with him," Craig said. "Maybe it's time you learn."

"I know enough to figure out when you two are planning to steal my food."

Damian switched to English. "I said, 'Come look at this.'"

Tristan stepped behind Damian and peered over his shoulder. Satellite imagery of the fortress filled the screen.

"Anything interesting?" Tristan took the seat beside Damian.

"Not yet."

"Put the images up on the TV so they're easier to see," Tristan said. "When was this taken anyway?"

"Right before I hijacked the helicopter," Quinn said.

"You mean when I hijacked the helicopter."

Craig shook his head. "What is it with you two and hijacking aircraft? This isn't a competition."

"If it were a competition, I'd be winning," Quinn said. "I hijacked the airplane when we were in Germany and the helicopter today."

"You're delusional." Tristan glanced around the room, expecting Brent to break up the brewing argument. The lack of his presence brought Tristan back to their current purpose. He focused on the screen, the Z-10 in the forefront of the image, several men moving into the woods in the background. "Damian, back it up to before we got to the Z-10. Maybe we can see what prompted the search."

Damian stopped the image and restarted it, but this time, it was before the Z-10 landed. Only a single guard patrolled the grounds, but he held a cell phone to his ear.

"His phone works." Damian pointed at the screen.

"Obviously, they have a way to protect their battery power," Craig said.

The guard pocketed his phone and used both hands to open the gate to the wide driveway. As soon as he rolled it aside, a van pulled through followed by a second and a third. The vehicles diverted away from the site of last night's explosion, stopping in front of the main entrance.

Doors opened, men piled out, each one carrying a rifle.

"Now we know where the extra men came from," Craig said.

Damian pointed at the top of the screen. "The gate is still open."

The words were barely out of his mouth when a car and another van pulled through. The guard rolled the gate back into place.

Tristan pointed at the screen. "See if you can push in on the new arrivals."

Damian zoomed in.

"I can't see any of their faces," Craig said.

"Me neither." Quinn stood and moved closer to the TV. "But these aren't amateurs. Look at how they're holding their weapons."

One of the new arrivals broke away from the rest and headed for the beach. The others went inside.

"Zoom out and speed it up," Quinn said.

Damian fast-forwarded until movement appeared on the third-floor balcony. He switched back to normal speed.

"How much time passed since the new guys showed up?" Tristan asked.

"An hour and twelve minutes."

"They've got casualties all over the yard. Why haven't they tended to them?" Craig asked. "Seems like if we showed up on a scene like this, we'd have someone assigned to forensics and removing the bodies."

"That is odd." Tristan focused on the man on the balcony. The man checked the position of the guards twice. Then he did something with the railing and climbed over it.

"That's a rope." Damian checked the screen in front of him as though confirming his conclusion.

"Looks like the professor wasn't the only one who wasn't happy to be there," Quinn said.

"Zoom in again."

Damian complied. The overhead image didn't reveal the man's face, but the rifle held in place by a sling told its own tale.

"He has to be one of Morenta's men, or he wouldn't be armed."

"Unless he was being held prisoner and managed to disarm a guard," Craig said.

"Also a possibility," Tristan conceded.

The man used the rope to lower himself to the ground. A second later, another man appeared on the balcony, this one without a weapon. He followed the same path as the first, but when he reached the ground, he headed in the opposite direction. He crept along the edge of the building until he turned the corner so he was out of the sight of both guards.

Damian manipulated the image on screen to track the man's movements until he disappeared into the trees.

"The first guy went toward our insertion point," Quinn said.

"The same direction the men were searching in after we got there." Tristan tapped his fingers on the table. "Damian, speed it up again."

The image fast-forwarded until the Z-10 approached the fortress. "We must already be in the woods at this point."

The rest of the scene played out as Tristan remembered it, right down to when they stole the Z-10. The image went black.

"Is that all we have?" Tristan asked.

"No, there's another one that picks up a half hour later." Damian pulled the new image up. "I don't know who authorized the retasking of the satellites, but I think having Whitmore in the White House is helping our intel."

"Yeah," Tristan said. "Let's make sure he gets the outcome he's looking for."

Quinn pointed at the wooded area visible on the screen, where three men emerged, two of them holding the third by his arms. "That guy didn't get the outcome he was looking for."

"The question is, Did they catch both of them?"

The guards escorted their prisoner inside, but no one else followed.

"They didn't kill him," Craig noted.

"Which means they need him for something," Tristan said.

"The other men there are still searching, so they must know two got away," Craig said.

"Damian, put in a request for intel to enhance the images of our guys who escaped. There might be enough of their faces visible when they climbed out of building to get an ID," Tristan said. "Craig, type up a summary of what we just saw and send it up the chain of command."

Craig shot a look at Quinn. "He's getting bossy all of a sudden."

"There's nothing sudden about it."

* * *

Vanessa walked through the wide hallway of the West Wing, her thoughts on her family. She had told Amy she would do anything she could to help. She hadn't considered that she would be faced with the possibility of going back undercover, the possibility of leaving Talia and Seth behind.

She and Seth had been so excited to move to DC to start their new positions in Washington's inner circle. Little had either of them known they would face such decisions so quickly. She might be able to make a difference, but at what cost?

The mere thought of going undercover again sickened her. This new job was supposed to give her more time with her daughter, not put her in the position of disappearing from her life for days, weeks, or possibly forever.

She couldn't think about that now. She needed to focus on the facts at hand. While she could see the benefit of having someone inside the fortress, the Saint Squad had already captured Morenta. Even if Osman were running the organization now, surely there wasn't a reason for her to risk her life. After all, if Tristan's analysis was correct, Brent wasn't at the fortress anyway. What possible reason could there be to send her back there? Except to learn whether another terrorist attack was being planned. Her stomach churned at that thought.

She went downstairs to the Situation Room, where she found Seth and Amy working in the conference area. "Anything new?"

"Actually, yes." Seth turned his laptop screen toward her. "Look at this."

Vanessa leaned forward, her gaze on an image of a man climbing off a balcony. "Is this at the fortress?"

"Yes." Seth clicked on his mouse to show a second man also using the rope to leave. "Damian sent a request to intel to enhance these images and run facial recognition. He cc'd Amy on his email."

"Do you have anything back yet?" Vanessa asked.

Amy shook her head. "They're running it now, but it may be a day or two before we get anything."

"Sometimes I really wish we could get everything back as fast as the fake intel officers do on TV," Vanessa said.

"Keep dreaming." Seth swiveled in his chair to face her. "How did it go with the president?"

"I think it's okay if you call him Jim when it's just us," Amy said.

"I'm trying to get in the habit of calling him Mr. President so I don't mess up when we're in public," Seth said.

"Fair enough."

"So?" Seth's eyes met Vanessa's. "What happened?"

"It looks like Osman Robleto took over for Morenta," Vanessa said.

"That didn't take long."

"No, it didn't, and quite frankly, I'm worried," she admitted.

"You know this Osman person?" Amy asked.

"I only met him once, but I heard his name a lot when I was undercover," Vanessa said. "He's a major player in the arms trade in Central and South America. He's also very good at staying off people's radars."

"What else do you know?" Amy asked.

"He's Nicaraguan. Before his sister was killed in the US, Osman worked as an electrical engineer for the main power company in Managua."

"What happened to his sister?" Seth asked.

"She was attending college in California and disappeared. Her body showed up a week later," Vanessa said. "The cause of death wasn't released to the public."

"Might be worth trying to shake that autopsy report loose," Amy said. "Understanding his motivation might help intel in the long run."

"I did one better. I pulled the police report," Vanessa said. "According to witness reports, she was last seen with an airline pilot at a bar in Hermosa Beach. He was questioned in her disappearance, and it looked like the DA was going to make an arrest, but then all of a sudden, the whole case against him was dropped."

"Do you think he killed her?" Amy asked.

"It's possible. The quick dismissal looks like a payoff to me."

Seth leaned back in his chair. "You really think a pilot would have deep enough pockets to bribe someone in the DA's office?"

"He didn't, but his brother did. The brother is a big-time exec at Citibank. If we were to check, I'd bet there's a large withdrawal right around the time charges got dropped."

"If Osman had similar suspicions, I can see why he hates Americans so much," Amy said. "He would see our entire judicial system as corrupt."

"Yeah. He would." At the moment, Vanessa was a lot more concerned with Osman's present and future than his past. "Bottom line is, whatever happened to his sister pushed him to change careers. He left the power company and started working with Akil Ramir, brokering arms deals. Morenta was one of his frequent customers. After Akil was arrested, Osman and Morenta joined forces."

"If he's in control of Morenta's empire, what will he do with it?" Amy asked.

"I have no idea, but I doubt it'll be good," Vanessa said. "He's bloodthirsty. If he can make Americans suffer, he will."

"We already have plenty of Americans suffering right now in Kansas City and North Las Vegas," Seth said.

A navy lieutenant entered the conference room. "Sir, I have those orders for you." He handed a paper to Seth.

"Orders?" Vanessa asked as the lieutenant retreated back the way he'd come.

Seth nodded and scanned the paper. "Amy and I are headed out to the *Truman*."

"You plan to go after Brent?"

Again, he nodded. "We've narrowed down the area where he could be hiding."

"How soon do you ship out?"

"Two hours."

Amy stood. "I'd better grab my go-bag."

"I'll be right behind you." Seth also stood. As soon as Amy left the room, he said, "I'm sorry I'm leaving like this. Do you think your mom can come watch Talia for a few days?"

"She's already planning on staying the week."

"Thank her for me."

"You can thank her yourself when you get back." Vanessa put her hand on his arm. "There is something I should tell you before you go."

"What's that?"

Vanessa drew a deep breath and fought against the turmoil of fear and uncertainty swirling inside her. "There's a chance Jim may send me into the fortress."

"What?" Seth took a step back, his gaze fixed on hers. "You can't go back there."

"I'm the last resort, but if we can't figure out what's going on with Osman, I may be the only option to discover what they have planned."

"My squad will get the intel." He took her hand and squeezed. "I don't want you to ever have to go undercover again."

"I'm praying I won't have to."

"So am I." He leaned down and kissed her.

When he drew back, she uttered a silent prayer for her husband and his squad. "Be careful."

"Always." He gave her another quick kiss. "I don't have much time before our ride comes to pick me and Amy up. Is there anything else I should know about Osman before we go back into Nicaragua?"

"He's arrogant, but he's also cautious," Vanessa said. "It would be wise for you and all of the Saint Squad to steer clear of him."

"I hope we can. Our primary objective is to find Brent and bring him home."

Vanessa looked at the computer screen again. Would the Saint Squad be able to stick with a single objective in Nicaragua? Or would intelligence dictate a new priority? With Osman in the mix, she was afraid to find out.

15

Amy rushed past the Secret Service agent standing outside the kitchen and hurried into her room. She grabbed her backpack, which contained her travel essentials, including two changes of clothes, then retrieved the small duffel she used for longer deployments. She had no idea whether this trip would last a couple of days or stretch into weeks, but she might as well be prepared. Even if they found Brent quickly, depending on the nature of his injuries, a lengthy hospital stay was a possibility.

Her chest tightened at the thought of what her husband must be going through. *Just let him be alive.*

Her hand went to her stomach, a reminder of their baby and that she needed food before she and Seth shipped out. If she was going to risk traveling, she needed to do everything she could to stay healthy, both for herself and for her unborn child.

She headed for the kitchen. The counters were all clean, the dishes put away. The only evidence of her mother's baking spree this morning was a gallon-sized bag of rolls propped beside the fruit bowl.

Amy grabbed the entire bag along with an apple and a banana. She slid the apple and the rolls into her backpack before she sat at the table and peeled the banana. She managed to eat three-quarters of it before her stomach protested.

A seed of doubt sprouted in her as she considered what she was about to do. Deploying to an aircraft carrier was normal enough in her job, but going out when she was already nauseous wasn't going to be fun, especially when working with five very observant SEALs. She looked down at the bag of rolls she had tucked into her backpack. Distraction techniques. That was what she needed.

She crossed to the freezer and took out two more bags of rolls, along with three gallon-sized bags of her mom's chocolate chip cookies. After storing the extra food in her duffel, she retrieved one more bag of rolls from the freezer and set it beside the fruit bowl, a replacement for the one she took.

"What are you up to?" her mom's voice carried from the doorway.

Amy looked up at her mom and opted for a full confession. "Stealing food."

"Why are you stealing food?"

"Because if I show up on the carrier with only one bag of rolls, the Saint Squad will eat them all. I want to make sure I have something that won't make me sick so the guys won't notice I'm not feeling well."

"The carrier?" Her mom took a step forward, effectively blocking the exit. "You shouldn't be deploying right now."

"I need to help the Saint Squad find Brent," Amy said. "Seth's coming too."

"Amy, I don't think this is a good idea." Her gaze lowered to Amy's stomach. "You have more to think about right now than just you and your husband."

"You're right. I do." Amy straightened her shoulders. "And I owe my child the chance to know his or her father."

"This morning you were questioning whether Brent is even alive."

"And you were right that I need to have faith that he is until I have proof to the contrary."

"I didn't mean go out and get the proof yourself."

"I'm not." She slipped her backpack over one shoulder and the strap of her duffel over the other. "I'm making sure the men who have that task will be fully informed before attempting a rescue mission."

"Amy . . ."

"Mom, I love you, but this is something I have to do." Amy leaned in and kissed her mom's cheek. "And I promise I'll be careful."

Before her mom could protest further, Amy slipped past her. "I'll see you when I get back."

"Are you sure you took enough rolls?"

"I did." Amy gave a slight smile. "Thanks, Mom."

* * *

Jim walked out the Oval Office door leading into the main hall. Despite his efforts to keep his schedule clear today, one crisis after another had cropped up, demanding his attention.

He crossed the hall to the Roosevelt Room, where Doug sat among several computers and three of his aides.

One of the aides noticed him first. She stood. "Mr. President."

"Please, sit down." Jim motioned at her chair.

The woman lowered back into her seat.

Doug swiveled to face Jim. "We're transporting more residents in Missouri over to the Kansas side, but I'm getting reports of looting in the downtown area."

"You were afraid that would happen."

"The police on the Missouri side are doing what they can, and the national guard has already arrived on the scene," Doug said. "They were able to drive all the way into the center of the city before we lost contact."

"How are you transporting residents out of there?" Jim asked.

"On foot, on horseback, and some are even using horses and wagons," Doug said. "We had truckers pick up as many of the wagons from local farmers as we could. They've all been working in shifts since this morning."

"What about the hospitals and the nursing homes?"

"We're focusing on ones that don't have gas heat." Doug's jaw clenched. "Unfortunately, we had three more deaths at local hospitals in Kansas City and two in North Las Vegas."

Five more senseless deaths. Jim blew out a breath. He glimpsed movement in the hall, his daughter's auburn hair and the backpack hanging from her shoulder catching his attention.

"Excuse me." Jim retreated to the hall. "Amy?"

She turned, a guarded look on her face.

"Where are you going?"

"To the Situation Room."

Jim's gaze dropped to the duffel hanging from her other arm. "You don't need luggage to go to the Situation Room."

"Seth and I are on our way to the *Truman*." Amy lifted her gaze to meet his, a steely determination reflected in her eyes. "We leave in an hour and a half."

Jim's protective instincts flared. "You aren't going to a carrier."

Her eyebrows lifted. "Excuse me? I already have orders."

"Orders can be changed."

Amy stopped by the door to the Oval Office. "Perhaps this conversation should be conducted in private."

The formal manner of her speech was enough to clearly communicate her anger.

"Perhaps you're right." Jim escorted her into the Oval Office and closed the door behind him.

As soon as they were alone, Amy turned on him. "Dad, I have a job to do, and I'm going to do it."

She was also his daughter, and he wanted her home and safe. "You're upset, and you aren't thinking clearly."

"Of course I'm upset, but that doesn't mean I can't do my job."

"What about your baby?" Jim asked. "Are you really willing to risk your health to go after Brent when we don't even know if he's alive?"

"I have to know." Amy's voice trembled. She swallowed hard and blinked against the sudden moisture in her eyes. After a moment, she drew a deep breath. "You gave the order to leave him behind. I'm trying to forgive you for that, but I won't let you stop me from making sure the Saint Squad has every tool possible for a successful mission."

The sting of her words hit home, and Jim had to take a moment to compose his own thoughts. "I had to give that order." He drew a deep breath. "And whether I gave it or not, it wouldn't have changed the outcome. That explosion still would have happened, but those thirty SEALs with him might not have made it had they not left when they did."

"I know. You were protecting the other men, but you need to let me protect the Saint Squad now." Amy lifted her chin. "I'm not just your daughter. I'm also a very capable intelligence officer. Let me be there for my husband and his squad."

Jim wavered. He wanted Amy to be safe, but he couldn't deny her abilities when working in the field. She was one of the best at what she did.

An errant thought pressed to the forefront of his mind. He leaned against the back of the couch. "Did Brent ever tell you what he said when he asked for your hand in marriage?"

"Just that he asked and you said yes." Obviously caught off guard, Amy narrowed her eyes. "Why?"

"After I said yes, he asked a favor of me." Emotions clogged Jim's throat, and he had to swallow before he could continue. "He acknowledged that the day might come when he didn't come home. He asked for my promise that I would make sure you were taken care of, that you would always have someone who would make you feel loved."

Tears surfaced in Amy's eyes.

"I have every intention of keeping that promise whether Brent comes home or not, but I can't make you see Brent's mission from my perspective, and I can't make you forgive me."

Amy sniffled. She stood rigidly for a moment. Then she opened her arms and stepped into his embrace. "I knew it might happen, but I didn't think it would be this hard."

"Sure you did, but we all prayed you would never have to go through this."

Amy clung to him for a long moment before she stepped back. "You aren't going to stop me from going to the carrier, are you?"

He wanted to. "I won't stop you if you promise to keep the lines of communication open. And be careful."

Amy's posture relaxed, and she wiped at the moisture beneath her eyes, where a few tears had escaped. She hugged him again. "I will."

16

BRENT PAINTED COPPER SHIELDING ONTO another battery and set it on the wooden cutting board Ghost had set on the kitchen table for them to use as a work surface. Copper shielding had been propped up on every side of it to prevent the working batteries from being drained before he and Ghost could add the extra protection.

For hours, the two of them had worked at melting down the copper shielding, then painstakingly coating batteries and the exterior of their equipment so they would be prepared for their surveillance and insertion into the fortress.

A sense of urgency rose within Brent. He could only imagine what his men and Amy were going through right now if they really thought he hadn't survived last night. If their roles were reversed, he would be frantic to get back to the fortress to see for himself what had really happened. That thought caused him to pause. Had his squad already gone back to the fortress?

The urgency simmering inside him heated to a slow boil. "Did you leave any evidence behind that would show my men that I survived?"

"I left the tracks of where I dragged you out of there," Ghost said.

Brent tensed. "You didn't cover our tracks?"

"I erased everything beyond twenty yards of where you went down," Ghost clarified. "If your men go back in, they'll find the sign I left for them. I assume they'll be smart enough to figure out that it wasn't the enemy since I pulled you away from the fortress, and the tracks disappeared."

"I hope so." Brent glanced at the window. Through the sheer curtains lining the back window, the last rays of sunlight filtered through the darkening clouds. "Of course, if it rains, our tracks will be washed away."

"Once we get you to Managua and on a plane, you won't have to worry about leaving cryptic signs of whether or not you're alive," Ghost said. "Your family will be able to see you for themselves."

"Yeah, but how far will we have to walk to find transportation?" Brent asked. Frustration tangled with the urgency. "The only engine I've heard anywhere near here today was from the helo flying overhead."

"A few vehicles came through earlier too."

"Any idea where they were going?"

"To the fortress." Ghost set another battery on the wooden cutting board. "Best guess is they were reinforcements."

"Reinforcements from where?" Brent asked. "Morenta has a solid network, but how expansive is it here in Nicaragua?"

"He's primarily kept to this area. The new arrivals are probably hired guns."

"Mercenaries. Great," Brent muttered. "I don't know which is worse. A professional army or zealots who blindly follow whoever's in charge."

"With Morenta's organization, there isn't much of a difference. They're all trained guns."

Brent had learned that himself last night.

Ghost set another battery on the cutting board. "That's the last one. By tomorrow night, they should be good to go."

Ghost picked up the tray and carried it to the cabinet. He slid it onto the empty shelf and returned to the table to collect the remaining copper shielding sheets. Once he set them inside the cabinet on either side of the newly coated batteries, he returned to the table.

"If those dry early enough, I'll go on a surveillance run at oh three hundred," Ghost said.

Brent checked the time on the stove clock. Seventeen thirty. Waiting another eight and a half hours sounded reasonable, but Brent couldn't deny the need brewing inside him to do something now. Was he simply impatient? Or was there a reason they shouldn't wait?

The questions repeated in his mind with a silent request for guidance. He pushed to a stand. "We need to check out the fortress tonight."

"I just said I was going to."

"No, I mean now."

"It's not even dark yet."

"I know it doesn't make sense, but I need to see what's going on there."

Ghost studied him for a moment. "Okay, but if we're going to do this, you need to change your clothes. You walk around in combat gear while it's light out and we're bound to draw the wrong kind of attention."

Brent sized up the man beside him. He was at least eight inches shorter than Brent. "I doubt you have anything that will fit me."

"I should have something that will come close. Let me look." He disappeared into the bedroom and returned a moment later holding a black long-sleeved shirt and black pants. "Here. Put these on. I'll check the perimeter of the house."

Brent held them up, surprised that the clothes did indeed look like they would fit. As soon as Ghost disappeared out the back door, Brent changed into the borrowed clothes. He then hobbled across the room to the cabinet and retrieved a holster. After slipping it into place in his waistband, he holstered his sidearm.

Ghost walked back inside. "You ready?"

"Yeah." Brent slipped his knife into the back of his waistband and adjusted his shirt over the top of it. "I'm ready."

* * *

Vanessa hugged Seth, holding him tight for a long moment. On the other side of the door, a car waited to take Seth and Amy to Andrews, where they would catch their flight. A short distance down the hall, Amy hugged her mom.

Seth kissed the top of Vanessa's head. "I'll call as soon as I can."

Vanessa swallowed hard and nodded. Deployments were never easy, but this one had her more rattled than ever before. Seth wasn't supposed to be deploying anymore, but here he was, not even two days into a job he wasn't supposed to start until next week, and he was leaving. And he wasn't just leaving. He was potentially going to the same place where he had lost one commanding officer and had another wounded—the same place the president could send her if Seth's squad didn't succeed.

Kel had survived his ordeal. Whether Brent would walk away from the last mission remained to be seen, but Vanessa couldn't deny that the fortress was the last place she would have chosen for Seth to insert for his first mission while in command.

"I love you." Seth's whispered words tickled her ear.

"I love you too." Vanessa squeezed him again before forcing herself to let him go. She glanced at Amy, who was standing beside her parents. The heartache and pain in her friend's expression was undeniable. Vanessa ached for her, and she couldn't deny her fear that she would suffer a similar fate.

Vanessa leaned back enough so her gaze could meet her husband's, despite more than a foot's difference in their heights. "Work smart out there."

"I will." Seth leaned down, and his lips met hers. Though brief, the kiss sent a thrill through her along with an underlying sense of home.

Vanessa's hand lifted to the back of his neck and drew him closer for one more kiss.

Seth's hands tightened on her waist for a brief moment before he released her. "Give Talia a kiss for me."

"I will."

Amy said her last goodbyes to her parents and approached. "Are you ready?"

Seth simply nodded and opened the door. He escorted Amy outside, casting one last glance over his shoulder before he let the door close behind him.

Vanessa's emotions swirled, a weepy sensation rising within her. She drew a deep breath and let it out slowly. This wasn't a military base where tearful goodbyes were common. This was the White House. She couldn't afford to be seen as overly emotional, especially not in her first week working here.

Beside her, Jim retrieved a handkerchief from his pocket and handed it to his wife.

Katherine dabbed at the moisture in her eyes. "I think it's easier when I don't get the chance to say goodbye."

It wasn't, but Vanessa didn't say the words.

"Let's go have some dinner in the residence," Jim suggested. "Vanessa, you're welcome to join us."

"Thanks, but I want to spend some time at home while Talia is still awake."

"If you decide you want to spend the night here, you're welcome to. Your daughter and mother as well," Katherine said.

"I appreciate that, but my mother staying in the White House would cause complications. She's not cleared, and this isn't a time when our president should have to worry about who's staying in his home."

"I'm afraid she's right," Jim told Katherine before turning to Vanessa. "But your guest room will be ready if you decide you want to sleep over here."

"Thank you." Vanessa took a step toward the door her husband had just walked through. "I'll let you know if I get any updates."

"And I'll do the same," Jim said. "Try to get some rest."

Vanessa took in the president's weary expression. "Maybe you should turn in early tonight. I seriously doubt any missions will happen with the Saint Squad until after Seth and Amy arrive."

"You're right. We should all sleep now," Jim said. "And you should go home and spend some time with your daughter. Who knows when the next lull will happen."

Vanessa checked her watch. Talia should be waking from her nap within the next half hour. "I think I'll take you up on that offer."

Katherine put her hand on Jim's arm. "Maybe you should take a nap. I'm sure Sarah can clear the rest of your schedule."

"I don't know. There's so much work to do," Jim said.

"Someone will wake you if there's another emergency," Vanessa said. "And trust me. If the Saint Squad is smart, they're all sleeping right now too."

17

Tristan stifled a yawn. He wasn't sure how many hours he'd been up, but his body was starting to feel the strain of back-to-back missions on a limited amount of sleep.

At one of the workstations, Craig tapped away on the keyboard, searching for new intel, while Damian dozed in the chair beside him.

"Should we wake him up and send him to his bunk?" Tristan asked.

Quinn's response was to lean back in his seat and slap Damian's leg.

Damian straightened instantly. "*Qué?*" He looked around, his dazed expression clearing. "What?"

"Go get some sleep," Quinn told him. "We should all hit the rack. Who knows when we'll get the go-ahead to insert again."

Quinn, a voice of reason again. They had all entered an alternate universe.

The hatch opened, and Commander Webb walked in. His gaze swept the room. "You all need to get some sleep."

"We were heading that way now," Tristan said.

"Good," Webb said. "I wanted to let you know my squad is shipping out."

"Where?"

"A problem in the Middle East is heating up," Webb said.

"Good luck," Quinn said.

"Thanks. You too." Webb disappeared back the way he'd come.

Tristan gave in to the urge to yawn. "Come on, guys. Time to get some sleep."

Damian and Quinn started toward the door.

"Hey." Craig motioned to his computer screen. "I think I found something."

"What?" Tristan moved to stand behind him.

"I've been tracking movement outside the fortress, trying to figure out where Brent could have gone."

"How?" Tristan asked.

Quinn and Damian stepped beside Tristan so they could see too.

"Yeah, the fog was too thick for the satellites to give a clear image," Quinn said.

"I know. That's why I went back to the few days before." Craig moved the cursor on the screen and clicked to start the recorded satellite feed.

He zoomed in to reveal a man slip across the road bordering the fortress and disappear into the thick trees beside the high wall encircling Morenta's property.

"Any idea where he came from?" Tristan asked.

"I've been scanning the village. Based on how long it would take one of us to travel through the woods between the village and the fortress, I think this is our man." Craig brought up a new image, this time rolling through the satellite feed at half speed in reverse. The man wore dark clothes, and a hat covered his head.

"He could be a local."

"A local who would willingly spy on Morenta?" Tristan shook his head. "I don't think so. Every time we've gone in there, all the villagers have steered clear of the fortress."

"Can you tell where he came from?" Damian asked.

"He keeps to the cover of the trees for the most part, but I'm pretty sure this is him here." Craig moved his cursor to display an earlier segment of the feed.

"If this is a guardian, you can be sure he's not taking a straight path," Quinn said.

"Keep looking," Tristan said. "See if you can find him leaving one of the houses."

"Or at least narrow it down," Damian added.

"Damian, see if you can help him track this guy," Tristan said.

Damian pulled up the satellite feed on the computer beside Craig. Quinn positioned himself behind Damian, while Tristan kept his focus on Craig's screen. Several minutes passed without any sighting.

"Wait." Quinn put his hand on Damian's shoulder. "Back that up. Half speed."

Craig continued his scan while Damian complied.

"Freeze it right there."

Tristan looked over at Damian's screen. Several houses clustered together on the edge of the woods, a dirt road cutting through the center.

"What are you seeing?" Tristan asked.

Quinn pointed at the center of the screen. "Punch in on that area."

As soon as the image enlarged, Tristan saw it, a shadow on the edge of one of the houses. "I can't believe you saw that."

"Eye of a sniper," Quinn said. "The shadow is about the same length as the one from the guy we saw before."

"I can't believe our intel right now is based on the length of someone's shadow," Craig said.

"That's what happens when we're tracking ghosts," Tristan said.

"Play it forward again," Quinn said.

"Keep it at half speed," Tristan added.

The shadow disappeared after only a few yards, as though the owner of it knew the sun's position and that he might be spotted from overhead.

"If that isn't a ghost, I don't know what is."

"See if you can pick him up again," Tristan said.

"Damian, give me the time stamp and coordinates of where you're looking," Craig said.

Damian gave him the information, and both men started working their way outward from the last potential sighting.

"I haven't seen anyone else moving around through here," Damian said.

"Other than a couple of people leaving in a car, I haven't either," Craig said.

Tristan moved to the worktable and pulled up the still image of the village. He returned to stand behind Craig and checked the coordinates. "Based on this, it looks like he had to have gone into one of these six houses."

"I agree." Quinn pointed at the quiet houses and empty street. "If he moved to the next cluster of houses, he would have had to cross the road, and there's a break in the trees if he continued farther north."

"Seems to me six houses is a target area we can work with," Craig said.

The hatch opened again, and the XO walked inside. "Did Webb talk to you before he left?"

"Yeah. He stopped by a little while ago," Tristan said. "Now that Webb's gone, who do we need to talk to for new orders? We've narrowed down where we think Commander Miller may be hiding."

"Where you *think* he may be hiding?" Commander Chang asked. "That's not very definitive."

"We know he was pulled out of the woods after the explosion, and we can't find any evidence of him going beyond the village," Tristan said. "We've narrowed his location down to six houses."

"That's impressive, but you'll need an officer present with you before you insert again."

"Why? Quinn and I are capable of running this op," Tristan said. "We don't need a babysitter."

"The last time you went in by yourselves, you stole a helicopter."

"An enemy helicopter," Quinn pointed out.

"And that helicopter is helping the navy figure out how to combat this battery drain problem," Tristan added.

"That's true, but I don't see the captain approving another op until you have a temporary commander assigned to you." The XO motioned to the computer stations. "Your squad has been working practically around the clock. Get some sleep. If the commander is still alive, he clearly has help. If he's not, there's nothing you can do for him. Either way, taking the time to rest isn't going to hurt anything."

Though Tristan couldn't shake the urgency rushing through him, arguing wasn't likely to get him closer to where he wanted to be. "We'll get some sleep, but can you put the wheels in motion for us to get back in to Nicaragua?" Tristan asked. "We're not trying to get into the fortress, so it will be far easier to get into position to set up surveillance."

"N4 is working on modifying some of our equipment," Commander Chang said. "I'll let them know what you'll need."

"And a ride to Nicaragua?" Quinn asked.

"I'll talk to the captain. In the meantime, hit the rack." The XO's gaze met Tristan's. "That's an order."

"Yes, sir."

18

Why was he doing this again? Brent followed Ghost through the shadows, each step a reminder of the wound he had suffered in last night's explosion. They had set out right before dusk, the fading light allowing them to remain invisible for all but a few yards of their journey.

Ghost stopped at the edge of the woods, where they could see the twelve-foot barrier that surrounded the fortress. As soon as Brent stepped beside him, Ghost jutted his chin toward the wall. "Best guess, the source of the problem is in that area of the fortress grounds."

In the fading light, Brent lifted his binoculars. He adjusted the focus manually until the top of the wall came into focus. "All I see are trees. How did you get inside when you hauled me out of the fortress?"

"Grappling hook," Ghost said. "I disabled a few of their perimeter alarms a couple days ago in case I needed to come in and provide support."

"They didn't fix them?"

"They hadn't as of the last time I checked," Ghost said. "I have no idea if they closed the breach after last night's invasion though. Who knows what kinds of precautions they're putting in place now."

Brent scanned the area again. Movement in one of the trees caught his attention. "Did you see that?"

"You're the one with the binoculars."

Brent adjusted the focus again. More movement, but this time he was able to make out the form of a man climbing from one branch to another. "There's someone in that tree."

Ghost stepped deeper into the shadows before he positioned himself for a better view. "Which tree?"

"My eleven o'clock." Brent kept his gaze trained on the man climbing down from the tree.

"I don't see him. What's he doing?"

"I can't tell. It doesn't look like he's armed."

A shout broke through the silence. Followed by several more.

"What are they saying?" Brent asked. "I don't speak enough Spanish to understand them."

"They're looking for someone."

A gunshot punctuated Ghost's words.

The man in the tree ducked behind a branch.

"If they want him dead, he must know something." Brent lowered his binoculars and drew his pistol.

Ghost retrieved his weapon from the holster at his waist. "Cover me."

Ghost shot once into the air and rushed across the road so he was pressed up against the wall. Then he yelled something in Spanish.

Brent was able to pick out enough words to know Ghost was offering the man help.

More gunfire sparked through the air.

Even though the shooters were safely behind the barrier, Brent returned fire.

The man in the tree froze, but the moment the gunfire stopped, he scrambled from his safe haven. He jumped down to the top of the wall, a bullet impacting the tree where he had been a moment before.

"*Apurase*!" Ghost said. Brent had heard a similar version from Damian often enough to understand that Ghost was telling the man to hurry.

The man slid down the outside of the wall to where Ghost waited. The moment they started across the road, Brent opened fire again, aiming at the top of the wall.

An engine came to life in the distance. With all the cars in the area stranded with dead batteries, Brent didn't have to guess that the noise was coming from inside the fortress walls.

"*Apurase*!" Brent called out, repeating the hurry-up order Ghost had issued a moment ago.

Ghost and his new companion reached the tree line. The man was younger than Brent expected, maybe twenty or twenty-one.

Ghost motioned them both forward. "Follow me." He repeated the command again in Spanish.

The man didn't have to be told twice. He quickly followed behind Ghost, leaving Brent to bring up the rear.

The engine drew closer, the swath of headlights spilling into the trees.

"Get down," Brent called out.

Everyone dove for cover. Despite the pain in his leg, Brent squatted and grabbed a tree branch. As soon as the light passed by him, he used the branch to brush away their tracks.

Ghost stepped back into view and motioned the younger man forward. They made it only fifteen yards before lights glared through the trees again. The brightness suggested the headlights of a vehicle were aimed directly at them.

The branch still in one hand, Brent pressed against a tree trunk. Footsteps crunched in the underbrush of the forest, each one growing louder.

Brent's fingers flexed on the grip of his gun. Limited ammo and they were likely outnumbered. Not to mention, they were protecting someone they didn't know anything about.

At the moment, none of that mattered. For now, they needed to neutralize the threat against them before one of their pursuers managed to put a bullet in someone.

Brent glanced at the path ahead of him where Ghost had been a moment ago. Ghost wasn't visible, but the man he had rescued now hid behind a tree ten yards away.

Trusting that Ghost was somewhere nearby to back him up, Brent concentrated on the approaching footsteps. Two men. Make that three.

Though he had to assume these men were armed, Brent wasn't in the habit of shooting people unless he was certain they were the enemy. Hoping to test them, Brent tossed the branch a few feet away.

Immediately, their pursuers opened fire. Brent waited until they stopped shooting before he peeked around the edge of the tree, sighted the nearest target, and squeezed off a shot.

The man grabbed at his shoulder, and his weapon dropped to the ground.

Brent rolled back out of view, this time lowering painfully to one knee. He peeked out on the other side of the tree and fired. Another man went down. The third returned fire and darted out of sight.

Brent rushed to the next tree and took cover. He listened for the last man's footsteps, but only silence greeted him.

Seconds ticked by, no one daring to move. If it was a game of patience, Brent had the stamina to win, but he doubted their pursuer was simply trying to wait them out. More likely, he was waiting for reinforcements.

Sure enough, the sound of another engine drew closer.

Not interested in being outnumbered again, Brent counted down in his head. With a prayer circling in his mind, he fired a shot as he rushed to the next tree, closing the distance between him and their new ally.

With his Spanish limited and Ghost not in sight, Brent used hand signals to urge the other man to continue deeper into the woods.

Brent used his fingers to count down. As soon as his hand closed into a fist, Brent fired two more shots. The man sprinted farther into the trees.

Their single pursuer peeked out just long enough for Brent to take aim, but before he could fire, another gunshot rang out. The man fell out of sight. A moment later, Ghost came out of the darkening shadows.

"Where did he go?" Ghost asked.

"That way." Brent pointed into the woods.

"I'll catch up to him. Can you get back to the safe house on your own?"

"Yeah. I'll cover our tracks."

"Be careful," Ghost said.

"You too."

19

Amy gripped the edge of her seat as turbulence forced the plane into an unexpected upward motion. Her stomach pitched, and acid rose in her throat. She swallowed hard and drew deep, even breaths to fight against the worsening nausea.

Beside her, Seth sat with his head back, his eyes closed, and his body completely at peace. How SEALs could sleep anywhere, she didn't know. Working with the Saint Squad for so many years, she had trained her body to sleep at odd times, but not the way the SEALs could. They had that uncanny ability to sleep anytime, anywhere.

The pilot's voice came over the intercom to announce they were on their approach. Seth's eyes opened.

"You doing okay?" he asked, his voice alert, as though he had been awake the whole time.

Amy nodded. Speaking might make her throw up.

The plane jerked again. Amy gasped, and her body stiffened.

"Deep breaths," Seth said with his slow Southern drawl. "Nice and easy. In. Out."

Too sick to worry about embarrassment, Amy closed her eyes and followed his instructions.

"Keep going. In." Seth paused. "And out."

Concentrating solely on the easy cadence of Seth's voice, she did as he instructed, and slowly, her body relaxed.

The pilot gave the final-approach warning. She and Seth took their positions, bracing for impact. The plane touched down, and her body jerked when the aircraft's tail hook caught the wire that jolted them to a stop.

Amy took several more slow breaths before she opened her eyes. When she did, she met Seth's concerned gaze.

"This isn't normal for you." He furrowed his brow. "Is this stress, or do you have good news to share?"

Amy looked down for a brief moment.

The silence stretched for several seconds.

"I understand," Seth finally said. "Brent doesn't know?"

Amy shook her head.

Seth studied her in his thoughtful way. Then he stood and collected both of their bags. "Come on. Let's get you some answers." He shouldered both of their duffels on one arm and their backpacks on his other. "Stress isn't good for anyone."

Amy unhooked her buckle and stood. Her legs trembled. She grabbed the back of her seat for a moment before she reached out a hand. "I can take my bags."

"I've got them."

Amy didn't argue. She led the way toward the exit, her hand gripping each seat back as she moved forward.

They reached the flight deck, where a seaman waited for them. Despite the protective ear coverings they all wore, the roar of a jet engine made communication impossible.

The seaman led them toward the doorway leading inside.

Seth gestured for Amy to go first. She nodded, taking care to step over the various cables on the deck. They walked down the catwalk and into the center of the ship. The seaman closed the hatch behind them, shutting out the worst of the deafening sounds.

Amy drew in a deep breath of air that was mostly void of engine fumes and pulled the protective gear off her head.

The seaman motioned them forward. "Follow me."

Instead of leading them to their ready room or their quarters, as Amy had expected, he headed for the bridge. As soon as they arrived, the captain greeted them.

"Your squad has been ordered to get some sleep, but they think they've identified where Commander Miller was taken."

Optimism rose within Amy and was reflected on Seth's face. She put her hand on Seth's arm. "Did they see Commander Miller?"

"No, but they tracked someone from the day before who may have been surveilling the fortress," the captain said. "If they're right, whoever it was may have been an intel officer working for us."

"When are we going in?" Seth asked.

"Work up a mission plan with your squad," the captain said. "I'll have a ride ready for you tonight. I suggest you both get some sleep. The seaman will show you to your quarters."

Seth nodded. "Thank you, sir."

Even though Amy would have preferred to go straight to their ready room, she left the bridge and fell into step behind the seaman.

She reached out a hand as she stepped over a bulkhead, her balance not as steady as it usually was.

Seth must have noticed because he said, "We'll take her to her quarters first."

"Yes, sir."

Seth hauled both of their bags down the narrow corridors until they reached the female quarters. "Can you give us a minute?" Seth asked the seaman.

The seaman nodded and moved down the corridor a short distance.

"Are you going to be okay?" Seth asked.

Fighting the nausea and weariness, she said, "I'm getting tired of answering that question."

"You know we're going to do everything we can to get Brent back, but we need your A game to make it happen," Seth said.

"I'll do my job," Amy said tightly.

"I know you will." Understanding and sympathy carried in his voice when he added, "I also know you need to forgive your father."

That was the last thing she had expected Seth to say.

"Your father made the same decision Brent would have. If you want to be mad at Brent for staying behind and making sure his teammates got out, go ahead, but the time may come that we may need your dad's help. Having the two of you on good terms will help us get Brent back so you can be mad at him in person."

Amy hoped that would be soon.

Not one to hammer a nail once it had been pounded in, Seth handed Amy her bags. "Get some sleep while you can. If we need anything before we ship out, I'll send for you."

"I'll try." Amy made her way to her stateroom and stored her bags. After a quick trip to the head, she climbed into her bunk. Tonight the Saint Squad would go after Brent, and Lord willing, they would bring him back to her safe and sound.

* * *

Jim flipped through the latest intel report, a photo of the electromagnetic weapon included. Though the inside contained complex wiring and circuitry, the entire weapon had been encased in a metal-sided suitcase, not unlike the larger bags one might see spinning on the baggage carousels at the airport.

Had these weapons come into the country as checked bags? Jim shook his head. Surely with all the screenings at the various airports, someone would have caught on that this wasn't what it appeared to be.

No, more likely it had come over the border in a different method—car, bus, or boat. Those were his best guesses. He supposed train travel was possible as well, but unless the terrorists had transported them in through Canada, that was unlikely.

Jim's desk phone rang, and he answered. "Yes?"

"Mr. President, I received a message that Lieutenant Commander Johnson has reached the carrier," Sarah said.

Which meant Amy had too. "Thank you."

"You're welcome. Also, Secretary Valdez is here to see you."

"Send him in."

Doug opened the door and poked his head inside. "Do you have a minute?"

"Yes." Jim set the report down and motioned for Doug to sit. "Any news from Kansas City?"

"More of the same. We have equipment en route to get the power restored, but in the meantime, we're focused on getting everyone into shelters until they can safely return to their homes." Doug sat in the chair beside Jim's desk. "We have buses and trains transporting residents to Omaha, Tulsa, Wichita, St. Louis, and Oklahoma City. We hope that will help us prevent the power grid in the nearby areas from overloading."

"What are the chances that the nearby power grids could fail?"

"Kansas City, Kansas, is already maxed out. This cold front is really pushing the limits."

"Can we divert power from other plants to help alleviate the strain?"

Doug shook his head. "All the surrounding areas are having similar problems." He slid a folder onto Jim's desk. "With your permission, I'd like to issue a public-service announcement to share emergency procedures in the event of additional power outages."

Jim weighed the pros and cons. He preferred to encourage preparation rather than deal with the lack of it, but the real possibility of creating a panic also had to be considered.

"You think this is the best course of action?" Jim asked.

"I do," Doug said. "I've met with the head of FEMA, and he agrees. Until we can modify enough emergency equipment and vehicles with copper shielding, we aren't capable of providing the support needed to evacuate another city. We're fortunate that North Las Vegas isn't also dealing with severe weather."

"What is happening in Vegas?" Jim asked. "Are you telling people to shelter in place?"

"As much as possible. Getting communications restored is still our top priority, but we're relying on volunteers from areas with power to go door-to-door to tell people what's going on. It's far from efficient."

Jim had spent months knocking on doors during his early political campaigns. He couldn't fathom trying to round up enough volunteers to get to so many homes in such a short period of time.

"Where are you getting your volunteers from?" Jim asked.

"Church and civic groups mostly," Doug said. "We've modified enough buses with copper shielding to take people in and out, and we've been able to evacuate the most critical cases from the hospitals."

Doug's creative solutions reinforced Jim's decision to bring him into his cabinet.

Doug motioned to the folder in Jim's hand. "This announcement will allow local communities to enact communication and evacuation plans now rather than wait until they don't have the means to use modern technology."

Because it was Doug, Jim asked, "Have you prayed about this?"

Doug nodded. "I have."

Warmth flowed through Jim, and he handed the folder back to Doug. "Then, make it happen."

"Thank you, Mr. President."

Jim stood and shook Doug's hand. "Thank *you*."

20

Brent zigzagged through the houses in the village, his leg throbbing with every step. He bypassed the safe house to ensure he wasn't being followed before circling back to it.

He finally reached the back door and knocked twice. A moment later, Ghost opened it and waved him inside.

After locking the door behind him, Brent took his first good look at the man they had helped escape from the fortress. Early twenties, Latino, his collared shirt torn at the right shoulder.

Brent jutted his chin toward their guest. "What's his story?"

"This is Moises. He thought he was being hired as a guard for the fortress."

"I gather that wasn't the case."

"No, and if he's telling the truth, we have a problem."

"We, as in you and me? Or we, as in the United States?"

"Probably both," Ghost said. "Turns out he and his buddy were supposed to be replacements for a couple of the men who were killed last night."

"Replacements to do what?"

"Help carry out a terrorist attack against the United States," Ghost said, his expression grim. "According to Moises, Osman has not only taken control of Morenta's business, but he also has an attack planned within the week."

"What kind of attack?" Brent asked.

"Moises here was supposed to deliver an EMP weapon to Orlando."

"Does he have a specific date for the attack?"

"Friday."

Brent did a quick timeline in his head. "Today's Tuesday?"

"Yeah."

"When was he supposed to leave for the United States, and how was he supposed to get there?"

Ghost relayed the question.

After some back-and-forth, Ghost said, "They're leaving sometime tonight, but he doesn't know how they're getting into the US."

"How many of them were there?"

Again, Ghost relayed the question.

Brent picked up the word *siete* in Moises's answer. "Seven?" Brent asked.

Ghost shook his head. "Nine. Seven plus him and his friend."

Brent dropped into an empty chair at the table. "Nine simultaneous targets, or nine people working in teams?"

This answer lasted longer than the last. When Moises stopped speaking, Ghost pushed out of his chair and paced across the room.

"Well?" Brent asked.

"He and his friend were given two different cities. He had Orlando. His friend had New York."

So many skyscrapers, so many people so close together, so many elevators that wouldn't be usable if the electricity went out. "A pulse weapon in New York would be devastating."

"Yeah. Based on the number of people in their briefing, he thinks they're working in teams of two. Sixteen men and two women." Ghost pressed his heel against the corner of a tile on the floor and leaned down to pop it out of place. He reached inside the hidden floor space and straightened a moment later, a folded map in one hand and a small plastic box in the other.

He crossed to the framed print on the wall and flipped it over to reveal a large bulletin board on the back.

"That's a neat trick." Brent moved to his side as Ghost used pushpins to mount the map of the United States to the corkboard.

Ghost pressed a red pushpin into the circle that identified Orlando. He added a second one to New York City.

"What other cities did he hear about?" Brent asked.

"He doesn't know. His friend only told him about his because he didn't want to go. Apparently, the guy has family in New York City, including a cousin who's being treated for cancer in a local hospital. Moises has family in the US too."

"What happened to his friend?" Brent asked.

"He isn't sure, but he thinks his friend was captured and taken back into the fortress."

Brent studied the map before him. "If they're going after these two cities, I have to think they're trying to cascade a power failure along the eastern seaboard."

"If that's the case, it's likely DC is also a target."

"And probably Boston, Philadelphia, Baltimore, and Miami," Brent said.

Ghost stuck a yellow pin in all four of those locations on the map. "Maybe Atlanta or Charlotte?" Ghost placed two more pins.

Brent looked at the streak of pins down the map and focused on where the largest gaps were—through Virginia and the Carolinas. Strategically, there was only one city between Charlotte and DC that had both the population and the significance to cripple the country's defenses: the Saint Squad's home. "Or Virginia Beach."

* * *

Vanessa walked into the kitchen, her mother at the stove, the scent of Moroccan spices hanging in the air, and Talia's happy babbles carrying through the baby monitor.

Her mom looked up from the pot she was stirring. "You're home early."

"Not that early." Vanessa closed the door leading to the garage. "Did Talia just wake up?"

"About five minutes ago. I wanted to get dinner in the oven before I went up to get her."

"I'll get her." Vanessa moved through the expansive kitchen into the great room. A book lay on the couch, revealing that her mom had found a little time to relax between babysitting and cooking.

Vanessa climbed the stairs. Even though she wanted to go straight to her daughter's room, she passed by it and moved into the master bedroom to change her clothes. No need to give her dry cleaner extra challenges if it wasn't necessary.

After she changed into jeans and a sweater, she headed back down the hall and pushed Talia's bedroom door open.

Talia looked up and squealed. "Mamama." The babble hadn't quite formed into a consistent word, but Vanessa understood the meaning well enough.

"Hey there, sweet girl."

Talia scrambled to stand, using the side of the crib to support herself. Her chubby little legs bounced up and down.

"Come here." Vanessa lifted her into her arms, and Talia snuggled into her.

Vanessa's heart melted. How could she leave this little girl to go into a place filled with evil and danger, especially while Seth was also in the field?

She couldn't. That answer flowed through her, and with it came both a sense of peace and a new flurry of questions.

Her country needed intel to defend itself against whoever Morenta had left in charge, and she was the fastest way to get it. Yet the sickening of her stomach she experienced every time she considered going undercover felt more like a warning than fear.

She set Talia on her changing pad. "Let's change your diaper." Vanessa performed the simple task, her thoughts still churning. Surely, there had to be another way to gain the information they needed.

Vanessa set Talia on her feet. The little girl tottered two steps before plopping down on the floor.

"Do you want to go downstairs to see *Jaddi*?" Vanessa asked, using the Arabic name for grandma.

Talia's response was to pick up one of her stacking cups and stick it in her mouth.

Vanessa laughed. "Or you can play here."

She sat beside her daughter and stacked the colored cups into a tower. Talia knocked it down.

Vanessa wished she could knock down Morenta's empire that easily. She stacked the cups again. "So, how do I?" She posed the question out loud.

Morenta was in custody, but Vanessa didn't hold out hope that he would give them any information. He didn't trust Americans, and he had no reason to share his plans.

He didn't trust Americans. That thought repeated in her mind. Morenta didn't think she was an American. He thought she was from a Middle Eastern family that had previously operated in Central America.

Vanessa's cell phone vibrated with an incoming text. She checked her personal phone first. Nothing. She pulled out her guardian phone.

K: Go feed the horses. Alone.

"Looks like I have chores to do." Vanessa picked up her daughter and carried her downstairs. Her mom sat on the couch, her book open in front of her. "Can you watch Talia while I feed the horses?"

Her mom set her book aside and held out her arms. "Come to *Jaddi*."

Vanessa settled Talia into her mother's arms. "I'll be back in a little while."

"Best wear a jacket."

"Yes, Mama." Vanessa opened the coat closet by the front door and pulled out a black overcoat. After slipping it on, she headed for the back door. "I'll be back in a little while."

"Don't be too long. Dinner will be ready in half an hour."

Vanessa stepped outside and followed the path through the trees toward the back of the Whitmores' property. She reached the clearing, where three horses grazed on what was left of the grass in the pasture. A tractor trailer occupied the open space beyond the stables.

Despite the trailer's lack of markings, Vanessa recognized the rig.

Kade stepped out of the stables. "Took you long enough."

"I only got your text five minutes ago." Vanessa walked past him into the wooden structure. "What's up?"

"The latest debriefing report for Yago Paquito popped up a few minutes ago. Turns out he helped build a dozen EMP weapons."

"A dozen?" The ramifications of so many sent a shiver of terror through her. "We've only discovered three."

"I know. It's possible the first three were used to see if they could crash the US electrical grid in one shot."

"But it didn't work."

"Not enough to satisfy Morenta, and the likelihood of Osman taking over for him doesn't bode well for us."

"You think we're looking at another attack." Vanessa dropped onto a hay bale. "Any sign of Osman's guards entering the country?"

"Nothing yet," Kade said. "Renee has been going through your notes from your time working undercover. We're flagging every name you came across while working for Ramir."

"That's a long shot."

"It's better than nothing."

"Where's your wife?" Vanessa asked. "And why are you here?"

"Renee's in the truck, resting. We came up to help you with Morenta."

"Help me with Morenta?" Vanessa repeated. They weren't going to pressure her to go undercover, too, were they?

"Renee still has her CIA credentials. We thought she could back you up when you visit Morenta at the interrogation center."

Vanessa looked up at him. Odd that he would share her idea about her speaking with Morenta. "I don't know that I'll have any more luck than the interrogators."

"I don't either, but it's worth a shot," Kade said. "I'm sure he knows who Lina Ramir is. Seems to me you have a right to demand your uncle's property back."

And it would keep her here in the United States with Talia. "Like you said, it's worth a shot."

"Just tell Renee when you're ready, and she'll set up an appointment for you to meet with him," Kade said. "By then, the Saint Squad should be back aboard ship, and we can pick up any more insight Commander Miller has for us."

"We're all praying he survived, but it's unlikely he knows anything beyond what the rest of his squad does."

"We'll find out soon enough," Kade said. "His squad inserts tonight."

"Most of his squad." Vanessa retrieved a leaf of hay and dropped it into the closest stall. "They're down both Brent and Jay."

"Not anymore."

Vanessa turned to face him. "What did you do?"

"The Saint Squad needs to go in full strength," Kade said. "Or as close to full strength as possible."

21

Tristan pushed the hatch open and stepped into his squad's ready room. He turned to the computer where Amy normally sat. If she were here, they would already have the latest intel reports. She'd probably also have decent food for them rather than the mystery meat currently being served in the enlisted mess.

The hatch opened, and Tristan braced against the storm of complaints that would arrive with his squadmates. The scent of fried chicken wafted toward him.

A seaman carried a tray into the room. Seth followed.

"What are you doing here?" Tristan asked.

"Making sure we don't have a revolt on our hands before we ship out tonight." Seth pointed to the worktable. "Seaman, you can set that over there."

"Yes, sir." The seaman set the tray down, a stack of what appeared to be chicken sandwiches stacked on top. As soon as Seth dismissed him, the seaman left the room.

Tristan sat at the table and grabbed a sandwich. "When did you get here?"

"A few hours ago. Amy's here too," Seth said. "I sent her to her quarters to take a nap, but she's probably pulling the new intel reports by now."

The hatch opened again, and Amy walked inside, a duffel hanging from her shoulder and shadows under her eyes.

Guilt welled inside Tristan. Realistically, he knew he couldn't have done anything differently two nights ago, but that didn't take away the regret or his determination to bring Brent back home. He waited until Amy set her bag down before he crossed to her and pulled her into a hug.

Her arms came around him, and she sniffled before she pulled back. She took a deep breath. "I just spoke with the XO. Your ride will be ready at twenty-three hundred."

Sensing Amy wasn't ready to talk about Brent, he asked, "What about our extraction?"

"Oh four hundred tomorrow," Amy said. "The backup will be one day later."

The hatch opened again. This time it was Jay who walked in.

In unison, Tristan, Seth, and Amy asked, "What are you doing here?"

Jay closed the hatch behind him. "I got a call." His jaw tightened. "Why didn't one of you tell me Brent was missing?"

"We've been River City," Tristan said.

Seth motioned to himself and Amy. "And we've been a little busy at the White House."

"You're supposed to be on paternity leave," Amy said.

"Like Brent wouldn't do the same thing in my place." Jay said the words and then looked at Amy. "Sorry, Amy. I didn't mean—"

"It's okay."

Jay turned to Tristan. "What happened?"

"We lost comm before we extracted." Tristan leaned against the table. "Some of Morenta's men showed up with missile launchers as we were trying to get out of there. Brent sent us ahead to make sure we got the professor out of there."

"What professor?" Jay asked.

"Yago Paquito. He was forced to develop a pulse weapon," Tristan said.

"Is that what caused the blackouts in Kansas City and Vegas?" Jay asked.

"We had blackouts in Kansas City and Vegas?" Tristan asked.

"Yes to both of your questions," Amy said.

"Since you're in command until we get Brent back, this is for you." Jay handed Seth a sealed envelope marked *Eyes Only—Saint Squad Commander*.

Seth tore it open, and his eyes widened. "Where did this come from?"

"It was delivered to me when I arrived at the airfield to fly out here," Jay said. "What is it?"

"An address in the village by the fortress." Seth picked up a folder off the worktable and flipped through it. "It's one of the houses y'all identified as being a possible hideout for Brent."

"It must have been one of the guardians who sent this," Tristan said. "If they had an operative staying there, they would know where he was."

"This will simplify our mission." Seth motioned for Jay and Tristan to sit. "I've been working up a plan. I didn't know we'd have Jay here, so that will give us an extra set of eyes."

"Please tell me I didn't leave my wife and daughter home because you need me to climb a tree."

"Okay," Seth said.

"We won't tell you," Tristan added.

* * *

Amy nibbled on a roll and read through the latest weather forecast for the fortress. At the worktable behind her, Seth, Tristan, Quinn, and Jay were hard at work reviewing their mission plan. Craig and Damian had been tasked with picking up their modified equipment from logistics.

Less than two hours before the Saint Squad would leave the ship to go in search of her husband and answers about what Osman had planned.

"I think you're right," Jay said. "Assuming a guardian is helping him, Brent has to be hiding out in the village."

The way Jay spoke as though Brent were still alive and well added to her hope.

"Amy, can you see if there are any updated satellite photos of the fortress and the village?" Seth asked. "Based on the time stamp on these, there should have been another pass an hour ago."

"Sure." Amy accessed the program she needed, but the updates weren't there. "Nothing yet."

"Any chance you can shake them loose?" Seth asked. "We need the latest on the movement in the area before we go in."

"I'll see what I can do." She picked up her phone and put in her request but wasn't surprised when the lieutenant on the other end informed her that the updated satellite images weren't available yet. Amy pushed back from her desk. "I'm heading up to CIC. I'll be back when I get the new images."

"Good luck," Seth said.

"Thanks." Amy navigated the maze of corridors, her stomach revolting with each step. She inhaled deeply. The underlying scent of jet fuel only served to increase her nausea rather than dissipate it.

She sidestepped two seamen heading toward her. Willing her stomach to settle, Amy continued forward until she reached her destination. She approached a lieutenant who stood by one of the comm units.

"I need to put in a request for the last satellite pass over Nicaragua." Amy handed the woman the information. "Here are the coordinates."

"Are you the one who just called?" the lieutenant asked.

"Yes," Amy said. "This is mission critical. We don't have a lot of time to wait."

"I can put the request in as a priority, but at this time of day, I'm not sure how quickly we'll get a response."

"Have you tried calling?"

"We're still River City," the lieutenant said.

"This is official communication," Amy said. "I'm sure the captain will approve."

"I'm sorry, ma'am, but I have my orders."

Orders the lieutenant was afraid to question. Amy stepped toward the door. "I'll be back."

Amy headed for the stairs and climbed the two levels to the bridge. The captain wasn't anywhere to be found, but the XO stood at the helm.

"Commander Chang, I need authorization for an emergency communication stateside," Amy said. "We need the latest sat photos for the Saint Squad."

"The captain is the only one who can authorize that," Commander Chang said.

"Where is he?"

"Sleeping. He'll be back before the Saint Squad inserts."

"We need this information before then," Amy said.

The XO hesitated briefly. Then he motioned to an aide. "Go wake up the captain."

Amy fought to hide her surprise. "Thank you."

Only a few minutes passed before the captain appeared.

"Captain on the bridge," one crewman announced.

The captain looked from the XO to Amy and back again. "What's the problem?"

"I'm sorry to disturb you, sir, but we need the latest satellite images of the fortress and the surrounding village."

"Commander Chang, make it happen," the captain said. "If you get any pushback, let me know."

The XO nodded. "Yes, Captain."

"Ms. Miller, I'd like a word."

Amy's already unsteady stomach lurched. She went toe-to-toe with XOs often enough, but she had a policy to avoid making waves with the captains of vessels.

The captain led the way off the bridge and into his office. As soon as Amy walked inside, he closed the hatch and strode past his desk in the small space. He turned to face her. "Is this going to become a habit, Ms. Miller?"

"I'm sorry, Captain. I'm not sure I know what you mean."

"I'm asking if you plan to use your family connections to influence my decisions in the future."

The pieces clicked into place, as did the source of the captain's annoyance. "You know who my father is."

"I do. I also know you're married to our missing SEAL." The captain gripped the back of his chair. "This entire situation is extremely unusual."

"It is, but all I'm doing is asking for mission-critical intel. I'm not using my White House connections to perform my duties this time, and I have more at stake now than ever. I hope that proves that I don't intend to use them in the future either."

A knock sounded at the door.

"Come," the captain called out.

Commander Chang opened the hatch and poked his head inside. "Sorry to interrupt, but the satellite photos are being sent now. We should have them within fifteen minutes."

"Thank you, Commander." The captain walked to the door and stood beside it. "Now, if you'll excuse me, Ms. Miller, I'm going to get some sleep before the Saint Squad launches. I'll see you in CIC after they leave."

"Yes, Captain." Amy stepped into the corridor. "And thank you."

* * *

Brent bit into his pupusa while he studied the latest satellite photo in front of him. The simple meal was a reminder that he needed fuel to function. The darkness outside signaled that the time to act was now.

With no current computer or internet access, they were relying on the photo Ghost had printed the day before Brent had been injured. He had to admit, this guardian was well prepared.

Brent looked up at Ghost, who was sitting between him and Moises. "Ask him where they keep their vehicles."

As soon as Ghost relayed the question, Moises pointed at the driveway situated between the main entrance and the helipad.

"There has to be somewhere else they have cars parked." Brent pointed to the corner of the building near where he had been injured. "The jeep with the rocket launchers came from somewhere behind the building."

"We don't have a garage visible on these images." Ghost rattled something off in Spanish to Moises, who simply shrugged.

Brent took a sip of water. "He doesn't know of anywhere else they parked?"

"I'm afraid not." Ghost leaned closer as he studied the ten-story building and the surrounding trees. "Your squad never came across any other structures besides the hideout while at the fortress?"

"No." Brent shifted to another photo, this one of the area the Saint Squad hadn't explored. "Either their vehicles must be housed in a parking garage beneath the building, or there's another structure over here."

"In the same area we think the power drain is originating."

"Which doesn't make a lot of sense," Brent said. "Why would Morenta deliberately put his vehicles close to a source of a power drain?"

"The power drain didn't start until last night," Ghost said. "My car battery was just fine before your squad showed up."

"But our comm gear and other equipment wasn't," Brent said.

"With the lack of traffic on the roads since you've been here, I suspect my car isn't the only one that's been affected here in the village," Ghost said. "Morenta or Osman must have turned up the intensity when they discovered trespassers."

"That would make sense." Brent shifted the photos again so they could see the entire complex at once, four images overlapping one another. "They obviously knew how to shield their batteries to keep the electromagnetic field from affecting them."

Ghost pushed back from the table and crossed to the corkboard. "If Osman really is planning to strike soon, we've got to get word out."

"I know. That's why we're looking at these."

"You keep working on your plan." Ghost headed toward the door. "I'm going for a walk."

"Where?"

"To see if the far side of the village is having battery trouble too."

Brent stood. "Do you need backup?"

"I'll be faster on my own," Ghost said.

Brent looked down at his leg. He couldn't remember the last time someone had said those words to him, if ever. Although Amy could have when he'd first met her. He'd been shot, but she had stayed by his side.

Brent focused on the map on the wall. "Fine. I'll stay here and work on our best options to borrow a vehicle from the fortress."

"Borrow?"

"Yeah." Brent shrugged. "I'll let them have it back after we get out of here."

Ghost chuckled. "I'll be back in a couple hours. Don't try leaving without me."

"I won't," Brent said. "Going on a walk without backup is one thing. If I have to go back into the fortress, I want someone else on my side."

"I don't blame you." Ghost slipped outside and closed the door behind him, and then the dead bolt flipped to the locked position from the other side.

Brent looked up at Moises. "What do you think? Hidden garage beneath the fortress or a garage by the pulse weapon?"

"*No hablo ingles.*"

"Right." Brent sighed. "I guess we're going to find out how much Spanish I've picked up from Damian."

22

Tristan held his night-vision binoculars to his eyes and scanned the coastline, the scent and spray of saltwater washing over him. A stretch of beach a mile from the village was their landing zone tonight, their course bringing them in from the opposite direction of where the fortress was located.

They didn't have to breach the fortress tonight. They wouldn't have to pick their way past countless motion detectors and security measures. Guards wouldn't be waiting for them, searching for them. And Lord willing, their modified equipment would work so they would have open communication throughout the mission.

Tristan identified their landing zone in the distance and mentally noted the course adjustment needed. He waited several seconds for Brent to issue the order to the boat captain to make the change before he remembered . . . Seth was in command.

Seth spoke into his comm set. "Adjust course five degrees starboard."

"Aye, sir." The boat pilot made the correction.

Four minutes later, they reached the beach. Tristan and Quinn hopped out and helped pull the boat onto the sand. The rest of the squad followed and secured the area.

As soon as they returned, Seth turned to the boat pilot. "We're good."

"Yes, sir." The pilot pushed the inflatable partway into the water.

Seth pointed to the boat. "Tristan, Craig, help him."

They moved to the part of the boat still on the sand and pushed until it was far enough into the water to retreat from shore. The boat motor engaged, and the pilot headed down the coast, where he would wait several miles away until he heard from Seth or until their designated extraction time, whichever came first.

Seth shifted his weapon to the ready position. "Craig, you're on point."

Craig nodded and took his position at the front of the squad. They rushed across the sand until they reached the palm trees and thick foliage a short distance away.

Tristan fell in behind Craig, Seth right behind him, with Damian, Jay, and Quinn bringing up the rear.

Craig deviated from their course to avoid some thick underbrush and then adjusted his heading to put them back on track. A mile and a half later, he stopped and waited for the others to catch up.

Craig pointed. "The house should be the third one from the end over there."

Tristan peered at the well-traveled dirt road before him and the line of houses across the street. He took a moment to adjust his image of the village in his head from the two-dimensional satellite photos to the three-dimensional reality.

"Quinn, find a spot behind the house to cover us," Seth said. "It looked like there was a garage or shed you should be able to climb onto. Tristan and Damian, cover him. We'll have you come in from the back." Seth turned to Jay.

"Let me guess." With a resigned look, Jay pointed up into the trees. "You want me to cover you from here."

"Sorry, but yes. I want to make sure we have a sniper ready in case we have company come down the road."

"I figured." Jay looked up before he moved to a tree that had enough branches. He started his upward climb while Tristan, Quinn, and Damian slipped across the road and into the shadows of the nearest house.

Tristan reached the back door of the house they had identified as Brent's suspected hiding place. Praying that they would find friendlies, including Brent, he checked the door for any sign of an alarm or booby trap. Sure enough, a small alarm was affixed to the top of the doorframe. "I've got an alarm on the back door."

"There's one on the front too," Seth said.

Though no one said the words, the fact that intel had sent them to a specific address suggested this house was indeed a safe house. Despite that likelihood, Tristan took the time to disable the alarm.

As soon as he finished, he pulled his lockpick kit from his combat vest and unlocked the door. "Back door is clear."

"Front door is clear," Seth said. "We're going in silent. On three."

Damian moved to the other side of the back door. Seth counted them down.

When the signal came, Tristan opened the door and lifted his weapon. Seth burst through the front door at the same time. A man sat on the couch, his back to Tristan. He immediately lifted his hands over his head and started speaking in rapid Spanish. Tristan caught the gist of the words: *Don't shoot.*

Craig rushed forward to search the man for weapons. Seth signaled for Tristan and Damian to search the rest of the house.

Silently, they moved forward. Two bedrooms, one bathroom. All empty. Tristan signaled to Damian to take one room. Tristan entered the other. He opened the closet door and pushed the clothes aside to ensure no one was hiding behind the assortment of black shirts, dark pants, and local clothing.

"Clear," Tristan said into his mic.

"Come take a look at this," Seth called out to him.

Tristan moved back into the living room. Facing him was a US map with pushpins in several cities along the East Coast. Red pins had been placed in Orlando and New York. Yellow pins had been placed in seven more cities, including Washington and Virginia Beach.

Tristan's breath caught. "Are these targets?"

"Two are," Damian said. "The others are guesses." He motioned to the man currently sitting on the couch. "According to him, nine more EMPs are being deployed to the United States."

"When?" Seth asked.

Damian spoke to the man in Spanish, his already serious expression turning grave. "Friday." Damian swallowed hard. "It's timed to coincide with a severe cold front moving across the East Coast."

Tristan's gaze whipped back to the map. A pulse weapon deployed where his family lived, where all their families lived?

His wife, his children, Jay's new baby. Would they survive an extended power outage?

Craig emerged from the hall holding a uniform that matched the one Seth currently wore. "Look what I found."

"That must be Brent's." Tristan's heartbeat quickened, and he motioned to the man on the couch. "Ask him if Brent was here."

Craig did the honors this time, holding up the uniform to show that one pant leg had been cut off.

The man shook his head and then pointed to the back door.

"He said he doesn't know anything about the uniform, but two men were here, and they left a few minutes ago." Craig's eyes lit up. "It sounds like one of them was Brent."

"Injuries?"

Craig translated the question.

After the man responded, relief swept over both Craig's and Damian's faces.

"He said Brent was limping but that he was okay," Craig said.

Tristan absorbed the news, relief pouring through him as well. He pressed a hand against the wall, amazement and pure joy bursting through him. They had prayed for a miracle, and their prayers had been answered.

Seth spoke to the man directly this time, not bothering to have Damian or Craig translate. "*Adónde fueron*?"

Tristan understood the question: Where did they go?

23

Amy stood beside the captain, the flat screen before them currently blank. The video feed from Seth's body camera had given them a firsthand look at the mission so far, but it had cut out a moment before he'd entered Brent's possible hiding place. Amy suspected the interruption had been deliberate to protect the guardian inside from being seen.

The communications officer in the corner hung up the phone. "The live feed should be restored any second."

Twenty seconds later, the digital image popped onto the screen, Tristan and Quinn visible in the foreground. Another man sat on a couch.

Amy had never met any ghosts operating in Central or South America, but she was quite certain this man wasn't one of them. The man on the screen appeared to be barely twenty and had a look of fear in his eyes, not exactly the expression Amy would expect of a guardian. Not to mention, guardians weren't prone to letting themselves get caught in front of a camera of any kind, even the body cam on Seth's uniform.

"What's the status?" the captain asked.

The comm officer relayed the question.

The response came over the audio from Seth's microphone. "Commander Miller isn't here, but we have a witness who said he left a few minutes ago. He has a leg injury but is otherwise okay."

Amy's pent-up breath whooshed out of her, and tears of relief sprang to her eyes. She lifted her hands to her mouth and fought back the sob trying to escape. She replayed Seth's words again to make sure she'd heard him correctly. Brent was alive. He'd survived when so many had thought such a miracle wasn't possible. And it was a miracle. Of that, she had no doubt.

Her ongoing prayers morphed from begging for his well-being to thanking the Lord for keeping him safe. She expanded that line of silent communication with God to add a continued plea that Brent and the rest of the Saint Squad be protected.

The captain's voice interrupted her silent prayer. "Does he know where Commander Miller is?"

Again, the comm officer repeated the question to Seth.

"We believe he's heading back to the fortress."

Amy's overwhelming joy transformed into a wave of panic. "What?"

"Why?" the captain asked in the same instant.

This time, Seth didn't wait for their questions to be relayed before he offered additional information. "Our intel here indicates there may be nine more EMP weapons in play. We have two confirmed intended targets: New York and Orlando. Projected date of attack is this Friday."

Nine more weapons, nine more cities, nine more potential blackouts.

Seth turned so that a map on the wall was visible. Pushpins dotted several cities along the eastern seaboard. "Our friend here has identified Orlando and New York as two definite targets. He doesn't know what the other targets are."

"Then, what are those cities identified on the map?" Amy asked.

The captain nodded at the comm officer to relay her question.

Seth responded a moment later. "We believe these are the locations Commander Miller has identified as likely targets." He stepped closer to the map so the image increased in size. "Request permission to continue our search for Commander Miller."

Amy looked at the captain, her silent prayers increasing in fervor.

The captain didn't say anything for several seconds. Then he nodded. "Permission granted."

* * *

Jim gripped his hands beneath the table in the Situation Room, Admiral Moss on one side of him and Sawyer on the other. Jim had managed a short nap after he'd sent Vanessa home, but now, here he was at two in the morning, watching a blank video screen. Prayers circled through his head, prayers for the safety of the Saint Squad, prayers for Brent's safe return, prayers that Amy and the rest of his family would be able to endure whatever came.

"What's the status on the live feed?" Admiral Moss asked the comm officer.

The young woman shot an apologetic look at the admiral. "I'm sorry, sir; the transmission is still blocked."

"Find a way to unblock it," the admiral ordered.

"Yes, sir." She tapped her fingers against her keyboard. "I'm contacting the *Truman* now."

Admiral Moss turned to Jim. "I'm sorry about this, sir. This should never happen."

"If we aren't getting the feed, I'm sure there's a valid reason why." Jim suspected the presence of a guardian might very well be that reason.

The comm officer straightened, and excitement filled her voice. "Mr. President, Commander Miller is alive."

"What?" Jim replayed the words against what he had witnessed in this room only two nights ago. Relief brought tears to his eyes. He placed both hands on the table and lowered his head until he managed to blink the moisture away. His chest tightened, and he prayed that the words were real and not imagined. "Are they sure?"

"We have a transmission coming in," the comm officer said. "It's a recording."

"Put it up." Jim motioned to the flat-screen.

An image of a living room popped onto the screen. Jim caught a glimpse of a man in military gear pass through the corner before the camera settled on a young man with dusky skin and dark hair.

Seth's voice played over the speakers as he described the witness's account of seeing Brent and another man. Amy's miracle had happened. His son-in-law was alive, his future still before him.

The view shifted to a map.

Jim didn't need to hear Seth's explanation to know the threat against the United States wasn't over. His insides shriveled, and fear threatened to overshadow all else.

Brent was alive. That was one miracle already this week. Now it was time to find another.

Seth moved closer to the map, little pushpins in it now visible. "We believe the commander identified other suspected cities." He continued, listing them off one by one.

"That would cripple the entire eastern seaboard," Admiral Moss said.

"And possibly cascade power failures across the country," Jim said.

The video ended with Seth's request to continue his search for Brent.

Jim looked over at the comm officer. "Was permission granted?"

"Yes, sir."

Then, the Saint Squad still had a chance of bringing him home. Focusing on the problems he could address, Jim spoke to Sawyer. "Get Doug Valdez on the line. Make sure he's aware of the threat."

"Yes, Mr. President." Sawyer stood and moved to the adjoining room.

"Sir, if I may," Admiral Moss began, "I suggest we go after these weapons before they come after us."

"What do you propose?" Jim asked.

"A missile strike." The admiral turned his laptop toward Jim. "According to the witness, Osman plans to strike on Friday. That means he has to be putting those weapons in transit any time now. If we target a missile at the fortress now, we can destroy the weapons and eliminate Osman and the threats from this organization once and for all."

Jim knew this day would come, the day when he would have to order a strike that would result in the loss of life.

As though sensing his hesitation, Admiral Moss added, "Sir, Morenta and Osman have declared war on this country. We have to defend ourselves."

"You're right." Jim pushed back from the table. "Prepare to carry out a strike against the fortress. And relay the order to the Saint Squad to retrieve Commander Miller and any other US operatives in the area. As soon as our people are clear, we strike."

"Sir?" Admiral Moss said the word with a question in his voice. "They already missed their scheduled rendezvous for today. Their next one isn't until tomorrow morning. By then, the weapons will already be on their way to the US."

"Then, send in a helicopter to pull them out of there."

"We almost lost our helos to battery failure last time they went in."

"Use one that's already protected against battery failure. That Z-10 is still on the carrier, isn't it?"

"Yes, sir, but we don't have any pilots trained on that aircraft."

"If the SEALs could fly it out of there, I'm sure we have a helicopter pilot who will be able to figure it out." Jim squared his shoulders so he was facing the admiral. "We strike after our people are safe. Not before." Jim tilted his chin up slightly. "Understood?"

Admiral Moss nodded. "Yes, sir."

24

Brent wasn't going to think about the throbbing in his leg or his reduced abilities. He picked his way through the woods, Ghost taking a parallel course. Brent had to give Ghost credit. The man knew how to stay invisible, and he had learned the art of being silent. If it weren't for the subtle scent of body odor, Brent likely wouldn't know he was there.

Ghost had returned from his walk around town with the news that he had indeed found a vehicle with a working battery. It was a motorcycle, but at least it would give them some transportation to the next village or to the nearest phone.

Brent reached the edge of the woods and pulled his binoculars out of his combat vest. He lifted them to his eyes before he remembered. Dead batteries, which meant the lighting mechanism wasn't working.

Frustrated, he pocketed them and listened for any sign of movement on the road before him.

Ghost stepped beside him and pointed at the twelve-foot wall. "The disabled motion detectors start over there and go for two sections of the wall."

"Okay, nice and simple. We go over the wall, plant the trackers on their transports, and get back out of there." Brent hesitated. "Unless we find an opening to take one of their vehicles without drawing fire."

"I doubt that's going to happen."

"I've already experienced one miracle," Brent said. "I'm being greedy in wanting another one."

"Yeah, you keep praying for that."

"I already am." Brent took another quick look at the road. "Let's go."

Brent checked both directions again and rushed forward as fast as his injured leg would take him. Ghost reached the wall first and pressed himself against it. Brent took position beside him, listening for any sign of movement on the other side. When he was satisfied there was none, he nodded at Ghost.

Ghost pulled a rope attached to a grappling hook out of the black backpack he carried. He took two steps back and threw the hook over the top of the wall. Quickly and steadily, he pulled at the rope until the hook caught.

Brent debated briefly whether he should go first or send Ghost. He grabbed the rope.

"Do you want me to go first?" Ghost whispered.

Brent shook his head. "Climb up as soon as I reach the top of the wall. I'll need the rope to get down on the other side."

Brent placed his foot on the wall, balancing on his injured leg. Then he used the rope to support himself as he climbed upward, wincing each time he had to use his injured leg.

He reached the top and lay down so he wouldn't be easily visible. Seconds later, Ghost was beside him.

He quickly adjusted the grappling hook and dropped the rope onto the other side of the wall. Ghost then gripped the rope and rappelled down the twelve feet.

As soon as Ghost took cover, Brent followed, taking care to land on his good leg.

They moved forward through twenty yards of trees. They were nearly to where they could see the open space surrounding the fortress when voices carried to them.

Brent could make out a few of the words, but not enough to put them into context. He crept closer, taking position behind some thick shrubs. He peered through the leaves. At least a dozen men stood beside the four SUVs parked in front of the fortress.

Out of the corner of his eye, Brent caught movement when Ghost ducked behind a thick palm.

Using his comm unit, Brent spoke quietly. "What are they saying?"

"Stand by." Ghost fell silent until the conversation stopped momentarily. "It sounds like they're getting ready to leave any minute."

"We've got to get trackers on those vehicles."

The front door of the fortress opened, and someone stepped out. Osman Robleto. With his hands lifted in the air to command everyone's attention, Osman began speaking.

The men gathered by the vehicles turned toward him.

Brent shifted to his right to make sure the vehicles were between him and the cluster of men in the yard.

Now or never. Brent sent up a silent prayer and spoke into his mic. "Cover me."

"Are you crazy?" Ghost asked.

"Probably." He took a second to make sure no one was looking in his direction. Then he silently rushed to the closest SUV and pulled a tracker from his vest.

Keeping his eyes on his surroundings, Brent pressed the tracker to the inside of the wheel well.

One down. He pulled another tracker from his vest and moved to the next SUV and repeated the process. Two down. Two to go.

* * *

The fortress. Tristan had hoped to never step foot on this soil again. Kel had been injured here. Brent had been injured here. Seth was in command tonight, and Tristan had no interest in letting him follow their example. No, tonight, they were unified in their objective to find Brent and bring their entire squad home safely.

Seth signaled to Jay and pointed upward.

Tristan fought back a smile. That was exactly what Brent would do.

To his credit, Jay didn't argue. Instead, he simply chose a tree near the edge of the clearing beside the fortress and started climbing.

Craig held up a fisted hand and pointed out a motion sensor. The squad bypassed the security device and continued to the edge of the woods.

A man's voice carried to him, the cadence like a football coach about to send his team onto the field. Or perhaps like a general sending his men into battle.

Tristan picked up his binoculars and scanned the crowd of men gathered around the man on the front steps of the fortress. Fifteen of them. Maybe twenty. And that didn't include the guards standing along the perimeter. Two visible on the far side of the yard by the beach, four at the main gate, and another at the corner closest to them, by where a burned-out jeep lay on its side. Though Tristan couldn't see the far side, he had no doubt another guard would be on duty at the other corners of the structure as well as at the entrances.

Sometime over the past day, the dead bodies had been removed, but the stench of death still lingered in the air.

Jay's voice came over his headset. "I've got movement by one of the SUVs. Third one in."

"What kind of movement?" Seth asked.

"Since it's a man who is staying out of sight of the guards, is wearing a combat vest, and is limping, my best guess is Brent is next to it."

"Brent?" Tristan fought the urge to leave his current position to see for himself.

"I can see his face." Excitement carried through Jay's voice. "It's definitely him."

Tristan's breath rushed out of him. So many days of wondering and worrying about Brent, and now they found him here at the fortress, the place they had feared he may have died? "What's he doing out there?" Tristan asked, the question intended more for himself than for Jay.

"I don't know, but he's moving to the last SUV."

A guard on the beach waved his hand in front of his face, as though swatting at a fly. His gaze turned toward the vehicles. He stared for a moment.

"I think Brent's been spotted," Jay said an instant before the guard shouted.

A flurry of shouts and movement followed. Both guards by the beach rushed toward the SUVs, and another guard appeared from beyond Tristan's view to take up a sentry post. Two of the gate guards rushed at the vehicles from the other direction. One fired toward the SUV.

"Cover him," Seth ordered.

Gunfire erupted instantly. Bullets impacted the ground between the vehicles and the guards coming from the gate. More interrupted the path for the two rushing from the beach.

Osman shouted to the men gathered by the entrance, all of them racing into the fortress rather than outside to engage with the intruders.

The guard by the corner of the building shot into the woods. Seth returned fire, and the man fell to the ground.

When another guard lifted his weapon and aimed at Brent's position, Tristan fired again. Two down.

"Take out the guards," Seth ordered.

The response was instant. Shots fired. The three guards in motion all fell to the ground.

The guards at the gate both took cover. So did the one who had emerged from the crowd at the main entrance.

Brent appeared at the edge of the nearest SUV. He fired off a single shot toward the guards by the gate and sprinted, or rather ran-limped, toward the woods.

The squad laid down more cover fire until Brent reached the safety of the trees.

Tristan traversed the twenty yards between his position and where he had last seen Brent.

When Tristan reached him, Brent wasn't alone. A shorter man dressed entirely in black knelt beside him. Seth stepped through the trees a moment later.

Brent looked up, and a flicker of relief crossed his face. "About time you showed up." Brent motioned to the man beside him. "Seth and Tristan, meet Ghost. He's my guardian angel."

"Thanks for watching out for him," Seth said before he turned his attention back to Brent. "What were you doing out there?"

"Planting trackers."

"Did you get all of them?" Seth asked.

"All but the one on the left." Brent held out his hand. "Let me have a grenade."

Tristan retrieved one from his vest and handed it over.

Brent pulled the pin and sent the grenade toward the vehicle that hadn't been tagged with a tracker.

"Take cover!" Seth ordered in the same instant.

The grenade exploded beneath the SUV. The vehicle flew into the air and came back down with a thud but didn't ignite.

Brent shook his head. "It must be armored."

"What's your exit strategy?" Ghost asked.

"An inflatable five miles up the beach. We'll rendezvous at oh four hundred tomorrow morning." Seth motioned to the wall behind them. "We need to get out of here while we still can."

The front entrance opened, and guards poured out, several of them firing into the woods.

"Great." Tristan ducked and sized up their opposition. Ten guards with a dozen more taking position on the balconies. "Looks like you just woke up the lion's den."

Brent did his own analysis and winced. "Sorry about that."

Seth simply shook his head and spoke into his mic. "Fire!"

Gunfire sparked behind him, his teammates sending a volley at the approaching guards.

The guards scattered, men diving behind the SUVs, others dropping to the ground to fire from a more protected position. The gunmen on the balcony used the concrete railings as a solid barrier between them and the Saint Squad's bullets.

Tristan pointed behind them. "It's time to get out of here."

"Agreed." Brent motioned twenty degrees to his right. "We left a rope and grappling hook on the wall over there."

"You go first. We'll cover you," Seth said. "Tristan, you go with him so we don't lose comm. You can cover us from the wall."

Ghost motioned to Seth. "I'll stay and help lay down cover fire."

Brent squeezed the man's shoulder, a silent gesture of good luck and gratitude. Then Brent moved toward the fortress wall. His limp was noticeable, but he moved with the same stealth typical of their squad.

They reached the rope, and Brent motioned to it. "You go first so you can cover me."

"Got it." Tristan adjusted his weapon, letting his sling hold it in place. He grabbed the rope and scrambled up the wall. When he reached the top, he moved to a spot behind a tree and shifted his rifle to the ready position. "On the wall," Tristan said into his comm set.

Seth's voice followed. "Everyone fall back. Tristan, cover us."

With no clear target in sight, Tristan took aim in the general direction of the fortress balcony, away from the tree that Jay had climbed, and squeezed off a round.

Brent climbed the wall. As soon as he reached the top, he flipped the grappling hook so he could use the rope to climb down the other side.

Quinn reached him, using a nearby tree to climb up to make it easier to scale the wall. As soon as he hopped from the tree to the top of the wall, he, too, took aim and sent bullets flying to keep the guards at bay.

Tristan pulled the grappling hook off the wall and threw the rope over so the rest of the squad would be able to use it to climb the wall quickly.

Damian and Craig came next, Damian pointing his rifle at any potential threat as Craig climbed the wall. Then Craig squatted and laid down cover fire while Damian scaled the wall and climbed down the other side.

Tristan signaled to Craig. "Go."

A motor rumbled in the distance as Ghost came into view, followed by Jay and Seth.

Bullets impacted the tree Seth had just passed, and Quinn fired. A thud followed, likely from a guard dropping to the ground.

Tristan squeezed off another shot as Ghost climbed up and over. Jay came next, followed by Seth.

"Fall back to the woods," Brent ordered.

He led the way as the rest of them climbed down from the wall and crossed the road into the nearby woods.

The engine grew louder, and Tristan identified the sound. "We may have a problem. Sounds like we have a chopper on approach."

"I'll check with command." Seth clicked off their frequency.

Tristan took cover in the woods beside Brent. Ghost hid behind a tree on the other side of him.

Tristan looked behind them for any sign of pursuit. Someone appeared at the top of the wall, right where they had climbed over. Tristan fired a shot, his bullet hitting the top of the cinder block. The guard ducked back down.

Brent looked up in the direction of the approaching aircraft. "This isn't good. It looks like a Z-10." Brent shifted closer to Tristan. "Have Seth call for air support."

Tristan nodded and relayed the message.

Seth didn't respond.

"He must still be on the other frequency." Tristan scanned the area beside him in search of Seth. He didn't see him, but a moment later, Seth's voice came back over his headset.

"The chopper is our ride." Seth gave the coordinates of their new extraction point, located less than a quarter mile away.

Craig waved at Brent. "Follow me."

Brent limped behind Craig, moving as quickly as he could. Tristan shot at the wall again to make sure Osman's men didn't follow. He waited another twenty seconds and fired again. Then he turned and sprinted after his teammates.

Tristan reached the landing zone, a spot along the road not far from the fortress. The helicopter landed, Brent's observations confirmed. It was most definitely a Z-10.

"That's our ride?" Jay asked.

Quinn stepped beside him. "Looks like it's a good thing I hijacked it."

"I'm the one who hijacked it." Tristan aimed his gun behind him. "Get everyone aboard."

Ghost stepped beside him and aimed his rifle at the woods behind them. "Go. I'll cover you."

"You're staying here?"

"I'll go pick up Moises and drive him out of here." Ghost waved at the helicopter. "Go."

Tristan lowered his weapon and put his hand on Ghost's shoulder. "Thanks for saving Brent."

"He would have done the same for me," Ghost said. "Any of you would have."

Tristan nodded. "Be safe." Then he turned and sprinted toward his ride home.

25

The satellite image of the winding road and empty beach filled the screen in the Situation Room. Jim sat at the far end of the table, his chief of staff on one side of him, his newly appointed secretary of state on the other.

The helicopter that had landed in the road was on the ground for only three minutes before it lifted into the air and moved over the water. Brent was coming home. That truth seeped into Jim, his relief beyond what words could express.

Admiral Moss stood beside the comm officer. Two more minutes passed before he said, "The helicopter has cleared the strike area."

The words were barely out of the admiral's mouth when the image of a projectile flew onto the screen.

"Incoming!" The pilot's voice came over the intercom in a near repeat of two nights ago when Brent had been left behind.

"Evade!" another voice commanded.

"Engaging countermeasures," the pilot said.

Something sparked behind the helicopter. An explosion followed.

Any reservations about striking the fortress vanished. Jim turned to Admiral Moss. "Attack."

"Yes, sir." Admiral Moss relayed the order through the comm officer.

A second image popped up, this one from one of the fighter planes, the structure of the fortress now on one side on the flat-screen and the satellite image of the helicopter on the other.

Another projectile streaked through the sky, but this time, it was headed toward land instead of coming from it. A second followed.

Half of the building exploded, and the other half looked like a toy structure that had been torn apart. A second missile hit the base of the building, new flames spearing out into the darkness.

"Direct hit," Admiral Moss announced, stating the obvious.

Jim's insides curled at the image on the screen, and he swallowed the burning sensation rising in his throat. This wasn't special effects from a movie or a still photo from a past operation. He had watched his orders carried out—he had watched people die because of his decision.

As though sensing Jim's inner turmoil, Doug put a hand on his arm. "You were protecting our troops. You were protecting your family."

Jim nodded. He focused on the helicopter that continued over the water until it finally disappeared from view.

He stood. "Everyone, thank you for your service tonight. Please, get some sleep," Jim said to his staff members present. He turned to the overnight duty officer. "And please notify me when the Saint Squad is back on the carrier."

"Yes, Mr. President."

Jim left the Situation Room, a Secret Service agent falling into place behind him. Jim began his forty-five-second commute from the West Wing to the residence. Time to wake up Katherine and give her the good news. And then he was going to try to block out the nightmare of the last few days so he could get some sleep.

* * *

Amy would have waited for Brent on the flight deck if the captain would have let her, but no one was about to let a civilian on deck during flight operations, especially not when that civilian's sole purpose was to welcome her husband home.

Amy settled for the next best thing: she waited in sick bay.

The only occupants at the moment were the doctor, two corpsmen, and three patients who had had the misfortune of consuming some contaminated nuts that had arrived in a care package. All three men were currently sporting IVs in their arms and a slightly greenish hue.

Amy suspected her coloring wasn't much better. Despite her efforts to ignore the nausea that had become her frequent companion over the past few weeks, the sensation had worsened since leaving Virginia.

She paced the open space of sick bay by the entrance, willing Brent to walk through the door.

The doctor finished checking on his current patients and approached Amy. "Maybe you should sit down."

Amy couldn't deny that her body needed rest, but the overwhelming need to see her husband overrode all else. "I'm fine."

"I hate to say it, but you look like you could use some Dramamine."

Amy doubted that would help, nor was she certain she could take it while pregnant. *Pregnant.* The reason for her discomfort hit her full force. She was finally going to be able to share her news with Brent. At least, she would be able to once they were alone. Surely they deserved to enjoy this moment in private.

Amy caught the concerned expression on the doctor's face. "I'm fine. Really."

The hatch opened, and Brent ducked to pass through the doorway. He spotted her and instantly extended his arms.

Amy's heart squeezed in her chest, pure joy enveloping her. She stepped into his embrace and pulled him close. Her throat closed, blocking any words she might say. Tears of relief and joy filled her eyes, and she clung to him.

Brent tightened his hold, and his body trembled as though he, too, were fighting back his emotions.

Silence stretched out for several seconds.

The doctor cleared his throat. "Commander. Let's take a look at that leg."

Brent ran his hand along Amy's spine before he swallowed hard and eased back. He looked down at her and blinked against the moisture in his eyes. Ignoring the doctor, he leaned down and pressed his lips against hers.

Amy slid her hand up to caress his cheek as she reveled in the kiss. Joy burst through her, her intense love bringing tears to her eyes. All too aware that they weren't alone, she eased back.

Brent reached out and used his thumb to wipe away a tear that had spilled over. "I didn't think you'd be here."

"Seth and I joined the squad yesterday." Amy helped support Brent's weight as he limped to the examination table. "How bad is your leg?"

"I took some shrapnel when the jeep exploded." Brent released Amy and pushed himself up onto the table. "A local stitched me up."

"You need to stop getting injured," Amy said. "Especially when you don't have a real doctor nearby."

"It always turns out okay." Brent put his hand on hers and squeezed. "Sometimes it turns out better than okay."

Amy had no doubt that he was thinking of their first meeting, which had resulted in Brent's getting shot. "I hope the local had more medical experience than me."

"I think so."

The doctor pulled a privacy screen into place and handed Brent a hospital gown. "Put this on. I'll be right back."

As soon as the doctor left them, Brent tugged on Amy's hand to bring her close. He leaned down, and his lips found hers once more. A shiver ran through her, and she lifted her free hand to the back of his neck. His strength, the miracle of his presence contrasted against all the fear and heartache she had suffered since he'd been left behind . . . He was here. He was whole. He was hers. Or rather, he was theirs.

Amy tightened her grip on his hand, and she smiled as she pulled back. The news of their pregnancy made it all the way to her tongue before she swallowed it back. Too many people were on the other side of the privacy screen.

Brent framed her face with his hands and stole one last kiss. "I missed you."

"I missed you too." Amy grabbed the hospital gown. "You'd better get dressed."

"Right." Brent changed into the gown, and Amy got her first look at the cuts and scrapes on his arms and torso. A nasty bruise covered the upper part of his arm, and a bandage hid the injury on his thigh.

The doctor rapped his knuckle against the metal frame of the privacy screen before moving past it.

Amy stepped back so he could conduct his examination.

The doctor removed Brent's bandage, the ugly wound repaired by even uglier black stitches. Amy's stomach pitched uncomfortably, and she turned her head away so she wouldn't have to look at it.

Pretending she could hear Seth's easy voice coaching her, she breathed in and out slowly.

After a few minutes, the doctor stepped back. "Your local did a decent job. We'll put you on some antibiotics, and I want you to stay here tonight so we can ventilate that wound."

"I'm fine," Brent insisted. "And I haven't gone through my debriefing yet."

"The debriefing can wait. You need hydration, rest, and antibiotics," the doctor said. "In eight hours, we'll talk about getting you back to your squad."

"But—"

"I'll be right back." The doctor moved to the edge of the screen and spoke to Amy. "Don't let him go anywhere."

Brent climbed down from the table. "Time to break out of here. There are more EMPs heading to the US."

"Were they still at the fortress?" Amy asked.

"Yes."

"The fortress isn't there anymore," Amy said. "They sent in a missile strike as soon as you were clear."

Brent gripped the side of the examination table. "You're sure?"

"I'm sure. I was in CIC when the strike hit."

Brent leaned back against the table and blew out a breath. "That was too close."

The doctor returned. "I have a couple of beds made up for you two."

"Both of us?" Amy asked.

"Your husband isn't the only one staying overnight. You're clearly dehydrated and suffering from seasickness."

"I'm not seasick."

"Dehydrated, then." The doctor jotted something on his iPad. "Either way, you two are staying here."

Brent lifted his eyebrows. "Trying to make sure my wife doesn't enlist my squad's help to break me out of here?"

"That thought did cross my mind, but your wife's color isn't her normal, and you'll both get back to full strength with IV treatments."

"I really hate IVs," Amy muttered.

Brent took her hand and spoke to the doctor. "She really does."

"Trust me," the doctor said. "You'll feel a hundred times better when we're done with you."

Amy swallowed the acid rising in her throat. "I hope so."

26

THE DOCTOR WAS GOING TO have a mutiny on his hands if he didn't release them soon. Brent recognized the light of rebellion in his wife's eyes and suspected the medical staff had less than ten minutes before Amy tried to take the IV out of her arm herself.

Brent reached out and laced his fingers through hers. The simple contact caused his chest to tighten at the overwhelming love that crashed over him. She clearly was too ill to be on the ship, yet she had come here for him.

At least her color was better than when he'd first seen her. He couldn't imagine the toll his disappearance had taken on her, especially when she hadn't been feeling well before he'd left on his last mission.

She turned her head, the determination on her face melting when her gaze met his. "I really wish we were home right now."

"Me too."

Brent had slept most of the past eight hours. He suspected his wife had as well. Now that they were both rested and feeling better, it was time for them to get the latest information and make sure the threat against the United States was really over. He was ready to get back to Virginia Beach, to his own home, where he could sleep in his own bed with his wife beside him.

The doctor approached with one of his nurses. "You two ready to get out of here?"

"Yes." Amy held out her arm that had the IV in it.

The nurse attended to Amy while the doctor examined Brent's wound. After he finished, he stepped toward the head of Brent's bed so the nurse could apply a new bandage.

"I'm approving you for limited duty, but you need to take it easy for at least a week."

Amy climbed out of the bed next to him and stepped beside the doctor. "Will he need crutches?"

"No, but no runs or swims until the stitches come out." The doctor spoke to Amy now. "How much longer are you on the carrier?"

"I'm going to check on our ride back as soon as I get to our ready room," Amy said.

"Stay hydrated. Plenty of fluids and no skipping meals."

Amy nodded.

His leg now bandaged, Brent stood and put a hand on Amy's shoulder. "I'll keep an eye on her."

The doctor held out a small duffel bag. "A member of your squad dropped this by. He thought you might need it."

"Thanks." Brent opened it and pulled out a set of fatigues. "About time I can finally get out of this gown."

"You two take care." The doctor moved to his next patient, and the nurse put a privacy screen in place so Brent could change his clothes.

As soon as he was dressed, he led the way to the door. "Where's our ready room?"

"This way." Amy headed down the corridor, checking behind her as though she weren't sure he could keep up.

He put his hand on her back and leaned forward. "I'm fine. Really."

"Thank the Lord for that."

"Oh, I have."

"Me too." Amy continued to the ready room.

They walked inside, the entire squad already present.

"You can't seriously think Arizona will get knocked out in the first round. They'll at least get to the Sweet Sixteen," Tristan said.

Quinn held both hands up and shrugged. "I'm telling you; they're going to choke."

Jay swiveled in his computer chair to face Quinn and Tristan. "My money's on Miami."

Craig laughed. "Your money's always on Miami."

Brent limped into the ready room and put his hand on Jay's shoulder. "And you don't bet."

"Fine." Jay grinned. "If I were betting, my money would be on Miami." He stood and offered Brent his chair. "We were wondering when you were going to show up."

"The doctor was being overly protective," Brent said. "And why are you talking about March Madness? It's barely February. You don't even know which teams will make it into the tournament yet."

"We were going to play Uno, but you weren't here to referee."

"You know, most civilized people can play that game without a referee." Brent took the seat Jay had vacated. "What's the latest on the fortress and the EMPs?"

"The missile strike leveled the fortress and the hideout. From what we saw from the satellite photos, it's unlikely anyone survived."

Amy sat at the computer beside Brent. "My poor dad. That couldn't have been easy."

"He knew this day would come," Seth said.

"I know." Amy logged in to her computer. "Any word yet on our ride home?"

"We were waiting on you two," Tristan said.

Amy glanced at Brent. "I'll see how soon I can get it."

"Let's say morning prayer first." Brent folded his arms. "I'll say it."

The moment he opened his prayer, a lump formed in his throat. Gratitude swelled inside him, and he had to take a moment to find his words to express his thanks for their safety. He continued the prayer, asking for the Lord to watch over them and guide them in their journey back home. He closed the prayer, and an echo of amens followed.

Amy immediately turned to her computer, but Brent suspected it was more to hide the tears pooling in her eyes than to get back to work.

The discussion about college basketball picked up again while Amy put in their transportation request.

"I just checked the weather forecast." Amy turned to face the squad. "If we don't get home by tomorrow, we'll probably be stuck here for another week."

"*¿Por qué?*" Damian asked.

"A bad storm system is moving in. It's due to hit the East Coast sometime Friday."

With the way the last couple of days had blurred together, Brent had no idea when Friday was. "What day is it?"

"Wednesday."

"I guess I should have prayed that we'd get a flight out today."

"I put us in for a priority return," Amy said. "With your injury and Seth's job at the White House, we have a fifty-fifty shot."

The squad chatted about their odds of success, but Brent's mind had gone back to Amy's comment about a storm hitting on Friday.

A thought niggled at the back of his mind, and he logged in to the computer in front of him.

"What are you doing?" Amy asked.

"Just checking something." Brent tapped on the keyboard and pulled up the program needed to locate the trackers he had planted on the vehicles at the fortress. Surely, they had been destroyed in the missile strike, but it wouldn't hurt to check.

Brent typed in the code that corresponded to the trackers he had used. Two signals popped up, both of them in motion, both of them heading north. "No way."

"What's wrong?" Amy asked.

Brent pushed back from the computer and limped to the worktable. "Seth, where are the satellite photos of the fortress?"

"Before or after the missile strike?"

"After."

Seth flipped through some folders, then handed one to Brent.

Brent rifled through the photos.

"What are you looking for?"

"The SUVs that were by the gate when we were there." Brent found one photo that showed an SUV on its side, likely the same one he had thrown the grenade at when they'd escaped.

He flipped to the next photo and the next. When he didn't find anything beyond the single SUV, he dumped the rest of the file onto the worktable. "Help me look. See if you can find any more vehicles."

"You're assuming we'll be able to tell," Craig said. "This is a mess."

"Their vehicles were closer to the gate than the building." Brent scanned several more photos. "I'm not seeing any more."

"Me neither," Seth said.

"Amy, we need to get a transport ASAP, and we need to talk to the captain," Brent said, urgency rushing through him.

"What's going on?" Jay asked.

"Some of those pulse weapons made it out before the missile strike."

27

So much for getting home today. Brent checked the map again, two blinking lights indicating where the vehicles were currently located.

"What's the plan?" Jay asked.

The possibility of his friends and family being without power in the middle of a cold front—of thousands, possibly millions, in the same situation—made the decision for Brent. They didn't have a choice. "We've got to stop them."

"This doesn't make any sense," Amy said. "If the attack is supposed to happen on Friday, why would they be driving to the United States? They wouldn't even reach the border until then."

"And they wouldn't have time to deploy the weapons to different cities," Craig added.

Seth stepped up behind him. "They must be catching a flight somewhere."

Brent zoomed out on his screen. "They have to be flying out of an airport somewhere in Honduras."

Seth pointed at the screen. "Tegucigalpa is the closest."

"It also has the most security," Amy said.

"Quinn and Damian, get us a list of all flights scheduled to leave out of Tegucigalpa over the next twelve hours." Brent pointed at the line of computers on the opposite side of the room. "Make sure you include the private charters."

"Got it." Quinn slid into the computer chair closest to him.

"Jay, check with N4 to make sure our gear is ready," Brent ordered.

"Tell them we need the shielded batteries," Seth added. "We don't know what we'll be walking into."

Jay nodded and rushed out of their ready room.

"What's the plan?" Tristan asked. "The Hondurans aren't going to let us land a military aircraft at their busiest airport without wanting to know why."

"So, we tell them why." Brent turned to Amy. "I hate to say it, but you need to talk to your dad. He may be the only person who can get us clearance fast enough. These guys will reach Tegucigalpa in less than three hours."

"This is more of a secretary-of-state job," Amy said.

"Yeah, but we don't have the secretary of state on speed dial."

"True."

Damian swiveled in his chair. "I think I found it." He pointed at his screen. "There's a private plane scheduled to fly to Dallas at fifteen thirty."

Seth glanced at the clock on the wall. "Four and half hours from now."

Brent did a quick calculation of their position. "The flight alone is going to take us at least an hour. Amy, make that call."

Amy stood and headed for the hatch. "I'll be back."

"Seth, Tristan, help me work up possible scenarios." Brent pushed back from his computer and moved to the worktable. "The Honduran government might let us land, but they aren't going to want us waging an all-out battle."

"First thing we need is the location of their plane," Tristan said.

"I'm trying to get that now," Damian said.

Quinn snatched a paper off the printer. "Here's the layout of the airport. It looks like the private planes fly out of this section over here."

Brent took the printout from Quinn and set it on the table. "These hangars will give us some cover."

"Assuming we can get there before Osman's men."

Brent studied the roads leading in and out of the airport. Focusing on the private section of the airport, he tapped his finger on an access road. "If they drive their equipment out onto the tarmac, they will come from here." Brent looked up. "Any idea how big these weapons are?"

"They fit inside a large suitcase," Seth said.

"Then, it won't take long for them to load."

"No. We need to get to that airport first."

* * *

Jim really missed his routine. Sleeping at night, meetings during the day, meals at regular hours, nightmares nonexistent. The fear for Brent had been replaced by the image of the missiles striking the fortress, the structure collapsing in a heap, and flames illuminating the fog-filled air.

The strike had been necessary, Jim reminded himself. Had he not ordered it, Brent and his team might not have made it out. The weapons intended to be used against the United States could have made it onto American soil.

Afraid to know why he was being summoned to the Situation Room for what felt like the thousandth time in the past week, he walked inside.

More flashes of the highs and lows of the week filled his mind, questions following of what he might have done differently. Brent was safe. Brent's teammates were safe. This country was safe.

Sawyer followed Jim inside. Only a handful of other people were present, including Admiral Moss and Doug.

Jim shook both of their hands. "I'm starting to think you live here."

"It feels like it," Doug said.

"What's the latest?"

"We just got here," Doug said. "I was hoping you could tell us."

"Mr. President," the communications officer said. "There's a call coming in from the *Truman*."

Jim stepped behind his usual chair at the head of the table. "Put it through."

A video of the bridge filled the screen, the captain front and center, Amy standing beside him.

"Mr. President, we have reason to believe some of the EMP weapons are en route to the United States."

"What?" Jim couldn't be hearing him right. "How?"

The captain nodded to Amy, signaling her to answer.

Amy edged forward. "The Saint Squad planted trackers on three vehicles. Two of those just crossed the border into Honduras."

"What do you need from me?" Jim asked.

"Satellite imagery of the road."

Jim signaled Sawyer to put that request in motion.

"We also need you to clear the Saint Squad to fly into Honduras," Amy continued. "We believe Osman's men are headed to Tegucigalpa."

"We have a transport standing by," the captain said, "but we need authorization to send the Saint Squad in to intercept the vehicles."

"Morenta and Osman are well connected," Amy added. "We don't have time for a joint operation with the Hondurans, nor can we risk a leak."

"Get them in the air. I'll make sure they're cleared to land in Honduras."

"Thank you, Mr. President," the captain said.

Jim nodded, but he shifted his focus to his daughter. His pregnant daughter. "We'll get those satellite photos for you shortly."

"Thank you," Amy said. "One more thing: the plane we believe is scheduled to take Osman's men to the US is scheduled to land at Dallas-Fort Worth around seven o'clock tonight. If we're right, that the attack is planned for Friday and that Osman has multiple targets, they'll likely have connecting flights planned from there."

"We'll look into it," Jim said. "Tell the squad to be careful."

Amy pressed her lips together and nodded. Jim didn't have to be a genius to sense the turmoil inside her. Amy's husband had been returned to her, and already, he was leaving again to put himself in harm's way.

The transmission ended, and Jim turned to Doug. "Orlando, New York, and now Dallas. This doesn't sound like only East Coast targets to me."

"Me neither." Doug closed the laptop in front of him. "I'll get my office working on likely targets."

"And I'll make sure the Saint Squad has the support they need," Admiral Moss said.

"Thank you." Jim moved toward the door. "And, Admiral, if you have any trouble with getting those satellites retasked, you let me know."

Admiral Moss's eyes lit with determination. "Yes, sir."

* * *

Vanessa followed a guard down the corridor of the detention center, willing her heartbeat to remain steady and her palms dry. When Kade had mentioned interrogating Morenta, he had neglected to tell her they had to fly to Denver to do so. An early morning on a government jet had allowed them easy passage between DC and Denver, but it had also given her far too much time to think.

The fortress had been destroyed, but the possibility that Morenta had another attack already in motion had pushed her to make this trip. The man was notorious for plotting multifaceted attacks, and now that she knew some of the EMP weapons had made it out of the fortress, she needed every ounce of information she could extract from this terrorist.

She still couldn't believe she was really doing this. She immediately corrected that thought. She wasn't Vanessa. She was Lina Ramir, daughter of convicted smuggler Fahid Ramir, niece of Akil Ramir, convicted arms dealer and owner of the fortress.

She lifted her chin and adopted an air of superiority. Lina Ramir wasn't afraid of Morenta. Okay, maybe a little afraid. Akil had certainly warned her about him, opting to keep her out of sight as much as possible when Morenta had visited the fortress while she'd been there.

The guard stopped beside a door and looked back at her. "He's in here."

Vanessa nodded.

He unlocked the door and led the way inside. "Your lawyer is here to see you."

Morenta looked up from where he sat beside the table in the center of the room. His hands were chained to the table, his orange prison uniform a stark contrast to his usual business suits and expensive casual wear.

Vanessa stepped past the guard. She lifted her chin a little higher. Imitating the Middle Eastern accent that had been common among the Ramir family, she said, "Leave us."

"I'll be right outside if you need me."

Vanessa didn't spare the guard a glance. Lina wouldn't have. She strolled across the room, set her briefcase down, and lowered into the seat opposite Morenta.

As soon as the guard closed the door, Morenta asked, "*¿Quién es?*"

"*¿No recuerda?*" Vanessa asked. "*Soy Lina Ramir.*" She leaned forward, waiting until his gaze locked on hers before she continued in Spanish, "My family owns the fortress, the property you have been using as though it were your own for the past five years."

Morenta's dark eyes narrowed. "Your uncle never complained."

"My uncle is dead." Akil Ramir wasn't dead, but Vanessa didn't need to tell him that the man she had pretended to be related to was still locked away in a maximum-security prison. "The fortress belongs to me, and I want it back."

Morenta lifted his hands, the chains rattling as he did so. "I'm in no position to help you." He lowered them again and leaned forward. "If you were to get me out of here, I might be able to facilitate your request."

"That may be possible."

Morenta scoffed, the disbelief on his face obvious.

Ignoring his skepticism, Vanessa opened her briefcase and retrieved a photo printed for just this occasion. No way was she was going to use her iPad this close to Morenta. It could turn into a weapon far too easily. "Kansas City and Las Vegas are still without power."

Morenta smiled.

The man truly was evil. Vanessa buried that thought. "My sources tell me Osman is planning another attack, one three times the size of the one you attempted." She leaned back in her chair, the picture on her lap. "He's trying to make a name for himself. He's trying to take over everything you created."

"He isn't taking over," Morenta said smugly.

Vanessa read between the lines. This man truly believed Osman's priority was to break Morenta out of this prison and restore him to his old life.

"If you think Osman is going to rescue you, you're quite mistaken."

"The guards will have a difficult time maintaining order once the power goes out, don't you think?"

Target number one: Denver.

"I think it will be difficult for your men to get to you without knowing where you are," Vanessa said. "I can help."

"Why?"

"Like I said, I want the fortress back." Vanessa turned the image toward him. "I have the schematics of this facility. I've seen their security."

"How did you get in here? You're no lawyer."

Vanessa smiled slowly. "Oh, but I am. I became Heather Elias shortly after she had an unfortunate accident after passing the bar."

Morenta stared at her for several seconds as though examining her for any hint of deception. A look of respect bloomed on his face.

"My network here in the States is extensive. Your plans threaten to destroy everything I've built," she said.

"I suggest you send your people on a nice tropical vacation very soon."

"You may not have access to the news in here, but Chicago and Detroit are both snowed in." Vanessa paused long enough to take in Morenta's reaction. At least one more target confirmed. Possibly two. "Minneapolis and Boston are both snowed in too."

No reaction on those.

"Maybe your people should consider driving to Canada for a few days."

"And my people in the Southwest?" Vanessa asked. "Los Angeles is a very lucrative market for me."

"And only a short drive from Mexico."

"Where else?" Vanessa asked.

"Perhaps you should pay a visit to my associates at your uncle's home," Morenta said. "You can share what you know, and my number two can give you the information you seek."

Aware that Morenta wasn't going to give her anything else, Vanessa stood. "I'll have my pilot prepare my plane."

"I suggest you leave now. The window is closing."

Vanessa nodded. She crossed to the door and knocked on it. The guard opened it a moment later.

She stepped into the hall and made her way to the exit, passing through the various security points along her way. As soon as she stepped through the final gate, she moved to where Kade had parked their rental car. Time to get the latest intel into the right hands. And time to leave Lina Ramir behind, hopefully forever.

* * *

Amy straightened her shoulders and lifted her chin. She could do this. She could give her husband the news that he and his squad had been approved for an intercept mission.

She prayed she could do this.

Brent was already injured. He should be staying on the carrier with her, but the captain had been willing to override the doctor's concerns in order to send the squad in with every available resource.

She reached the ready room, where the whole squad had reconvened, each of them dressed in their battle fatigues. Brent zipped the pocket on his combat vest, where he kept the miniature version of the scriptures. Then he slipped the vest on.

"When do we leave?" Brent asked her.

"As soon as you get to the flight deck."

"You heard her, men." Seth waved everyone forward. "Let's go."

Amy swallowed her frustration. Couldn't she get one minute alone with her husband? But she knew the answer. They were aboard ship, and yet again, he had a mission. Needing whatever connection she could steal in this moment, she leaned in and kissed him. "Be careful."

"I will." Brent put his hand on her cheek. "I love you."

"I love you." Amy eased back. To fight against her fears, she focused on the obstacles still before them. "I'll keep monitoring Osman's men. I should have new satellite photos shortly."

"Thanks, Amy." Brent leaned down for another kiss. Then he turned and disappeared through the hatch, closing it behind him.

Amy stared at the doorway for several long seconds before she moved to her computer and sat down.

Brent and his squad were going in unprepared. She had less than ninety minutes to find everything they needed to ensure they had a successful mission . . . and would come home alive.

28

Vanessa approached Sarah's desk and glanced at the closed door leading to the Oval Office. "I need to see him. It's urgent."

"I'm starting to think it's urgent every time you need to see him."

"Sorry. Looks like that's the nature of my job."

Sarah picked up her phone and hit a button. "Mr. President, I have Vanessa Johnson here to see you. She—" She broke off and hung up.

"Go right in."

"Thank you."

Vanessa opened the door, expecting Jim to be meeting with Sawyer or maybe Doug. Instead, she faced a room full of Jim's most trusted advisers: Sawyer, Doug, Director Gibson, Admiral Mantiquez, Jim's new secretary of defense. The director of the FBI, the chair of the joint chiefs, and the secretary of the navy were also present, as was Kel Bennett, the former commander of the Saint Squad and current secretary of Veteran Affairs.

Jim stood and motioned Vanessa inside.

Vanessa stepped forward and closed the door. "I'm sorry to interrupt, Mr. President, but I've identified some more potential targets."

"Where?"

"Los Angeles, Denver, Chicago, and Detroit," Vanessa said. "I couldn't tell with Chicago and Detroit whether it was both of them or only one. Sorry."

"That gives us seven possibles," Director Gibson said. "If we assume each of the vehicles that came out of the fortress has three EMP weapons, that means we're likely looking for six targets."

"Unless the tracker isn't working on the third vehicle, in which case, we could have nine," Jim countered.

"Regardless of the number of weapons, I believe we can take Boston and Minneapolis off the list," Vanessa said.

"Where did this intel come from?" the FBI director asked.

"Morenta." Vanessa sidestepped the fact that she had been the one to extract it. "He was interrogated this morning, and we were able to pull this information from that session."

"He willingly gave up Osman's plan?"

"He believed he was speaking to someone he could trust," Vanessa said.

"He could be playing us," the FBI director said.

"Mrs. Johnson's intelligence sources have always proved to be reliable for me in the past," Kel said. "Am I correct in assuming you witnessed this interrogation?"

Vanessa loved that he phrased his question so she could answer honestly without admitting she had been the trusted source. "Yes. Morenta also believes the attack is happening soon."

Jim stood and retrieved a chair that had been pushed against the wall. He set it to the right of where he had been sitting. "Vanessa, take a seat. I'd like to have your input as well."

Doug tapped his pen against the notepad in his hand. "So, if our intel thus far is correct, we have Los Angeles, Denver, Dallas, Orlando, New York, and either Chicago or Detroit, possibly both."

"Best guess for the others?" Jim asked.

"At least one must be somewhere in the west." Doug tapped his notepad again. "Three targets are on the East Coast: Orlando, Detroit, and New York. Then we have Dallas and Chicago in the Midwest; plus, Kansas City is still without power."

"So is North Las Vegas," Jim said. "With Los Angeles as a new target, we would have to think they would have at least one more in the west."

"My guess is they'd go after San Francisco and Seattle," Doug said.

"Both areas have large populations," Admiral Mantiquez said.

"And they both have strong IT sectors."

"Doug, work with your people to provide extra security at the power plants in both of those cities," Jim said.

"They're already on high alert, but we'll do what we can to modify the generators and batteries for our emergency services and hospitals."

"What's the latest on the computer virus?" Jim asked.

"We have our best hackers working on it. We believe we can get a fix to the core electronic manufacturers so they can send out an update to counteract it."

"How long is that going to take?" Jim asked.

"Apple and Samsung are both close. They'll run tests tomorrow. If all goes well, they could have a fix as early as next week."

"Apple is headquartered in the Bay area," Vanessa said. "If they get hit, the fix could be wiped out before it's shared with their consumers."

"Samsung's US headquarters is in striking distance of New York," Doug said.

"Sounds like they need to be given some protection as well."

"I'll get the information to them on how to protect themselves against the pulse weapon," Doug said.

"Thank you, everyone." Jim stood. "Keep me updated."

The response of "Yes, Mr. President" echoed through the room.

Vanessa stood, but Jim motioned for her to remain behind.

"Kel, can you hold back for a minute?"

"Yes, sir."

Kel followed the others to the door and closed it when the last of them left.

"The Saint Squad is heading into Honduras to head off Osman's men." Jim motioned for Vanessa and Kel to sit back down. As soon as they did, he continued. "The secretary of state is working on getting them permission to land in Tegucigalpa, but I need to know from the two of you what support we can give them once they get there. The president of Honduras isn't going to want a shootout in the middle of his largest airport."

"We need to give them resources on the ground," Kel said. "A way to blend in."

"How do we get them the support they need without possibly tipping off Osman's organization?" Jim asked.

"I have an idea," Vanessa said.

"So do I," Kel added.

"Good. You two, work out the details. You know the squad better than anyone else." Jim stood again. "We can't afford to miss this opportunity."

With nine large cities as potential targets, Vanessa couldn't agree more. "We'll get them what they need."

* * *

Brent prayed they would be granted clearance to land. The backup plan of parachuting out of this plane would mean making a choice between sending his squad into Honduras without him or risking further injury to his leg. With as much as their country had at stake, they couldn't afford to have anyone slowing them down.

Brent glanced at his watch. Based on his calculations, they should be nearing Honduran air space.

He spoke to the pilot through his headset. "What's our position?"

"We're preparing for our final approach."

One prayer answered. "Any updates on our target's position?"

"Sixty-five miles out."

"This is going to be close," Jay said.

Brent pulled the printed image of the airport from his vest pocket. Not a lot of places to hide, and no trees for Jay to climb to keep watch with his sniper rifle.

From the seat beside him, Jay asked, "How do you want to handle this? We don't want to go in shooting, not with civilians around."

"And we don't want one of those weapons to be turned on," Seth added. "Losing power at an airport would not go over well."

Brent didn't want to think about the chaos that would cause. "Damian and Craig, I want you to see if you can board the plane before Osman's men show up. Jay and Quinn, set up by the hangars on either side to cover them."

"What about the rest of us?"

"We're going to commandeer a couple of airport vehicles to use for cover," Brent said. "That's the only way we'll be able to get close to the plane without being completely vulnerable."

"Any chance we can radio ahead and get some of those cover vehicles in place before we get there?" Craig asked. "Requesting a luggage tug shouldn't raise any questions."

"That's a good idea." Brent relayed the request to the pilot.

The pilot spoke a minute later. "We're beginning our final approach, but we have new mission parameters."

"What are they?"

"The Honduran president is allowing us to land, but he has dictated that we can't use lethal force."

Seth shook his head. "If we capture them and turn them over to the Honduran government, it's only a matter of time before they're freed."

"We need a new plan." Brent glanced at his watch. "In the next thirteen minutes."

"How many tranq rifles do we have?" Seth asked.

"Three," Jay said.

"I say we take a page out of Quinn's playbook." Craig waved his hand toward Quinn. "Let's hijack the plane."

Seth's eyes lit up. "With Osman's men on it."

Quinn's hand shot into the air. "I'm flying it."

Brent ignored Quinn's enthusiasm. "Craig, you're brilliant."

"It's a win-win." Craig shrugged. "We won't have to worry about extradition issues, the Hondurans won't have to deal with the extra security of keeping them in custody, and the weapons will be delivered intact to the US to be studied."

"Okay, so, new plan." Brent's mind raced. "Quinn and Craig, you're going to replace the pilots."

A huge grin flashed on Quinn's face. "Oh yeah." He gave an exaggerated nod, repeating it twice. "I get to hijack a plane."

"Tristan, you take Quinn's spot on sniper duty with Jay," Brent said. "The two of you and Seth, take the tranquilizer guns." Brent leaned forward so he could see Damian past Seth. "Damian, as soon as we land, find some kind of airport uniform you can change into. I want you to play airport personnel."

"I can do that."

"What about the two of us?" Seth asked. "Maybe I should play pilot and have Damian pretend to be a steward."

"If they have a steward, that would work," Brent calculated the angles. "We can have our pilot play lookout, and I'll find somewhere else to set up to cover."

"Are you sure you want to hand lookout duty to someone else?" Seth asked. "He won't be able to park too close since there are US markings on our plane."

Rely on someone outside their squad to feed relevant information to them from a distance, or take on the task himself? Brent looked down at his leg. As much as he wanted to be out there with his squad, Seth was right. He was back in command, and he needed to put his squad in the best situation for success.

"If we can find another plane to park beside Osman's, you could spot for us right through the cockpit window," Seth suggested.

"And the pilot can keep an eye out for any activity coming toward us from the airport." Resigned to staying inside, Brent nodded and spoke to the pilot. "Lieutenant Rhodes, do we have enough fuel to fly from Tegucigalpa to Dallas without cutting into our reserves?"

"Yes, sir."

"Good. Clear a flight plan for us. When my men take off in Osman's plane, I want to be right behind them."

"Yes, sir."

29

Tristan had a bad feeling about this. If they had uniforms to blend in with the airport employees, they'd have a decent shot of pulling this mission off. Without them, they were at a huge disadvantage.

Their plane came to a stop, and Tristan disarmed the door. He pulled it open as a portable airstair rolled toward the side of the plane.

"Looks like someone was expecting us," Tristan said, not sure if that fact was good or bad. The man steering the airstair climbed out of the tug, a duffel bag in hand. He started up the stairs, and recognition dawned. It was the same guardian who had helped Brent in Nicaragua.

"Hey, guys. We have a ghost."

"What?" Brent looked over his shoulder. "How in the world did he end up here?"

"I have no idea." Tristan moved back to let him into the plane.

"I thought you might need this." Ghost handed the duffel to Brent. "It's uniforms so you'll blend in."

"Bless you." Brent reached out and took it from him. He handed the bag to Seth, who immediately unzipped it and started handing out uniforms.

"The pilots got delayed in security," Ghost continued. "If we hurry, you should be able to get to the plane before them."

"What's the position on Osman's men?" Brent asked.

"They're twenty minutes out, give or take."

Brent turned toward the rest of the team. "We've got to move."

Tristan slipped a bright orange safety vest over his uniform. Seth did the same.

"There are a couple of pilot uniforms in there and some staff ones," Ghost said. "Sorry, there weren't a lot that fit people over six feet."

"That's okay," Brent said. "The only people who are going to be in sight will be able to use what you gave us."

"There are a couple of guards next to where Osman's plane is parked," Ghost said.

"How many?" Brent asked.

"Two, both heavily armed."

"Our best bet is to drive Quinn, Craig, and Damian out to the plane and hope they can pass as staff."

"I have a truck down there that I can use to drive them," Ghost said. "And there's a luggage tug down there too."

Brent turned to Seth. "You drive the luggage tug over there. Jay and Tristan can hide in the back. The three of you cover them if things go south."

"What about our orders?" Seth asked. "Nonlethal force, remember?"

"We try to stick with that, but use your judgment. Don't take a bullet because we were asked to play nice."

"What about you?" Ghost asked Brent.

"I need a plane I can use to park next to Osman's."

"There are a couple of Cessnas in the hangar next to where Osman's plane is parked." Ghost motioned to the truck below. "You can hide in the back. I'll drop you off in the hangar before I take the others to the plane."

Brent nodded. "Tristan, you're with me. You can cover from the hangar."

"If I'm doing that, I'm not wearing this." Tristan took the vest back off.

"Seth, you and Jay get going. Those tugs are a lot slower than the truck."

Ghost handed Seth a cell phone. "I pinned the plane's location on that. Keys are in the ignition."

"Thanks." Seth jogged down the stairs, Jay right behind him. A few seconds later, the engine turned over, and they pulled away.

"What frequency are you on?" Ghost asked, pulling a comm earpiece from his pocket.

Brent gave him the frequency. Then he moved to the door. "Let's go."

Brent grabbed the railings and used them to hop down the stairs using his good leg.

Tristan, Ghost, and the remaining members of the squad followed. Tristan and Brent climbed into the bed of the truck and lay down so they were out of sight. The afternoon sun beat down on them, and sweat beaded on Tristan's forehead.

"It doesn't feel like February down here," Tristan muttered.

"We'll be in the shade soon," Brent said.

Doors opened and closed as Ghost, Quinn, Craig, and Damian climbed into the front. The vehicle went into motion. Four minutes later, Ghost pulled into the hangar, the heat just as intense beneath the corrugated metal structure as it was outside.

"You're clear," Quinn said.

Tristan climbed out of the back, his tranquilizer rifle in hand. He positioned himself beside the hangar door while Brent headed for the closest of the two Cessnas housed inside.

Tristan peered out at the sleek jet waiting a short distance away. Two men stood beside it, one by the tail and the other near the center of the plane.

"Confirmed," Tristan said. "We've got two guards by the plane. Looks like both have pistols holstered at their waists."

"Seth, what's your position?" Brent asked.

"Almost there. ETA two minutes."

Brent did a quick check of the engine and then climbed into the small plane. "I'll get into position first."

Brent started the engines. Tristan wasn't sure whether the keys had been in the aircraft or whether Brent was demonstrating his abilities in hot-wiring, but either way, he had accomplished his objective.

The luggage tug came into view, Seth in the driver's seat with his bright vest, Jay hidden in one of the three carts pulled behind.

"I've got a visual on Seth," Tristan said.

The man by the tail of the plane moved his hand to the front of his belt.

"These guys look antsy," Tristan said.

"Ghost, go now," Brent said. "Craig, take out the first guard. Tristan, as soon as he makes his move, take out the other one."

"Roger that," Craig said.

Ghost pulled out of the hangar and stopped beside the plane as Seth approached. Quinn, Damian, and Craig stepped out of the truck.

Quinn said something in Spanish to the closest guard, but Tristan didn't understand the words. Tristan lifted his tranquilizer gun and took aim. The tranq wouldn't immobilize the guard as quickly as the sedative Craig would use, but hopefully, it would stun him enough for Tristan's teammates to disarm him.

Craig stepped past the guard as though to pull open the airstair at the same time Damian moved toward the guard at the rear. The rear guard held up his hand as though to warn him off. Damian spoke, also in Spanish, his hands held out to his side so as to appear nonthreatening.

Before the conversation between Damian and the rear guard could continue, Craig turned suddenly and slapped his hand against the other guard's shoulder, no doubt where he plunged a needle through his sleeve and administered a high dose of a fast-acting sedative.

Tristan squeezed the trigger, his tranquilizer dart impacting the rear guard's leg.

The man cried out and grabbed for his weapon. Damian rushed forward and kicked the man's hand, knocking the pistol to the ground. The man leaned down for the gun, and Damian kicked him again, this time in the ribs.

The guard fell down and reached for his pistol. Jay fired, his bullet hitting the gun and sending it skidding away from the guard.

Damian leaned down and put his knee in the man's back, then pulled the man's arms behind his back. The lack of resistance from the guard indicated the tranquilizer was taking effect.

Damian dragged the man to the back of the truck, and Ghost helped put him into the truck bed. Craig and Quinn lifted the other guard in beside them.

"If you're all good, I'm going to take these guys back to the airport," Ghost said. "I need to pick up the actual pilots to make sure someone else doesn't bring them out here."

"Thanks, Ghost," Brent said.

Lieutenant Rhodes's voice came over Tristan's headset. "Osman's men are approaching the gate."

"Okay, everyone," Brent said. "Showtime."

30

Brent taxied out of the hangar and headed toward the empty space beside Osman's plane. He parked so he could see the airstair and cargo doors. "Damian, take the guard's place. They'll expect someone to be protecting the plane."

"Roger."

"What about the second guard?" Craig asked.

"Seth, step in for him," Brent ordered. "Jay, you take Seth's place as the luggage-cart driver."

Seth handed Jay his vest and stripped off his combat vest so his attire would look more like the men they had just sedated. The rumble of car engines neared, competing with the sound of an airplane on approach.

Brent pulled his binoculars from his vest and peered through them until he spotted the SUVs from the fortress. "They're here."

The two vehicles parked beside the plane, and men piled out of both of them. Brent did a quick head count. Ten men total.

One of them approached Damian. He motioned to the plane and spoke in rapid Spanish. Brent picked out enough of the man's question to figure out he was asking whether the plane was ready.

Damian responded in the affirmative and waved toward the cockpit.

The man speaking to Damian turned and motioned to the rest of the men. Four of them moved to the back of the SUVs. Within seconds, they had opened the trunks and were unloading silver cases, which undoubtedly contained the pulse weapons. Smaller duffels joined the weapons on the tarmac.

Damian opened the rear luggage compartment of the plane, and the men loaded the weapons and their gear into it.

Brent counted the weapons as they were loaded. "I only see five cases. Where are the other weapons?"

"Maybe they were destroyed in the missile attack," Tristan said.

If they were lucky. But if they weren't . . . Brent's blood ran cold as he finished the thought. "Or half of Osman's men are flying out of a different airport."

"I hope you're wrong," Tristan said.

"Me too." Brent turned his attention to his men on the ground. "Seth and Damian, see if you can find out where the other vehicles were headed."

Seth clicked once into his mic.

One of the men secured the rear storage compartment. Then he turned and tossed Seth a set of keys. Another man handed Damian his keys.

The one by Seth ordered the rest of the men to board. The command to prepare the airplane followed.

As soon as the men were on board, Damian secured the airstair, folding it up until the door closed into the side of the plane.

"Sorry, Brent," Seth said. "They told us to take care of the vehicles. We didn't get a chance to pull information out of them."

"Wait until the plane pulls away. As soon as they're clear, we'll use their vehicles to drive to our ride." Brent focused on Quinn and Craig, who were visible in the cockpit. He was sending them with a bunch of armed men on a flight that would take over four hours to arrive at their destination. He prayed they would arrive safely, without incident.

"Quinn and Craig, we'll meet you in Dallas," Brent said. "Be careful."

One of them clicked into his mic. Then the aircraft went into motion and pulled slowly toward the runway.

Damian and Seth rushed toward their prospective vehicles.

"Seth, you pick up Tristan from the hangar. Jay, hold your position."

"It's getting pretty hot down here. I think I'd rather be up a tree."

"That's saying something." Brent waited until Quinn moved Osman's plane forward enough that the passengers would no longer be able to see him through the windows. Then he climbed down from the Cessna. "Jay, we're clear."

Damian started the engine, and Brent and Jay jumped into the waiting vehicle. Brent slapped the dashboard. "Let's go."

Damian hit the gas and followed Seth, who was already well on his way to where they had left their plane.

"Ghost, do you read me?"

"*Sí.*" Ghost's use of Spanish instead of English suggested he had company.

"The plane is on its way to the runway. As soon as you're clear of Osman's pilots, I need you to get a message out. We're missing four of the EMPs. Only five are on the plane."

"*Sí*," Ghost said again.

"Good luck," Brent said.

"Why are you having Ghost send the message?" Damian asked. "We can send the message through our pilot."

"Yes, but Ghost may be able to get the intel into Jim's hands faster than the navy can," Brent said.

"He's right," Seth said from the back seat. "Vanessa will make sure Jim knows of the potential danger."

"Let's pray they can find the second plane," Brent said.

Seth gripped the back of Brent's seat. "I already am."

* * *

Vanessa studied the map of Central America at the kitchen table in the trailer of Kade's truck. Kade sat at his desk in the corner of the living space. Renee sat at the desk beside him.

Vanessa did a search on driving times to the fortress as well as flight times from the nearby airports to Dallas. "Why would Osman's men fly out of Honduras instead of Nicaragua or Costa Rica?"

"I don't know," Renee said. "I've been wondering the same thing. Managua is a six- or seven-hour drive from the fortress, and San José is around eight."

"Yet they chose to drive to Tegucigalpa, over twelve hours away."

Kade looked up from his computer. "They didn't fly out of Managua because Osman knew President Aviles had an alert out for him and his men."

"What about Costa Rica?" Vanessa asked. "The flights from there to Dallas are about the same length as the ones from Tegucigalpa, and it would have saved Osman's men several hours of driving time."

"Not to mention, Osman has connections that would make it just as easy to cross into Costa Rica as Honduras," Renee said.

Vanessa's phone rang, and she pulled it from her pocket. "It's Manuel." She hit the Talk button. "Did the Saint Squad intercept the weapons?"

"They hijacked the plane with Osman's men and weapons on it."

"They did what?" Vanessa let out a heavy sigh. Leave it to her husband and his teammates to improvise.

"They were ordered not to use lethal force while in Honduras. This will give them the chance to get these men to the US and give us control of the weapons."

Vanessa couldn't fault that strategy. "I'll let the president know the latest."

"There's one more thing."

"What's that?"

"We only saw five weapons when they loaded up. We're missing four."

Vanessa looked at the map again. "They must have split them up."

"Or some of the weapons were destroyed in the missile strike."

"I hope that's the case, but we can't count on it," Vanessa said. "Thanks for the update."

"You're welcome," Manuel said. "I'm heading back to the fortress. I'll see if I can find any evidence of the missing weapons."

"Thanks. Let me know if you find anything."

"I will." Manuel ended the call.

Vanessa looked up at Kade and Renee. "Four of the pulse weapons are missing."

Renee tapped on her keyboard.

"Are you looking up flights out of San José?" Kade asked.

"Yeah."

Vanessa did the calculations on when Osman's men would have left the fortress, then she mapped the most direct route. "According to this, they should have arrived in San José around four or five."

Kade stood and moved behind Renee. "What have you got?"

"I'm narrowing them down to private planes going to the US." Renee clicked on her mouse. "Looks like we have four."

"What are the destinations?" Vanessa asked.

"San Diego, Houston, Miami, and Atlanta."

"It could be any of those." Kade leaned down to look over his wife's shoulder. "They all left within an hour of each other."

"What time was that?" Vanessa asked.

"The first one was at four forty-five," Renee said. "That would have been within the window of when Osman's men would likely have arrived at the airport."

Kade moved back to his desk. "I'll see if we have any satellite footage of the airport. Maybe we'll be able to see what vehicles are parked beside these planes."

"I'll look up which hangars the planes were parked at," Renee said.

"See if you can pull up the pilots' names too. That might help us narrow down if any of these were connected to Osman."

"I'm going to run correlations on the possible target cities," Vanessa said. "There has to be a reason Osman picked them."

"If Morenta's right, Osman is taking the overkill approach in trying to go for a cascade effect in our power plants," Renee said.

"Yes, but there has to be something that ties them together besides that," Vanessa said. "If we can find a common thread between them, maybe we can figure out the other targets."

"How soon are you going to talk to the president?" Renee asked.

Vanessa debated. At the moment, she had little more than suspicions, but those suspicions could have a significant impact on the readiness for a potential terrorist attack. She pulled out her phone and dialed the White House. As expected, Jim's secretary answered.

"Hi, Sarah. It's Vanessa Johnson. Is the president available?"

"I'm sorry. He's in a meeting."

"Can you please have him call me. It's important."

"Of course." Sarah took down her number, even though Jim already had it.

Vanessa ended the call. "He's in a meeting."

"He may be in meetings all day."

"If I don't hear back from him by tonight, I'll drive over to the White House after rush hour dies down," Vanessa said. "I'd like to have more details on where we really stand before I talk to him anyway."

"Let's hope we have some for you by then," Renee said.

Vanessa nodded. "I'm praying we will."

31

Amy waited in the Ready Room, willing a new update to appear on her computer screen. The vehicles she'd been tracking were now parked at the airport in Tegucigalpa and hadn't moved for the past fifteen minutes. On another screen, she checked the local news reports for Honduras. The fact that she didn't find any breaking news was promising. If a shootout had occurred at the airport, she suspected something would have popped up by now.

Her stomach grumbled, and she pulled out the bag of rolls she'd hidden in her desk drawer. Only two rolls left. That didn't bode well for spending much more time on the carrier. Since the doctor had forced her to rest in sick bay last night, the queasiness had eased to an irritating constant, mild enough that she could function as long as she could keep from thinking about her stomach.

She took a roll from the bag and broke off a piece. Taking small bites, she ate the first one and debated eating the second. The rumble in her stomach made the decision for her. She wasn't leaving her desk until she had news, and her body needed fuel.

She leaned back in her chair and let her head fall back against the headrest. Possible ways of telling Brent of her pregnancy filled her mind. The gift of a little baby outfit with Daddy scrawled across the front, or perhaps a printout of her test results from the doctor. A stuffed animal, a bottle of prenatal vitamins, an eating-for-two T-shirt. Ideas continued to flow, but the one constant in all her scenarios was that she and Brent would be in the same room without a potential terrorist attack looming on the horizon.

Amy's phone rang, and she snatched it up. "Amy Miller."

"Amy, it's Commander Chang. We just got word that your boys are in the air and headed for Dallas."

"What happens when they get to Dallas?"

"They'll work with the FBI to take Osman's men into custody."

Amy did a quick search for the flight time between Tegucigalpa and Dallas. Her squad would be in the air for the next four hours. There was no reason for her to stay on the carrier.

"How fast can you get me stateside?" Amy asked.

"There's a transport heading to Andrews in a half hour," Commander Chang said. "That's the best I can do."

If she got to DC, it would be easy enough to grab a ride to the White House. After how cold she'd been to her father when Brent had disappeared, she needed to at least stop by long enough to apologize. "If you can get me a seat, I'll take it."

"Consider it done."

"Thank you." Amy glanced at the worktable where her squad had left the satellite photos and printed material they had been working from. "One more thing. I need authorization to carry classified documents."

"Get me an inventory and meet me in my office," Commander Chang said. "Better make it quick."

"I'll be right there." Amy hung up and shut down her computer. After gathering all the work materials her squad had printed, she made a quick list, secured material in a folder, and stamped it Top Secret. A quick stop at her quarters to grab her bags came next. When she reached the XO's office, she had only ten minutes until her flight was scheduled to leave.

A little breathless from her rush, she handed over the inventory and her file. "Here you go."

Commander Chang scanned the inventory and flipped through the documents. "Make sure you secure these at Andrews until you can arrange for a secure transport. We don't want you getting nailed for mishandling classified documents."

"I will. Thanks."

Commander Chang handed her the file and the paperwork authorizing her to get on the flight to Andrews. "You better get going. You don't have much time."

Amy nodded. She unzipped her backpack and pulled out the protective ear covering she would need before walking out onto the flight deck.

"Thanks again." Amy left his office and hurried toward the catwalk leading to the flight deck.

She showed her paperwork to the appropriate personnel and boarded the plane with less than two minutes to spare. Her heart still pounding, she stored one bag in the overhead and belted her backpack into the empty seat beside her. No way she was letting her classified material out of her sight.

She clipped into her own harness, and one of the crew members instructed her and the handful of other passengers on board to prepare for takeoff.

The engines revved, and seconds later, the plane shot forward into the air. Amy's body jolted from the sudden acceleration, and her stomach pitched. Maybe she shouldn't have eaten that second roll.

* * *

Tristan was going home. Sort of. He had lived all over Texas during his childhood, pawned off to whichever family member would take him when his mom was deployed. While he associated the most with San Antonio as his hometown, he had spent the majority of ninth grade in Dallas with his uncle. A little rebellion against curfew had ultimately resulted in him moving in with his newly starred admiral mother in northern Virginia. That incident had paved the path for him to meet Quinn and eventually move in with Quinn's family for the better part of his high school years.

"When was the last time you were in Texas?" Seth asked.

"Not since I brought Riley to San Antonio to meet the family."

"You have two kids," Seth said. "Maybe it's time to arrange for another trip."

"Yeah. Maybe."

Brent approached from the cockpit. "I just got the latest update from the FBI. They've identified twenty-three flights over the next eighteen hours that could be going to potential target cities."

"It sure would help if we knew which cities we were trying to protect," Damian said.

"For now, we're planning a new kind of mission."

"When aren't we planning a new kind of mission?" Tristan asked.

"Okay, good point," Brent conceded.

"What do you have in mind this time?" Seth asked.

"We don't want to risk the pulse weapons being deployed, but the FBI wants to follow Osman's men to their prospective planes rather than take them into custody when they land."

Damian straightened in his seat. "They're trying to wrap up the whole operation?"

"Yes." Brent sat beside Seth, across from Tristan and Damian. "Our mission is to drive beside Osman's plane when it lands, unload the weapons, and replace them with look-alike cases that have hidden transponders in them."

"We're going to unload a plane while it's still moving?" Tristan repeated.

"And load it again." Brent nodded. "All of this without being seen."

"This should be fun."

"Air traffic control is having Quinn land on the outermost runway. That will give us more time to accomplish our goal."

"What if one of these guys looks out the window?"

"Unless they're trying to look behind them, we shouldn't have a problem," Brent said.

Shouldn't. Not a word he particularly trusted.

"Has the FBI already talked to Quinn?"

"Yes. He'll match our speed at twenty miles per hour."

Tristan leaned forward. He was up for a new challenge. "Okay, who's doing what?"

Brent's gaze met his. "I'm glad you asked."

32

Alone. Finally.

Jim didn't know how many back-to-back meetings he had endured. He wasn't sure he wanted to know.

Exhausted, he leaned back in his desk chair in the Oval Office and rubbed his eyes. The lack of sleep was catching up to him. If only he could take a nap and then wake up to find the world at peace, everyone's electricity on, and the outside temperature a nice sixty-eight degrees.

Based on the latest reports, that wasn't going to happen. Nine potential targets, only two of which had been positively identified. Of course, that was assuming all their intel was correct and that Osman hadn't made any changes to Morenta's original plans.

With the power companies still unable to restore electricity in Vegas and Kansas City, Jim couldn't imagine what would happen if even more cities suffered similar fates. And in truth, until the cellular service and electronics companies could come up with a way to destroy the virus that had infected so many devices, new power outages could cascade through the entire nation and cripple their efforts.

A knock sounded, and Jim's door opened a moment later. Sarah walked in carrying a stack of messages. "I thought you'd want to see these. I sorted out the ones that can wait until next week."

"Thanks, Sarah." Jim flipped through the messages from various members of his cabinet, senators, admirals, congressmen. He reached one from Vanessa and put it at the top of the stack. "Can you get Vanessa Johnson on the line for me?"

"Yes, Mr. President." Sarah retreated from the room and closed the door behind her.

A moment later, his phone rang. "Vanessa, any updates?"

"I'm afraid so."

"This doesn't sound promising."

"I just got word that only five weapons were loaded onto the plane heading for Dallas."

"I thought there were nine."

"That's what we've been told," Vanessa said. "We've been going over the possibilities. We think Osman split up his men so they flew out of two airports, half from Honduras and half from Costa Rica."

Jim rubbed his forehead in a futile effort to combat the headache forming there. "This is a nightmare."

"We're analyzing flights coming out of San José. We haven't identified which one might be Osman's men, but I wanted to let you know that the threat goes beyond whatever weapons are flying into Dallas."

"I'll talk to Doug and let him know," Jim said. "Once we know where the first five weapons are headed, that will narrow down which cities are still at risk."

"We already put in a request for the CIA to help research flights out of Managua and the other airports in the area in case Osman risked sending the other weapons out of there."

"Keep me informed."

"I will."

Jim ended the call. A knock sounded on his door a moment later.

"Come in."

The door opened, and Amy walked in. Instantly, some of his tension eased.

Relieved to have her home, Jim stood and rounded the desk. "I didn't know you were back."

"I just arrived. I have to admit, it's nice to be on solid ground again."

"I'm sure."

With an uncharacteristically sheepish expression on her face, Amy hugged him and held on a moment longer than expected before she stepped back.

"How's Brent?" Jim asked.

"Way better than expected. Just some bumps and bruises and a few stitches in his leg."

"Thank goodness," Jim said. "The Lord truly was looking out for him."

"Yes, He was." Amy stepped back and sniffled. "Dad, I'm so sorry."

"Sorry for what?"

"It wasn't your fault Brent was MIA. It would have happened whether you were president or not." She let out a sigh. "I shouldn't have blamed you."

"This has been a rough few days for all of us." Jim put his hand on her back and guided her to one of the sofas in the center of the room. "I'm just grateful Brent's okay." They both sat, and Jim asked, "Does he know about the baby?"

"No. We didn't have much time together aboard ship, other than when we were stuck in sick bay, and there were too many people around to have a private conversation."

"You'll get the chance soon enough. If he's not already in Dallas, he should be there any minute."

"What's the latest?" Amy asked.

"Vanessa just called. Four weapons may still be in play."

"Oh no."

Jim recapped the latest information Vanessa had given him.

"Maybe I should help with the search. Is there an area I can work in?"

"I think Doug may be using the Roosevelt Room, but the Cabinet Room is open. Or if you'd rather work in the residence, you can take a secure laptop up there."

"I'll work down here until you go upstairs," Amy said. "If Vanessa and the guardians are already working on flights, maybe I can go through surveillance video at the airports. I might recognize someone from the footage off the body cams from the Saint Squad."

"That's a long shot at best."

"I know, but until the squad comes out of the field, we don't have anyone who was there who can look."

"There was a guardian down there, but I don't know how close he got to Osman's men."

"Based on the mission reports, Brent probably had the best view," Amy said. "Seth may have seen some of them when he was undercover years ago. Vanessa too."

"In that case." Jim stood and crossed to his desk.

"What?" Amy asked.

Jim picked up the phone. "Sarah, I need to speak with Admiral Moss."

"Yes, sir."

"Why do you want to talk to the admiral?" Amy asked.

"Because we need Brent and Seth here, where we can take advantage of what they've seen."

* * *

Tristan should have been the one to hijack the plane. If it hadn't been for his height, blond hair, and inability to speak Spanish, he could have gotten away with it. Instead, here he was on the back of a pickup truck, going twenty miles an hour, picking a lock.

He leaned forward, both hands busy with his lockpick tools. Seth's hand gripped the back of his shirt to keep him from plunging into the void between the truck and the plane.

The lock clicked open. "Got it." Tristan dropped his tools onto the truck bed. No time to put them back where they belonged.

Tristan twisted the handle of the luggage compartment and pulled the door open. A duffel bag slid out, dropping to the ground.

"We lost a bag." Tristan used one hand to prevent the next one from sliding out and his other hand to keep the door from banging closed.

Brent's voice carried over Tristan's headset. "I'll have one of the FBI guys grab it. Quinn, maintain your speed."

"You ready?" Seth asked.

"Yeah." Tristan drew a deep breath. "Now!"

Seth let go of his shirt, and Tristan used the door to hold his weight as he leaped forward. One foot caught the edge of the open doorway, and he used his upper-body strength to balance himself while he put his other foot in place. Then he threw his weight toward the cargo hold and tumbled on top of the luggage.

He took a moment for his heartbeat to settle before he pushed the personal bags aside so he could reach the silver cases containing the pulse weapons. He picked up the first one, turned toward where Seth and Damian stood in the back of the truck, and chucked it over. Seth caught the case and handed it to Damian.

Damian tagged the case with a red sticker to identify it as an actual weapon and set it behind him.

Tristan grabbed the next silver case and sent it flying. Seth snagged it, and he and Damian repeated the process of tagging it.

One by one, Tristan unloaded the weapons.

Once that task was complete, Damian handed Seth a replacement case. Seth held it out to Tristan, waiting for him to grab it before letting go. Tristan stacked the case behind him and turned to grab the next one. They loaded three without incident.

On the fourth, the door swung at Tristan, and the case crashed to the ground, the hinge busting on impact, the case falling open. "Dang it!"

"What happened?" Brent asked.

"We lost one of the cases."

Quinn's voice followed. "We're running out of time."

"I'll have the FBI grab it too. We can load the missing bags when Quinn makes the turn toward the terminal."

"I don't think that one is going to pass inspection," Tristan said. He reached out his hand. "Get me the last one."

Seth handed it over, this time making a successful transfer.

"We need a fifth case," Tristan said.

"I've got an idea." Damian leaned down and pulled the sticker off one of the weapons. He then opened it and removed the weapon from inside.

"It's going to be too light," Seth said. "They'll notice it."

"You're right." Damian pulled off one boot and then the other and stuffed both into the foam casing that had held the weapon in place.

Seth pulled a tracker from his combat vest and passed it to Damian. Damian tucked it into the foam padding and closed and latched the case. "Here."

Seth took the case from Damian and passed it to Tristan.

Tristan placed it with the others. "Okay, we're all set. I just need the missing bag."

"The FBI will have it for you by the terminal," Brent said. "Quinn, we need you to go really slow when you approach so Tristan has time to store the bag and close up the luggage bay before anyone has the chance to deplane."

Quinn clicked into his mic.

"Tristan, the FBI agent will have a safety vest for you so you can blend in with the ground crew. Stay near the plane in case Quinn and Craig need backup."

"Roger."

Brent eased off the gas, and the pickup fell behind the plane. When Quinn made the final turn toward the terminal, Brent continued forward, undoubtedly to deliver the weapons to the FBI.

The plane slowed to five miles per hour. A luggage tug pulled alongside Tristan's position, two men sitting in front, both wearing bright-yellow vests. The one closest to Tristan held up the bag that had fallen from the plane and passed it to Tristan.

Tristan stored the bag. Then he jumped down to the ground. Walking alongside the slow-moving aircraft, he secured the door and stepped back from the plane. "Quinn, I'm clear."

One of the men on the tug tossed him a security vest. "We'll cover the rear of the plane. You take the front."

"Roger." Tristan slipped the vest on and walked beside the plane until it came to a stop. Then he moved to the front and waited for the door to open. If all went well, the men inside would deplane without incident, and the FBI would be able to follow them to their intended targets.

33

FROM HIS SPOT IN THE driver's seat, Brent looked through his binoculars as Osman's men unloaded their bags. Seth had taken the spot beside him, and Damian and Jay remained in the back of the truck. Tristan had faded into the background of the other workers, all of whom were likely undercover FBI agents.

"I haven't seen Quinn or Craig yet," Damian said, his voice coming over Brent's headset.

"They're probably waiting for everyone to clear out before they join us," Jay said.

"Quinn, Craig, do you copy?" Brent asked.

One of them clicked into his microphone. The nearly silent response told Brent what he needed to know. Someone was still on the plane.

Brent kept his focus on the bags being unloaded. One of the men charged with that task secured the luggage compartment.

"Only four of the weapons have been unloaded. That plane must be heading to one of the other target cities."

Quinn or Craig clicked again.

A fuel truck approached. "Tristan, maintain your position. You may need to give Craig and Quinn some support."

Quinn's voice came over the radio. "*¿Donde vamos?*"

Brent recognized the phrase Damian used often: Where are we going?

Quinn rattled off something else, but Brent couldn't pick out the meaning.

"Damian, what did he say?"

"He said he needs to file the flight plan before he can take off," Damian said. "I couldn't hear his response."

"We need to know where that plane is headed so we can narrow down what other targets might still be out there," Seth said.

Seth was right. As much as he hated to do it, Brent faced the facts. They wouldn't find out that information unless the plane were allowed to leave. "Quinn, Craig, are you up for flying to the next location?" There was a slight pause before one of them signaled in the affirmative. "We'll track your progress and meet you at your next destination."

A work truck pulled up beside Brent, two men visible inside. The Latino man sitting in the passenger seat rolled down his window. Brent followed suit.

The man hooked an arm over the edge of the window. "Do your men know where the plane is supposed to go?"

Even though the man appeared to be an airport employee, his words identified him as FBI.

"They were told they'd be given their destination in the air," Brent said.

"They're going to have to stay with Osman's men until they get to the target city."

"I already told them as much," Brent said. "We need to get our plane fueled up so we can provide support."

"Negative. You and Commander Johnson are being recalled to Washington."

Brent narrowed his eyes. "I understand Commander Johnson's needing to go back, but why me?"

"You're injured." The agent passed a paper to Brent. "Those are your orders. Lieutenant Wellman will take command of your squad until they return to Virginia Beach."

"Lieutenant Wellman is supposed to be on paternity leave."

Jay climbed out of the back of the truck and stepped between the two vehicles so he could join the conversation. "Special Agent—"

"Hernandez," the man said.

"Special Agent Hernandez," Jay began again. "Doesn't it make sense to keep our squad together? Those are our teammates flying with Osman's men."

"I'm just relaying orders," Agent Hernandez said. "My partner and I will join your squad on the flight to follow Osman's men. We have four other teams who will track the other weapons."

Though Brent wasn't thrilled with the new orders, at least Jay would have someone with the authority to arrest Osman's men backing up his squad. "How are Commander Johnson and I supposed to get back to DC?"

"There's a flight leaving for Washington-Reagan in ten minutes. We're holding the flight."

Which meant their gear was staying on the original plane. There was no way they would have time to retrieve it. "Where's the plane?"

"Gate C16. Special Agent Burns here is going to drive you over there." Agent Hernandez climbed out of the truck and held the door open for Brent.

Brent made sure the safety was engaged on his rifle. Not willing to risk Osman's men seeing his weapon, he left it in the cab of the truck and climbed out to speak to Jay. "You'll need to take care of our rifles and gear."

"No problem." Jay said the words, but Brent sensed Jay's uneasiness with the change in plans.

"Handle the next stop just like this one."

"Without the luggage exchange," Jay said.

"Yes, without that." Brent put his hand on Jay's shoulder. "You've got this." He tapped his headset. "Give Quinn and Craig the update."

Jay nodded and took Brent's spot behind the wheel. Agent Hernandez circled the car and took Seth's spot, while Seth and Brent climbed into the truck.

Through his headset, Brent listened to Jay give Quinn and Craig the details on the personnel changes and the plan for when they arrived at their destination.

Brent and Seth's driver navigated out of the private section of the airport, past commercial airplanes, and around luggage carts and ground personnel. When they reached the correct gate, he parked beside the nose of the plane.

"We'll take you up this way." Agent Burns motioned to the metal stairs leading from the tarmac to the Jetway.

"Thanks for the lift." Brent climbed the stairs, using the metal railing to reduce the amount of weight he was putting on his leg.

Seth followed him. "Think they'll let us on without boarding passes?"

"We're about to find out."

Brent reached the top and opened the door into the empty Jetway. It took him only a few steps to reach the open airplane door.

The moment he stepped onto the plane, a flight attendant approached, his beard trimmed close to his face. "Commander Miller and Commander Johnson?"

"That's right."

"You're in seats 1A and 1B." The flight attendant pointed at the two empty seats in the front row.

"We're in first class?" Brent asked.

"Yes, sir."

"Thank you," Brent responded.

"Thank you for your service." The flight attendant nodded before he moved back to the front door.

Brent took the seat by the window, and Seth sat beside him.

They had barely fastened their seat belts when the flight attendant's voice came over the intercom. "Doors armed and crosschecked."

Brent leaned back in his seat. "This sure beats sitting in the back of navy transport."

"Agreed." Seth glanced at him. "The real question is, Who decided we needed to go to DC?"

"And why?" Brent added.

34

Amy looked up from the airport video feed playing on her laptop when the door to the Cabinet Room opened.

Her mother entered, a butler following her with a tray in his hands.

Amy closed her laptop. Though she trusted her mother implicitly, her mother did not have clearance for classified information.

"You can set that down there." Her mom motioned to the empty space beside Amy's laptop.

He set the tray down. A bowl of chicken and rice soup, saltine crackers, a roll, and a glass of ginger ale.

"Thank you, Brandon," her mom said.

"You're welcome, ma'am. Let me know if you need anything else."

"We will."

The butler retreated from the room and closed the door behind him.

"What's all this?" Amy stood and gave her mom a hug. "I didn't think you even knew I was back."

"One advantage of having Secret Service agents all over the place is that they tend to know everything that's going on."

"I can imagine." Amy sat back down.

"How are you feeling?"

"Hungry." Amy pulled the food closer and picked up a saltine cracker. "Thank you for this."

"You're welcome." Her mom put her hand on Amy's shoulder. "Make sure you don't stay down here too late. You need your rest."

"I told Dad I'll go up to the residence when he does."

"Good." Her mom moved to the door. "I'm sure you still have work to do. I'll see you later."

"Thanks, Mom."

As soon as her mom left, Amy opened her laptop again. She hit the Play button to restart the security feed.

Slowly, she ate her dinner while watching for familiar faces. She'd been at this for nearly an hour, and so far, she had yet to find any hint of anyone flying out of Costa Rica to the US who had also been seen at the fortress. Her dad was right. Brent and Seth might be the only ones who would be able to identify the terrorists.

She finished her meal and pushed the tray toward the center of the table.

The door opened, and her dad walked in. "Any luck?"

"No. If any of these guys are Osman's men, they aren't ones who were caught on the body cams, at least not well enough for me to recognize them." Amy leaned back in her chair. "I wish we had surveillance feed on the planes the guardians identified as possibles."

"Me too."

"I hate to say it, but I think our best bet is to pull security feed from the airports where they landed," Amy said. "We'll need some more eyes on this."

"We already have Homeland Security searching, but if I'm not mistaken, extra help just arrived." Her dad leaned toward the door and peeked into the hall. He waved someone forward. "In here."

Amy's heartbeat quickened. "Is Brent here?"

"Did I hear my name?" Brent asked as he walked in.

Amy pushed out of her chair as he moved toward her. His arms came around her, and Amy pulled him close. "Welcome back."

"Thanks." Brent held her for a moment before he stepped back. "Any word yet on the rest of the squad?"

"Last we heard, they were heading for the San Francisco area."

"I didn't expect that." Brent turned to her dad. "I assume you have a specific task for me and Seth?"

"Yes." Her dad motioned to Seth, who stood beside the door. "Go ahead and close that."

Seth pushed the door closed, and they all sat at the table.

"Vanessa and the guardians have identified four planes that could have been carrying the missing four weapons," her dad said. "Amy and the guardians have been searching through the airport security feed in Costa Rica but haven't found anything."

"The external camera views are limited, especially where the private planes are loaded and fueled," Amy said.

"If that's where they flew out of, Osman's men probably never went into the terminal," Seth said.

"He's right." Brent stretched his arm out and rested it on the back of Amy's chair. "They drove straight to the plane in Tegucigalpa."

"I want the two of you to search through the airport security feed for the possible airports here in the US."

"Which cities?"

"San Diego, Houston, Atlanta, and Miami."

"With the pattern we've seen on our suspected targets, I doubt they would hit Houston since it's only a few hours from Dallas," Brent said.

"If Houston is a target, they could drive a weapon there from Dallas," Seth added.

"Miami and San Diego are the most likely targets," Brent said. "They both have a higher population than Atlanta."

Her dad nodded. "You can work in the Situation Room, or I can have a couple secure laptops brought in here."

"We'll have easier access to Vanessa and the guardians if we work here," Seth said.

Brent nodded. "I agree."

Her dad stood. "I'll have some dinner sent in for you as well."

"Thanks, but we ate on the plane." Brent tilted his head to the side. "Do we have you to thank for our upgrade to first class?"

"That wasn't me." Her dad headed for the door. "Sounds like someone at the airline must have wanted to show their appreciation for your service."

"It was nice to get a meal and catch a nap while we were in the air," Seth said.

Brent motioned to Amy's laptop. "Especially since it will likely be a late night."

Amy stifled a yawn. It would be a late night for Brent and Seth. And even though her mother was right, that she needed rest, more than anything, they needed to find the remaining weapons and identify the targets.

35

Albuquerque, Las Vegas, Oakland, San Francisco. Tristan was tired of guessing their end destination. So were Damian, Jay, and the two FBI agents accompanying them.

Agent Burns returned to his seat from his latest consultation with the pilots. "I've got agents at both the Oakland and San Francisco airports. It has to be one of those two."

"The bay area is heavily populated. It makes sense," Jay said.

"Not really." Tristan shook his head. "I thought Osman was trying to hit areas that would suffer from severe weather. San Francisco isn't it."

"Yeah, but there are a lot of tech companies in the area," Jay said.

"No power would kill the economy in the area," Damian added.

"It's like they're waging a multipronged attack using a single weapon," Tristan said.

"They are," Agent Burns said. "The power outages in Vegas and Kansas City have already caused nine deaths and cost the US millions, both in emergency-response needs and in lost enterprise."

"Right now, I just want to get our teammates back and get those guys behind bars," Tristan said.

"I'd like to get home to my wife and daughter too," Jay added.

"How are we playing this at the airport?" Damian asked. "Are we posing as ground crew again?"

"This is FBI jurisdiction," Agent Burns said. "We'll handle taking Osman's men into custody and securing the weapon."

Tristan opened his mouth to object, but Jay spoke before he had the chance to. "You can have jurisdiction as soon as my men are off that plane. Until then, you're stuck with us."

"I don't think you understand—"

"No, you don't understand," Jay countered Agent Burns. "We work with those men day in and day out. If there's a problem, we're the ones who will recognize their signal." Jay gripped his rifle. "Our job is to bring them back home safely, and that's what we're going to do."

"Look, we understand where you're coming from," Agent Burns said, his tone placating. "Really, we do, but the navy has no jurisdiction on US soil."

"We aren't asking for jurisdiction," Jay said. "We just want to make sure we're in position to protect our teammates."

Suspecting the argument was going to continue, Tristan motioned toward the cockpit. "Look, if you can't grant permission for our involvement, we know who can."

"Who?"

"Doug Valdez."

"The secretary of Homeland Security?" Agent Burns eyed Tristan skeptically. "You know him?"

"Yes." Tristan hoped dropping Doug's name would keep them from needing to bother Jim at the White House.

"What's it going to be?" Jay asked. "Are you willing to let us help, or do we need to make a call?"

"*I'll* make the call." Agent Burns stood again and headed for the front of the plane.

Five minutes later, he returned, a stunned look on his face. "Secretary Valdez granted permission for you to back us up."

"That's all we ask," Tristan said.

"If we're going to work together, you'll need to be on our frequency." Jay pulled a paper from his vest and jotted down the correct one. "It's the only way we'll be able to easily communicate with you and our men on the plane."

Agent Burns took the paper from Jay. "Just remember, the FBI's in charge."

Tristan glanced at Jay. Whether the FBI wanted to admit it or not, until Quinn and Craig were off that plane, Jay was calling the shots.

* * *

Jim pushed aside his dinner plate and took a sip of water. When this threat was over, he was going to make a point of eating every meal with Katherine for a week straight, lunch included. But first, he needed to know every other American had that ability too.

The electricity crisis had yet to be resolved in Kansas City or Las Vegas. Almost three days with no heat or any other modern conveniences.

Why was this happening? His prayers had led him to run for president. Inspiration and good people had paved the way for him to take office. Now, not even a month into his presidency, the nation was under attack, with millions of people vulnerable to power outages and the next wave of attacks by Morenta's—or rather, Osman's—people.

Doug stepped into the office doorway and knocked on the open door.

Jim stood. "Please tell me you have good news."

"I have good news and bad news."

Jim was tired of bad news. "I'll take the good news."

"The electricity has been restored in Kansas City."

Relief flowed through Jim. "That is good news. How close are we on restoring power in North Las Vegas?"

"That's the not-so-good news. We tried to keep the power usage stable, but too many people from North Las Vegas have crowded into Vegas proper."

"You're about to tell me the rest of Las Vegas lost power, aren't you?"

"Only one section, but unfortunately, the part that's affected includes the airport."

"One of the busiest airports in the country, out of power as we're going into a weekend?" Jim shook his head. "How long until we can restore power?"

"My people are working on it, but it looks like the reason they lost power was that the virus was transferred into the power grid at the airport," Doug said. "They think they can get North Las Vegas back up within the next few hours, but the rest of Las Vegas is vulnerable."

"What's the latest on overriding the virus?"

"I've spoken to several of the top tech companies," Doug said. "They're close, but the soonest anyone will be able to get the update out there is Monday or Tuesday."

"Let's pray that we can find the missing weapons before Friday."

"That's a constant prayer," Doug said. "I have the latest update from the FBI too. They've taken Osman's men in Dallas into custody as well as the ones who flew to Denver and Chicago."

"So, Vanessa was right about Denver and Chicago being targets." Jim leaned forward. "What about the other two flights we're tracking out of Dallas?"

"Best guess, one is heading for Los Angeles and the other for San Francisco."

"Where is the Saint Squad?"

"On the plane heading for San Francisco," Doug said. "The FBI has been monitoring flights into Detroit, New York, and Orlando as well as the other heavily populated areas we've identified as possible targets."

"Two more targets to find."

"Two targets, four weapons."

"Is it too much to hope that they were destroyed in the missile strike on the fortress?"

"I've been hoping for that, too, but so far, we don't have any intel one way or another to indicate whether those other vehicles got out before we attacked."

Four more weapons. Finding those was the key to moving past this crisis so the rest of the country could get back to living a normal life. As for him and his family, he suspected *normal* was a word they wouldn't be identifying with anytime soon.

36

Tristan sat behind the wheel of a luggage tug, his rifle beside him so it was in easy reach without being visible to anyone passing by. He'd parked beside a private plane that had landed at the San Francisco airport over an hour before because it was next to the spot where Quinn and Craig would be parking momentarily.

Once they had finally ascertained where they were going, Agent Burns had coordinated with airport security and the FAA to allow Tristan's plane to land before Quinn and Craig's.

Damian had donned a safety vest and taken on the role of ground-traffic control along with three FBI agents. Jay had assigned himself sniper duty. Instead of climbing a tree, he'd climbed onto the roof. Two more agents sat in a nearby work truck.

Agent Burns's voice came over Tristan's earpiece. "The plane is taxiing in from the runway."

"Roger," Tristan said, Damian and Jay echoing his response.

"I see the plane," Jay said. "Quinn, do you read?"

Quinn clicked into the mic.

"Stay in the cockpit until everyone gets off," Jay instructed. "Then sweep the passenger compartment to make sure no one is hiding in there."

"Negative," Agent Burns said. "The FBI will clear the plane as soon as everyone is off."

"We aren't debating the mission," Jay said calmly. "Our men can check the cabin without raising suspicions. Quinn, Craig, you have your orders."

Both men clicked into their mic.

The plane came into view from behind a jumbo jet parked a few spots away.

Tristan put his hand on his rifle. "I've got a visual."

"Okay, people," Agent Burns said. "We wait until everyone deplanes before we move in."

The plane approached slowly, as though Quinn were making sure everyone had time to get in position for their arrival.

As soon as the plane came to a stop, Damian moved forward and put the blocks on both sides of the front wheel to keep the aircraft in place. He then waited by the nose of the plane.

The door opened, and the airstair unfolded until it landed on the tarmac. One of Osman's men walked halfway down the stairs, a second peeking out from the plane.

One of the FBI agents looked up and stared.

The man on the stairs froze. Then he backed up a step.

"We've been made," one of the agents said.

All three agents on the ground pulled their weapons. "Federal agents. Freeze!"

Damian repeated the command in Spanish. Tristan lifted his weapon, reminding himself that he was only backup on this op.

The man in front reached for a weapon. He swung it toward the agent nearest him, but the agent fired before he could take aim. Osman's man tumbled down the stairs and landed in a heap at the bottom.

The other man shouted something in Spanish.

"Damian, what's he saying?" Tristan asked.

"He's telling someone to close the door."

A click came over Tristan's headset.

"Hold your fire," Tristan said. "It may be one of our guys closing up the plane."

"Did you all get that?" Jay asked. "Hold your fire."

Agent Burns repeated the command to ensure his agents didn't subject Quinn and Craig to any friendly fire.

Craig appeared at the edge of the open doorway. He retracted the airstair slowly. The door was halfway up when a thump reverberated over the comm unit. The stairs suddenly dropped down again.

Quinn's voice came next. "Enemy secure. We're coming out."

His pistol pressed against the enemy's temple, Quinn pushed Osman's man forward and escorted him down the stairs.

Two of the FBI agents rushed forward. One evaluated and disarmed the injured man, while the other handcuffed the man Quinn handed over.

Craig followed Quinn out of the plane.

"I don't know about you guys, but I'm starving." Quinn rubbed his stomach. "I say we grab some pizza."

"Quinn, you find us some dinner," Jay said through the comm units. "Tristan, check with command to find out where they want us tonight."

Tristan approached Quinn, Craig, and Damian. "I think Jay's getting the hang of this command thing."

"Yeah," Quinn said. "He didn't even have to climb a tree."

"No." Tristan pointed at Jay's current position. "Just a building."

37

Vanessa tucked Talia into bed, clinging to this little moment of normalcy. Her quick trip to Denver had been productive, but between that, her research with Kade and Renee, and the trip to the White House, she felt like she had jammed a week's worth of work into one day.

Kade and Renee had returned to their home-on-wheels, which was once again parked by the stables. Knowing the two of them, they were probably watching airport video feed as their before-bed entertainment.

Vanessa ran her hand over Talia's tight little curls before stepping back and leaving the room. She cast a glance at her own bedroom. The idea of going to bed early held an appeal, but she doubted she would be able to sleep until she checked for the latest intel updates.

She headed downstairs to the office. Her mom appeared in the entryway as she reached it.

"I'm going to read for a little while before bed." Her mom kissed her cheek. "Don't stay up too late."

"I'll try not to." Vanessa would try. She just couldn't make any guarantees.

"See you in the morning."

Vanessa nodded. "Thanks again for helping out."

"I'm happy to be here." Her mom started up the stairs before turning back to look over her shoulder. "And I'm serious. Get some sleep tonight."

"I will." *Eventually.*

Vanessa walked into the office and closed the door. She retrieved her secure laptop from the vaulted cabinet in the closet and set it on Jim's desk. Technically, it was her desk now that she was living here.

She logged in to the guardian database, the one place she could get the latest intel from all of the US government agencies as well as any analysis the eight guardians and their various support staff members performed.

A flash message appeared from Kade, announcing that power had been restored to Kansas City. Thank goodness.

Grateful for that tidbit of good news, Vanessa pulled up the latest message from Manuel, which he'd posted only five minutes ago. He had returned to the fortress to survey the damage. Several photos accompanied his analysis: only one SUV had been present at the time of the strike.

Vanessa's heart sank. Even though she, Kade, and Renee had spent the better part of their day researching flights from Costa Rica and considering possible destinations for Osman's men, the whole time she had hoped the exercise was unnecessary, that the missing four weapons had been destroyed.

She grabbed her guardian cell phone and pulled up *M* in her contacts.

Manuel answered on the second ring.

"How sure are you about the vehicle destroyed in the missile attack?"

"Ninety-five percent," Manuel said. "I only found one engine, one radiator, and four tires. The SUV remains were far enough away from the fortress that most of the pieces were still intact."

"Could any of the others have been closer to the fortress?" Vanessa asked.

"I looked, but I didn't find any other evidence of vehicles in the area where they were loading," Manuel said. "My guess is that when the Saint Squad blew up that vehicle, it knocked the tracker off the one beside it."

"Which would explain why Brent only found signals for the two you all tracked to Honduras."

"Any luck yet finding a plane leaving Costa Rica?" Manuel asked.

"We've narrowed down the possibilities to four, but all of them were boarded away from security cameras," Vanessa said. "We've moved on to searching traffic-camera feed for vehicles leaving the airport."

"What about outgoing flights to the possible target cities?" Manuel asked.

"The CIA is working on it. They're looking through possibilities from Nicaragua, Honduras, Belize, El Salvador, and Costa Rica."

"I'll check the ships leaving from Honduras and Belize too. It's a long shot, but someone could have hopped on a cruise ship to Miami."

"Or a private charter."

"I'll look into it."

"Thanks, Manuel." Vanessa ended the call and set her phone aside. An alert popped up in the guardian message board, this one from Kristi, the group's financial expert. At the same time, Vanessa's cell phone buzzed with an incoming text, also from Kristi.

URGENT: Financial breach—Ryan National Bank. Check the message board for details.

Vanessa scanned Kristi's post, which detailed thousands of unauthorized withdrawals from customers, all of them residents of Kansas City and North Las Vegas.

Vanessa dialed Kristi's number.

Kristi answered on the first ring. "You saw my message."

"Yes. How did this happen?"

"I'm not positive, but it looks like someone has used Ryan National Bank's app to access customer accounts," Kristi said. "The bank started getting complaints this morning, but their call center has been going crazy for the past half hour. Most of the calls are coming from Kansas City."

"What about the customers in Las Vegas?" Vanessa asked.

"Only a handful of complaints have come in from there, but the number of suspicious withdrawals is in the thousands."

"Kansas City has their power back on. North Las Vegas doesn't."

"I know this sounds crazy," Kristi said, "but I think Morenta set this up to hack into people's accounts while they were without power so they wouldn't see the transactions until it was too late to do anything about it."

"When did the transactions start?" Vanessa asked.

"This morning."

"For anyone who didn't evacuate their homes, they probably would have lost battery power on their phones by then." Vanessa let out a frustrated sigh. "How much money are we talking about?"

"Eighty-four million dollars."

"Oh wow."

"I'm starting a search through other banks that are common to both areas, but needless to say, if we have more power outages, especially if they happen in larger cities, Osman will easily triple that amount," Kristi said. "Ryan National Bank is working on a fix for their app, but if they can't find one and we have another power outage, we may have to force them to disable their app and their debit-card system, which will prevent their customers from accessing their funds at a time when they may need them the most."

"What a nightmare. I'll get the CIA on this to see if they can trace the money."

"Better put the FDIC on alert too. Nearly all of this money is insured."

"I'll take care of it. Thanks, Kristi." Vanessa hung up and crafted emails to both the CIA and the FDIC describing the problem. As soon as she finished, she picked up her phone again and called the White House.

After Vanessa spoke with both the White House operator and one of the president's executive assistants, Jim answered.

"Sir, I'm sorry to be the bearer of more bad news, but we have a banking crisis brewing," Vanessa said.

"Banking?" Jim repeated.

"Yes." Vanessa relayed everything she and Kristi had discussed. "I don't know what bank you and your family use, but you may want to make sure your personal funds are secure."

"We spread our money among several different institutions, including Ryan National." Jim sighed. "But if I pull money out of there, it will be like participating in insider trading on the stock market."

"Insider trading is illegal. Pulling money out of your own bank accounts isn't."

"You're right, but we need a fix on their banking system so others are protected as well," Jim said.

"Kristi is working with them on it right now. If they can't fix it, they'll have to disable it," Vanessa said. "That should protect people's money, but it will prevent them from having access to it when they're in the middle of a crisis."

"So, anyone using that bank wouldn't be able to rent a hotel room or use a debit card at the grocery store?"

"No," Vanessa said. "They wouldn't."

* * *

Brent rubbed at his eyes. "I'm not seeing anything."

"Me neither." Seth tipped his head back and yawned. "Ready to call it a night?"

"Yeah. Might as well." Brent closed his laptop and pushed back from the table. "It's already nine. Do you want to stay here tonight? I'm sure Jim and Katherine won't mind."

"They've pretty much given me an open invitation, but I'm going to head home. I'd like to see my wife and daughter while I have the chance."

Brent felt the dart of disappointment. He could see his wife, but children might never be in his future. He tamped down his jealousy and nodded. "I'll see you tomorrow."

Seth motioned to his laptop. "Do you mind securing this for me? If I stop in the mil aides' office, who knows if I'll really make it out of here tonight."

"No problem. I have to secure mine anyway." Brent picked up both laptops, slid them and the cords into the soft-sided briefcase they had been delivered in, and carried the case into the hall.

Seth gave a last wave and headed for the West Wing exit that led to the Eisenhower building. Brent turned the other direction. He made it as far as the mansion before a Secret Service agent stopped him.

"Sir, can I help you?" the agent said.

"I'm just heading to the residence." Brent motioned in the direction of the door that led outside to the rose garden.

"I'm sorry, sir, but the mansion is closed to visitors. No one is permitted to enter without advanced authorization."

Or a badge. Like the one stashed in Brent's duffel on the plane that had taken him to Dallas.

"I'm sorry. I didn't have the chance to grab my badge before I came into town," Brent said. "I'm Brent Miller. I'm on the list of authorized guests."

The agent moved to the security desk behind him and typed in Brent's name on his computer. The monitor dinged, and the agent straightened. "Do you have any ID?"

Brent pulled out his military ID and passed it to the agent.

"Thank you." The man checked his name and glanced up at him before handing it back. "I'm sorry about that, sir. You can go ahead."

"Thanks."

Brent walked outside and passed through the West Colonnade to the White House mansion. He had barely stepped through the door when another Secret Service agent blocked his path.

"Do you have a badge?" the woman asked.

Brent shook his head. "Sorry, I don't have it with me."

He went through the process again of giving his name and showing his military ID. Again, he was given permission to proceed. He climbed the stairs to the second floor, where yet another Secret Service agent was posted. Thankfully, this one recognized him.

Brent nodded a greeting and headed toward the east bedroom, where he and Amy were assigned when they visited.

Katherine appeared in the main hall before he could cross it. "Brent. Thank goodness you're home safe."

Brent turned toward her, not surprised when his mother-in-law hugged him. "It's good to be back." Katherine released him, and he said, "I assume Amy's already in our room."

"Yes." Katherine waved toward the hall that led to the east and west bedrooms. "Jim mentioned that you arrived without any luggage. Amy said you already had a change of clothes in the dresser, but I had a fresh uniform delivered for you."

"I appreciate that. If I can get security to give me a second badge, I'll be all set."

"Did Secret Service give you a hard time on your way up?"

"They're just doing their jobs." Brent nodded at the man standing a short distance away. "Only a handful of them know I'm married to your daughter."

"After you disappeared in Nicaragua, I can understand how smart you and Amy were to keep your identity out of the press." Katherine stepped back. "I'll let you get some sleep. And I'll call security about getting you that new badge. It might be best for you to have one they can keep here in case something like this happens again in the future."

"Thanks, Katherine," Brent said. "I really appreciate it."

He entered the short hall that separated his and Amy's room from Charlie's guest room. Brent opened the door, surprised that the light was already off. He checked his watch. Only nine thirty.

He closed the door behind him and turned on the bathroom light before continuing into the bedroom. In the wash of light spilling into the room, he made out Amy in the bed, her auburn hair contrasting against the white linens. He secured the laptops in their closet and slipped off his boots, leaving those in the closet as well.

He peeked at Amy again. She hadn't stirred. A new disappointment washed over him. He had hoped for at least a few minutes alone with his wife while they were both awake.

Turning, he headed back toward the bathroom. Time to grab a shower and wash away the grime from his long day of traveling. Tomorrow, they would find the last of Osman's weapons, and he and Amy would finally get their lives back.

38

Amy's eyes fluttered open, and a smile bloomed on her face. Brent was home, and he was lying beside her. She reached out and draped her arm across his chest. Lazily, his eyes still closed, he lifted his hand and laid it on top of hers.

"Are you awake?" Amy asked.

"Mmm." He stretched out his arm and drew her closer.

She snuggled into his side, her head resting on his chest. His steady heartbeat thumped beneath her, further proof that her prayers had been answered.

"Sorry I fell asleep so early last night." Amy brushed her hair back from her face. "I didn't even hear you come in."

"Seth and I stayed in the Cabinet Room watching airport-surveillance feed until after nine."

"Any luck?"

"No. We'll start looking through the feed from Houston and Atlanta today." Brent lifted his hand and checked the time on his watch. "What do you have planned for today?"

"I'm not sure." Amy sat up and reached for her cell phone on the nightstand. Five messages, one from each of the remaining members of Brent's squad. "It looks like my first order of business is to get the rest of the squad home. They got stranded in San Francisco."

"They should be able to assign the plane they went in on to take them to Virginia Beach."

"It's being recalled to the carrier."

"Make Jay the priority. He never should have been on this mission in the first place."

"I know, but I'm glad he was there."

"Yeah, me too." Brent sat up. "I should get dressed. Knowing Seth, he's already on his way over."

Amy checked the time: 6:12 a.m.

"I don't know," she said. "If he didn't go home until after nine, Talia was already in bed. I'm sure he'll want to see her before he comes to work."

Brent's expression clouded for a brief moment. "Yeah, you're right." He climbed out of bed and put on his uniform.

The news of her pregnancy bubbled inside her. Even though she had thought of so many ways to tell Brent, she couldn't wait any longer. Words jumbled inside her, anticipation building. She climbed out of bed. "There's something I want to talk to you about."

"What's that?"

She took his hands in hers. "You know how I went to the doctor the day you shipped out?"

"Yeah." Concern flashed in his eyes. "You're okay, aren't you?"

"I'm fine," Amy assured him. "The doctor said I should start feeling better in a few weeks."

"That's a relief."

A knock sounded at the door.

Amy let out a sigh. Did someone always have to show up every time she wanted to share the good news? She grabbed her robe from the closet and pulled it on.

Brent opened the door. Seth stood in the hall.

"What are you doing here so early?" Brent asked. "We figured you'd stay home long enough to play with the baby this morning."

"I did." Seth grinned. "She was nice enough to wake up at five."

Amy's earlier irritation faded, and she couldn't help but laugh. "You know, most parents don't consider their children waking up at that hour a good thing."

"Maybe not, but it gave me the chance to play with her a bit before I had to leave."

"She must have known you were home," Amy said.

"Maybe." Seth turned his attention back to Brent. "Sorry to come by so early, but I wasn't sure if you'd heard the latest."

"What latest?" Brent asked.

"Looks like Morenta's organization set up a huge hack into Ryan National Bank. Millions have been siphoned out of accounts from customers in the areas affected by the power outages."

"Oh no." A wave of dizziness hit Amy, and she put her hand on the wall to steady herself. "Does my dad know?"

"Yeah. Vanessa called him last night."

"Has the FBI located any of the missing weapons?" Brent asked.

"Not yet. They're staking out the main power plants in the cities we think they're planning to hit, but so far, nothing."

"We'd better get started on the rest of the airport security feed." Brent retrieved the computer bag from the closet. He leaned in and kissed Amy. "Can we talk later?"

Amy fought back her disappointment and nodded. "I'll let you know when I get the squad's travel sorted out."

"Thanks." Brent stepped out into the hall with Seth. "I'll see you later."

He closed the door, and Amy sat on her bed. Another twenty-four hours until the attacks were supposed to begin. Another forty-eight hours until they would know whether they'd successfully stopped them.

Amy headed for the shower. The sooner she took care of the Saint Squad, the sooner she could help Brent and Seth search for the latest needle in a haystack.

Her cell phone buzzed. She laughed when she read the message from Quinn. *Can we come home yet?*

Rather than text, she called him.

"Oh good," Quinn said when he answered. "You're up."

"It's almost six thirty here. Why are you awake?"

"We think that if you can get Osman's plane fueled for us, we can hijack it so we can get home."

Amy laughed. "What is it with you and hijacking planes?"

"Craig's claiming credit for the last hijacking because it was his idea, and Tristan hijacked the helicopter. I think it's my turn."

"Let me see what our options are." Amy pulled up the scheduled military flights for the next few hours. Nothing in the San Francisco area heading to Virginia. The first commercial flights would leave in a few hours, but with the weaponry the squad was surely carrying, that could get complicated. "Give me an hour to make some calls. I'll see if I can get the FBI to authorize you to fly the plane here to Virginia."

Quinn let out a long-suffering sigh. "Fine."

"And, Quinn, don't wake everyone else up until I have a ride for you."

"Too late," Quinn said repentantly. "We're heading back to the airport in a few minutes."

"Tristan is going to strangle you if this doesn't work out."

"So, make it work out," Quinn said.

Amy just shook her head. "I'll call you later." She hung up the phone and dialed Doug's cell number.

Doug answered on the third ring. Thankfully, he sounded awake and alert. "Hey, Amy. Is everything okay?"

"Yes, but I'm hoping you can do me a favor."

"What's that?"

Amy explained the situation. "Is there any way you can authorize the Saint Squad to fly Osman's plane here to Virginia?"

"I'll take care of that if they'll do me a favor."

"What's that?"

"I want whoever isn't flying the plane to help look through the video footage from the airports," Doug said. "The Saint Squad are the only ones who have seen any of these people in person. From what I understand, a lot of Morenta's men weren't caught on camera, which means they'll have the best chance of recognizing our terrorists."

"You get the video footage and computers to the airport, and they'll make that their in-flight movie."

"Great. I'll have Special Agent Burns meet them at the airport. He can get them what they need."

"I'm not sure he'll be thrilled to find out the squad wants to leave as soon as the plane is fueled."

"It won't be a problem," Doug said. "I spoke with him a few minutes ago. He's been up all night, interrogating Osman's men."

"Any luck?"

"Best we can tell, they don't know anything beyond their individual assignments."

"That's consistent with the witness statement Brent got in Nicaragua. The man who escaped only knew what city he was supposed to attack."

"Which is why we need to find where the rest of Osman's men came into in the US."

"I'll call the squad and let them know what's going on," Amy said. "Thanks for your help."

"No problem, but do me a favor now."

"What's that?"

"Tell them to let Special Agents Burns and Hernandez sleep on the flight. They've had a rough night."

"I'll do my best."

39

What a morning. Over an hour of Vanessa receiving updates from Kristi after Seth had left for work. That had been followed by another hour playing with Talia while Vanessa's mom had gone grocery shopping and another two hours reading through the latest updates from the various intelligence agencies. Then there had been the hour of traffic while driving to the White House. Why everyone had felt the need to be on the road at ten thirty in the morning was beyond her.

Vanessa walked into the Cabinet Room, where Seth, Brent, and Amy had set up their temporary office. The Saint Squad working in the White House—who would have thought when they'd started out together nearly a decade ago that they would end up here, all four of them, with badges that granted them access to every corner of this historic building? The names of the rest of the squad and their wives had also been placed on the list that allowed them access to the first family without additional background checks. It was amazing how far this miraculous group had come.

"Any luck yet?" Vanessa asked.

Seth looked up from where he sat at the far side of the table. "No. We're running out of places to look."

Vanessa closed the door behind her.

Amy swiveled in her chair. "Have the guardians come up with anything new?"

"Nothing except confirmation that the weapons made it out of the fortress before the missile strike." She circled to take the seat beside her husband and pulled her laptop from her bag.

"What about the banking problems?" Seth asked.

"The guardians found two more banks that were hit during the night," Vanessa said. "They're trying to trace the funds."

Brent looked up from his laptop. "How much did Osman's guys get?"

"Another hundred forty-two million," Vanessa said.

"Oh man." Brent groaned.

"We have got to find Osman," Amy said.

"And I'm here to help." Vanessa opened her laptop and logged in. "Can one of you send me a link to the airport surveillance?"

"You can help me look through the Atlanta airport. You can start with cameras nine through twelve." Seth sent her a secure email, which popped up on her screen a second later.

"Got it." Vanessa opened the link and accessed the surveillance feed.

She opened all four camera views and studied them. Two were exterior views of terminal gates. The others were of the interior. Suspecting Osman would avoid going into the actual airport, where he might be spotted, she expanded the image of one of the external views. She sped it up to eight times the usual speed, slowing it every time someone new appeared.

Fifteen minutes passed in silence.

"I've checked the flight plans for the private planes that came into Houston and Atlanta," Amy said. "Only six refueled and left within four hours of arriving."

"Where were they going?" Vanessa asked.

"From Houston, there were four: Vancouver, Orlando, Philadelphia, and Boston."

"And the ones from Atlanta?" Brent asked.

"Another one to Orlando and one to Detroit."

"All of which could be targets," Vanessa said. "Do you have the gate locations for the two planes in Atlanta?"

"Neither of them came to the actual terminal, but I have the locations of where they were refueled. I'll send those to you." Amy tapped on her keyboard. A moment later, a new email showed up on Vanessa's screen.

"I'll take the one in Atlanta going to Orlando," Vanessa said.

"I'll take the other one," Seth said.

"Amy, send me the ones for Houston," Brent said.

"Already did. I sent the refueling times too. That should narrow down the window you need to look through." Amy pushed back from the table. "While you three start on those, I'm going to see what I can do to get us some food. I'm about ready for a lunch break."

Vanessa pulled up the correct video feed based on the information Amy had sent her. "Sorry. I should have picked something up on my way in. I didn't expect it to take so long to drive over here."

"I think my dad will be okay with us asking for the kitchen to make something for us." Amy headed for the door. "I'll be right back."

"I think she's adjusting to her new role of First Daughter," Seth said.

"As long as we don't have to deal with that title outside these walls, I'm okay with it," Brent said.

Amy returned a moment later. "Sarah's going have something delivered from the Navy Mess."

"Thanks, Amy."

"No problem." She sat back down.

Vanessa located the security footage she was looking for and fast-forwarded to the time the plane in question had landed. Then she slowed it to four times the normal speed. When there wasn't anything on the screen beyond the empty tarmac, she sped it up again, not slowing it until the plane came into view and the door opened.

She hit the button to play at normal speed, zooming in on the now-open airplane door. Several men deplaned, two of them heading for the luggage compartment at the back of the plane. They opened it and started unloading. Suitcases came first, followed by a silver case that matched the description she had read in the intel reports. "I may have something. Seth, look at this."

Seth leaned closer. "That looks like the cases they had the pulse weapons in."

The men pulled out an identical case and set it beside the first.

"There's another one," Amy said.

Brent gestured to the screen. "If there are four, we have our plane."

The men unloaded a few more bags, including one more silver case, then they closed the luggage compartment.

"They only had three."

"That makes sense," Amy said. "If the plane is continuing to another target city, they would leave one in the cargo hold."

Another man walked down the airstair to the tarmac, and Vanessa zoomed in. "Oh, wow."

"What?"

"I think that's Osman."

Seth's eyes widened. "Sure looks like him to me."

Brent stood and circled the table so he could look over Vanessa's shoulder. "I don't believe this."

"What?" Vanessa asked. "That Osman came himself?"

"No." Brent waved in her direction. "That we've been working on this for hours and you find Osman in less than thirty minutes."

"She must be living right." Seth winked at Vanessa.

Amy moved to the phone. "I'll let Doug and my dad know."

"Vanessa, let intel know where to focus our search," Brent said. "Atlanta is probably a target city. And we need to know where that plane went next."

"And what other planes flew out of Atlanta that could be carrying the other three weapons."

Vanessa nodded. "I'll get the word out."

40

A MEETING WITH HIS PRESS secretary, followed by an update by his intelligence advisory committee, and then a strategy session with Doug. Jim's head was spinning, and he was ready to get off this merry-go-round of chaos.

Sitting on the couch across from Doug in the Oval Office, Jim leaned forward and rested his elbows on his knees. "Is there anything else we can do to protect the remaining cities we expect to be affected?"

"We've added copper shielding to all the main substations, and FEMA is sending emergency provisions to New York, Detroit, and Orlando. They have more trucks ready to roll once we identify the final target."

"Brent and Seth are working on that now."

Doug's cell phone rang. "Sorry about that." He pulled his phone from his pocket and glanced at the number. "I'm sorry. It's my office. Do you mind if I take this?"

"Go ahead."

Doug answered. "Valdez." Only a few seconds passed before his jaw clenched. He listened for several more seconds. "Thanks for letting me know."

As soon as Doug ended the call, Jim asked, "What's wrong now?"

"The power situation in Las Vegas has expanded to include three more sections of the city, including the strip." Doug shook his head. "They don't know if they'll be able to get power restored to the airport or the strip before Sunday."

"The weekend starts tomorrow, and Las Vegas has gone dark." Jim ran his hand through his hair to work out some nerves.

"I'm afraid so," Doug said. "At least we've intercepted all of Osman's men who were set to attack the western targets. That should prevent further cascading power outages in that part of the country."

"I hope so."

Jim's phone rang. Since he was closer to the door leading to his secretaries' office, he opened the door rather than answering the phone.

Amy stood beside Sarah's desk. Sarah hung up the phone, and Amy moved toward him. "I have new intel you need."

"Come in." Jim waited for her to pass through the door, then closed it behind her. "What's going on?"

"Vanessa found another target. Osman and his men landed in Atlanta, Georgia."

Doug stood. "Osman is here?"

"Yeah. Vanessa's alerting the FBI and CIA so they can focus on tracking where Osman and his men went from Atlanta."

"Make sure she shares whatever facial images she can capture off the surveillance feed," Doug said.

"I will," Amy said.

Doug pulled his phone from his pocket. "I'll get FEMA rolling to Atlanta."

Jim nodded and turned to Amy while Doug made his phone call. "You're sure it was Osman?"

"Yes."

Jim sat on the couch. "So, that missile strike was a waste after all." They had been so close to stopping all this before it had even started.

"The strike wasn't a waste." Amy sat beside him and put her hand on his arm. "You made sure Osman wouldn't have more support, and we have a good idea of how many of his men are still on the loose."

"Two men per city?" Jim asked.

"That's our guess."

Doug hung up the phone and reclaimed his seat across from Jim. "How many of Osman's men did you see get off the plane?"

"Ten. And they unloaded three of the silver cases, which we believe are housing the weapons."

"You're guessing the fourth weapon remained on the plane?" Doug said.

"It would make sense," Amy said. "That plane continued on to La Guardia. They would have left one weapon to attack New York."

"What's our next step?" Jim asked. "Obviously, Osman and his men are already in place to strike."

"According to our intel, we have until tomorrow before that's going to happen," Doug said.

"But we don't know what time tomorrow," Jim said. "It could be six in the morning or six at night."

"We'll work on tracking down their hotel accommodations," Doug said.

"Assuming they're staying in hotels." Jim had seen enough during his time on the Senate Intelligence Committee to know that well-thought-out plans were put in place long before they were executed. "Morenta was a planner. He likely has some longer-term rental that started months ago."

"He's right," Amy said. "We don't have a lot of time to stop him."

"But we have a lot of manpower to try," Doug said. "We can track their movements through traffic cameras and search through rental agreements that started after Yago Paquito was taken hostage."

"I assume you already have enhanced security at all of the power plants," Amy said.

"Yes, but it might not be a bad idea to add some more," Doug said.

"What did you have in mind?" Jim asked.

"The Saint Squad," Doug said. "They're in the air now, on their way back to Virginia Beach. I recommend diverting them to Atlanta."

"Why Atlanta?" Jim asked.

"Because it's the closest city to their homes," Doug said. "If we have any cascade effects from a successful attack, that's the location that would be the most likely to affect their families."

"What can they do that your agents can't?" Jim asked.

"They've seen Osman and his men in person," Doug said. "And honestly, I wouldn't mind having their inspiration and skills where Osman was last seen."

"I can't fault you there," Jim said. Inspiration might be the only way they would stop the attacks in all four cities, and the Saint Squad was one of the best special ops teams in the military. "Amy, what do you think? They've been on one mission after another for days."

"I'm sure they slept last night, and Doug's right. If they have the chance to help protect their families, they'll want to be involved."

"Then, make it happen," Jim said. "Let me know if you need my help."

"We will." Doug stood.

Amy stood as well. "I'd better get back in there. We're going to watch the rest of the Atlanta security feed to see if we can narrow down where Osman and his men went."

"I'll get Homeland, the FBI, and the CIA on board with the search."

"Good," Amy said. "The more eyes we have on this, the better. We're running out of time."

Jim stood as Doug and Amy walked out of his office. The grandfather clock across the room struck one. Amy was right. They were running out of time.

41

Tristan sat in the back of the private plane, the seating area resembling a cozy living room rather than a traditional commercial aircraft. Damian and Craig sat at a small table, snacking on the food they'd picked up at the convenience store on the way to the airport. Jay had taken the copilot's seat, with Quinn piloting the plane. Their two FBI agent passengers chose seats in the back of the plane, both of them now awake and busily working on their laptops.

From his seat beside the window, Tristan stared out at the puffy white clouds beneath them. Another hour and they would be home. Or at least at their home base. If he was lucky, he'd be able to swing by Riley's work to see her on her afternoon break before stopping at the babysitter's house to pick up the kids. He missed them.

The plane adjusted course.

Damian and Craig both looked up.

"Did you feel that?" Craig asked.

"Yeah." Tristan unbuckled his seat belt and stood. "That wasn't a minor course correction."

"What's wrong?" Agent Burns asked.

"I don't know, but I'm going to find out." Tristan walked to the cockpit and opened the door that separated it from the passenger compartment. "What's going on? Why did we change course?"

"New orders." Quinn's focus never deviated from the instrument panel.

Jay looked over his shoulder at Tristan. "We're being redirected to Atlanta. Osman was seen there last night."

"And?" Tristan glanced at their FBI passengers. "Don't tell me we're making a detour just to drop our FBI friends off."

"No." A flicker of disappointment crossed Jay's face. "They want us there too."

Tristan shook his head. "Sorry, Jay."

"It is what it is." Jay motioned toward the back of the plane. "Can you let Agents Burns and Hernandez know what's going on?"

"Yeah, but I don't think they'll be happy about having us involved," Tristan said. "They've been so territorial during this whole operation; I doubt that's going to change now."

"They spend their careers dealing with who has jurisdiction over what," Jay said. "Obviously, a bunch of navy SEALs don't have jurisdiction in the US."

"If we come across Osman and his men, it doesn't matter much who stops them," Quinn said.

Tristan stared at his brother-in-law. "Are you okay? You've been surprisingly logical ever since the carrier."

"I've hijacked a helicopter and two planes this week. I'm great."

"Technically, I hijacked the helicopter," Tristan countered. "And you've flown this plane twice with government permission."

"Fine. I hijacked this plane twice and helped hijack a helicopter, right, Jay?" Quinn said.

"Don't ask me. I'm not getting involved in your petty arguments."

Quinn shot a grin at Tristan before he focused on Jay. "You have to."

"Why?"

Tristan's own grin formed. "Because you're in command."

Jay narrowed his eyes for a brief moment. "Okay. Tristan, go tell the FBI guys what's happening and then bring me and Quinn something to eat. I'm hungry."

"Yes!" Quinn's grin widened.

"I'm not sure I like the in-command version of Jay," Tristan said.

Jay's only response was to give the next order. "Have Craig and Damian do an inventory on our weapons, and see if the FBI can get us some more ammo. Best to be prepared."

Tristan furrowed his brow. "I think I just turned into Jay's secretary."

"Hey, someone has to do it," Quinn said. "I'm still busy hijacking a plane."

* * *

Brent rolled his head from one side to the other to stretch his neck. He, Seth, Amy, and Vanessa had been staring at screens for hours, but since Vanessa's discovery of the plane that had landed in Atlanta, they hadn't found any evidence of where Osman's men had ended up beyond the plane landing in New York.

Amy looked up from her laptop. "I don't see any sign of Osman or any of his men leaving on another flight from Atlanta."

"Maybe the plane to New York dropped a few people off and continued to Detroit," Seth suggested.

"I don't think so." Vanessa waved at her screen. "The FBI is at La Guardia now. The plane is still there."

"Vanessa, put in the request to Homeland to search for private planes from La Guardia to Detroit," Brent said. "Better have them check JFK while they're at it. It's not hard for someone to fly into one airport and leave out of another."

"It's not easy either," Amy said. "It's worth checking though."

Brent's phone rang. Jay calling. "Hey, Jay. Any luck finding Osman's men?"

"None. We can't find a second plane leaving here with them on it," Jay said. "The FBI agents we flew in with are working on getting us the video feed for the external cameras and the rental car area."

"You think they drove out of there?"

"If Atlanta is one of the targets, two of them would have stayed," Jay said. "I'm wondering if the ones headed to Orlando chose to drive. It's a seven-and-a-half-hour drive from here."

"They could have driven down last night and still had plenty of time to get to wherever they're planning to plant the weapon."

Brent debated how to best use the squad's resources. Have his men search through video feed, or search the likely target areas in the city? "Let the FBI handle the surveillance feed for now. They can send it up to us, and we'll help."

"What do you want us to do?"

"Drive over to the main power plant and visit other likely targets," Brent said. "If the attack is tomorrow, Osman's men will likely scout out their target today."

"That's a long shot."

"I know, but we might get lucky," Brent said. "Or inspired."

"We'll be sure to pray before we set out," Jay said.

"And, Jay, I'm sorry we couldn't get you home."

"Like you said, the attack is supposed to happen tomorrow. We stop it, and we can all be home for the weekend."

"Positive thinking. I like it." Brent leaned back in his chair. "Keep me informed."

"I will."

Brent hung up and gave everyone the latest from Jay.

"If Osman's men did drive to Orlando, that would explain why we couldn't find another plane," Amy said.

"Technically, they could have driven from New York to Detroit, too, but that's got to be at least a ten-hour drive."

"But still doable on their timetable," Vanessa said.

"But why would they use private planes for all their strike teams who flew into Dallas, but only have one for the teams who flew into Atlanta?" Amy asked.

"Maybe they had to adjust based on the number of planes they had access to," Vanessa said.

"Or the number of pilots," Seth said.

"That would make sense," Brent said. "The targets on the western side of the country are a lot more spread out. Driving wouldn't be a viable option."

"Sounds like we need to shift to looking for the cars they might have used," Amy said. "Do you want to split up again? Two of us can take Atlanta, and two can take La Guardia."

"Yes. Naturally, we should have two vehicles at both airports." Brent opened his email. Jay had already forwarded the links for the Atlanta surveillance feed. "Amy and I will take Atlanta. Vanessa, see what you can do to get what you need for La Guardia."

Vanessa picked up her phone and sent a text.

"While we're waiting for the extra camera angles for La Guardia, do you want me to go find us some dinner?" Seth asked.

"Amy, can you text your mom? Maybe she can have someone send something over for us."

"No problem." Amy sent the text. A moment later, her phone chimed. "Mom said dinner will be here around six."

Brent checked the time on his computer screen. Half an hour until dinner. "Great. Seth and Vanessa, want to help us look at the Atlanta airport until you get what you need?"

"Might as well," Seth said. "Send it over."

Brent forwarded Jay's email to Seth, Vanessa, and Amy.

"I really hope we can spot them soon," Amy said. "Ideally, with their cars' license plates."

"That would be nice," Vanessa agreed. "A little GPS magic, and we can have these guys behind bars before the day is out."

Brent stifled a yawn. "I'm already praying for that."

42

Amy zoomed in on the image of four men approaching a white SUV.

All the men were in their twenties and thirties, all fit, all of average height and build. Their dress ranged from khakis to cargo pants, exactly the type of casual wear that would make it easy to blend in.

A driver climbed out and opened the back. The men stepped off the curb, and Amy got her first good look at their luggage: two silver cases, a carry-on bag, and three soft-sided duffels.

"I think I found them." Amy rewound the image to where the men and their luggage were clearly visible. She froze it and hit the Print button.

Brent leaned close. He pointed at the man on the edge of the screen. "I remember that guy from the fortress."

Relief filled Amy. They were getting close. She zoomed in on the man Brent indicated. "I'll print images of their faces to send to the local authorities."

"Get as many views as you can," Brent said.

The printer in the corner of the room whirred to life once again as Amy printed several more images.

"If we get lucky, the FBI can run facial recognition and ID these guys," Amy said.

"Hoping they can ping their cell phones?" Seth asked.

"That would be nice." Brent moved to the printer across the room.

"You're assuming they have personal cell phones with them," Vanessa said. "It's more likely Osman would give them all burner phones. That's what Morenta would do."

"Probably." Amy zoomed in on another terrorist and hit Print.

"Can you see the license plate?" Seth asked.

"No. The jersey wall is in the way, but they're in a Toyota Highlander."

Seth shook his head. "One of the most popular SUVs in the country."

Amy jotted down the camera number and time stamp and handed it to Brent. "Here. You can try to pick them up on the next camera when they're leaving. I'll see if the license plate is visible when they arrive." She rewound it again, only going back four minutes to when the SUV arrived. She zoomed in. "Dang it. A car shielded the license plate when the SUV pulled up to the curb."

"I've got an idea." Brent pulled up the list of security images and retrieved the feed from a parking lot.

"Where's that?"

"The cell phone lot. If these guys waited for their buddies to call them, we might get lucky."

"Amy, see if they might have circled through the pickup area," Vanessa said.

"Good idea."

Amy backed up the image again, slowing it every time a white SUV passed by. "Do you have any idea how many people drive white SUVs?"

"I know four are parked in the cell lot."

"Get me the plate numbers, and I'll run them all," Seth said.

"The only two I can see are the wrong make and model," Brent said. "I'll see if I can pick up the other two when they leave the lot."

Amy spotted another white SUV and confirmed it was a Highlander. She zoomed in and identified the driver as the man who had opened the trunk. She hit Pause. "Found it."

"Got him," Brent said an instant later.

"You got the plate?" Seth asked.

"North Carolina plates. The first three are alpha zulu charlie. It looks like the next one is a seven."

"It is. The last four are seven one two six."

"I'll call Doug," Seth said. "He'll be able to pull the registration and get the FBI to track the GPS."

Seth made the call and relayed the license number and their suspicions that some of Osman's men could be driving to Orlando and Detroit.

Someone knocked, and the door swung open. Amy's mom walked in, followed by her dad and a butler pushing a serving cart.

"Is everyone ready for a dinner break?" her mom asked.

"Perfect timing." Amy looked up at her dad. "We just found the license plate of the car that picked up Osman's men in Atlanta."

Her dad's tense posture relaxed slightly. "That's great news."

Seth ended his call. "Doug's having the FBI track down the vehicle. We should hear something within the next fifteen minutes or so."

"You can fill Jim in while we eat," her mom said. She motioned to the far end of the conference table, which was currently empty. "Let's set up down here."

"Yes, ma'am." The butler moved the cart to the far side of the room and set out six place settings. He then transferred several covered dishes to the center of the table.

Amy debated whether she should insist on eating beside her laptop. After all, they still hadn't found Osman's men in New York.

Brent put his hand on her back. "I think we can all use a little break."

Following Brent's lead, she closed her laptop and moved to an empty spot at the end of the table.

As soon as everyone was settled, her mom folded her arms.

"I'll say the blessing," Amy's dad said.

Everyone bowed their heads. Her dad offered a prayer, both of gratitude for the progress they had made and of pleading for the Lord's guidance over the coming days so they could protect their country.

After he added a blessing on the food and the amens were said, he looked across the table at Brent. "Any word from your squad?"

"They're in Atlanta, working with the FBI," Brent said. "Once the FBI tracks down that SUV, I'm sure they'll want to be involved when they go in to take Osman's men into custody."

"Doug specifically asked for the Saint Squad to be on the front lines," Amy's dad said. "I'm sure he'll pave the way."

"Good," Brent said. "At times like these, the more trained personnel we have available, the better."

"I agree."

* * *

Tristan followed Agent Burns out of the airport to the passenger pickup area, his duffel bag over his shoulder and Quinn and Craig on his heels. He had no idea where Jay and Damian had disappeared to, but Tristan wasn't about to let the FBI slip away while their commanding officer wasn't present.

Agent Hernandez waited outside, the trunk open, keys to their rental car in his hand.

Agent Burns dropped his bag into the trunk. "Sorry. We have our orders, and you aren't included in them."

Agent Burns didn't sound the least bit sorry.

Tristan fisted his hands and fought against his frustration. "We're coming with you."

"How many times do we have to go over this?" Agent Burns slammed the trunk closed. "You have no jurisdiction."

"And without us, you're shorthanded." Tristan pointed at himself and then at Quinn and Craig, who stood beside him. "And Secretary Valdez wants us on this."

"He wanted you involved when you had people on the plane with Morenta's men. That was then. Now it's time for you to sit this one out." Agent Burns opened the passenger side door. "We'll let you know what happens."

Tristan stepped forward, but Craig grabbed his arm.

"Let them go," Craig said. "We have an inside track to get the location."

"Planning on us calling Doug again?" Tristan asked as the two FBI agents pulled away from the curb. "I'm not sure he'll take our side on this."

A van pulled up beside them, Jay in the passenger seat. The side door opened.

Damian poked his head out. "*Vamanos*."

Tristan stepped forward to see who was driving. His eyes widened. Ghost. Not the Ghost who had helped them in Nicaragua and Honduras but the one who they worked with occasionally in Virginia.

"What are you doing here?" Tristan asked.

Jay didn't give Ghost a chance to answer. "Get in. We'll talk on the way."

Craig and Quinn went first. Tristan dropped his duffel inside and followed. After he pulled the door closed, he settled into the seat behind Jay.

"Ghost thought we might need some backup," Jay said before Tristan could ask his question again.

"The FBI guys just left."

"I figured they wouldn't want you around," Ghost said. He put the car in gear and pulled into the flow of traffic leaving the airport.

"Do you have the location?" Tristan asked.

"We got it," Ghost confirmed. "It's only ten minutes from here."

"Check your weapons," Jay said. "We'll let the FBI take their shot at Osman's men, but I want to be ready in case any of them try to make a break for it."

Nine minutes later, Ghost pulled into a hotel parking lot. He chose a spot at the front corner where they could see the main entrance as well as one of the side entrances.

"Now what?" Craig asked.

"We watch and wait," Jay said. "Agent Burns and Agent Hernandez know what we look like. We don't need an obstructing justice charge leveled against us."

"They don't know what I look like." Ghost slipped a comm earpiece into his ear and opened the van door. "I'll be back."

"Here." Jay handed Damian and Tristan an earpiece each. Then he handed Tristan two more. "Pass those back."

Tristan handed two to Quinn and slipped his in place.

No one spoke for several minutes. Then Ghost rounded the far side of the hotel and headed toward them.

"Any luck?" Jay asked.

Ghost didn't respond until he reached the car and opened the door. "Osman's men aren't here. Looks like they dumped the car and switched vehicles."

"How did you figure that out?"

"The FBI is searching the hotel, and they have a forensics team already on site. There weren't any fingerprints on the SUV."

"And there's no reason to wipe it down unless they aren't going to use it again," Tristan said.

"Can you pull the security feed for the parking lot?" Craig asked.

"I already put in the request," Ghost said. "My wife should have it for us by the time we get to the power plant."

"That's where you want to look through video?" Quinn asked. "Wouldn't it make more sense to find a hotel somewhere to set up a temporary office?"

"We don't want to use a hotel's Wi-Fi, and I have a place where you can at least get some sleep tonight." Ghost started the car and pulled out of the lot.

Less than three minutes later, he turned into another lot, this one beside a park, and pulled up beside a tractor trailer.

"Come on." Ghost opened his door. "Bring your stuff with you."

Tristan climbed out of the van and grabbed his duffel.

Ghost waited for everyone to join him by the semi. Then he locked the van and looked around as though making sure no one was watching. "Follow me. And make sure no one sees you." He ducked under the truck.

"What are you doing?"

"Going inside."

Tristan glanced over his shoulder. No one was visible besides his squad. He followed.

To Tristan's surprise, Ghost pushed open a hatch beneath the truck's trailer and climbed inside. Tristan joined him.

Tristan stood in the back of the trailer, and his jaw dropped. The interior looked like the inside of a high-end motor home. A kitchen to one side, complete with a table. A couch stretched along one side, with two desks at the back of the trailer. A hall led to what was likely a bathroom and bedroom.

Quinn entered next. "Whoa."

"You live in the back of a tractor trailer?" Tristan asked.

"Sometimes," Ghost answered.

The rest of the squad joined them, and Ghost closed the hatch behind them. "It'll be a little tight, but you can work at the table or on the couch."

"What about the desks?" Jay asked.

"One is mine." He motioned toward the hallway. "The other is hers."

A dark-haired woman emerged. She wore a baggy sweater over her slender frame, but her rounded stomach suggested she was several months pregnant. It took only a moment to recognize Renee, one of the intel officers they had worked with in the past. "Welcome. It's good to see you all again."

"Renee will set you up with secure laptops." Ghost turned to her. "Were you able to get us hooked up for the utilities?"

"Yes. We have electric, waste, and water."

"How did you manage that?" Craig asked.

"There are a couple of hookups here in the park for tiny houses." Renee shot an apologetic look at Ghost. "I had to bribe someone to let us have this one."

"That's okay. We needed this location."

"Why?" Tristan asked.

"Because the main power plant is down the street."

"In that case, Craig and Damian, go scout out the area," Jay said. "Evaluate whatever surveillance the locals and the feds have set up."

Craig nodded and opened the hatch again. He and Damian disappeared through what was essentially the middle of Ghost's kitchen floor.

"The security footage just came in from the hotel," Renee said. She opened a cabinet behind the desk, retrieved three laptops, and handed them to Jay. "Here you go. Make yourself comfortable, and help yourself to anything in the fridge."

Jay passed a laptop to Tristan and another to Quinn. "Get started. When Craig and Damian get back, we'll set up a schedule for watching security feed and running surveillance."

"You'll want to sleep too," Ghost said. "There are four bunks in the back of the cab."

Working in a trailer and sleeping in a truck. Not a bad deal for a stakeout.

43

Jim looked around the table. Had it not been for the laptops on the other end and the terrorist threat looming over them, this could have been a typical meal when Brent was in town. Family and friends, good food, interesting conversation.

Jim looked forward to when that conversation would include something other than talk about security feed and power plants.

"Any idea how many people are guarding the various power plants?" Seth asked.

Jim shook his head. "Doug is supposed to be getting me the latest on that sometime this evening."

"Has he even been home the last few days?" Katherine asked.

"Long enough to sleep, but I don't think it's been much more than that," Jim said. "After we get through all this, I think we may need to have a little getaway to Camp David for a few days. We can have Doug and his family join us, along with any of the Saint Squad who would like to come."

"After so many back-to-back missions, I'm sure command would give us all leave for a week or so," Brent said.

"I need to talk to personnel about extending Jay's leave." Amy sipped her ginger ale. "He shouldn't even be working right now."

"We were lucky to have him when we went in after Brent," Seth said. "It would have been rough to go in shorthanded."

"Has anyone talked to Carina lately?" Jim asked, referring to Jay's wife.

"I've spoken with her a few times," Katherine said. "Both of her sisters are there helping out. So are Jay's parents."

"Thanks for checking in on her," Vanessa said.

"Yeah, thanks, Mom," Amy said. "I feel bad that I didn't think to call her."

"You've all been busy," Katherine said.

Vanessa's phone chimed with an incoming text. "Sorry. I should check this." She pulled out her phone and read the message. "The rest of the Saint Squad is staking out the power plant in Atlanta."

Another text chimed. Vanessa smiled. "And it looks like Jay is enjoying being in command. He sent Craig up a tree."

Jim chuckled. "Poor Jay. It seems like every time I read one of your after-action reports, there's something in them about Jay spotting something from a tree."

"He's got a great eye," Brent said.

The door opened, and Doug walked in. "Sorry to interrupt your dinner, but I thought you might want the latest updates."

"Yes." Jim waved at the empty chair beside Brent. "Have a seat."

"Doug, have you eaten?" Katherine asked.

"No, but I'll grab something later." Doug sat beside Brent.

"Don't be silly. We have plenty of food to go around." Katherine glanced at the butler, who was waiting beside the serving cart.

Her words prompted Brandon into action. He abandoned his station beside the cart and carried a place setting to where Doug now sat. He set out the plate and silverware.

Brent passed the chicken Tetrazzini down to Doug.

"Thanks." Doug accepted a glass of water from the butler before he turned his attention back to Jim. "The latest from Vegas is that they've been able to contain the power outages to North Las Vegas and the four sections of Vegas that lost power."

"So the strip is still dark?" Jim asked.

"Yes, and the airport is still without power." Doug dished some pasta onto his plate. "The FAA has issued cancel orders for all Las Vegas flights."

"I'm sure the airlines are dealing with a lot of upset passengers," Vanessa said.

"No doubt." Seth nodded.

"Any luck finding any of Osman's men?" Jim asked.

"Not yet." Doug twirled some pasta onto his fork. "We traced the car in Atlanta to a hotel near the main power plant. It was wiped clean. We think they switched cars so we wouldn't be able to use GPS to track them, but we have a contingent of agents staked out and undercover police officers patrolling the area."

"What about the other cities?" Jim asked.

"Those are a little tougher." Doug plucked a roll out of the basket beside him and broke it in half. "We haven't found them on any surveillance cameras yet, but we're still combing through traffic cameras. Unfortunately, we can't be sure if they'll hit one of the power plants or a substation, but the local police have units in the critical areas."

Jim prayed that their preparations would be enough.

"Do we have any new information from Paquito, the man who created these weapons?" Brent asked.

"Nothing." Jim shook his head. "The last debrief from him suggested that he only knew he needed to extend the range of the weapons as much as possible, but he never knew what the targets were beyond batteries and electrical grids."

"How close was the car to the Atlanta power plant?" Brent asked.

"Less than a mile away."

"Then, it's possible they could be on foot," Jim said.

"I doubt it," Seth said. "They'll have a vehicle somewhere as part of their exit strategy."

Brent speared a piece of chicken with his fork. "Probably a car that's been adapted to include copper shielding on the engine to protect it from the pulse weapon."

"The police have patrols on foot as well as others canvasing the area in unmarked cars," Doug said. "If they don't spot them by the power plant, hopefully the FBI or the Saint Squad will. I assume that's where the Saint Squad is hiding out."

Jim pondered his answer. He had little ability to lie, and he'd chosen Doug to serve in his cabinet for a reason: he trusted him. "If I tell you the truth, is it going to cause problems between them and the FBI?"

"I'll smooth any ruffled feathers," Doug said. "And I'd rather know where they are so I can utilize my resources more efficiently."

"Then, yes, they're watching the power plant in Atlanta."

"Good. I'm glad I guessed correctly," Doug said. "I'll let the authorities know they're on site."

"If you could put in a good word about cooperating with them, that could go a long way," Brent suggested.

Doug nodded. "I'll take care of it."

"I assume we haven't had any luck finding Osman's men in Detroit either," Jim said.

"Nothing."

"They've probably gone into hiding to make sure they're ready to attack."

Doug angled his chair to face Brent. "Did your source in Nicaragua say anything about what time the attacks are supposed to happen tomorrow?"

Brent shook his head. "He didn't know."

"Logically, they would all occur within minutes of each other if they want to create a cascade effect," Vanessa said.

"So, what time would be the most efficient for that?" Jim asked. "Middle of the night when people need heat the most?"

"If that's the case, it could be early tomorrow morning or late tomorrow night," Brent said.

"They would want it to happen while people are awake," Vanessa said. "It would create more of a sense of panic. People driving, who suddenly have no power, parents trying to get to their children, who are in school, workers trapped in the top of tall buildings without a working elevator."

"Not to mention that a successful attack in New York while the stock market is open would have international ramifications," Amy said.

"She's right," Doug agreed. "A middle-of-the-night attack isn't as effective if they want to create real chaos."

"With the time differences, I think they'll try sometime around midday here on the East Coast," Seth said.

"I agree," Brent said. "Anytime from noon to two would mean schools would be open across the country, the stock market would be open, and there would be plenty of people on the road."

Though he hated to choose, Jim said, "We need to make New York a priority. It has the highest population of all the cities still at risk."

"We're already sending in extra agents from headquarters and the Boston office," Doug said. "And we have more than a thousand people searching for Osman and his men, both at local hotels and on every traffic and security camera we can find."

"Thanks, Doug," Jim said. "I know you're doing everything you can."

"We'll find them," Doug assured him.

Jim tried to believe him.

* * *

Vanessa led the way to the third floor of the White House residence. Though she desperately wanted to go home and spend time with Talia, by the time she and Seth would have arrived home, their baby would have been fast asleep, and they would likely have had to leave before Talia woke in the morning.

"Sorry we didn't make it home tonight," Seth said, clearly sharing her thoughts.

"Me too, but my mom is loving every minute with Talia."

"I'm sure she is."

They reached the guest room that had been assigned to them, and Vanessa led the way inside. She set her laptop on the table next to her side of the bed. Seth put his in its usual spot on the desk.

"Do you think we'll ever get used to having our own room in the White House?" Vanessa asked.

"Good question." Seth toed off his shoes and put them in their closet.

Vanessa sat on the side of the bed. "Do you think Amy has told Brent that she's pregnant yet?"

"I don't think so." Seth turned abruptly to face her. "How did you know Amy's pregnant?"

"I'm a woman who was newly pregnant less than two years ago. I recognized the signs." She narrowed her eyes. "How did you find out?"

"Amy doesn't usually turn green when we fly out to the carrier." Seth changed out of his uniform and put on his pajamas. "I think she may be waiting until this whole national emergency blows over before she tells him."

"She hasn't had much of a chance yet, that's for sure."

"That's true." Seth sat in the office chair and opened his laptop.

"What are you doing? I thought we came up here to get some sleep."

"I want to take another look at the pickup area at La Guardia," Seth said. "I keep thinking I missed something when we looked earlier."

New York. Jim's earlier comment about prioritizing the largest city repeated through Vanessa's mind.

Of the four remaining targets, it was the only one in the top ten as far as population. Detroit was in the top twenty. Atlanta was, too, barely, so why had those two been chosen?

Vanessa did a quick search on her cell phone of the largest cities in the US by population. As she suspected, Detroit was smaller than both Boston and Columbus, either of which would serve a similar strategic location as Detroit if trying to create a cascade power outage.

Vanessa looked up from her phone. "Why did Osman choose these cities?"

Seth's focus remained on his laptop screen. "Large populations, strategic locations to create a possible nationwide outage."

"Then, why not hit Miami instead of Atlanta? Or Jacksonville?" Vanessa asked. "Denver isn't that big. If they hit Phoenix instead, it would affect a lot more people."

"Is it possible we're wrong on these last cities?" Seth asked. "All the other ones we had confirmed turned out to be accurate."

"I don't know." Vanessa went over the list of remaining cities in her mind along with where the intel came from. "Orlando and New York both came from the same source. It makes sense that New York would be a prime target, so that makes me think the intel on Orlando is accurate too."

"And we know Atlanta because that's where the plane landed."

"Right. That leaves Detroit." Vanessa paused. "And that one could be wrong."

"Why do you say that?"

"I asked Morenta about Chicago and Detroit at the same time," Vanessa said. "He reacted, but he might have only been reacting because I mentioned Chicago."

"Which we confirmed was a target," Seth said.

"Yeah. I lumped the two locations together because they would both be severely affected by the coming cold front if they lost power. At the time, we were focused on the largest cities in the East and the Midwest. I should have pressed him when I figured out Denver was a target too."

"You should tell Jim."

"The president needs sleep." Vanessa picked up her phone.

"Who are you calling?"

"Doug." Vanessa scrolled through her contacts. "He can make sure the FBI knows there is a possible unknown target city."

"You should probably tell Ghost too. He can get the word out through his resources."

Vanessa hit the button to call Doug. "I already planned to."

44

Brent awoke slowly and reached out his hand in search of his wife. He opened his eyes when he found nothing but cool sheets beside him. He pushed up on his elbow and scanned the empty room. Light spilled onto the carpet from beneath the bathroom door.

"Amy?"

The toilet flushed. The faucet turned on and then off. Amy emerged from the bathroom, her dark hair spilling loosely over her shoulders.

"Are you okay?"

"Yeah." She climbed back into bed, but rather than lie down, she grabbed an extra pillow and propped herself up so she was nearly sitting upright.

Brent sat up and turned on the bedside lamp. He could see the signs of illness now—the pale skin, the puffy eyes. "Amy, what's wrong? Have you been feeling this bad since before I left?"

"It comes and goes."

A trickle of fear seeped through him. If Amy was suffering from another bout of exhaustion, she would tell him. This was something new, something unexpected.

Though he wasn't sure he was ready to hear what she had to say, Brent bent one leg and shifted so he was facing her. "What did the doctor say?"

To his surprise, a little smile illuminated her face. She turned, opened her bedside drawer, and pulled out an envelope. "Here."

Thoroughly confused, Brent took it from her. "What's this?"

"It's from the doctor." Amy motioned to it. "Go on. Open it."

Brent studied her face for a clue before lowering his gaze to the plain, white envelope. He pulled open the flap and slipped an oddly shaped paper from inside. He unfolded it to reveal a series of black-and-white ultrasound photos.

He had seen photos like this before—each time one of his teammates had had a pregnant wife. "Is this . . . ?"

Amy's smile bloomed fully. "That is our son or daughter."

"You're pregnant?" Brent dropped the ultrasound photos and grabbed her hand with both of his. His chest tightened in the same way it did when he was about to parachute off a high-flying aircraft. "You're sure?"

"I'm sure."

His mind froze, unable to comprehend what she'd just told him. A baby? A tiny life that they had made together? It was almost too much to hope for. Holding a tiny body that would fit in his hands, cuddling a soft bundle late at night, playing on the floor with a toddler, watching his own child grow and develop their own personality and interests—all these moments of wonder flashed through his mind in an instant.

Brent let go of Amy's hand and pulled her into his arms. He blinked several times against the sudden moisture in his eyes. He was going to be a father. Finally, after so many years of praying for this moment, they had received a miracle they'd thought would never come. He held her for a long moment. "I can't believe this."

"I couldn't either when the doctor first told me." She pulled back so she could see him. "I found out right after you left."

Right before he went MIA. "I am so sorry I wasn't here to share in the good news."

"You came home." Amy linked her fingers with his. "That's what's important."

A knock sounded at the door.

"That must be Seth." Amy climbed out of bed and slipped on her robe. "He usually shows up every time I think about telling you you're going to be a father."

Brent barely managed to smother his smile when he opened the door. Sure enough, Seth stood on the other side. "You're late."

"Late for what? It's not even six." Seth's gaze landed on the ultrasound photo. His eyes lit up, and he focused on Amy. "You told him?"

"What?" Brent looked from Seth to Amy and back again. "You already know?"

Amy put her hand on Brent's arm. "He guessed."

"Who else have you told?"

"You're the only person I've told." Amy looked at him apologetically. "But my parents guessed too."

"So did Vanessa," Seth said. "She admitted it last night."

Brent supposed he should be annoyed that his friends and family had learned the news before him, but his joy overshadowed all else.

"Seth, if you're knocking on our door before six in the morning, you must have news," Amy said.

"Yeah, and it's good news, for a change," Seth said. "Relatively good news anyway. I went over some of the New York airport security feed again last night, and I spotted a couple of guys who could have been in Atlanta before that."

"Were you able to track them?"

"They got into a cab, so I handed it over to the FBI. They're searching the area where they were dropped off."

"We're running out of time."

"One more thing," Seth said. "Vanessa thinks we might have one of the cities wrong. She's second-guessing whether Detroit is really a target." Seth explained Vanessa's thought process.

"Maybe Vanessa and I can look for commonalities among the targets we've identified," Amy said. "We might be able to narrow it down."

"Vanessa is already in the West Wing going over the intel reports that came in last night."

"I'll meet you down there as soon as I shower and change," Brent said.

"Sounds good." Seth took a step back. "And congratulations."

Brent's heart lifted. "Thanks." He closed the door and turned to Amy. "You should get some more rest."

"I'll lie down while you shower, but I want to help."

Brent wanted to argue, but he knew he wouldn't win. "Fine." He leaned down and kissed her, unable to resist drawing her close. The spark of attraction ignited, and his heart soared. A baby. They were having a baby. When he pulled back, he tucked a lock of Amy's hair behind her ear. "I want you to promise you'll take care of yourself."

Amy smiled and kissed him again. "I will."

* * *

Amy lay in bed for the fifteen minutes it took Brent to shower, dress, and check in with the rest of his squad. Once he left their room, she gave up trying to fall back to sleep. Even though her night had been less than restful, her mind was spinning and wasn't going to calm down until she was sure she'd done everything possible to help her father and her country.

Fighting the latest bout of nausea, she showered and changed. But when she sat on the side of the bed to put on her shoes, her stomach roiled uncomfortably.

She drew a slow, deep breath and tried to ignore the sensation. She didn't have time for this right now. Today was the day that could change everything. If they didn't stop the attack, this could be another 9/11.

Not if she could help it. She pushed to a stand.

Willing her body to cooperate, she left her room and made her way to the kitchen as the clock struck the half hour. Even though it was only six thirty, she wasn't surprised that her mother was at the table, her breakfast in front of her, her cell phone in her hand.

Her mom looked up, empathy shining in her eyes. "You had a rough night."

Amy didn't know how her mother knew the morning sickness had kept her up, nor did she ask. Her mom had a sixth sense when it came to these things. "On the plus side, I finally told Brent."

"I'm sure he was thrilled."

Amy couldn't help but smile. "Yes, he was." She opened the freezer and pulled out a roll. When she put it in the microwave, her mom stood and poured her a glass of ginger ale.

"Here. Try some of this. It should help settle your stomach."

"Thanks." Amy sipped it slowly as she sat across from her mom at the table.

Her mom's phone chimed with an incoming text.

"Who's texting you so early in the morning."

"Kendra."

Charlie's wife, Amy's pregnant sister-in-law. "Don't tell me she's having morning sickness too."

"No, she's past that stage. She had a concert last night and hasn't gone to bed yet."

"I really hope she's on the West Coast." Three thirty was way later than Amy would want to be going to bed, but it was better than being awake until after the sun was up.

"San Diego," her mom said. "She was supposed to fly to New York this morning."

"What?" Amy set her glass down abruptly. "She can't."

"I know. I already asked her to avoid flying until we give her the all-clear," her mom said. "She'll stay where she is until we let her know everything's okay."

"Thank goodness." Amy took another sip of her ginger ale. "Could you imagine what would happen if she were midflight when the power went out in New York?"

"It's terrifying." Her mom sent another message to Kendra and set her phone aside. "Sometimes, I think it was easier when I didn't know what was going on behind the scenes. I don't know how you handle the stress."

"After spending two days not knowing if Brent was alive, I kept wondering how my friends deal with the uncertainty every time the squad ships out."

"I guess that means you'll want to keep working once the baby is born."

"I don't know." Amy tried to picture it, being home and not having the insight to Brent's missions, not know where he was or when he was coming home. She weighed that against the possibility of finally having the child she so desperately wanted and leaving him or her in the care of another every day.

And what about deployments? Could she stand to leave her child in someone else's care every time the squad shipped out and needed her present?

"It's a lot to think about," she finally said.

Her mom put her hand on Amy's. "You don't have to make that decision today. The right choice will come to you, especially if you hand the question over to the Lord."

Her mom was right. It wasn't a decision she needed to make now. Today, her focus needed to be on helping her squad and her father find Osman and his men.

45

Top-twenty lists filled one side of the enormous conference table in the cabinet room. Vanessa highlighted her latest printout, this one of cities with the largest tech company headquarters.

What a day. At a time when they should be celebrating Amy's good news, they were faced with a puzzle that had so many pieces, they couldn't find the edges, much less fill in the picture.

Amy walked in, her face a little paler than normal. "What's all this?" She glanced at the laptops on the other side of the table. "And where are the guys?"

"They're down in the Sit Room getting the latest update."

"And all this?" Amy waved at Vanessa's current research project.

"I'm looking for the missing target," Vanessa said. "I think I was wrong about Detroit."

Amy picked up one of the papers off the table. "The largest cities in the US."

Vanessa held up her highlighter. "The highlighted cities are the confirmed targets. I'm hoping that if we look at the main categories that could be of interest to Osman's group, we can narrow down the other possibilities."

"Want me to start making a list for each city to see how many categories they pop up on?" Amy asked.

"That would be great." Vanessa debated how to best utilize her time. "If you can do that, I'll start looking at the surveillance feed again."

Amy set her computer backpack on the chair in front of her. She unzipped it and began rummaging through the middle pocket. "Do you really think you'll see anything new? Hundreds of intel officers have been searching them."

"I know, but I just keep getting the feeling that I might catch something other people would miss," Vanessa said. "Plus, I'm one of the few people who has seen Osman in person."

Amy looked up. "I didn't know that."

"It was when I was deep undercover." Vanessa moved to the far end of the table and opened her laptop.

"When you were Lina Ramir?"

Vanessa nodded. When she wasn't allowed to be herself.

"Do you ever miss that life?" Amy asked.

"At times like these, I always wonder if I would have seen or heard something that could have stopped the threat before it started, but I wouldn't want to go back to living the lies."

"But you almost did." Amy pulled out a package of sticky notes and set it on the table. "The CIA was going to send you to the fortress to gather intel on this attack and to help find Brent."

"How did you know that?"

"I may not have been fully functioning when Brent was missing, but I heard enough to put together the pieces." Amy sat at the table. "Would you have really done it?" she asked. "Could you have left Talia, especially while Seth was in the field?"

"No." Vanessa lowered into her chair and swiveled so she was facing Amy. "I'm sorry. I know I said I would do anything to help find Brent."

"I didn't expect that 'doing anything to help' included putting yourself in harm's way. You have nothing to apologize for."

"I'm glad you think so, but being Lina again was a means to an end."

Amy's eyes lit with understanding. "You questioned Morenta."

Though Vanessa would have denied it to nearly everyone else, Amy was one of the few in her inner circle of trust. "Yes." She explained her questioning tactics and her concern about the misinterpretation of Morenta's reaction to Detroit.

"You've already done half the work here." Amy motioned to the printouts. "I'll get it narrowed down."

"I hope so." Vanessa started the security feed in Atlanta again, this time reviewing it as though she hadn't already witnessed it. Meanwhile, Amy jotted information down on sticky notes, using the wall to organize the squares.

Over an hour passed without any progress on Vanessa's part. She pulled up a different camera for when Osman's plane was unloaded and scanned through the footage at the plane. She let it run until well after the cases were unloaded. Three cases. She paused, rewound the feed, and played it again. Three silver cases. Three weapons.

She hit the Play button, her focus on the weapons rather than the men surrounding them. The bags were gathered. The cargo door was closed. None of the weapons was loaded back into the plane.

Quickly, Vanessa pulled up the feed from when Osman's men had been picked up from the airport. She viewed it twice to confirm the anomaly.

"Amy, I think found something."

"What?"

"When Osman's men loaded their luggage into the car that picked them up, they only had two weapons." Vanessa pointed at her screen. "But they unloaded three."

"There's a plane or another car that we missed."

"That's exactly what I think," Vanessa said. "Do you still have your research on where the private planes from Atlanta flew into?"

"Yeah." Something sparked in Amy's expression. She pulled her cell phone from her pocket and started typing on the screen. "You don't have the list of the largest airports here."

"No." Population, proximity to nuclear power plants, number of power plants, industry types, but not airports.

"Vanessa, I think this is it." Amy held up her phone, the screen illuminated with her Google search. "Listen to this: The cities with the largest US airports are Atlanta, Dallas, Chicago, LA, Denver, New York, Las Vegas, Charlotte, Orlando, and San Francisco."

Vanessa checked off the target cities as Amy read them. Every single one had either been confirmed a target or was on their list. Except for Detroit.

"Charlotte," Vanessa said. "The third weapon must be there."

Amy pulled out her laptop and set it on the table. "I'll check again for private planes that went down there after Osman and his men landed in Atlanta."

"I'll look for them in the pickup lane," Vanessa said. "It's not that far to drive from Atlanta to Charlotte. They could easily make it in less than a day."

Brent and Seth walked in. "How's it going?"

"We think Amy found the common thread," Vanessa said. "Airports."

"Airports?" Seth sat beside her.

"Every target we've confirmed is one of the largest in the country." Vanessa pulled up the video feed of the pickup area at the Atlanta airport. "We think Charlotte might be the missing city."

"If they're going after the airports, the power plants might not be the primary targets," Brent said. "Can you imagine what would happen if we had planes taking off and landing in the middle of a strike? With the range of these weapons, it could crash every aircraft within a couple of miles."

Seth nodded. "And as high as ten thousand feet."

Brent pulled out his phone.

"Who are you calling?" Amy asked.

"Jay. They need to find the best strike point for the airport's electrical grid."

As Brent made his call, Seth asked Vanessa, "What can I help with?"

"Help me look through this. I'm on camera seventeen. Maybe you and Brent can take some of the other areas of the pickup lane."

Seth glanced at her screen. "We should start with the time that we spotted the other car," he said. "We looked through everything before that point."

"Good idea." Vanessa fast-forwarded.

Brent hung up the phone. "Jay and the rest of the squad are heading back over to the airport. They said the locals and the FBI have the power plant well covered."

"You should call Doug too," Vanessa said. She picked up her phone and tried calling Jim only to have his secretary tell her he wasn't available.

The printer in the corner of the room whirred to life. Amy crossed to it and retrieved the pages. "I have a list of private planes that flew to Charlotte after Osman and his men landed."

"Let Brent start on those," Vanessa suggested. "You should go find your dad and see if you can bypass his secretary. He's going to want this update."

Amy nodded. "I'll be right back."

Brent finished updating Doug and hung up. "Why did you send Amy? I could have gone."

"Yes, but walking around will help her feel better." Vanessa looked up. "By the way, congratulations."

The corners of Brent's mouth lifted into a smile. "Thanks."

"You know, once we get Osman and his men in custody, we can have a nice dinner to celebrate," Seth suggested.

"I'd like that," Brent said, then let his smile fade. "But for now, we still have a lot of work to do."

46

Four cities at risk and not one of Osman's men had been spotted near the power plants in the target areas. Jim had so hoped to have at least some progress by now. He walked into the Oval Office, not sure he wanted to know what all was scheduled for this morning. Only eight thirty and, already, he'd gone through his daily brief, a meeting with Doug, and another with his intelligence advisory committee.

Jim barely reached his desk when Brandon entered holding a serving tray.

"Mr. President, your wife asked that I bring you something to eat."

Had he forgotten breakfast again?

The scent of eggs and sausage wafted toward him. His stomach grumbled. "Thank you, Brandon."

"Of course, sir." Brandon set the tray on a side table and lifted the covered plate from it. He set the plate down and took off the metal dome to reveal a breakfast sandwich comprised of an English muffin, a fried egg, and sausage beside a helping of mixed fruit. He then brought Jim a set of utensils rolled in a cloth napkin along with a glass of orange juice. "Please let me know if I can get you anything else."

"I will. Thank you."

The butler left as Amy walked inside. "Dad, we think we figured it out."

"Figured what out?" Jim took a bite of his sandwich.

"What the target cities have in common." Amy closed the door before continuing. "Every one of these cities has one of the largest airports in the country."

"Osman is going after our electrical grid *and* our air travel?"

"I think so." Amy sat in the chair beside his desk. "Could you imagine what would happen if the major airports in four cities all of a sudden couldn't take incoming flights? Even if the power outages don't cascade to the surrounding areas, the overload of redirecting flights would be a nightmare."

"It would, but I don't think creating travel inconveniences is what Osman is looking for." Her dad shook his head. "The helicopters that brought the SEALs out of the fortress when they had to leave Brent behind barely made it back safely. The pulse weapons could very well crash any aircraft that's too close to it."

"That would be devastating." Amy drew a deep breath and let it out slowly. "Combined with the power outages and the repercussions from that, a significant number of Americans would be affected."

"If we have planes dropping out of the sky, the fear factor alone will be unimaginable."

"That's true," Amy said. "Assuming we're right about the airports being the reason for those cities becoming targets, we think Charlotte is the other target, not Detroit."

"Does Doug already know?" Jim asked.

"Brent was calling him when I left the Cabinet Room," she said. "And Mom already checked with Kendra to make sure she postponed her flight to New York."

"Thank goodness for that." Jim didn't need any more family members in danger, especially not now, while so much uncertainty hung over him. "I have to imagine that if they're going after airports, they'll try to take out the power for both JFK and La Guardia."

"I agree," Amy said. "The plane we traced to New York landed at La Guardia, but JFK is the larger airport. They'll likely make that one their primary target."

"Their plane is still parked at La Guardia, right?"

"Yes."

"I want the FBI to check it out again."

"If there was anything to find, I'm sure they would have found it by now."

"Can't hurt to take another look." Jim picked up his phone. "Sarah, can you get Doug Valdez on the line?"

"Yes, sir."

A phone rang in the hall outside. A knock on the door followed.

"Come in."

The door opened, and Doug walked in. "I have the FBI coordinating with the local authorities in Charlotte."

"Thanks." Jim put his phone back down. "How bad will it affect air travel in the rest of the country if one of these cities goes dark?"

"New York is the biggest challenge since it has two major airports. Atlanta, Orlando, and Charlotte rely primarily on one each." Doug's expression turned grave. "Unfortunately, our projections of potential cascade effects shows that if Atlanta loses power, it will likely ripple through all of North Carolina and at least all the way up to Richmond."

"Including Virginia Beach?" Amy asked.

"Virginia Beach and Norfolk."

"Where a good chunk of our naval forces are stationed." Amy stood and stepped back. "Dad, you should send as many naval vessels out to sea as possible. Now."

"That's not a bad idea," Doug said. "If they're far enough away from the coast, there's a good chance they won't have any infections from the virus, and that will protect them from any effects from the EMP."

"I'll call the secretary of the navy and get the ball rolling," Jim said. "I want them to suspend air exercises too. No reason to have planes in the air unless absolutely necessary."

"Planes in the air." Amy said the words as though testing them out rather than speaking to him.

"What are you thinking?" Jim asked.

Her eyes widened, the way they did when the pieces of a puzzle clicked into place. "Remember a few years ago when the FAA's system shut down and it caused all those flights to be grounded?"

"Vaguely."

"I remember," Doug said. "The FAA's Notice to Air Mission system crashed."

The same system that created notifications for flight operations, such as informing air-traffic controllers about a power outage at an airport.

"Charlotte might not be the target after all," Amy said. "What if DC is?"

"DC doesn't have any airports," Jim said. "They're all in Virginia or Maryland."

Doug exchanged a look with Amy before speaking. "But if Osman's men took out our power and the FAA's systems were down—"

A new terror clawed inside Jim. "Those planes would be in the air with no idea where to go. It would affect far more flights that just the ones near the target airports."

"I'm afraid so." Doug nodded. "Maybe it's time to suspend all flights, at least along the East Coast."

Interrupt the lives of thousands for a threat that may or may not happen, or let the planes into the air, knowing that they could be flying into a trap, or worse, that they could lose power and fall from the sky, possibly killing thousands of people if the pulse weapon affected them. "Have we had any luck finding the terrorists?"

"Not yet."

"Can I play devil's advocate here?" Amy asked.

Jim needed someone to do it. He nodded.

"If you shut down these airports, it will make the news." Amy paced the room until she stood beside Doug, directly in front of Jim. "If Osman's plan is to kill air travel, you'll be doing the job for him."

"But if people are in planes when the EMPs are deployed, planes could come crashing out of the sky."

"Did we have any plane crashes when Vegas and Kansas City lost power?" Amy asked.

"There was a minor incident with a plane that was landing when the power went out, but other than that, we got lucky," Doug said.

"Which was probably because the planes that were off the ground were high enough that their batteries weren't affected," Amy said.

"Yes, but only the Kansas City airport lost power, and the FAA was able to divert all the other planes," Doug said.

"What's worse?" Jim asked. "Causing a panic now and preparing against an attack that we hope won't come, or letting those planes take off, knowing they're at risk?"

"I say we take a middle ground." Amy motioned to the clock. "It's already after nine. If we're right, the soonest the attack will hit is at noon eastern time."

"Three hours from now." Jim's chest tightened. Only three more hours for multiple miracles to happen to stop a potential disaster.

"Yes. So, let all the flights leave the target airports until a little before noon," Amy said. "For incoming flights, the FAA can give all of them an alternate landing spot in the event of a disruption in communication."

"And when we hit the expected window of attack?" Doug asked. "It might happen at noon, but it could be several hours later."

"We delay flights that are supposed to leave between noon and three."

"Why three?"

"By then, a good number of the schools have let out on the East Coast," Amy said. "Based on the psych profile for Osman, he'll most likely strike when parents will be separated from their children."

"Which will create more chaos than if he strikes during the night when families would be home together," Doug said.

"Right."

What Amy proposed was risky.

She took a step back. "You know what we do in the Saint Squad when facing these kinds of decisions?" She didn't wait for Jim to answer. "We pray." She looked from Jim to Doug. "What do you think? Are you willing to ask for some divine guidance on this? We need the extra help."

"You're right." Jim stood. Though his instinct was to offer the prayer himself, his gaze remained on his daughter. She and her team had faced countless dangers. "Amy, would you say it?"

She folded her arms. "I'd be happy to."

* * *

Finally, they had a direction. After spending all night watching for intruders with a dozen police officers and several FBI agents, Tristan was ready to leave the stakeouts to the locals and do something—anything—that would get them closer to resolving this situation. And the only true resolution would be when Osman and all his men were in custody.

Sitting in the back of Ghost's van, Tristan slipped his new communication earpiece into place, a gift from Ghost. "You're sure these won't crash if the pulse weapon is deployed?"

"I'm sure." Ghost pulled onto the airport service road.

"If we do get cut off, meet back at the parking lot at three."

"Here. You'll need these too." Ghost pulled up to a stop sign and reached over to open the glove box. Moving efficiently, he handed each of them what appeared to be a thin wallet, opening each before he handed them over.

Tristan accepted his. Inside was a badge and an FBI ID, complete with his name and photo. "Where did these come from?"

"I made them," Ghost said.

"You're sending us into a potential terrorist zone with fake credentials?"

"They're real enough," Ghost said. "We don't have time for anyone to throw barriers in your way."

"Everyone clear on their assignments?" Jay asked.

"We got it," Quinn said.

Ghost pulled up to the drop-off zone, and everyone climbed out, except for Jay and Quinn. The two could hardly walk through the airport holding sniper rifles without drawing unwanted attention. Instead, Ghost would drop them at a service entrance that would give them easier access to the roof.

Taking command of the others, Tristan said, "Check out the main power conduits. I'll make sure security's been briefed on our suspects."

Craig and Damian split up, each going in opposite directions. Tristan headed for the security office.

The moment he entered, he approached the young woman at the desk and flashed his fake FBI credentials. "Tristan Crowther. I need to see your security chief."

A man approached from behind the counter. "Who are you?"

"I'm with the FBI." Tristan glanced at the handful of customers in the lobby area. "Is there somewhere we can speak privately?"

The director leaned closer to inspect Tristan's badge. Then he tilted his head toward a hallway. "My office."

Tristan followed him down the hall and through the door of a modest-sized office. He closed the door. "I assume you received the alert on Osman and his men."

"Everybody has." The man sat behind his desk and gestured for Tristan to take one of the seats across from him. "We showed the images to our airport security in this morning's briefing, and we included all the other wanted criminals."

The man's casual manner and his mention of other criminals sent a warning blaring through Tristan's brain.

"Did you emphasize that Osman and his men could be making a move today?"

"You're with the FBI. You know these reports hit us practically every day." The man held up both hands. "We do our job. Our people review the most-wanted and special-alert photos at the beginning of every shift."

"That may be, but this isn't an everyday event."

"They never are."

Frustration bubbled inside Tristan. "Where's your control center?"

"You aren't authorized to be in there. TSA personnel only."

"Today, you're going to make an exception."

"Sorry. Those aren't my rules. The only way you're getting into that control booth is if Homeland Security gives approval."

"I can take care of that." Tristan pulled out his phone and dialed Doug's number.

"Any luck?" Doug asked in lieu of a greeting.

"Not exactly. I need a favor." Tristan explained the Homeland Security rule preventing him from doing his job.

"Let me talk to the director," Doug said.

Tristan held out his phone. "Someone wants to speak to you."

The man took the phone. “This is Kevin.” His eyes widened briefly before he glared at Tristan. “You don’t really expect me to believe that this agent has the director of Homeland Security on speed dial.”

Tristan didn’t know what Doug’s response was, but Kevin jotted something down on the paper in front of him. He then hung up, a furrow of confusion creating a line between his bushy eyebrows. He pulled a book out of his drawer, flipped it open, and dialed a number.

“Yes.” The director cleared his throat. “I’d like to speak with Director Valdez please. This is Kevin Matza from the Atlanta airport.”

A moment later, the director swallowed hard. “Yes, sir. I’m sorry for the confusion.” He hung up the phone and stood. After handing Tristan his phone back, he said, “Follow me.”

Tristan tapped on the comm earpiece. “Headed to the security room now.”

“Almost in position,” Jay said.

Everyone else relayed a similar message.

The director tapped a code into the cipher lock and leaned forward to allow the retinal scanner to work its magic. Then he opened the door.

Tristan walked in and scanned the dozens of wall monitors. Apparently, his stakeout wasn’t over yet.

47

VANESSA LOOKED UP WHEN AMY rushed into the room. "What's going on?"

Amy closed the door before speaking. "We think DC may be a target."

"Here?" Seth furrowed his brow. "We don't have any airports within the city limits."

"No, but we have three within striking distance. And we have the FAA," Amy said. "If we have major airports lose power and the FAA can't send out notices—"

"That would be a disaster." Brent pushed out of his seat.

Amy moved to her laptop. Without sitting down, she typed in her pass code. "Doug is increasing the alert status for Reagan National, Dulles, and BWI, but we need to figure out the most likely place they'll strike."

"If I wanted to take out an airport and the FAA, I'd probably go for National airport," Brent said.

Seth stood. "We should head over there."

"I'll head over to the FAA," Vanessa said.

"What about me?" Amy asked.

"You should stay here," Vanessa said.

"She's right," Brent said. "You can be our command center. It will help to have a direct line to the White House if things go south."

"Assuming we don't lose comm," Amy said. "I know the Secret Service has been working to put copper shielding on the backup generators here at the White House, but I don't know which systems they've already protected."

"We aren't relying on anyone else for comm." Vanessa opened her backpack and pulled out four communication earpieces, each one in a protective case.

Seth opened his. "Where did you get these?"

"Ghost." Vanessa took hers out of the case. "They've already been treated with copper shielding."

"Good." Brent took Amy's hand and leaned down to kiss her. "Let your dad know what we're doing, and make sure he keeps you in the loop."

"I will." Amy hugged him. "Be careful."

Brent nodded and headed out the door.

"I'll watch his back," Seth said before following Brent into the hall.

Amy turned to Vanessa. "You be careful too."

"Don't worry about me," Vanessa said. "The only risks I'm likely to face are from papercuts when I sign in to enter the building at the FAA."

"Are you sure about that?" Amy asked. "For all we know, Osman could go after the FAA instead of the power grid."

Vanessa shook her head. "I doubt it. He'll want to wipe out the whole city. It would help hide his real purpose."

"I hope you're right."

A little seed of doubt planted deep inside Vanessa. She grabbed her back-pack. "Me too."

* * *

Brent turned off George Washington Parkway into the maze of roads that wound through Reagan National Airport, Seth sitting in the passenger seat beside him. Brent debated where to start their search. "Where do we look first?"

"If their goal is to disrupt air operations, it has to be the tower," Seth said.

"Or the tower's power source." Brent stopped at the red light. "Which way? Do we try to access the service area of the airport or the passenger side?"

"Passenger side," Seth said. "That will be their easiest point of entry."

Brent nodded in agreement. He pulled into the parking structure, going up several levels so he could park close to the skybridge that connected the garage to the terminal.

He found a spot and hurried to the skybridge entrance. He glanced at the cars driving on the lower level, people picking up passengers. Above the street level, the elevated rail of the Metro ran parallel to the drop-off zone on the upper level, the tower rising just beyond. Brent stopped.

Seth stopped beside him. "What?"

Brent motioned at the tower. "If I were planning a EMP attack on this airport, this is where I would do it. It's close to the tower and the subway station. It's not far from the planes in the main terminal."

"What time is it?" Seth asked even as he pulled his phone out to check for himself.

"Almost eleven."

"If they're striking at noon, they could be here by now."

"The question is, Where?" A couple passed by, both rolling carry-on bags.

"The weapons are disguised as luggage." Brent watched the couple continue.

Seth shook his head. "They could literally be anywhere."

"Not necessarily." Brent turned and headed back toward the garage.

"Where are you going?"

"People are more aware of their surroundings when they travel, at least when it comes to unattended luggage."

"Well, yeah. They have announcements reminding passengers to inform security if they see anything odd."

A prerecorded voice sounded over the loudspeaker, punctuating Seth's point. Seth held up a hand. "See?"

"Right." Brent motioned back toward the parking garage. "The range on the pulse weapon is at least two miles. If the weapon were left in a trunk here at the airport, it would take out the airport's power, the cars below, a portion of George Washington Parkway and I-395—"

"And the Pentagon." Seth picked up his pace until he reached the parking structure again. He put his hand on one of the thick concrete pillars. "They wouldn't want all this interference down here. They would go for the top level."

"Let's go." Brent rushed to the stairs and raced up them. He reached the top and surveyed the half-filled lot. "They'd likely try to park close to the tower."

"Agreed." Seth headed toward the cars parked a short distance away. "I'll take this row."

Brent angled toward the next row over, the one that ran along the edge of the parking structure. He searched for any occupied cars, finding no one in the first dozen he checked. He passed a large pickup truck and slowed so he would be able to see inside whatever car was parked on the other side of it. The next car was empty, but Brent caught a glimpse of movement inside the blue sedan parked three spaces over. A man sitting alone.

Brent slowed his pace even further. The likelihood was that this man was simply waiting to pick up someone at the airport, but Brent leaned down to get a better look anyway.

The man looked up, his face familiar. It took only a moment for Brent to recall where he'd seen this man: on the surveillance video in Atlanta.

Brent reached for the pistol holstered at his waist. "Seth."

That was as far as Brent got before the man shoved his door open and came out firing.

Brent dropped behind the pickup. "Found one."

48

Gunshots sounded through the communication device in Amy's ear, a striking contrast to the heavy security of the White House. Trying to remain calm, she asked, "Status?"

Brent responded, his voice low. "Single target, blue Honda Accord, Maryland license plate XTR 5578."

"I'll alert the police and run the plate."

Brent gave her their detailed position in the parking garage at the airport.

Amy made the call to 911 and relayed the situation as well as the shooter's location. After ensuring that the authorities were aware of Brent and Seth's presence, she put the phone on speaker so the 911 operator would be able to hear updates as Amy received new information.

Amy accessed the FBI's system and typed in the plate number. The results popped up. "The car belongs to a rental company. It was rented in Atlanta a week ago."

"That's before Osman and his men arrived," Seth said.

"He must have already had people here laying the groundwork," Brent added.

Another shot fired.

"Status?" Amy asked again.

"No change. The shooter has taken cover behind his car," Brent said. "Amy, get word to Doug and the rest of the squad. Let them know to check the parking garages at the target airports. Maybe we'll get lucky, and that's where all of Osman's men will set up to strike."

"I'll take care of it." Amy looked down at her phone sitting on the table. "Do you need me to relay any more information to the authorities before I hang up with the 911 operator?"

Seth answered this time. "Have the cops block off the parking garage. We don't need any civilians up here."

"The skybridge too," Brent said.

"I'll take care of it."

Amy relayed the information to emergency services and ended the call. She then called Doug.

When Doug didn't answer, she hung up and dialed Jay. Again, no answer. She tried Tristan next.

"Hey, Amy, I'm a little busy right now. Can I call you back?" Tristan said.

"No. Brent and Seth found one of Osman's men at Reagan National." Amy headed for the door that connected the Cabinet Room to the office where her father's secretaries worked. "Brent wants you to check the top level of the garage at the Atlanta airport. They'll probably be in the section closest to the tower."

"Roger that."

"Keep me updated."

"Roger."

The call ended, and Amy opened the door and entered the office where her father's secretaries worked. She passed by the first two and stopped at Sarah's desk. "Do you know where Doug Valdez is?"

"He's in the Roosevelt Room."

"Thanks." Amy turned away from her father's door and crossed the hall to the Roosevelt Room. Sure enough, Doug was inside with four other members of his Homeland Security team.

"Doug, Brent and Seth found one of Osman's men." Amy gave the location and the specifics.

Doug turned to the man beside him. "Get the word out. I want agents scouring the parking areas closest to the airport towers."

The man picked up the phone as Doug did the same.

"Who are you calling?" Amy asked.

"The FAA. I want all flights grounded until we get Osman's men into custody."

Amy looked at the clock: 11:32. The attack could happen within minutes.

Doug ended the call and tried again. Again, he hit the End button. "It's not going through."

More gunfire sounded through Amy's earpiece. "Brent?"

"We've got him pinned down."

Doug picked up the phone in the corner of the room and dialed once more. Frustration filled his expression. "The phones at the FAA are down."

* * *

Nearly two hours in meetings with the FAA only to discover what they could have told Vanessa over the phone in less than five minutes: Upgraded, copper-shielded generators to provide backup electricity in case of a power outage, a backup computer network that ran independently of their main internet connection to avoid any shutdowns of the flight data center. Their security at their main entrance was adequate, and a badge system was in place.

Vanessa approached the entrance now with Ross, the security officer who had shown her around.

"Thank you again for your time." Vanessa turned and shook the man's hand.

"Anytime."

One of the guards motioned to Ross. "Sir, I just wanted to let you know the technician for the emergency generators arrived."

"What technician?" Ross asked.

"The man had a work authorization signed by you."

"I didn't authorize anyone to work on the generators." Ross took a step toward the guard. "Where is he now?"

"He should be inspecting the generators."

"What did he look like?" Vanessa asked.

The guard motioned to his partner. "Pull up the security feed for when the tech showed up."

The other guard tapped on his computer keyboard and turned his laptop toward them.

"I don't know him," Ross said.

Vanessa stepped closer. "I do. That's Osman."

"Call the police," Ross told the guard.

Vanessa reached into her purse and pulled out the earpiece Ghost had given her. She pressed the button to turn it on, then slipped it into place. "Seth, Brent, do you read me?"

"They're a little busy right now." Amy's voice came through clearly.

"They need to get unbusy. Osman is here at FAA headquarters."

"What?" Amy asked.

"Say again," Seth said.

"You heard me. He snuck in disguised as a technician. We think he's going for the backup generators."

A popping sound carried over the comm device. "Is that gunfire?"

"Yes," Seth said. "We found one of Osman's men."

"Maybe you should get him to stop shooting so you can help me find Osman."

Brent responded this time, sarcasm carrying in his voice. "We'll get right on that."

Vanessa clicked on the button to mute the comm unit. Even though she wanted to keep listening to what was happening with her husband, she didn't want her conversations to distract Seth from getting out of the situation safely.

The guard hung up the phone on his desk and pulled his cell phone out. "Ma'am, the main phone lines are down."

"Is your cell working?" Vanessa asked.

He nodded.

While the guard called the police, Vanessa turned on her earpiece again. "Amy, the main phone lines are down at FAA headquarters."

"I'm here with Doug right now. Hold on."

While Amy spoke with Doug, Vanessa turned to Ross. "Where's the generator room?"

"This way."

49

Sirens rang out as Brent peeked over the hood of the truck he was currently using for cover. As expected, Osman's man fired.

Brent ducked back down. He didn't know how much ammo the man had brought with him, but he had used a good bit over the past few minutes.

Seth had used the row of cars opposite Brent's position to circle to the other side of Osman's man, but every time he passed between cars, the man fired. As though Seth were going to let him get a clean shot.

"In position," Seth said.

Brent spoke into his earpiece. "Amy, what's the status on the police?"

"They've shut off the entrance to the garage, but they need another minute to secure the elevators and skybridge."

The elevator dinged. Brent could barely make out the sound of the doors sliding open.

"We've got company," Brent said.

"Friendlies?" Seth asked.

"I can't tell yet." Brent dropped onto the ground and looked beneath the vehicles between him and the elevator. He couldn't see anything, but the sound of wheels against the concrete carried to him. Not wheels of a car. Something else, something lighter. A luggage cart maybe?

Brent crept to the back of the truck so he could see who was coming. A woman pushing a stroller, a toddler bundled inside.

"Seth, cover me." As soon as Seth fired, Brent popped up so the woman could see him. "Gun! Go back!"

The woman's eyes flew wide, and she froze.

Another newcomer, a man in his twenties, appeared behind her. Brent started to shout another warning, but then his gaze lowered to the man's right hand and the gun gripped there.

"Take cover!" Brent aimed at the man behind the woman and child. "Federal agent! Freeze!"

The woman didn't move, but the man immediately jumped to the side so the civilians were in the line of fire.

Seth fired at the man by the sedan, away from the woman and child, to keep Osman's man by the car at bay. Brent rushed forward. He fired once at the man and then pushed the woman toward the row of cars opposite him. Her grip remained firm on the stroller, and it tipped precariously.

Brent fired again and used his free hand to grab the stroller. He picked it up and carried it between an SUV and a Mini Cooper. Brent set the stroller down. Immediately, the toddler went from startled to screaming. Brent gripped the woman's shoulder and pushed her down behind the car. "Stay down."

"Brent?" Amy's worried voice came over his comm unit.

"Advise the police. We've got two civilians pinned down up here. A woman and her child." Bullets sparked off the SUV. A window shattered. "And a second shooter."

The child's wails intensified. The woman gasped for breath.

Brent focused on her face. "Ma'am, look at me."

She did, but the wild look in her eyes told him she was barely functioning. "What's your baby's name?"

More gunfire.

The woman screamed.

"Ma'am, I'm going to get you out of here, but I need your help." Brent waited for her to look at him again. "Talk to the baby. Tell him it's okay."

She focused on the child, and something seemed to click. "It's okay, sweetie." The woman's voice trembled. "It's going to be okay."

"Don't move from here. The police are on their way."

"I thought you were the police."

Brent didn't want to dispute her assumption. "My backup is on the way." He tapped on his earpiece. "Amy, how close are they?"

"There are four officers heading your way. ETA two minutes."

Brent peeked out at the latest arrival. He'd taken cover between the vehicles parked by the railing and was moving toward his partner.

"Seth, he's working his way toward you."

"The other one keeps trying for the trunk."

"That's probably where the weapon is." Brent's hand flexed on the grip of his pistol. "We can't chance them using it."

"Agreed," Seth said. Another shot fired, and Seth's irritation came through in his next words. "I've had about enough of this."

"Me too."

The new arrival passed Brent's position and reached the pickup Brent had been hiding behind earlier.

"Get ready. I'm going to see if I can give you some targets." Brent turned to the woman again. "Remember what I said: Stay here until the police tell you it's okay."

She nodded.

Keeping his head down, Brent moved to the edge of the Mini Cooper. He waited until both shooters were out of sight before he rushed forward.

Brent reached the barrier, both men finally visible as one approached the car and the other squatted behind it, the trunk now open.

A car engine echoed from the garage below and then the squeal of tires taking a corner too fast. The police were here, but Brent couldn't afford to wait.

"Freeze!" Brent shouted.

One turned, leading with his gun. Brent fired, and the man dropped. The other man swung his pistol at Brent, but before he could fire, a shot rang out.

Osman's man jerked backward and grabbed the edge of the car. He reached into the trunk, and Brent glimpsed a flash of silver inside.

"Don't do it!" Brent shouted. When the man continued to reach for the weapon, Brent took aim and fired.

50

Tristan raced behind the security director on the way to hourly parking.

Jay's voice came over his comm unit. "The parking lot is packed. I don't know if we'll have time to search it all."

Five SEALs and possibly some airport security searching the top deck was doable, but it was time to give them a better advantage.

Tristan grabbed the security director's arm. "I need a chopper."

"All flights are grounded until further notice."

"I'll get clearance."

The director nodded. "This way."

"What are you doing?" Jay asked.

"I'm going to go up in a chopper and act as a spotter."

"Better make it fast," Jay said. He then said Quinn's name, but Tristan didn't listen to the order that followed. He was already dialing Doug's number.

"Through here." Kevin unlocked a security door and led Tristan into a long hall.

Doug picked up, and Tristan explained his plan while sprinting forward. By the time Tristan reached the helipad, the tower had already cleared him.

Tristan pulled on his headset, warmed up the engines, and did a quick check of the helicopter. He wasn't going to think about the shortcuts he was taking to get up in the air quickly. If he didn't go now, he wouldn't have the chance.

He checked the time. Less than twenty minutes until the suspected strike window opened.

Another minute, maybe two before he would be airborne. He checked in with the tower to clear his takeoff. As soon as he was cleared, he switched frequencies and checked in. "Prepping for takeoff. What's our status?"

"No visual yet on Osman's men," Damian said.

"I'll be airborne in sixty seconds."

"Quinn's heading your way," Jay said.

"What?" Tristan looked up as Quinn rushed toward him, his rifle slung over his shoulder. He reached the helicopter and climbed into the back.

"What are you doing here?" Tristan shouted. "This is a solo flight."

"Negative," Quinn shouted back. "I'm your sniper." He snatched the second set of headphones in the copilot's seat and slipped them into place.

"You realize that if that EMP is deployed, this chopper could go down."

"I hope you're good at crash landings, then."

"Quinn, stay here."

"Get in the air," Jay ordered over the comm set. "You have until eleven fifty-five to spot. After that, I want you both on the ground."

Quinn strapped into the back seat, leaving the door open. "You heard him. Let's go."

Tristan was about to take off with his brother-in-law, knowing a weapon was nearby that could quickly take out their engine. If his wife could see him now, she'd kill him. Tristan grabbed the throttle. If he survived the day, this was one secret he would definitely be keeping.

* * *

Possible reasons for Osman's presence inside FAA headquarters raced through Vanessa's mind, but none of them made any sense. If Osman wanted to use his electromagnetic weapon, he could activate it just as easily from outside.

Vanessa reached the door to the generator room and pulled out her cell phone. The phones. Maybe that was what he'd been after, ensuring that the FAA would lose their ability to communicate.

Ross started to open the door, but Vanessa held up her hand. "Wait."

"Why?"

"Because Osman may have been here." Vanessa shone the flashlight from her phone along the edges of the door but didn't see any sign of tampering. "Okay. Go ahead and open it."

Ross gave her a skeptical look before swiping his badge and unlocking the door. Slowly, he pulled it open.

Vanessa stepped inside and looked around the room. Two large generators lined the wall to her left. Huge vents opened to the outside. Vanessa did a quick search of the nearly barren room. Nothing.

"Where's the main junction for your phone system?"

"Just down the hall." Ross led Vanessa past two doors and across the hall before stopping beside an open door. A technician stood beside an open junction box.

"What's the deal with the phones?" Ross asked.

"I don't know yet."

Vanessa pulled up a photo of Osman on her phone. "Have you seen this man?"

The man in his fifties pulled off his glasses and leaned forward. Then he straightened and slipped his glasses back in place. "Yeah, he was in the hall when I came down here."

"Where did he go?"

"I'm not sure." He motioned toward the front of the building. "I think he headed for the stairs."

"Thanks." Vanessa rushed out of the room toward the stairs. "What's above us?"

"Just offices and a couple of storage closets," Ross said.

"We'll check the storage closets first." Vanessa led the way to the second floor.

"What are you looking for?"

"I'm hoping not to find anything, but Osman had a reason for breaking in here," Vanessa said. "We need to know what it is." She focused on the storage closet situated above the utility room. Without waiting for Ross, she checked the door and opened it.

"That should have been locked," Ross said.

Vanessa suspected as much. Rather than turn on the light, she used her phone's flashlight to illuminate the closet's interior. Shelves on one side, an open space on the other. A conduit box that appeared to continue from the room below occupied the far wall.

"The light switch is on your right." Ross started to reach past Vanessa to turn it on at the same time she turned her light on that part of the wall. The light plate hung slightly askew, and a wire ran to the floor.

"Don't." Vanessa grabbed his hand to stop him.

"What's wrong?"

"The switch looks like it's wired to something besides the light."

"What?"

Vanessa followed the wire with her flashlight to the floor and followed it along the baseboard. Carefully, she pushed aside a box of printer paper. Another box sat behind it. Vanessa lifted it, surprised that this one didn't have any weight to it. Moving slowly, she pulled it toward her and turned it to reveal the hollow underside. She shined her light on the wire again, now able to see where it disappeared into a block of C4, a detonator attached to the side of it.

"Did you find something?" Ross asked.

"Yeah." Vanessa looked over her shoulder. "Call the bomb squad."

Ross stepped back. "There's a bomb?"

"Yes." Vanessa dropped to her stomach so she could get a better look. "Clear the building, and see if the tech downstairs has a pair of wire cutters. Two pairs would be better."

"And if he doesn't?" Ross asked, already dialing his phone.

"Then get me the sharpest knife or pair of scissors you can find."

* * *

Brent put his hand to his ear to block out any extra noise from the police officers who were now dealing with Osman's men and the weapon that had indeed been in the trunk. He could have sworn Vanessa had just said she found a bomb.

Seth mimicked his action. "Vanessa, say again?"

"I found a bomb."

Seth took off running toward the stairs.

"We have to go!" Brent shouted at the nearest officer as he started after Seth. "Make sure you secure the weapon, and tell your guys to open the gate for us."

"Vanessa, we're on our way," Seth said.

Brent raced down the stairs and hit the fob to unlock their car. He and Seth both jumped inside, and Brent hit the Start button. He pulled out of his spot and sped down the four levels to the exit the police currently flanked.

"Tell me what you see, Vanessa," Seth said, his voice deceptively calm.

"It's a block of C4 that's been wired to the light switch," Vanessa said, her words coming out quickly.

"The light switch?" Seth asked. "Why would he do that?"

Brent lifted his hand to signal he was exiting. Thankfully, someone opened the gate and the police let them through.

"The phones are out here. I think this may be one of the places they can fix the lines."

"So they would have let whatever phone tech on duty trigger the bomb for them," Seth said. "Is there a detonator or a timer?"

"There's a timer. I've got fourteen more minutes," Vanessa said. "It's set to go off at noon."

"Get out of there," Seth insisted. "Let the bomb squad handle it."

Vanessa didn't respond, but a moment later, Seth's phone rang. He pulled it from his pocket. "Vanessa is FaceTiming me." He hit the button to accept the call.

"Here. Now you can see what we're dealing with."

Brent pulled onto the GW Parkway and headed for I-395. "What have we got?"

"Looks like a straight timer with a secondary line hardwired into the light switch."

Though Brent hated to ask the question, he did anyway. "Can she disarm it?"

"Yeah, can I?" Vanessa asked.

Seth blew out a frustrated breath before he spoke. "I think so."

51

Jim checked the grandfather clock across the room. Only twelve minutes until noon.

Doug appeared in the open doorway and gave a cursory knock on the doorjamb.

Jim stood. "What's the latest?"

"EMP weapons were found in Atlanta and at Reagan National." Doug crossed the room until he stood opposite Jim's desk. "We have helicopters searching the tops of the airport parking decks in Charlotte, Atlanta, New York, Detroit, and Miami."

"If New York goes dark . . ." Jim shook his head.

"I know. We're doing everything we can," Doug insisted. "Local police are working with the FBI. They're searching all levels of the parking areas as well as cars parked along the pickup and drop-off lanes."

"What about flight operations?"

"We've already grounded all flights in Atlanta," Doug said. "A half dozen more flights are cleared to leave New York, but both airports there will shut down at eleven fifty."

Ten minutes before the expected attack, just enough time for the local planes to clear the area before the weapon deployed.

Amy rushed in and closed the door behind her. "There's a bomb at the FAA headquarters."

Doug whirled to face her. "What?"

"Are you sure?" Jim asked.

Amy nodded. "Seth and Brent are almost there. They're trying to talk Vanessa through disarming it."

"What about the bomb squad?"

"They're on their way, but we aren't sure they'll get there in time." Amy looked up at the clock. "It's set to go off at noon."

"Osman's men must be planning to activate their weapons around the same time," Doug said.

Jim put both hands on his desk. "We need to get those helicopters on the ground."

"We have a couple more minutes." Doug pulled his phone out of his pocket.

"But—"

"Dad, he's right," Amy cut Jim off. "We need to give the authorities as much time as possible to stop these attacks. It could mean the difference between life and death for a lot of people."

"Those helicopter pilots are at risk if the weapon is activated while they're in the air," Jim said.

"Give them five more minutes," Amy said. "If the weapon is anything like what the SEALs experienced at the fortress, the engine failure won't be immediate. They should still have a couple minutes to land."

Jim straightened and studied his daughter and his director of Homeland Security. He had chosen Doug for this role because he trusted him. Amy had proved repeatedly that she had a unique wisdom in crisis situations.

"You both think I should wait?" Jim asked.

They both nodded.

"You can have your five minutes for the helicopters, but I want flight operations grounded until that bomb is defused."

Doug nodded. "I'll take care of it."

* * *

Vanessa shined her phone flashlight on the bomb, sending the image to Seth through FaceTime. Even though she had undergone basic training in how to defuse a bomb, her husband had a whole lot more experience than she did in this department.

The fire alarm blared, making it nearly impossible to hear Seth's voice over the phone. Thankfully, his words were relatively clear through her earpiece.

Ross appeared in the doorway, holding a toolbox. "The tech took off when the fire alarm sounded, but he left behind his toolbox."

"Are there wire cutters in there?" Vanessa asked.

He set the toolbox on the floor and rummaged through it. "Yes." He grabbed a pair and handed them over.

Vanessa took them with her free hand. "What's the status on the bomb squad?"

Ross repeated the question into his phone before answering. "Nine minutes."

Vanessa shook her head. Nine minutes and seven seconds left until the bomb detonated. If she were driving, she could shave a minute or two off that. "I need a lamp and an extension cord."

Ross disappeared down the hall, his footsteps pounding against the linoleum floor.

"Vanessa, let me see where the wire goes into the detonator from the light switch," Seth said.

She angled the phone to give him the view he wanted.

"How far out is the bomb squad?" Brent asked.

"Eight, maybe nine minutes."

"What's taking them so long?" Seth asked. "The District isn't that big."

Amy answered. "The DC police had three bomb threats scattered all over town this morning."

"Three?" Seth repeated.

"Best guess is Osman called them in to keep the bomb squad occupied and away from the FAA building."

"He's stretching our resources to make sure no one interferes with his plans," Vanessa muttered.

"Too late for that," Brent said.

Ross reappeared in the doorway. He held out a desk lamp, an extension cord gripped in his other hand. "Here."

"Set it over here, and plug it in for me." Vanessa motioned to the floor beside her.

He put the lamp down, plugged it into the extension cord, and hurried into the hall to plug it in. The lamp turned on. He peeked through the doorway. "What else do you need?"

"Nothing." Vanessa motioned toward the exit. "Go ahead. Get out of here."

"What about you?" Ross asked.

"I don't need anyone around if I have to defuse this on my own."

Ross hesitated slightly before stepping back again.

Vanessa grabbed the lamp and moved it closer to the bomb so she could see it more clearly. Before she could ask Seth for instructions, a gunshot echoed in the hallway.

Vanessa turned as Ross cried out and grabbed the doorjamb. His phone slipped from his hand and fell to the floor in the hall.

Vanessa dropped her phone and leaped to her feet. She grabbed Ross and pulled him into the utility room, slamming the door behind her.

Struggling to hold Ross upright, she flipped the lock.

"Was that gunfire?" Seth asked, his concern obvious.

Vanessa supported Ross's weight as he slid to the ground, his hand pressed to his left shoulder. In the wash of lamplight, the dark red of his blood colored his fingers.

Three more shots fired, each impacting the steel door but not penetrating it.

"That was gunfire," Vanessa confirmed.

A heavily accented voice carried to her. "False alarm. It isn't a bomb."

"And I think I found Osman."

52

Amy paced the length of her father's office, her mind racing. Tristan and Quinn were in a helicopter, an electromagnetic pulse weapon could be activated at any minute, Vanessa was facing a bomb and an armed man—likely Osman—and Amy's husband was rushing toward the danger.

"Why would Osman come back if the bomb is about to go off?" Amy asked.

"He probably went back to find out why the fire alarm was pulled." Doug pulled out his phone. "Shots fired inside the FAA headquarters. I need police presence on the second floor, southeast corner." He lowered his phone briefly. "Is Vanessa armed?"

Amy repeated the question through her comm unit.

"No. I came straight from the White House," Vanessa said.

"Brent, how far away are you?" Amy asked.

"Four minutes." Sirens blared in the background. "Assuming the cop following us doesn't cut us off."

"What cop?" Amy asked.

"The one who didn't appreciate me driving 110 miles an hour on 395."

Amy turned to Doug. "Can you tell the cops to call off the unit chasing Brent? Or better yet, have it escort him."

"License plate?" Doug asked.

Amy relayed it.

Her father paced the room opposite her. "This is like living in a thriller movie."

"It's time we get to the happy ending," Amy said.

Doug ended his call. "Tell Brent the police unit will lead the way."

"Brent, did you hear that? The police are escorting you to the FAA building."

"Roger," Brent said. "ETA three minutes."

More gunshots echoed over Amy's earpiece. "Vanessa? Are you okay?"

"The door is holding, but I lost my light again," Vanessa said. "Osman must have unplugged the extension cord."

"Can you see the bomb using your phone?" Seth asked.

"Yeah."

"How much time is left?" Seth asked.

"Six minutes."

"Hang on," Seth said. "We're almost there."

* * *

Tristan circled above the parking garage for the third time. A half dozen police officers were searching the cars on the top deck, and more were searching lower ones. Damian and Craig worked their way through the area closest to the tower.

"I don't see anything," Craig said.

"Quinn, what about you?"

"Nothing."

"Maybe they aren't hitting this airport," Tristan said. The moment the words escaped him, he knew he was wrong.

"That wouldn't make sense," Jay said. "Why fly to a city they aren't going to target?"

"They must have another spot they've set up." Tristan adjusted his heading and flew over the pickup and drop-off lanes. "Quinn, anything down there?"

"There are too many possibilities."

"I can see the pickup lanes from here," Damian said.

"And I've got the drop-off lanes covered," Jay said.

The air-traffic controller cut into their communication. "This is air-traffic control. You are requested to land. Land immediately."

"Great." Tristan checked the time on his instrument panel: 11:53. Technically, they still had two more minutes until they had to be on the ground.

He made one more pass over the pickup and drop-off lanes, circling wide so he would be able to utilize the time he had remaining.

"Nothing," he said. His stomach tightened. Five SEALs, all with intimate knowledge of the terrorists, and they had failed to complete their mission.

Disheartened, he flew around the back side of the airport, planes parked at nearly every terminal below.

"Got something," Quinn announced. "Your three o'clock."

Tristan looked down at the pickup truck with the airport logo on the side. A man stood by the tailgate, a silver case open beside him.

Another man emerged from the cab of the truck, an automatic rifle gripped in his hand.

"Gun!" Tristan shouted.

Gunfire sparked against the front of the helicopter. Several bullets whizzed through the open door, impacting the ceiling of the aircraft.

"Quinn!" Tristan shouted, unable to see whether his brother-in-law had taken a hit.

"Jay, a little help?" Quinn said, his voice steady.

A single shot rang out, and the gunman dropped to the ground.

"I don't have a clear shot on the other one," Jay said.

"Tristan, circle around," Quinn said.

Tristan blew out a breath and adjusted his headset. "Circling."

* * *

Brent skidded to a stop beside their police escort, both vehicles a hundred yards from the FAA building. Emergency vehicles blocked the rest of the street, hundreds of people loitering beyond the safety barricade that had been set up. Brent and Seth both pushed out of the car and sprinted forward.

A police officer tried to stop them, but the policeman who had been escorting them shouted, "Let them through!"

Ignoring the pain in his leg, Brent dodged past the officer on one side of the barricade. Seth leaped over it on the other side.

Brent burst through the door into the empty lobby and rushed past the security station, turning down the corridor, Seth's footsteps pounding beside him.

"Where are you?" Vanessa asked through their comm units. "There are only three minutes left."

"We're almost there." Seth spoke the words in time with his steps.

On the ride over, Seth had told Vanessa which wire he thought would disarm the bomb, but none of them wanted her to test his theory, not without them getting a closer look at the device.

Brent and Seth were nearly to the stairs when a man rushed out.

Brent slowed and reached for the gun holstered at the back of his waistband. Seth mirrored his move as he realized the man was Osman.

Osman already gripped his gun.

Brent aimed his pistol. "Freeze!"

Osman darted back into the stairwell. An instant later, his gun hand reappeared.

Brent and Seth both pressed against the opposite walls of the hallway. Both fired in tandem as Osman shot at them.

Osman pulled his arm back, and footsteps pounded upward.

"What's going on?" Vanessa asked. "I hear gunfire."

"Osman is still here."

"Why would he still be here?" Vanessa asked. "The bomb is going to go off in less than two minutes."

"He was leaving," Brent said. "We got in his way."

"He'll try to get to the other side of the building to make sure he's clear of the blast," Seth said. "You go find him. I'll help Vanessa."

"No." Vanessa's voice was firm. "You two get Osman. I'll disarm the bomb."

"I'll come—"

"No," Vanessa interrupted Seth. "I don't want both of us in the blast zone in case this doesn't work."

Brent hated that Seth had this choice to make. "It's your call."

"Seth, I love you," Vanessa said, steel in her voice, "but I need you to do this for me."

Seth's jaw clenched, and he took two deep breaths. "I'll follow him up these stairs. You try to cut him off on the far side."

Brent nodded. "Vanessa, Seth will be running past you in about twenty seconds."

"I'll wait until time is almost out to cut the wire," Vanessa said. "I want both of you out of here. Every child should get a chance to know their father."

Seth's whispered response came through clearly. "And their mother."

* * *

Vanessa picked up the wire cutters and adjusted the light. Footsteps pounded down the hall, past the utility closet, and quickly faded.

"You're really going to disarm that by yourself?" Ross asked, his breathing labored.

"Yes."

A shot fired. More pounding footsteps.

"Seth?" Vanessa asked.

"I'm passing you now." His footsteps slowed before increasing speed again. "I love you."

"I love you." She read the numbers counting down on the detonator. "Fifty-nine seconds."

"Wait until you get to ten," Brent said, his voice low.

Vanessa turned to Ross. "Can you walk?"

He nodded.

"Good. Get out of here." Vanessa nodded toward the door. "And leave the door open."

"But—"

"If you can't get down the stairs, go to the far side of the building." Vanessa set the phone down, trying to position it so it would shine on the bomb without her needing to hold it.

Ross propped the phone up so it was more firmly in place for her. "I hope you know what you're doing."

"Me too." Vanessa pointed. "Go. Now."

Ross nodded and disappeared from the room.

Vanessa watched the time tick down. Sixteen seconds. Fifteen. She slipped the wire cutters into place as the seconds continued to count down. Giving Ross as much time as possible to get clear of the danger zone, she waited until the timer was at ten seconds.

Sending up a silent prayer, she drew a deep breath and blew it out. Then she squeezed the wire cutters in one quick motion.

53

Tristan moved back into position to give Quinn the best shooting angle. Osman's man was at the back of the truck again, the silver case still open.

"Ten degrees to the starboard, and I'll have it," Quinn said in his no-nonsense voice.

Tristan made the adjustment, and Quinn fired as the man grabbed his weapon and ducked behind the truck. He popped up shooting a second later.

Bullets sparked off the front of the chopper.

A gust of wind pulled at the aircraft, and Tristan fought against the sudden turbulence.

Quinn fired in that same instance. "Dang it. I missed."

More gunfire filled the air. Quinn sent off a round, but the target shifted his position and fired again. Tristan pulled up and maneuvered out of range.

"I'm coming around again," Tristan said. "Jay, lay down some cover fire so I can hold it steady."

"Roger," Jay said. "Better make it quick. He's going for the case."

"If he activates that thing while we're this close, this chopper is going down," Quinn said.

As though Tristan needed the reminder. Nor was he going to explain the aerodynamics of autorotation or an emergency helicopter landing right now. "If you shoot him before he activates it, we won't have to worry about it." Tristan increased his speed and pulled around again. "Five seconds to target."

"I have him in my sights," Quinn said.

"He has the case open," Jay said, urgency in his voice.

"One second," Quinn said. "Firing."

A single shot competed with the noise of the helicopter engine and the whirring of the blades.

Tristan glanced below him, but he didn't have the right angle to see the truck or the shooter below. "Status?"

"He's down," Quinn said. "Let the police know they can move in and secure the weapon."

"I'll call it in," Jay said.

Quinn secured his rifle and climbed into the seat behind Tristan. "You can land now. This thing is finally over."

* * *

Brent slowed when he passed the elevator located in the middle of the long hallway, a set of stairs beside it. He had already checked the stairs on the East Wing near where the bomb had been planted. Seth remained on the second floor, the last place Osman had been seen.

Brent glanced at the elevator again. Would he try to use it or the stairs? The stairs. No way would Osman wait for the elevator with Seth behind him.

"Anything?" Brent asked.

"I haven't seen him since the last time he shot at me," Seth said. "He has to be in one of the stairwells."

"Which one?" There were three stairwells on this hallway alone.

"I don't know. I didn't hear a door close," Seth said.

"I'll check the one by the elevator. You check the next one."

"Got it."

His pistol gripped in his hand, Brent reached for the door handle. He pulled it open in the same moment someone rammed into the door from the other side. Brent stumbled back as Osman rushed into the hall. Osman lifted his pistol, but before he could take aim, Brent flung his hand out to block Osman's intended movement. Osman's gun dropped.

Not giving Osman the chance to retrieve his weapon, Brent kicked it down the hall to keep it out of reach.

Too close to use his own weapon accurately, Brent took a step back, but Osman charged at him, tackling him around the waist. Brent fell to the ground, and his gun skidded across the floor.

Osman jerked his fist up into the bottom of Brent's jaw, and Brent's head flew back against the hard floor. Dazed, he shook his head to clear his vision as Osman straddled his waist and lifted his hand above him, a knife now fisted between his fingers.

Flat on his back, Brent lifted both hands to keep Osman from thrusting the knife downward.

Osman grunted as he struggled to overpower Brent, using all his weight to try to drive his weapon into Brent's chest.

Brent bent his legs and threw his weight to one side. His efforts knocked Osman off him, the two men grappling as they rolled on the floor and broke apart. Brent grasped for the handle of the knife, but Osman pulled it out of reach and plunged it toward Brent's chest once more.

Brent struck out with his hand to block the attack, the blade slicing through the skin on his forearm. He cried out in pain and kicked to create distance between them. Quickly, he scrambled to his feet. Osman stood as well, his knife outstretched as he jabbed at Brent again.

"You aren't getting out of here," Brent said, not sure if Osman even spoke English. "The bomb's been disarmed."

Fury flashed in Osman's eyes. He darted forward again, swiping at Brent with the knife another time.

Brent jumped back, the blade cutting through the fabric of his shirt. Irritated on principal, Brent took another step back, this time creating enough distance to kick out and knock the knife loose.

Osman grabbed for the loose knife, but Brent stepped on it and shoved Osman backward. Unfortunately, Osman dropped to the floor right beside his gun. He scrambled to his feet, gun in hand.

With only one possibility for cover, Brent ducked into the elevator doorway. Osman fired, and a bullet impacted a half inch from Brent's head.

A door opened down the hall.

"Freeze!" Seth shouted.

Brent peeked out as Osman glanced behind him.

Brent scooped the knife off the floor as Osman turned and swung his weapon toward Seth. Brent hurled the knife at Osman at the same time Seth lifted his pistol and fired. The knife impacted Osman's shoulder, and his body jerked forward. He looked at Brent with surprise. Then his eyes glazed over, and he dropped to his knees before collapsing to the floor.

* * *

Jim stood beside his desk as the clock struck twelve. Two weapons still unaccounted for.

Amy had given him the update on the bomb at the FAA. Vanessa had disarmed it, and Brent and Seth had killed Osman.

Amy's phone chimed. "Jay just texted. The police have secured the weapon at the Atlanta airport."

Only one more to go. Jim turned to Doug. "Any word yet on New York?"

"Not yet." Doug's phone rang. "Sorry. I need to take this."

Jim nodded.

Sawyer walked into the Oval Office. "It took nearly three hundred police officers, but they found the weapon at JFK and the people who planted it. In this case, it was two women."

Jim sagged with relief. "That's all of the weapons, then."

"Thank goodness." Amy sank onto the couch.

Doug lifted the phone he held. "The bomb squad has removed the explosive device that Vanessa disarmed." He focused on Jim. "With your permission, I'd like to have the FAA resume operations."

"By all means." Jim sat beside Amy and looked at the clock again. "That was far too close."

"But we got the job done." Amy put her hand on his arm. "You put together a good team, and everyone worked together when it really mattered."

"She's right," Sawyer said. "That's the sign of a great president."

"If it's all the same to you, I'd prefer not to demonstrate any greatness in these kinds of situations again," Jim said.

"I don't blame you." Amy leaned heavily against the back of the couch. She rolled her head to look at him. "But you might want to have this conversation with your intelligence council. They're the best for preventive measures."

"You could be right."

"Dad, you should know by now, I'm always right."

Jim couldn't help but smile. "Just like your mother."

54

Amy curled up beside Brent on the couch of the cabin they had been assigned at Camp David.

Over the past week, the virus that had aided the spread of the unique electromagnetic weapon had been virtually eliminated, and the FBI had managed to track down two more of Osman's men, who had been trying to escape over the Canadian border.

The crisis was over, her father had finally managed a few good nights of sleep, and Amy's morning sickness had settled to occasional bouts of nausea when she didn't eat often enough.

Brent caressed her shoulder the way he did when his mind was wandering.

"What are you thinking about?" she asked.

"Us."

Amy shifted slightly and tilted her chin up so she could see his face. "What about us?"

"I keep thinking about Vanessa defusing that bomb." Brent shook his head. "It about killed Seth to leave her to it, to make sure that if things went south, at least one of them would survive."

Instantly, Amy was transported back to that private moment broadcasted through her earpiece. "He made the right choice."

"Yes, he did, and thankfully, it all worked out, but it got me thinking about what it will be like once the baby comes."

"You're wondering if I'll want to keep working."

"Not just that. I'm wondering if I should keep working."

Amy shifted away so she was facing him fully. "Define 'keep working.' Are you thinking about leaving the navy?"

"Not necessarily the navy, but I could step back from the SEALs."

Amy tried to imagine it. Brent coming home from work every night, keeping regular hours, his biggest danger coming from the traffic on the freeway.

In theory, it sounded wonderful, except for one major issue. "You would be miserable working behind a desk."

"Yeah, but at least you wouldn't have to go through knowing that when I leave, I might not come back."

"We've been living with that reality for six years." Amy took his hand. "Is having a baby going to make leaving that much harder on you?"

"It's not me I'm worried about," Brent said. "Our situation is different now, not just because you're pregnant. Your father is now president." He put his free hand over hers. "I know you blamed your dad for me going MIA." He let out a sigh. "If something had happened to me, that would have come between you at a time when you needed your family the most."

She couldn't deny the truth of that. "What happened this time wasn't just because my father gave the order to leave you behind."

"Then, what was it?"

"It was because I watched it happen." Amy pulled her hand from his and stood. The memories crashed in on her, all the feelings of despair and disbelief and the faint glimmer of desperate hope.

She paced several steps away before turning back to face him. "I was in the Situation Room watching the mission on screen. I saw you by the jeep. I saw the explosion. And I sat there while everyone offered their condolences, so sure you were dead."

Brent stood and crossed to her. "Amy, I'm so sorry." He pulled her into his arms, and Amy wrapped her arms around his waist. He held her for a minute in silence. He swallowed hard before he spoke again, a clear sign that he was fighting his emotions. "I hate that you went through that. I hate that you had to wait to tell me you're pregnant."

Amy eased back and reached up to kiss him. Her lips met his, the connection between them enveloping her just as it had the first time he'd kissed her. She knew then that he would never be a man who worked nine to five. She couldn't let him change now. "Brent, I love you for who you are, and I don't want to be responsible for changing you or getting in the way of you doing what you love."

"I won't always be a SEAL. I'm already thirty-one."

"I know, but you need to walk away when the time is right for you, not because I got scared," Amy said. Hope illuminated his eyes, confirming what she already knew. "You aren't ready to walk away."

"What about you?" he asked. "Do you want to stay with the Saint Squad, even if you wouldn't be able to deploy with us?"

"I don't know, but we have another seven months to make that decision." She slid her arms up to encircle his neck. "That's seven months for me to pray about what I want and for us to pray about what will be best for our family."

"It's a big decision," Brent said, his voice low.

"Yes, it is." Her lips curved slowly into a grin. "And me getting pregnant is a big miracle. I never want to forget that."

"Me neither." He kissed her again. "And just so you know, I'll support whatever you decide."

She already knew as much, but hearing him say the words gave her a deeper comfort she hadn't known she needed. "I love you." She ran her hands down his arms and linked her fingers through his.

"I love you too." His eyebrows lifted, and so did the corners of his mouth. "You know, the first time I was left behind enemy lines without my squad was when I met you."

"I remember."

"This time, I came home to find out you're pregnant." His smile widened. "If we decide we want to go for baby number two, you can always have my squad abandon me again."

"Not a chance." She shook her head. "At least, not unless I'm with you and we're getting abandoned in the Bahamas or somewhere equally safe."

"The Bahamas," he repeated, nodding. "I can live with that."

"Good." Amy pushed up on her toes and kissed him.

Brent pulled her closer once more, proving what she hoped would always be true: He was alive, he was well, and he was hers.

EPILOGUE

Thanksgiving Day

Amy stood beside the window and gazed out at the North Lawn, her baby on her shoulder and her heart filled to overflowing. Today would be her first Thanksgiving at the White House, her first Thanksgiving as a mother. She ran her hand over her son's head. Little Cameron snuggled closer, burying his head in the curve of her neck.

Down below, several members of the Saint Squad tossed a frisbee around, Tristan's son, Dixon, and Seth's daughter, Talia, chasing after their fathers. Amy missed being part of that camaraderie, always knowing where the squad was and what they were doing. She even missed breaking up the arguments over who stole Craig's lunch and who was cheating at Uno.

A rather vigorous throw by Dixon went straight up and landed in a nearby tree. Amy laughed when Jay climbed up to fetch it.

Brent walked in behind her. "What are you laughing at?"

"Jay. He's up a tree again."

Brent's laughter joined hers. "At least if he gets a splinter, Carina is here to bandage him up."

Cameron's body grew heavy as he gave way to sleep. Amy rubbed his back and swayed to make sure he wouldn't wake up the moment she set him down. "It's been so strange being at home the last three months."

"It's been strange not having you at the office." Brent motioned to his squad downstairs. "The guys miss having you just as much as they miss Seth."

"I miss them." She also missed the puzzles that so often came with their intelligence work and the team atmosphere that encompassed the Saint Squad.

Satisfied that her son was really asleep, she lowered him into his bassinet. She stared at his perfect little form. "I can't imagine going back to work and putting Cameron in day care, but it's hard to envision staying home too."

"Maybe it's time to consider a less traditional approach." Brent took her hand in his.

She looked up and met his gaze. "How so?"

"Mei Lien has been doing a great job filling in for you, but word is they're going to pull her to a new squad within our unit."

"We knew that they would need to reorganize after the fiasco we had with Commander Gardner."

"Yes. Part of that reorganization could include you." Brent squeezed her hand. "If you and Mei Lien worked together, she could deploy with whichever squad needs her the most, and you would be able to stay stateside."

Which meant Cameron would never be without a parent close by. "Riley and Taylor's mom said she would be willing to watch Cameron if I decided to go back to work," Amy said, referring to Tristan and Quinn's mother-in-law.

"She's pretty much created her own day care for the squad."

"She is great with kids." Amy glanced down at Cameron before looking up at Brent once more. "Would you be okay with me being a working mom?"

"I'll be okay with whatever decision you make." He released her hand and slipped his arms around her. "As long as your choice makes you happy."

The joy of motherhood. The challenge of intelligence work. Standing by her husband's side at home as well as on the job. And always knowing where he was and when he was coming home.

"I'll call personnel next week. I want a couple more months at home with Cameron, but after that, I want to come back."

"Really?" Brent's face lit up.

Amy slid her arms around his neck. "Really." She reached up and kissed him, her heart full. So much had happened over the past year, but never had she found so much joy.

A knock sounded on her door, and her mom's voice followed. "Dinner's ready."

"Be right there," Amy called out.

Her dad's voice carried to her too. "Will someone please tell Jay to get out of that tree?"

"I think that's your cue." Amy stepped out of Brent's embrace.

"I'll get Jay out of the tree." Brent opened the bedroom door. "You can keep Quinn out of the desserts until after dinner."

Amy couldn't help but laugh. "Right. Because you always give me the hard job."

Brent leaned in for another quick kiss. "Always."

ABOUT THE AUTHOR

Traci Hunter Abramson, a former Central Intelligence Agency officer, was born in Arizona, where she lived until moving to Venezuela for a study-abroad program. After graduating from Brigham Young University, she worked for the CIA for six years until she resigned to raise her family. She credits the agency with giving her a wealth of ideas and the skills needed to survive her children's teenage years.

Traci is a popular writing instructor and keynote speaker and enjoys sharing her knowledge with aspiring writers. She recently retired after spending twenty-six years coaching her local high school swim team and now spends a lot of time traveling, which she loves.

She has written more than forty best-selling novels and is a 2022 and 2023 Silver Falchion Award Mystery/Suspense finalist, 2022 Rone Award finalist, and eight-time Whitney Award winner, including Best Novel of the Year in both 2017 and 2019. She received the 2021 Swoony Award for Best Mystery/Suspense Romance.

She also loves hearing from her readers. If you would like to contact her, she can be reached through the following:

Website: www.traciabramson.com

Facebook page: facebook.com/tracihabramson

Facebook group: Traci's Friends

Bookbub: bookbub.com/authors/traci-hunter-abramson

X: @traciabramson

Instagram: instagram.com/traciabramson